I0561772

OLYMPUS: A NEW ORDER
THE WRATH OF OLYMPUS TRILOGY
BOOK ONE

ISAMAR MIRANDA COLÓN

Copyright © 2025 Isamar Miranda Colón

All rights reserved.

No part of this publication may be reproduced, distributed, or transmitted in any form or by any means, including photocopying, recording, or other electronic or mechanical methods, without the prior written permission of the publisher, except as permitted by U.S. copyright law.

The story, all names, characters, and incidents portrayed in this production are fictitious. No identification with actual persons (living or deceased), places, buildings, and products is intended or should be inferred.

❀ Formatted with Vellum

DISCLOSURES / TRIGGER WARNINGS

This is the first installment of The Wrath of Olympus Trilogy.

This book, or any in the series, is **not** meant to be a retelling of any Greek myth. There will be references throughout the book, but that is the extent of myth involvement in the story.

TRIGGER WARNINGS:

This book features the following in various degrees:

- Graphic Violence / Gore
- Emotional and Physical Abuse
- References to Suicide
- Sexual Language / Situations
- Abuse of Power (to include, religious abuse)
- References to Abortion
- Sacrifices

This story is not suitable for young audiences. Reader's discretion is advised.

CHARACTER PLAYLISTS

These playlists were carefully curated to highlight our protagonists' transformations throughout the story in an emotional and cinematic way.

JOSEPH ARGYROS

A journey into shadows and awakening. These tracks trace a soul pulled toward something powerful and consuming—where longing becomes obsession, peace fractures into conflict, and the fight to hold on turns into the fight to rise. The feel is haunted and hungry: a pulse of quiet worship, rising tension, and finally, a violent catharsis. It's emotional in a dangerous way—where beauty meets brutality, where grief turns into teeth, and where inner battles spill outward in fire and steel.

A soundtrack for falling into the abyss and learning to breathe fire there.

1. The Apparition - Sleep Token
2. Look to Windward - Sleep Token
3. Specter - Bad Omens
4. Take Me First - Bad Omens

5. Shadows - Tommee Profitt (ft. Sam Tinnesz)
6. Enemy - Tommee Profitt (ft. Beacon Light & Sam Tinnesz)
7. The Death of Peace of Mind - Bad Omens
8. Serpent - Tommee Profitt (ft. Jung Youth, Sam Tinnesz)
9. Caught in the Fire - Tommee Profitt (ft. Sam Tinnesz)
10. Hell You Call a Dream - The Warning
11. Darkest Hour - Tommee Profitt (ft. Sam Tinnesz)
12. Deception - Tommee Profitt (ft. Sam Tinnesz)
13. Billy No Mates - Knocked Loose, Counterparts
14. Insanely Illegal Cage Fight - Dal Av, Jackson Rose
15. Heaven and Earth - Tommee Proffit (ft. Sam Tinnesz)

KATERINA FAYE ARGYROS

A descent into forbidden longing and war-forged rebirth. This playlist follows a soul that wakes from numbness only to drown in desire, doubt, and desperation and rises again armed with fire, ruin, and resolve. From fragile beginnings to chaos and battle drums, each track pulls you deeper into the struggle between temptation, self-destruction, and the will to survive what changed you. By the end, there's no softness left... only the slow, sacred fury of someone who has survived their own undoing and now stands in the echoing silence.

For hearts that have burned, fallen, and learned to sharpen the ashes into armor.

1. Blue - Billie Eillish
2. Alkaline - Sleep Token
3. Can you see me in the dark? - Halestorm (ft. I Prevail)
4. Daylight - Tommee Profitt (ft. Sam Tinnesz)
5. Dangerous - Sleep Token
6. Whose Side Are You On? - Tommee Profitt (ft. Ruelle)

7. Animal - Emeline
8. Forbidden Fruit - Tommee Profitt (ft. Sam Tinnesz, Brooke)
9. Doubt - Twenty One Pilots
10. Lost - Tommee Profitt (ft. Sam Tinnesz, Billy Ray Cyrus)
11. Going Under - Evanescence
12. Taking Over Me - Evanescence
13. In my blood - Tommee Profitt (ft. Fleurie)
14. Desolation - Tommee Profitt
15. Sound of War - Tommee Profitt (ft. Fleurie)

ZEUS

From the first spark of divinity to the slow corruption of ego. When the heart of empire begins to grind its own maker, rebellion ignites, shadows whisper betrayal, and the crown grows heavier than the kingdom it commands. Each track builds a throne from steel and sacrifice, calling armies to march, enemies to kneel, and fate itself to obey.

But power is a living thing, and it demands blood.

1. Empire - Tommee Profitt (ft. Steven Malcolm)
2. The Summoning - Sleep Token
3. Throne - Bring Me The Horizon
4. Feed the Machine - Red
5. V.A.N. - Bad Omens (ft. Poppy)
6. What it Cost - Bad Omens
7. Like a Villain - Bad Omens
8. Blood//Water - Grandson
9. Courtesy Call - Thousand Foot Krutch
10. Concrete Jungle - Bad Omens
11. Ready for War - Tommee Profitt (ft. Liv Ash)
12. Running Out of Time - Tommee Profitt (ft. Staars)
13. Spiral - Tommee Profitt (ft. Our Last Night, Sam Tinnesz)

14. The Fall - Tommee Profitt (ft. Sam Tinnesz)
15. Exile - Tommee Profitt (ft. Sam Tinnesz)

For everyone who believed and supported me since day one.
I couldn't have done this without you.

Mount Eventide
Governess Estate
Moonist
Sylene
Euxine Sea
Governess Estate
Heartfen Citadel
Syrell
Aeshelyn
Liverfron
Forest
Nanneau Cove

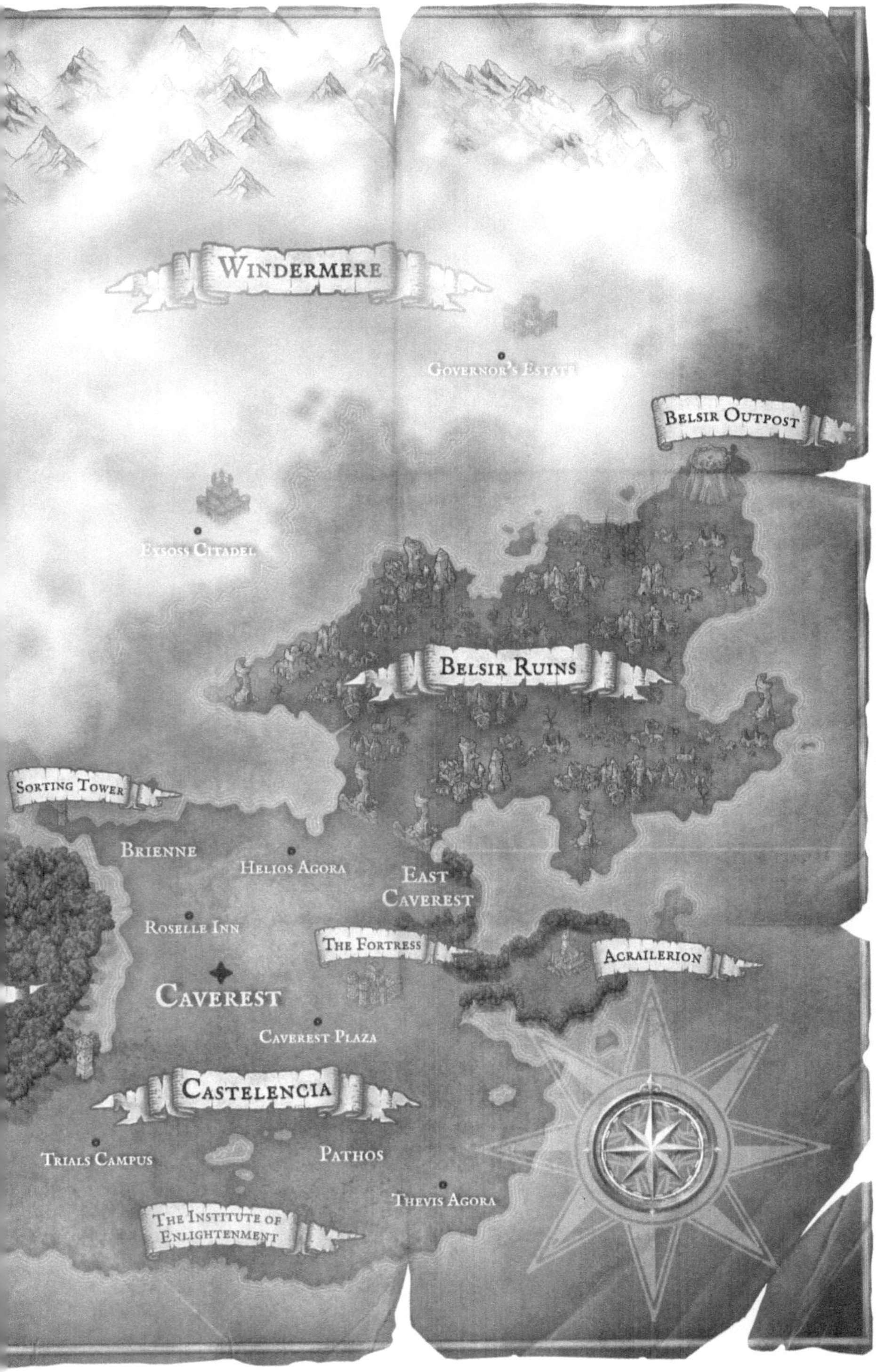
Windermere
Governor's Estate
Belsir Outpost
Exsoss Citadel
Belsir Ruins
Sorting Tower
Brienne
Helios Agora
East Caverest
Roselle Inn
The Fortress
Acrailerion
Caverest
Caverest Plaza
Castelencia
Trials Campus
Pathos
Thevis Agora
The Institute of Enlightenment

PROLOGUE

THE HYMNS OF THE CHOIR ECHOED AS MEN, WOMEN, and children alike bowed their heads as the priest worshiped their Savior and knelt before the altar.

"Let us hold our hands as we repent and be forgiven for our sins as the dark times are to be upon us."

The congregation held their hands with force as they took in his spirit and essence.

Some nodded their heads, pursed their lips, and others rocked their bodies to the rhythm of the toubeleki. The priest, Quinn, stood clasping the ceramic bowl at the peak of the altar. "May we be coated in your salvation," he whispered, before placing his lips against the bowl, taking a sip of the blessed waters.

"We, your humble servants, come toward you coated in regret. Our choices. Our actions. Our day to day. We come humbly to you, seeking forgiveness and salvation. We are sinners. We are Dirty. We are corrupted."

"That's right!" A woman shouted in the distance.

The cloudy skies rumbled, and droplets of rain fell onto the vaulted glass ceiling. The orange glow of the scattered candles slowly consumed the creeping darkness on each column, but the primary source of light was the golden chandelier that hung from the center.

"The polluted, the provocatives, the *rebels* do not appreciate what you've done for us!" he emphasized, sending the crowd into a cheering frenzy. "And how *you* will lead us to Divine Salvation. You will guide us on the path of righteousness. You—" Pieces of wood and metal flew across the room as the entrance blew off its hinges; making the priest halt and the congregation freeze.

The Commander stood in the doorway. An air of arrogance surrounded him. Darkness presided over the Temple of Light as he walked through the fearful crowd, soldiers piling through behind him and surrounding the area. His face was hidden behind a golden Corinthian helmet that matched his cuirass.

He looked around the room. The silence was deafening. No one dared to look in his direction. He took notice of a woman— blonde, fair skin in a worn forest green gown who fidgeted with her fingers as her eyes remained fixed on the ground. Her body trembled under his piercing gaze.

"Can I h-help you?" Quinn asked with all the confidence he could muster.

The Commander slowly turned away from the woman and approached the priest. The thunderous rain intensified by the second, drowning the muffled screams coming from outside the church.

"Please don't stop on my account." The Commander stated as he walked around him, making Quinn squirm. An amusing feat.

Drops of sweat trailed down his face as the semi-silent cries of the congregation got drowned by the intense beats of his heart. He subtly scanned the room—all eyes were glued onto him. *Hope*, and silent pleas all around. Any sudden movement would guar- antee the end of him and his people, he thought. Drawing a shallow breath, he peeked at the Commander who hovered around the altar.

Ares.

Shaking in his boots, he continued with the sermon. The people stared at him dumbfounded, while others cautiously glanced at the soldiers that surrounded them.

"Let us hold our hands and repeat after me."

The congregation cautiously held onto each other, tightening their grips.

"May Apollo guide us in this uncertain time. May he grant us strength and light in the times of utter darkness..." He took a breath. "Praise be to Apollo."

"Praise be to Apollo," the congregation echoed.

Ares chuckled as he stepped away from Quinn, approaching the fidgeting woman and pulling her out of her seat.

"No! Please! Please! I have a family. Please! Let me go!" She pleaded frantically, pulling her body away from his solid hold.

"Whatever it is you're looking for, you won't find it here," urged Quinn as his palms gestured for him to stop.

"Aren't I?" Ares asked amusingly as he forcefully pulled the woman's body against his and traced a dagger against her now flushed face and neck. Tears streamed uncontrollably down her face. "You think you can force your way onto our grounds and leave unscathed?"

Quinn's brows furrowed, confusion painting his face. Yet, he remained silent. The congregation held its breath as its eyes jumped back and forth between Quinn and Ares.

"For the sake of your legacy, see this through." A voice in his head said.

Keeping his gaze locked on him, Quinn summoned complete and utter darkness... a darkness that never came. *No fucking way.* He tried again... and again... each time more urgent than the last, but the light remained. His heart dropped to the pit of his stomach. *This can't be happening.* He peered down at his bare hands, cursing this retched day as Ares laughed.

Ares asked him about someone, but Quinn was so involved in his mind that he didn't seem to catch it. "Who?"

Ares scoffed, applying pressure to the blade, warm blood

trickling down the woman's neck, staining her dress. Her cries intensified.

"Alright! Enough! Please!" Quinn pleaded, but he continued. "I don't know who that is! I swear it!"

"Pity." In a swift, practiced movement, Ares slashed her throat, covering his armor with blood. Dropping her limp body, he turned to his men. Screams tore through the crowd.

"Barricade the doors." Ares said, standing as the woman bled out behind him. They could not help looking over his shoulder as they obeyed.

———

ARES STEPPED INTO THE POURING RAIN AND approached his obsidian steed. Men, women, and children alike could be seen fleeing from all parts of the town. The Temple of Light, the eternal symbol of protection and hope, had finally succumbed to the raging inferno. On the streets, a crazed fanatic ranted on about the end times, about a great uprising, a fallen kingdom.

The Olympian Army scattered and seized each building, raiding everything they considered of value and burning the rest. Wild embers consumed everything in their path, building upon the sea of smoke and flame that threatened to devour a once sacred town rapidly being mutilated and warped into rubble and ruin.

IN LOVING MEMORY OF
QUINN R. PETRAKIS
The Hero of the Dammed Souls
The Sovereign of the Paragons of Light & Castelencia
Caverest, CA

POST-WAR HIERARCHY

CASTELENCIA
Leading country in Eseron and primary suppliers of fresh produce.
Government: The Paragons of Light

SOVEREIGN
Joseph Argyros

LADY
Rena Vitalis

PRINCESSESS
Katerina Faye Argyros
Jezebelle Delí Argyros

THE ACRAILERION
The sacred space of Eseron's record-keeping & a sanctuary for women across the continent.
Currently under the Paragons of Light's Administration

|

THE VERENNA
High Priestess of the Sisterhood

|

THE DENAI
Advisor of the Verenna & Liason to the Sovereign

WINDERMERE
Country distinguished by their exemplary craftsmanship of weaponry.

|

GOVERNOR
Lazaros Tatiades

SYLENE
Country distinguished by its contributions to medicine.
Haven country as deemed by the *Sanctuary Treaty.*

|

GOVERNESS
Nesielle Verois

AESHELYN
Known for the unrelenting support to the Olympians.
Primary suppliers of fresh water.

|

GOVERNESS
Faviola Kiarelli

15 Years Post-War | Sovereign Joseph Argyros (50) & Lady
Rena Vitalis (41) | Princesses: Katerina Faye Argyros (15) &
Jezebelle Delí Argyros (11)

CHAPTER
ONE
KATERINA

TWENTY-EIGHT YEARS LATER

Katerina's heart thundered against her ears, drowning the heaving in her chest. *Steady... keep your breathing steady.* Sweat dripped down her face and burned her eyes as she reached the massive crowd gathered around the marbled plaza.

Was it almost time already? She slowed to a walk, squeezing through the array of bodies. Refreshing mist fell on her face as she passed the center fountain. She would've preferred to run without having a piece of fabric plastered to her mouth and nose; but even in the middle of autumn, even at the crack of dawn, the sun was unforgiving. Dare she say brutal.

Pulling down the mask from her face, she secured it in her pocket and smiled at the people she passed, keeping a friendly demeanor and as much as a low profile as she could; but her attention was focused on finding a way out of this place and sneaking through the back entrance unnoticed.

People from all over the country were already lined up with baskets of offerings in hand, waiting expectantly to be let into the Acrailerion for the evening's mass.

What never ceased to amaze her was that the temple was almost a 30-minute walk from here and the plaza was almost filled to capacity. She couldn't help the warmth that bloomed in her chest. *We've saved so many, but we still have a long way to go.*

Katerina may not be the one in the public eye, but she'd been privy to the conversations her father has had in the past. Things were tense outside the capital, and it was an outright miracle most of the people standing here made it. It was rumored that the rebels were killing everyone related or in close relation to their faith. *It's not right.* But she believed that her kind would prevail. She was certain of it.

Red, orange, and yellow leaves crunched beneath her boots as she approached the back of the Caverest Plaza. Picking up pace ever so slightly, almost at a power walk, sent a burning sensation radiating through her calves; but she couldn't stop. Not when it was a matter of time before they came to her room and escorted her and her sister to mass.

Her younger sister, *Jezebelle,* the one who was in the public eye.

Her heart's rapid tempo slammed against her chest as the foliage-adorned pathway to the Fortress' golden gates slipped into view. Soldiers of the Light Militia patrolled the area; dressed in their signature black house security uniform with golden trims that bared the faith's crest on the right sleeve: a black shield with a bold golden trim. Behind it, lie crossed spears at the top and a subtle olive branch wreath at the bottom. In its center, a sun was displayed, bearing two snakes opposing each other and a lightning bolt at the bottom, signifying their rebirth and renewal after the war against the Olympians.

Her attention drifted to a man who yelled obscenities to and about the Sovereign as he got dragged out by two soldiers. He looked feral and ready to kill anyone he got his hands on. His clothes were torn in all places, peppery hair ragged and falling across his bony face. A lost soul.

Katerina suppressed a shudder. There weren't many of them left here, but the few that have managed to slip through the cracks haven't stopped trying to lead the good astray. They were just bitter and refused to believe the truth: that her father and their Savior led them to prosperity when there was nothing but ashes and ruin coating their country with no fathomable way out. Zeus, Ares, and all the Olympians were the sole cause for the war and bloodshed to begin with. The rebels were just too stubborn to see it.

Made from white Pentelic marble veined with faint gold, that gleamed under sunlight, roofs clad in bronze-gold tiles that caught the sun like a fire on the mountain, and a broad sacred ramp ascended to the highest terrace. The Fortress served as a reminder to the rebels that their faith was able to withstand anything that crossed their paths, from sieges, storms, and even divine wrath.

Trees lined her view along with the second set of golden gates, a clear indicator that she was well within reach of the back entrance. She shoved a hand into her pants pocket and pulled out a small leather pouch, coins clinking with each step.

"Here," she tossed the pouch into the hands of Johan, who gave her an amused chuckle as he opened the back gate.

"The Sovereign is bound to find out if you keep this up." He said, tossing the pouch and catching it repeatedly.

"Then it's a good thing I'm paying you." She laughed, aiming toward the mahogany door.

"I don't know why he hides you; you're bleeding him dry with this stunt."

"It does have its perks." She flashed a smile over her shoulder and slid inside the dark storage room, locking the door behind her. She crouched next to the loosened tile, prying it open.

She partially enjoyed her current standing. It gave her a sense of autonomy, to a degree. Many would've protested if their father were to tell them that, moving forth, they'd be limited to certain outings, to maintain security amidst tensions on the continent; but she found it liberating. She didn't have to be subjected to the majority of public events, save for the ones hosted at the Fortress, which weren't many to begin with.

Gently, she placed the tile next to her, pulled out her maroon satchel and removed the sage dress and sandals from within. Without wasting more time, she took off her brown running boots, pants and hooded top, tossing them into the hole.

I'll come back for it later.

The sage dress was loose and allowed the chill air to bite into her skin as she tied her sandals.

She kept her raven braid in a crown and tossed the satchel into the hole with the clothes. Quietly, she placed the tile back in its rightful place and headed toward the door that led to the corridor.

Normal composure.

You did nothing wrong.

Act normal.

Opening the doors, she assumed a nonchalant demeanor and strode toward her bedchamber. She was in desperate need of a bath, but she couldn't run. It would draw too much attention, and with that came questions. If her father found out that she'd been going out unescorted or without his permission—she suppressed the thought. She didn't want to entertain those options. Katerina slithered through the array of housemaids with their hair neatly secured, their grey dresses and golden aprons swaying with each step. Her gaze followed their direction of movement. All were headed to the foyer.

Cursing under her breath, she quickened her pace, ignoring the lingering stares and managed to slip into her room.

The morning sun bathed the space in golden light, highlighting the adornments and marble flooring. Judging by the unmade bed, none of the housemaids had come yet, which meant that she wasn't as late as she thought. A relieved sigh escaped her lips and headed into the bathroom.

Before she knew it, she was shoulder-deep in lukewarm water. She closed her eyes, tipping her head back against the copper tub. Jasmine and pear filled her nose, allowing her to relax.

Three miles done today. She remembered when she tried running for the first time—it was torture. But now, it was her escape from the everyday, mundane duties. Plus, it gave her a quick look into what was happening outside. Not that there was anything eventful in the capital. They knew everything that's happening six to twelve months out: from imports/exports to who entered and left the country without prior clearance from her father. But she couldn't help feeling like she wanted some excitement. Everything was so repetitive.

She woke up, had breakfast at the Dining Hall, lounged around the grounds, read for most of the day, then when dinner came, she and her sister would be summoned by their father to discuss any relevant information he'd be willing to share or follow up on any tasks he'd assigned to either of them.

She was tired of the same old routine. What's the point of not being subjected to most of the diplomatic gatherings if she wasn't even allowed to step off the grounds? She longed for something different, to see what's beyond Caverest... if things were different, she could...

There were times when she'd fantasize about seeing the continent, new landscapes, trying other cuisines... going somewhere on her own. No escorts. No formalities. No secrets about who she was. No dangers. No threats. No—she took a deep breath. It was wishful thinking. That was all it was.

Repeated knocks grabbed her attention.

Wishful thinking... no matter how short-lived.

INTRICATELY PLACED TOWERS OF TOMES, SCROLLS, AND maps fill the library, accompanied by an abundance of greenery and polished wood. Sunlight filtered through the mosaic glass window panes, each displaying Castelencia's distinguished landmarks: the Fortress, the pier, the Acrailerion, and the Liverfront Forest.

When her father mentioned he would fix up the library, she would never have imagined that this was what he had in mind, considering how his study was a stark contrast of this—all gloomy, dark and cold.

Creaks echoed throughout the space as Jezebelle balanced herself in a mahogany and scarlet chair, reaching for a book in the upper left corner.

"Be careful," Katerina warned. "I don't want people to see you all bruised up." Her eyes fell to the bottom of Jezebelle's lilac dress and how a simple misstep could make their father go haywire.

With a loud thump, she landed on her feet, book in hand, and a gleeful smile. "I'm fine, see?" She outstretched her arms and twirled before plopping next to Katerina, golden brown locks falling over her shoulders. "You worry too much."

"*You* make me worry too much." Katerina nudged her arm.

She wouldn't need to if Jezebelle were the more cautious type. She *did*, in fact, have the reputation of being quite the klutz; despite her best attempts to—Katerina shook her head. No need for that now.

She turned back to Jasmine, whose ocean eyes remained on her.

"I'm sorry, you were saying..."

"That the commitment is unparalleled, and it is a great honor," Jasmine's voice was as smooth as honey. "Once you're inducted, you can't just take it back and call it quits."

"I know and I *am* happy—truly."

"I can see that you are, but something also troubles you."

"No, I'm just excited. That's all." Katerina responded vaguely. She loved her to death, but she didn't want her to start with her lectures. "How does it work? Will I come back here after the ceremony?"

Jasmine shook her head, blonde hair shimmering against the light. "No. You'll be required to move to the Re'Veillite Wing inside the Acrailerion. The section of the wing assigned to you depends on the type you align with."

A place outside the Fortress... heaviness weighed on Katerina's chest. All her life, she'd wanted to be a Naturopath and help others, but... the thought of leaving... her stomach hollowed... in this world they lived in... besides, what if she didn't align with it? What then?

"What's on your mind?" Jasmine's eyes gleamed with a hint of worry.

"Nothing," she lied. "Just nervous."

"You'll be alright." Jasmine gave her a reassuring hand squeeze. "I was nervous too when I first joined."

But it wasn't mere nervousness that plagued her mind. She glanced at her sister. At her delicate warm ivory limbs, her wavy golden brown hair, her peach-stained cheeks, her naïve face. *How is she going to survive without me?*

"Just relax." Jasmine tightened her grip, pulling her out of her thoughts. "You have a great opportunity that others would die for. You passed the trials and—"

"Everyone passes the trials." Katerina retorted.

"Although that may be true, you were worthy enough to be afforded this position. You know, other women would kill to be in your place. Do you realize how hard it is to be slotted here? Consider yourself lucky."

Lucky... consider myself lucky... lucky because of the fact that I passed the trials based on merit alone or family ties?

The Trials were a post-graduation requirement implemented by the Institute of Enlightenment alongside the Sovereign. Graduates would go to an off-site campus, and the evaluators would assess them in different categories: cunning, adaptability, trauma response, empathy, temptations, critical thinking, strength and endurance, knowledge, and the ability to learn quickly.

Depending on the scores each graduate got by the end of the week, they'd be slotted into different jobs in the country. Many aim to score as top performers because it would secure the best occupations, such as High Ranking Officer in the Light Militia or Strategist among the Sovereign's inner counsel.

People who scored average but had a strong sense of empathy

and trauma response would be housemaids or work in the fields in agriculture. In the rarest of cases, the Acrailerion would accept women in this category as *Initiate-Sisters*, but only after being vetted by the Verenna, the convent's high priestess.

The Herald would offer jobs to everyone else, dividing them between Military Enlisted, Maintenance Technicians, or other options available.

An itch festered within Katerina. She couldn't doubt... she did her best, but her scores were pitiful, if even that. She didn't want to doubt... she shouldn't... but she knew damn well that her father was not above doing things to get his way. Not to mention the image it would bring upon him if there was any record of either her or Jezebelle as subpar. He wouldn't allow it. She shoved the thoughts away.

The *Re'Veillites* were a highly respectable sisterhood inside the Acrailerion. Women prepare themselves since childhood just for the sole purpose of becoming one or finding their calling; whether it's being a Sister, Naturopath, Chronicler, or High Re'Veillite, they would do it just for the opportunity.

Only those classified as Sisters wore a distinct all-white, floor-length robe with intricate dark red celestial and floral embroidery along the hems, cuffs, and high collar. The entire ensemble resembled silk or fine linen, and a modest capelet draped over their shoulders, and a fitted bodice transitioning into wide sleeves and a full skirt. A veil that matched their ethereal ensemble always covered their hair. Everywhere they went, they were symbols of divine purity and fidelity. A true image of class and purity.

"Easy for you to say. You were a Re'Veillite yourself. A *High Re'Veillite,* might I add." Katerina folded her arms across her chest. "Ms. Resilience."

Jasmine laughed. "Perhaps."

High Re'Veillites were a rare type of Sister. Upon induction, their personality or experiences gave them an opening into receiving unique abilities, which is why not everyone that applies becomes one; aside from the basic requirements of virtue. Perhaps one to two percent of women are chosen in a lifetime. The odds were insane to think. The ability of reactive adaptation made Jasmine one of the most resilient of the Sisters.

"But that doesn't devalue what I said." Jasmine added. "You *are* lucky and you *are* blessed."

Katerina's body softened; but there was still an itch lingering in the back of her mind that she wasn't able to dismiss so easily.

"I suppose." Katerina turned to her sister, who was absorbed in the book in her hands. "Since when are you so fond of history?"

To her surprise, Jezebelle's cheeks turn a bright shade of pink. "Can't I just be interested?"

"No, no," Jasmine gasped amusingly. "Judging by how flushed you are..."

"Oh, Savior, help me," Katerina muttered.

Jezebelle, her face now as red as a tomato, closed her book and smiled coyly.

"Oh, come on, Jezy, you know you're dying to tell us." Katerina inched closer to her, taking a hold of her hands. "What is it?"

"Is it a boy?" Jasmine asked jokingly.

"Is it?" Katerina gasped.

"Alright, alright." Jezebelle laughed as she swatted the air in an attempt to make them calm down. "But you mustn't tell anyone. If word gets to father about this—"

"It won't, we assure you." Katerina interrupted. *Now, who's the one worrying too much?*

"Yes, I've been talking to someone." She murmured between the squeals of excitement that reverberated across the room. They were mainly from Jasmine, while Katerina remained silent, stunned. "Shhh! Keep it down." Jezebelle said with another blush.

"So, who is he? In what area does he live? Is he from the capital?" Jasmine asked rapidly, getting a head start.

"Funny thing..." Jezebelle threw a quick side glance at Katerina.

Oh, don't you even...

"He's not from here..." she admitted.

Katerina's heart dropped to her stomach as if someone had poured ice-cold water over her. *You better not.* She turned to Jasmine; both gave each other an understanding look.

"Where is he from, Jezebelle?" *He better not be one of them or I swear...*

"Kate... please don't—" Jezebelle began.

"Where is he from?" Katerina asked again, colder this time.

Jezebelle glanced at Jasmine, who looked at her with a worried glint in her eyes.

"Jezebelle, I swear if you—" Katerina drew breath, eyes still locked on her sister. "May our Savior be my witness, if you are in communication with one of the... I don't even want to think about it. Where is he from?"

With a sigh of defeat, Jezebelle looked back at Katerina and said, "He's from Sylene."

Katerina's mind stirred and an overwhelming sense of... fear? Worry? She couldn't place it, but it rushed through her, claiming every inch of her body. Sylene may be the sanctuary country in the event of a war; but that didn't guarantee that their people would be receptive to *them.*

Not with their reputation, at least.

Katerina may be inside most of the time, but she still tried to keep herself informed, aside from the evening meetings. She was no stranger to how they were perceived outside of the country and the lengths rebels would go to—she relaxed but kept a cool expression.

"I won't tell father if that's what you're worried about," Katerina reassured.

"Even knowing that he's from another country?" Jezebelle questioned.

Knowing how their father would react... she'd much rather deal with this between themselves.

"How did you even meet? We're not allowed to leave Caverest, let alone travel to another country." Jasmine hinted, sparking yet another wave of curiosity inside Katerina.

"It was quite funny actually... and unexpected, to be honest. Um... to make it short, he sent me a letter. I still have it somewhere in my room. But... he wrote about how he saw me when we were doing charity work at the Thevis Agora and, at the time, he was just visiting Castelencia and that's when he saw me... I mean, us."

"But how did he get your name? Your address?" Katerina countered, brows furrowed. She was all for romance and a nice meet-cute and whatnot, but she couldn't help but be cautious. What if Jezebelle piqued his interest because of the connection to their father, the Sovereign of the Paragons of Light and Castelencia, which obviously made them high-value targets?

"I assume he asked one of the many people we were with that day," Jezebelle replied dismissively. "I just found it commendable that he went through all that trouble *just* to send me a letter."

"I'd say be careful," Jasmine interjected.

"Not *only* to be careful, but have you even seen this man? Do you even know his name?" Katerina demanded. "Don't get me wrong, I am happy that you may have found someone you may feel content with, but—"

"Yes, I know his name." She stated matter-of-factly. "Rhei Khol. We haven't seen each other *yet*, but... we will soon."

"And how are you possibly going to do that?" Katerina's gaze hardened, and Jezebelle frowned slightly in return. This was precisely why Katerina had to be the way she was. Her sister was so naïve... so damn reckless.

"I have to concur with your sister here, Jezy," Jasmine added. "It's all about your safety. Your father has many enemies outside the country, let alone in the capital. They would do anything to harm him. If any of them were to find out that you or Kate are his daughters..." She sighed. "Savior knows what would happen."

"I am absolutely certain that he is a good man," Jezebelle said in a reassuring tone.

"You hardly know him." Katerina retorted. "Basic correspondence barely qualifies you to say how much of a supposedly good man he is." She picked up the book sitting in her sister's lap and placed it back in its rightful place.

"Jezy," Jasmine began. "I know that this feeling is something... good. It brings joy. But my recommendation to you, and I am certain that Kate would agree, is to slowly detach yourself from this man."

Katerina shot her a disapproving look. "Not slowly." Her eyes reverted back to Jezebelle. "You *will* end this immediately."

Jezebelle slipped her hands away from Jasmine's hold. "You don't get it." Hurt swept across her face.

"Actually, Jezebelle, we do. *I* do." Katerina held her sister's challenging stare, and it felt like looking in the damn mirror—only four years younger and with subtle differences.

Jezebelle's honey-doe eyes screamed nothing but pure pleas to make her sister understand, while Katerina's emerald gaze was unrelenting. They were similar but so different in their own right.

"May I remind you what father did to me when he found out I was talking to a man who was not from our community? A man I loved dearly?" Pools threatened to form in the back of Katerina's eyes, but she quickly willed the tears away and let out a sigh. "I'm not saying this to... to make you hate me. On the contrary, I want you to be safe. You can't be trusting a man you hardly know, let alone one you've never seen in person. For your own good, lay this to rest."

"The fact that father didn't approve of your union with Byorn has nothing to do with me." She hissed.

"You think father would approve of yours?" Katerina challenged. "Let's ask him."

"No! Please!"

"Kate," Jasmine cautioned.

"But weren't you confident that this union would gain his blessing?" Katerina scoffed. "You may not get it now, but I'm stopping you from making the biggest mistake of your life."

Before Jezebelle could respond, Jasmine interjected once again. "We need to get moving. The evening mass will start in ten minutes, and you know how the Sovereign gets when someone is late."

Right... "But isn't someone supposed to get us?"

"While the both of you were bickering, one of the soldiers came in and gave me the notice."

Katerina nodded and turned to Jezebelle. "I won't tell father. But for your own sake, let this go. Or else you will give me no choice but to bring this up to him myself." They headed toward the door, and Katerina reached for her sister's hand, making Jezebelle turn to meet her gaze. "You know I'd die if something were to happen to you, right?"

"It won't." Jezebelle nudged her arm. "I still love you, though."

And I you.

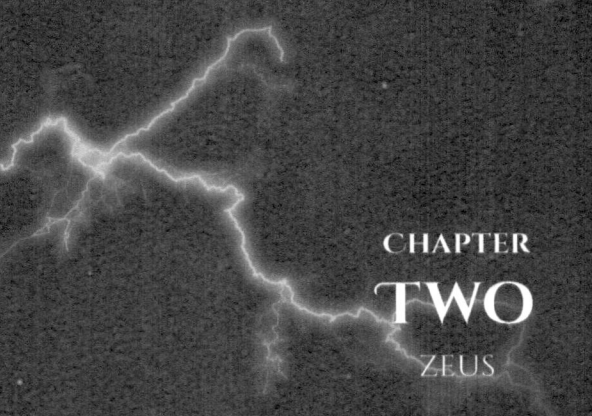

CHAPTER
TWO
ZEUS

ZEUS' BLOOD BOILED, REQUIRING IMMENSE RESTRAINT to stop himself from summoning a catastrophic thunderstorm that would destroy Castelencia, ripping it from its core. He stood near the center of the War Room, breathing heavily, maintaining his composure as Argus, his strategic advisor, circled the sand table, moving pieces and rearranging their manpower across the continent, analyzing each and every position before reassigning.

Ares stood near it, silent and unmoving, dark eyes fixed on it while Themis sorted and read through rolls of parchment at a table near the exit.

"That makes five now..." Argus finally broke the silence, steel eyes flickering back and forth between the Fortress and silver figures slightly north. "Five temples have been destroyed between Brienne and East Caverest." Argus took a step back, eyes still on the map. "Not to mention the statues that have been vandalized, beheaded, hanged—" he tipped over broken red figures in different areas of the Brienne and East Caverest territories.

"Were those the only towns?" Zeus asked through gritted teeth, approaching the mockup.

"As of now." Ares responded, his onyx hair gleaming in the firelight. "Brienne and East Caverest may be the ones leading, but

Pathos is joining their crusade with countless of our devotees being turned in to the Sovereign to await *punishment*."

"Supposedly, the Sovereign is paying the mayors a generous sum for their compliance." Argus added.

"Why not threaten, kill, or injure them into submission?" Ares asked, snickering. "Seems like a waste of coin."

"Because it creates dependency and incentives for loyalty." Zeus answered, eyes landing on Caverest, then the Fortress.

Coin bought livelihoods, patronage networks, and expectations. Governors and Mayors, would be more inclined to be and stay in the Sovereign's good graces, in hopes that he'll increase their wages, promotions, or whatever else they're into. All to reduce the possibility of a rebellion; which he'd grown successful in. It's smart. Zeus gave him that.

"I suppose." Ares said dismissively.

Argus shrugged, turning back to Zeus. "I advise we focus on Brienne, who's leading the crusade. Once they fall, the rest will follow suit shortly after."

"It won't be that simple." Themis interjected as she lifted her gaze from the crumpled parchment in her manicured, chocolate hands. "That will just solidify the Sovereign's view of us—of *you*." Her gaze seared into Zeus. "You'll be adding fuel to the fire."

"And what do you propose we do?" Argus raised his eyes to meet hers. "Hold a tribunal? We're past diplomacy at this point. They think—no. *He* thinks he can order his men to destroy *our* temples, our agoras, kill our people and not suffer consequences for it? Please."

Themis stood, squaring her shoulders. "Violence and brute action are never the first choice."

"It was when he threw the first stone at our people and succeeded in taking control of the country; something his predecessor never fully achieved."

"The bastard doesn't want to take the continent?" Ares snorted, plunging onto a seat.

"I wouldn't put it past him." Zeus inched closer to the table.

Silver figures were strategically placed on each of their citadels closest to the borders of Castelencia. One in Aeshelyn and one in Windermere. None inside Castelencia.

Zeus pondered over the idea of establishing a citadel in one of the villages around the capital but, in the middle of the unknown and the many questions that still lingered, he couldn't risk it. Not yet. It may appear cowardly, but that was far from it. He was saving his assets and manpower for something he knew they'd face eventually.

He'd already unleashed catastrophic storms upon Castelencia, executed their leader, destroyed the rebellion, and yet... here they were. Back at square one. As if Quinn had risen from the dead, and with it the rebellion.

"Aeshelyn is strengthening its perimeter in light of what's happening in Brienne." Zeus moved silver figures from the Eyross Citadel in Windermere. "Soldiers will likely need to be transferred to the Heartfen Citadel, or they'll be severely outnumbered if Joseph decides to ambush them."

While others referred to Joseph by his mortal title, Zeus refused to give him any validity or further recognition. Calling him by his name reduced him to nothing but a mere mortal. Not a Sovereign others felt intimidated by. He was nothing when compared with the power Zeus held.

"Castelencia has alliances throughout the continent. I'm surprised Aeshelyn hasn't been attacked at this rate." Ares commented.

"What will you do with the Eyross Citadel? You can't leave them unmanned." Argus asked, surveying the sand table carefully.

"Nothing." Ares responded curtly. "Windermere won't be attacked unless the Governor acts foolishly, given his current relationship with the Sovereign."

Zeus lifted his gaze. "What's the status of the other countries?"

They already had soldiers on each of the territory borders, coasts, and some patrolling within each country, save for Castelencia. Sending more men would be futile and a waste of resources.

"They're remaining neutral. As Ares mentioned, Windermere has an alliance with Castelencia, so they won't attack unless provoked. Currently, Sylene has no affiliation with them, maintaining their neutral standing. Perhaps because of the Sanctuary Treaty in place." Argus answered. "Our focus should lie with Aeshelyn and a way to neutralize the Sovereign's influence. Because if not—with time—they could easily break through our borders."

Zeus scoffed, annoyance rushing through him. This again reiterated how far Quinn had planned this. How far ahead he thought of this. How was it possible that a mere mortal outsmarted him?

"And you seriously consider them a powerful enough threat?" Themis waved her manicured hands dismissively. "They may make it to the entry point, but will die as soon as they walk through those gates."

"But they already did." Zeus admitted through gritted teeth. "They came in like they fucking owned the place and challenged *my* authority and destroyed *my* grounds."

Themis opened her mouth but was immediately stopped by Argus.

"While you were touring all throughout Sylene, we were here defending our grounds from this same group you consider insignificant." He hissed.

"I don't appreciate your tone." She glared.

"I can't seem to find it reason enough to give a fuck." Argus locked eyes with her blazing gaze. "If you can't see the severity of this, then why are you even here?"

"We need to look at a better way to sort this." She countered. Seemingly, trying to make him change his mind; but he isn't the one she should be trying to convince.

Zeus was seconds away from destroying every inch of Castelencia, even if it was the last thing he'd do.

"What do you think their Sovereign is going to do as a result if you attack? Back down?" She raised her hands.

"And I suppose *you* expect us to back down?" Zeus challenged. "Cower under pressure."

"May I remind you of what happened last time you went in full force and hotheaded into this mess?"

"Last time, we won." Zeus stated.

"Barely."

"They've declared war on us, and it's out of your hands, Themis." Argus approached her, stopping merely inches away.

"The Law is the Law." She glared.

"The law doesn't apply here, sweetheart." Argus smiled smugly.

He towered over her, but she didn't cower. He had trimmed his copper hair, shaving the sides almost completely, but the top was longer, and rogue strands fell over his eyes.

"Did you ever find out the hand Apollo had in this?" Zeus interjected to stop the bickering between them.

They could argue or fuck some other time for all he cared. He needed answers. He needed to know how they had got onto Mount Olympus all those years ago and how likely they'd be to do it again.

"Aside from what we already know. No." Argus stepped away from Themis and ran a hand through his ragged coppery hair, taming the rogue strands. "There were very few things I could do."

Of all the Olympians that Zeus could've assumed would have the nerve to go up against him, never did he once believe Apollo would be the one. He was the most decent of his offspring. Zeus gave him everything he wanted, and this is how he repaid him?

"Do better, try harder, I don't care. Just get me the information." Zeus ordered. "Because how the fuck, after Ares killed Quinn, did this guy revive Quinn's regime and took control of the entirety of Castelencia in the span of twenty-eight years? Something Quinn never accomplished."

Also, how and when the hell did his son get the balls to rebel against him? As if he could. He remembered when Ares brought Quinn's body to him with an impaling wound in his torso. He was dead. He *did* die. So, what the fuck was this?

"You know what? Just kill him and be done with it. Turn Castelencia into ruins. Make them an example of what happens when they challenge you." Ares suggested.

"It's not that simple." Themis warned.

"Care to elaborate, or do I have to force it out of you?" Ares threatened, and Zeus could've sworn he noticed Argus inch closer to her.

She rolled her sassy eyes at him. "You forget, Quinn did something before his death that made his successor attain the power he had. We don't know whether the Sovereign did the same. So, outright killing him would just bring us back to the same problem we have now."

Fucking great. Rubbing his temples, Zeus gestured to his servant to bring him a chalice full of ambrosia, which he downed almost instantly and requested another.

"We could send soldiers to Caverest; they'd be able to get more insight into what is happening in the next couple of days." Ares suggested.

"Already ahead of you." Argus answered proudly. "I sent four men to Castelencia on special orders, two in the Caverest and two in surrounding villages. They are our direct eyes and ears on the ground."

"A bit out of your depth, aren't you?" Ares taunted.

"When were you planning on mentioning this?" Zeus questioned.

"What about our current problem?" Themis asked. "Are you just going to let them keep destroying the town?"

"*Now* you want us to take brute action?" Argus replied smugly, which she scoffed in response.

"What division are the men from?" Zeus turned to Argus.

"The Blood Legion."

"The fuck is wrong with you?" Ares snapped.

Zeus' gaze snapped toward Ares, confused and in utter disbelief of his reaction.

"Tell them to stand down now." Ares ordered.

"Why?"

"Don't fucking question me." He barked. "Tell them to retreat."

"I can't. They're already with their targets."

Zeus watched Ares intently. He clenched his fists, and a muscle contracted in his strong jaw. His eyes grew dark and menacing. He drew a sharp breath before glaring back at Argus and inching closer to him. Ares towered over him, who didn't back down in the slightest.

"What did you make them do?"

"They are getting information." Argus responded vaguely.

Ares grabbed a handful of Argus's dark jacket and slammed his athletic body against the nearest wall, pressing his tan forearm against his neck. "Don't fucking come with me with that superficial shit."

Themis gaped at Zeus. "Aren't you going to do anything?"

"Fuck no," Zeus snorted. He'd much rather do her. "Not my problem to handle." Besides, he was enjoying the show, in addition to her company.

His eyes trailed from her defined half-pinned onyx curls to her full lips down to her teasing chocolate body. A glint of silver drew his attention back to Ares and Argus.

"I don't go around ordering your men to clean up the fucking grounds, make the food, or do their fucking job. What makes you think you have the authority to do it to mine?" Ares placed the tip of the sharpened blade against Argus's jaw.

"You weren't doing shit." Argus sneered, pushing Ares' muscular body off. "If you would've done your job, we wouldn't be in this predicament to begin with."

"You think you can run my division better than me, you filthy ingrate?" Ares' tone lowered to steel, his eyes piercing through Argus's core.

"Judging by what's going on, you tell me." Argus cocked a brow.

"Did you have other plans for these men?" Zeus asked.

Ares didn't turn or answer, for that matter. He unclenched his jaw and took a step back, heading out. But before he reached the doors, he turned to Argus. "Careful, half-breed."

The entrance slammed shut, and Zeus' gaze fell back on Argus, who was fixing his clothes. Zeus scanned the room, and they were alone.

Apparently, Themis had left during this entire ordeal. Zeus had seen Ares angry and displeased; he hated when others tasked his men without his knowledge because it would hinder any mission he'd planned. But Zeus had never seen him act this way, save in war.

"I need to get going. I have a few things pending to be done." Argus said, heading to the door.

"Before you go," Zeus said, and Argus turned. The stubble on his face was more prominent now, matching his hair. "I need you to travel to the Eyross Citadel and find out Windermere's standing with Castelencia. I know they're the ones supplying their weapons. However, I require more information."

Argus nodded and left.

CHAPTER
THREE
KATERINA

"This is precisely why we must look within ourselves and ask, *how can I serve others better, despite my own views?*And yes, I know what you must be thinking. *Why should I put in extra effort to assist those who hate us? They corral us everywhere we go. They call us heretics and so on.*" Her father, Joseph, pointed out. "'*Thou shalt not forsake the wicked, for a path toward righteousness is to be paved.*' Page 524, paragraph 16, verse 23 of the Codex Lux Aequitatis."

"You tell them!" A woman shouted from a distance, applauding her father.

He chuckled. "Our faith implores us to help others and bring them into our community. How can we *save* these rebels if we are not there to light their paths? To guide them to the right choice." He remained silent for a second, assessing the crowd and running a hand through his salt-and-pepper hair.

Katerina grimaced at the thought of *them*. They weren't even grateful for their services. She understood where her father was coming from; it was the bread and butter of their community. They had to be the beacons of positivity and whatnot, but she wanted to be able to go somewhere and not feel like she was a target or a topic of conversation. There were moments when she wanted to switch places with her sister, just to spare her from the name-calling at a minimum; circling back to the names they called her at the Institute of Enlightenment. The things they said about her family.

Like, how could she even sleep at night? The daughter of a dictator. The daughter of a tyrant. The uptight, temperamental, cruel daughter. *The Heretic's Daughter.* How she will burn from the core. How they blamed her for their families' suffering outside the capital. Among other things, she didn't want to recall.

None of them dared to call her these things in public due to the public scrutiny they'd face; but at every corner, every free period, there was always one who managed to sneak in an insult her way. She'd brought this up to her father when things got out of hand, hence why he didn't enroll Jezebelle for secondary level and opted for private tutoring at the Fortress until she came of age and assumed her duty as the public figure.

Katerina took a quick glance at her sister, and her chest warmed at the sight of how in awe she was with every single word their father preached, the sheer and absolute untainted innocence that she needed to protect, in full display. Perhaps the world had been kind to her.

Katerina noticed Jasmine's hands, which she had clasped together so tightly it drained the color from them.

"Are you okay?" Katerina mouthed to her once her gaze pierced Jasmine's invisible shield, to which she replied with a silent nod and a kind smile, slowly unclasping her hands.

Claps erupted around them, and her father's smile radiated nothing but pure glee. In an instant, he moved behind a circular pit on the stage, and his smile dropped, and with it went the lights. They became so dim that Katerina could hardly make out anything, apart from his stoic expression and hair painted by the orange glow of the scattered flames resting on each of the pillars around the Worship Hall.

"The Olympians have ruled this world, and it has brought nothing but peril across Castelencia, not to mention the rest of the continent..." Her father hesitated. "They raided our home; killed my closest friend and his family..." He scoffed. "Zeus believes that this is how we should rule. In fear and complete and utter submission to his tyrannical ways..."

The surrounding air thickened. Her father was nothing if not passionate, especially when it came to their faith—more so after the passing of Quinn. Katerina never got a chance to meet him, but ever since she could remember, she'd been told that he was a legend. The hero of the damned souls. The one who ended the corruption of the McClaren government.

"Covered by the mantle of light given to us by the Savior himself, we are the beacons of light. *The Paragons of Light.* Our fire can never be extinguished. The Olympians might've killed my friend—my brother. But his legacy will carry on forevermore..."

The community honored Quinn's entire lineage for their contributions. If Katerina recalled correctly, his grandfather, Weston Petrakis, founded their community. He was the one who completed and founded the Institute of Enlightenment, rendering it almost fifty years since its opening.

Katerina wondered why no one targeted the institute during the war. Perhaps they were lucky, or they thought of it as insignificant since the war took place in Belsir, which now lies in ruins.

Cheers rippled through the crowd, and her body filled with liveliness. They've truly come a long way, which was something people outside the community could never understand. From starting off as a small group, they've been able to expand their faith and save so many... even if they called them *heretics* outside of Caverest, even if they tried to demoralize her—them, because they didn't follow the Olympian way of life. If not worshiping Zeus and his tyrannical ways was the price she had to pay to bring others to utter bliss and peace, she had no problem doing so.

"We must be better than the rest. We *are* better than the rest. Which is why I implore you to hold hands as we ask for strength and resiliency these upcoming days as we embark on our journey to a higher understanding."

The congregation held their hands and bowed their heads in unison. Katerina held on to her sister, giving her a reassuring squeeze. Noticing that Jasmine was clasping onto her own, she reached out and held hers as well, even if it meant that she had to contort her body uncomfortably. *We are one. Regardless of what others think, we are one.*

Her father recited a passage from the Lux Aequitatis and then spoke in a foreign dialect. Katerina assumed he was growing adept in the ancient language of Calastalli, since she was able to pick up a few words like: strength and promise.

He ignited a small fire in the pit in front of him and ended his prayer by prompting the newcomers to step forward.

A man and two women approached the flames, each with a single item in hand. It was tradition and a momentous occasion for newcomers to take the item they held dear and offer it to their Savior in exchange for protection, cleansing, penance, and a fruitful future. A clear sign of devotion to him and commitment to being reborn.

Katerina's gaze swept over them as they took center stage next to her father, who fixed his black and gold suit.

"The new faces among us are a blessing, brothers and sisters. To those who have entered the Worship Hall for the first time, know this: you are not strangers here. You are already part of our family, bound together not by blood, but by faith, hope, and the light of the Savior." Her father spoke to them. "Here, we walk not in perfection, but in honesty. Each of us has stumbled, each of us has carried burdens, and each of us has found renewal through the grace of this community. We are strengthened not by hiding our flaws, but by revealing them, so we can be healed, uplifted, and restored together. As you stand with us, I invite you to take the first step into this fellowship. Speak aloud the weight you carry, the wrongs you repent, and the shadows you wish to leave behind, followed by the sacred burning of the past. In confessing before your brothers and sisters, you are not judged. No. You are cleansed. Let your words be the symbol of your penance, and let this community receive you with open hearts."

The crowd cheered briefly, offering words of encouragement. Katerina smiled. *This* was what this was all about.

The first to go was a brunette woman, who looked no older than 35. She wore a maroon dress with medium-length sleeves, and in her hands, she had a stuffed doll. Katerina couldn't tell if it was an animal or a person, but the woman held on to it with dear life.

"I'm Willie," she said tremulously. "I... I..." her lips trembled. Was she going to cry? "Some of you may look at me and wonder why I'm holding onto a rag doll?" She raised the item. "It used to belong to my mother, and I was supposed to pass this on to my daughter..." she hesitated, looking down at the doll. "They took her from me..." she uttered loud enough for Katerina to hear. She raised her gaze. "They took her from me." She said louder. "They took her from me because I wasn't loyal enough..."

Who? Did the Olympians do this to you? Katerina's heart broke.

"Margarette was supposed to turn six today... and the rebels took her from me." She wept. "I'd like to put this pain and past behind me and not be constantly reminded of my failure as a mother." She tossed the doll into the fire apprehensively. "Thank you." She muttered.

Joseph placed a hand on her shoulder. "Losing a child is not something I'll be able to comprehend, but I have lost a loved one. You will heal. You will find peace." He hugged her. "Welcome home."

Willie bowed her head in what appeared to be gratitude and made her way back onto her seat. People reached out, cradling her arms as she passed.

Katerina's eyes welled, but she blinked the tears away as she turned her attention to the next one. A blonde girl with shoulder-length hair, seemingly in her early twenties.

"The man I loved gave me this." She displayed an emerald and gold ring. "He wasn't who I thought he was."

The words struck Katerina, her attention now seared onto the girl.

"I'm Raven, and he was one of the leaders of the rebellion." Silence fell. "He almost killed me." She croaked. "All because I expressed my gratitude to the Re'Veillites one time...just once. Threatened that he would make my life miserable if he ever found me talking to the *other side* again." She threw the ring into the fire. "I want to be free. I don't want to fear for my life. I want peace and not to constantly look over my shoulder. Thank you."

"I commend you for your bravery." Joseph placed a hand on her shoulder. "Our community will help you heal, and you being here with us granted you your freedom. Welcome home." He hugged her and sent her off to the congregation.

Katerina's heart was with them. It was a hard thing to do, but it's the right choice. *Here marks their journey of letting go of who they were and becoming anew. Praise be to our Savior, and may his light coat these beautiful souls.*

Katerina's gaze finally landed on the last newcomer. A tall man with ginger hair and freckled skin, in a long navy blue cloak with a subtle sheen, fastened by a delicate silver clasp in the shape of intertwined vines. The pants are practical yet elegant, crafted from what appeared to be dark, soft leather with silver accents along the seams. His boots were knee-high with silver buckles. He had a slender, graceful build, with a subtle silver pendant hanging from his neck.

Praise be to our Savior and the work you are doing today to these men.

He stepped forward.

"I'm Rhei Khol—"

Someone grabbed Katerina's arm forcefully, only to find it was Jezebelle, her eyes as wide as a frozen fish. Her stomach hollowed. *What are the damn odds?* She snickered, ignoring her sister's firm grip. Katerina glanced at Jasmine's stunned face. *Thank Savior I'm not the only one at a loss of words.*

Jasmine leaned in over Jezebelle and whispered, "What are we going to do?"

Katerina peered at Jezebelle, whose face was filled with astonishment. *Oh, Jezy... this is going to hurt.* Claps erupted around them, completely missing when Rhei went back to the crowd and their father had extinguished the flames.

"How I love it when we have new members join our cause and believe in our faith," Joseph cheered, moving toward the podium. "Here lies the first step toward salvation. Praise be to our Savior!"

"Praise be to our Savior!" Everyone echoed.

"Please, at this time repeat after me as we recite the Plea of Salvation."

They all joined hands and closed their eyes as they recited in unison.

We vow our fealty, bound in flame.
We offer not doubt, but our unwavering name.
Through silence and sacrifice, we are made whole.
Through loyalty unbroken, we give our soul.
Keeper of the Embers, shelter our flesh.
Watcher of the Flame, sear us afresh.
Purge us of weakness, rid us of shame.
Let only the loyal remain.
For we are the devoted. The unyielding. The chosen.
Our breath is *Your* will, our blood is *Your* ocean. In fire, we rise. In ash, we stand.
No fear, no falter, no trembling hand.
By the Plea of Salvation, we are sealed.
By the Embers of Purity, we are healed.
Grant us the path, ablaze and divine.
And we shall never stray from *Your* light.
We are Yours.
We are Yours.

We are Yours.

"Praise be to our Savior." Joseph blessed, and once everyone echoed, he concluded the mass.

As everyone stood and greeted the newcomers with the warmest of welcomes, Jezebelle grabbed Katerina and Jasmine, leading them toward the back of the room by their wrists.

"I cannot believe he is actually here!" Jezebelle squealed, releasing her hold. Her eyes scanned around, possibly to ensure that he wasn't within earshot, but Katerina couldn't precisely tell.

"Good, you can end it here. Now." Katerina jeered.

"Didn't you say that he was coming to see you?" Jasmine cocked a brow, disbelieving Jezebelle's innocence, as did Katerina. "He must've mentioned something in his letters."

"I knew he was coming, but I just didn't know *when*." Jezebelle's gaze moved back and forth between Jasmine and her sister, but it lingered more on Katerina.

"Are you planning on talking?" Katerina asked.

"Please," she waved a hand dismissively. "Look at all these girls ogling him already. I'm just gonna wait until he's alone."

"Jezebelle Delí Argyros!" Katerina scolded. "You are not to go near him unless it's to end it. Do you understand me?"

"We've been talking for months now. Do you really expect me to just throw it all away?" Her voice cracked, but her eyes displayed complete and utter disdain. "Look at them." She nodded to the crowd of girls.

"There's a difference between you and them." Jasmine commented. "You're the Sovereign's *daughter*."

"So I keep getting reminded..." She grunted as her eyes locked in the distance. "You have to be kidding me..." Her eyes narrowed and lips curled into a snarl. Katerina knew that face all too well.

Katerina's gaze followed, falling upon a girl—blonde with waist-long hair and a muted yellow dress. Her delicate hands traced Rhei's forearm. "Jezy—"

"I know what you're going to say." She lifted a hand at her

sister, attention still on the blonde. She let out an amusing scoff before saying, "I feel that with him being here, it'll give him a chance to get into father's good graces."

So help me... Katerina's blood simmered at the defiance and grabbed Jezebelle's arm. "Don't you ever think of what may happen if things go wrong between you?"

Jezebelle pulled out of Katerina's grasp. "I guess we'll have to find out, shall we?" she trotted over to him before Katerina could stop her, her lilac dress flowing behind. Her movements were fluid and graceful, slightly unhurried.

Katerina looked at Jasmine, who was equally dumbfounded. Jezebelle had never been the defiant type. That was a title *Katerina* had earned throughout her life. But it was because *life* made her that way. Jezebelle was kind. The fact that she mentioned that she'd been talking to him for months didn't seem to ease Katerina's doubts. What have they talked about? How much does he know of their family? How did he even get here?

Both Katerina and Jasmine turned to look at Jezebelle, who was three steps away from the crowd. The blonde girl turned her attention toward her upon noticing her presence and instantly gave her a half-assed bow before scurrying away.

Rhei gave Jezebelle a warm smile at first. But after a while, his eyes widened. In an instant, he pulled her into an embrace, bringing her body up and twirling her around in his arms. Her laughter echoed around the open space.

A heaviness filled Katerina's chest. *No. Stop.* She shoved the unpleasant feeling away as she scanned the room for any sightings of their father but, fortunately; he was nowhere in sight. *This is going to be harder than I thought.*

"And you." Jasmine turned to Katerina, her eyes narrowed. "You cannot give in to impulses if you want to be a Re'Veillite. You must remain pure."

"You say this as if I already got a man." Katerina chuckled.

"I'm not talking about a man. I'm talking about your temper."

My temper. Katerina snorted.

"I get that you are being protective of her, but she is no longer a child and you won't be around for much longer."

I am very aware... "I'm not just protecting her. I'm protecting *us.*"

"That's no longer your burden to carry, Kate," Jasmine said softly. "Look at her."

Their eyes fell on Jezebelle and Rhei, who held each other tightly as if they'd never see each other again. Katerina's heart caved in further.

"She looks happy. It's been a while since we've seen her that way."

"I just don't want her to get her heart broken..." Katerina sighed.

"Heartbreaks are inevitable. We both know that. But for now, let's give her this moment. Jezebelle is smart; if things are not going well, she'll leave him."

"She is also naïve... naïve and in love." *A deadly combination.*

Perhaps it was Katerina's overprotective nature toward Jezebelle or her bias with relationships in general, but she wasn't going to let this go lightly. She couldn't. Not until she could make sure that he would not harm her, or had ill intentions. For her sake, for Katerina's sake, for their family's sake.

"Perhaps, but I'd be more careful if I were you."

Katerina raised an eyebrow.

"You think I don't know about you leaving the grounds?"

Ice ran through Katerina's veins. *How?* "I don't know what you mean."

"You think Johan doesn't tell me anything?" She whispered.

There goes her runs. No more. "He trusts you; that's why he's telling you. If he would've told my father, he would've already dealt with it. So, I'm fine."

"Kate, be careful. I'm not telling your father if that's what you are worried about."

I'm not worried about that. Katerina knew she could trust

Jasmine, but she didn't want to entertain the subject any further and risk anyone else overhearing.

"Do you still keep in contact with your friend who works in the Chronicler Wing?" Katerina asked.

Jasmine's shoulders slumped, and gave her an incredulous look. "Is this going to make you let it go?" Even looking displeased, she looked ethereal with her golden locks cascading down her porcelain shoulders.

"If you find me what I need, yes."

CHAPTER
FOUR
ZEUS

THE SKIES RUMBLED OVER BRIENNE, SLOWLY devouring the blazing sun. Villagers stored away their displayed belongings, spices, and other materials in their makeshift market-place, while others hurried indoors upon feeling the first droplets of rain.

All over the village, boulders and debris were bunched to the side of the streets, leaving behind a paved way for passersby. The remnant base of the Olympian statues were now replaced by the statue of the *Savior* of Castelencia.

My ungrateful son.

A handful of their temples became a public holding area for unwanted items such as furniture, clothes, or miscellaneous items. The columns and walls were vandalized to the brim, displaying *'Death to the Olympians'* in red and black, along with other obscene imagery and sheer blasphemy. Zeus could feel the weight of his power simmering beneath his fingertips.

Other temples were taken over by the homeless, who pissed on his statue's feet in defiance and retaliation for their circum-stances in life. How they blamed him for their demise. The place has succumbed to nothing but a hellish pit of sorrow as they rebuild their village into one approved by the fucking Sovereign.

Rapid trotting captured the attention of onlookers who still remained outside. Their eyes widened and, dropping everything, they sprinted in the opposite direction, warning everyone they saw to hide. Rain poured down from the sky, snuffing out the surrounding fires the homeless used to keep warm or cook their stolen food.

Olympian soldiers charged into the village, showing off their division's insignia on their left sleeve—the *Thunder Guard*. While some soldiers dismounted their steeds and raided each home, soldiers from the Blood Legion destroyed every glimpse of the Savior of Castelencia—from statues to newly built temples.

Men fought against the soldiers, holding weapons of their own and defending their homes from invasion, while the rest tried to escape the bloodshed outside their homes. But it was futile. Olympian soldiers tore through them as if there were nothing but soaked parchment, sealing their fate and showing them what happens when they go against the divine and follow a worthless mortal.

Ares commanded the soldiers to be merciless. Everyone was to be treated as a traitor.

Zeus, on the other hand, made his way to his piss-stained and vandalized temple. Nothing but pure terror shone in the homeless people's eyes as they stumbled upon him in all his divine splendor, who was about to pulverize their very bones. If they wanted to destroy the temple and everything in it, who was he to deny them the pleasure? They could succumb with it.

He launched himself into the air, hovering over the wretched temple. His attention shifted to the villagers who fought against them as they huddled into various establishments in attempts to escape the ravaging hands of his men.

He couldn't help the amusement growing in his chest. *Too easy, so damn predictable.*

Thunder rumbled and electrifying power rushed through him as he released his wrath onto every single blasphemous temple in the vicinity, taking everyone down with it.

Ares, blood-covered and grinning, took the lives of all who dared to go up against him, and the occasional ones just because he could.

Zeus returned to the ground, gravel crunching beneath his boots, as he and Ares swept the remaining parts of the village. Ares was about to kill the surviving few that scrambled to their feet when Zeus stopped him and addressed the two men.

"Let this be a warning." He said to the trembling Castelenian folk. "Next time, I won't be as merciful."

Deep crimson covered the streets. Homes were consumed by a raging fire that refused to be snuffed by the rain. Bodies lined every inch of the village, piling on top of each other. Zeus's blood simmered. All these people supported Joseph. What did he have? How did he sway them to follow him?

They turned toward a street that led to the last part of the village. Mostly homes and one or two shops lingered—he stopped, eyes darting slightly upward.

Zeus' eye twitched at the sight of bodies... bodies hung and lined, one next to the other in various states of decomposition—men, women... and children...

His chest caved, but it wasn't in horror. No, it was rage. White hot rage that grew hotter by the second as his eyes drifted to the gold and black banner beneath the hanging feet.

Behold the fate of those who defy the Sovereign. Let their end be your warning.

"Come on." Zeus's lips graze the nymph's ear from behind.

She groaned, molding her body to his. He traced his fingers down her soft, light blue skin. A gasp escaped her lips as he turned her, making her turquoise eyes meet his. Her face radiated nothing but pure desire, and her delectable body made him want to have her in every way and everywhere possible. A pinch to her nipple made her whimper.

Navaiah has been a favorite among the gods, mainly because of her beauty. Deep hues of dark blue crept up her long iridescent hair, matching her big round eyes. A beautiful peach tone painted her cheeks, contrasting with her flawless skin and her soft, plump lips that begged to be kissed. Her curvaceous body held enough power to bring any god and mortal to their knees. And he was the only one ravishing her. *Exclusively mine.*

He held on to her chin with his thumb and index finger; her mouth parted slightly, sucking in a shallow breath.

"Tell me what you want." He whispered.

Her gaze trailed from his eyes to his lips. She looked like she was carved out of clay, a true art form that not even Aphrodite could replicate. She gnawed on her lower lip before uttering the words he wanted to hear. "You."

A smirk slithered onto his mouth as he hovered his lips over hers. "Kneel."

She fell to her knees, and her hands wandered, setting him free. *Good girl.*

Sneaking his hand to the nape of her neck, he pushed deep into her mouth in slow repetitive moves. The way she effortlessly took all of him again and again just made him want to go rougher. But he couldn't get carried away. *Not yet anyway.* He let her savor him for a little longer before hoisting her up and bending her over the bed.

Thrusting into her, satisfying cries filled his ears. Her wetness intensified the deeper he thrust, savoring how delicious she felt on him.

"Please," she whimpered.

He tightened his grip on her hips, driving himself further into her. *I need more.* His hand snaked through her hair, grabbing a fistful at the base and pulling hard enough to arch her back. The sight was one to fucking behold.

He ignored the knocking sound at the door. Whoever it was

could wait. He released her hair and pulled her body toward his; her damp back pressed against his torso. He grabbed her face and turned it toward him, kissing her deeply. *Fuck.* He growled as he got harder and muffled moans filled his body.

The knocking continued, this time quicker, more urgent. *Go Away.* A loud groan escaped his lips.

He pushed her down and pinned both arms behind her back with a hand. She moaned as his free hand slapped her precious ass and pulled it toward him, burying himself inside her once again.

The bang of the door slamming against the wall had him pulling out of her. Unhurried and annoyed, he covered himself from the waist down and met Hera's death-ridden glare.

"I tried to stop her—"

Zeus raised a hand to the clerk and dismissed him with a glance. There's nothing he could've done to stop her, anyway. She would've broken the door down if that's what it took.

Zeus picked up the thin iridescent dress from the ground and tossed it to Navaiah, his eyes still on his wife, who now gave her a murderous look.

Navaiah scrambled to get dressed, and before he knew it, she was out the door. Not daring to look back at him or at his enraged wife, who looked gorgeous with her dark brown hair pinned and adorned with her golden diadem that matched her delicate jewelry. Even angry, she was breathtaking. Her rose lips scowled in disgust as she beheld him, and Zeus could've sworn a glint of desire flashed in her eyes for a millisecond.

"This could've been you." He shrugged, pouring himself some ambrosia from the decanter atop the dresser.

"Ugh." She rolled her eyes. "As if I wanted scraps."

Ouch. He winked at her. "As if you don't enjoy my attention."

"Frankly, I do not."

He snorted, bringing the chalice up to his lips. "You sure as hell weren't complaining when I had you sprawled in that—"

"Don't even finish that." She lifted a manicured finger.

Smiling against the rim of the cup, he downed the rest of the amber drink. "Why are you here? You didn't even let me get dressed. Come to scold me about my extracurriculars?"

"I gave you ample time to get decent." She countered, taking a seat and crossing one leg over the other under her blue and white gown. He knew her body like the back of his hand, and she knew it. "Anyway, Hestia and I are to travel to Aeshelyn in the next couple of days."

He poured himself some more ambrosia. "And I need to know this because?"

"I'm not ignorant of what is happening in the mortal lands." She cocked a brow as he handed her a chalice, which she reluctantly took. "The problems may be primarily in Castelencia, but I doubt that Sylene and Windermere will remain neutral for long. Aeshelyn is one of our only allies, and it's only a matter of time before—"

"We already have men on the Aeshite-Castelenian border and on the Sylenian front. What are you worried about?"

She took a sip of the drink. "You know I hate not knowing what I am dealing with, and you are not passing information."

"There's no information to pass." Zeus shrugged.

"Oh, don't give me that." Her gaze sliced through him. "I won't allow myself to be in the same position I was during the war." She downed the rest of her drink.

Her position in the war... in the war that cost him almost everything. He could still hear them pleading for mercy as he unleashed countless lightning bolts on their territories. Hera was one of the few who came out partially unscathed and who actually put up a fight against Quinn's goons.

That was one of the few moments he was genuinely worried about her... and when he found her, all bloody, shaking, and filled with rage and torment, that's when he realized the things she had to endure to survive and make her move.

"What are you going to be doing in Aeshelyn?" Zeus asked.

"Blossom peak season. I am to bless the expectant mothers, women in childbearing years, as well as the infertile."

"Let's do this." He began getting properly dressed; it was getting ridiculous still being half-naked and getting no action. "I'll send men to accompany both of you during your time there. I assume you're staying?" He pulled up his trousers.

"Possibly." She placed the chalice down. "This may be a week-long thing, but I don't have to be there for the entirety of it. Maybe just the first three days."

"Then it's settled." He pulled the linen shirt over his head; the sleeves snug against his biceps. "They'll remain with you until you return and, before you ask, yes. I'll ensure that the men are top of the line and not recently converted soldiers."

"Did you really have to wear servant's attire to bed a nymph?" she snorted.

"Deal?" He dismissed her question, and she nodded once.

"It was a pleasure doing business with you." She stood, aiming for the door.

"It would've been a pleasure if—"

"Don't." She warned, and without a moment to spare, she left the room.

Zeus snickered and couldn't help but replay the time he had her all to himself. She could argue and complain all she wanted; but that entitlement vanished in an instant once he was in between her legs.

Once out of ambrosia, he opened the door, only to find Hermes just about to knock.

"To what do I owe the pleasure?"

"You're being summoned to a Council Meeting."

CHAPTER
FIVE
JOSEPH

LEAVES RAINED DOWN THE OPEN MAUSOLEUM, LEAVING behind a thin coat of scattered flora on the stony surfaces in the chill night.

Glancing up at their *Savior's* statue, Joseph couldn't help but scoff. Years upon years of this bullshit and he still had to do it every single damn time. Pay reverence to someone—some *thing*, Quinn pledged fealty to. The mausoleum gave just enough privacy the Fortress didn't. The only downside was that the sky was on full display, no cover overhead whatsoever. He took off his black and gold jacket, staying in just his onyx short-sleeve shirt.

How did you do it, Quinn? All this time. How? Joseph knelt before the statue and bowed until his forehead touched the cold, gritty concrete. *How did you keep up this façade for so long? How come no one questioned anything?* He discarded the thoughts.

"I'll never understand why you did this... why you chose me..." he muttered. "I know I gave you my word... but things are getting out of control outside these walls." He drew a shallow breath, suppressing the pathetic feeling blooming inside him. "Shit." He slammed a fist on the ground.

Joseph lifted his gaze, landing on the small picture frame at the base, and his throat clenched as he reached for it. *Why did you have to do this?* A single droplet fell onto the glass, atop the image of him and Quinn, who had his arm around Joseph's shoulder, smiling. Quinn's long dirty blonde hair was untamed, and his eyes were as dark as night. But even then, when Quinn had just ascended into power and Joseph was no more than his trusted advisor, they looked normal. Untainted. Unburdened.

We had peace once. A long damn time ago. But you had to go, and get yourself involved with questionable things... questionable beings. He scratched his head. *I did promise. I did vow... It's not like I had a choice, anyway.*

"I will not fail you." Was the last thing he muttered before rising to his feet, picture still in his grasp.

He'd been his closest friend and brother even before he was adopted by Quinn's father. Joseph genuinely believed that Quinn's family had been wrongfully treated by their distant relatives, hence why he stood by him, even when faced with absolute hatred and disdain. Was it pity? Maybe. But between him, Quinn, and Marcus, they did a hell of a great job in building the foundation of their community, alas tearing down the McClaren government.

How after the war, thanks to their early efforts, Joseph was able to rebuild their country from the ground up. He gave the people something to believe in aside from the Olympians, who refused to lend a helping hand, even when compensated and worshiped for it. Even when the people desperately needed them and approached them with penance and regret in their hearts. Joseph grimaced at the reminder.

Quinn's sudden death took him by surprise and, after learning who was responsible for it, it only fueled the fire further. He couldn't let this die.

"THINGS ARE BOUND TO GET UGLY," QUINN SAID *amidst a swig of wine. "If something were to happen to me—"*

"It won't."

"If it were." He continued, emphasizing the first word. "I need you to do something for me." Quinn put down the wine and walked over to the cabinet in his desk, pulling out a wooden box with an intricate sun carved at the top.

I eyed him closely, heart racing and suddenly dropping at the sight of a black and gold dagger with a red trim.

"I have bounties on my head, courtesy of my former relatives." He played with the blade in his hands, checking the tip for sharpness. "I cannot let this die. Our hard work cannot go to waste."

JOSEPH SHOOK HIS HEAD, TRYING TO DISMISS THE reminder, and glanced back at the vine-covered statue.

"SWEAR TO ME THAT EVEN IF I DIE, YOU WILL CONTINUE to fight for this. For our efforts." Quinn added. "That if I were to die, you would step in as Sovereign and make our cause a force to be reckoned with." He pointed the sharpened tip at me, merely at arms-length. "They cannot fucking win." His eyes darkened, lowering the blade.

"Quinn, isn't it easier for you to have an offspring? I can find—"

"Swear to me." He ordered.

"What about Bernadette?" I stood my ground. Surely his sister can give him a nephew or something.

"Bernadette has her role to play." He closed the box, dagger still in his hands. "Now, enough with the questions." He pointed the blade back at me. "Vow to me."

Joseph's eyes trailed down to the diagonal scar on his left forearm. *The vow. The fucking promise.* Placing the picture back, he paced around the lonesome space.

"I swore to him..." he muttered. "I can't fail. I fucking can't." His mind trickled back to the order he'd given. *Destroy everything. Temples, agoras, Olympian statues. Anything from anyone who pledged fealty to the Olympians.* This was a clear sign of war, and Joseph didn't have the same amount of power Quinn had, which had him shaken to the fucking core. It was only a matter of time before they sent a counterattack. It was bold. Stupid and irrational. But, bold.

What can he do if they do? His men were at the outpost near the pier. He could relocate a battalion over... he cursed under his breath. "If fucking only..."

"How precious." A woman's voice emerged from the shadows.

The hair on the back of his neck stood, making him freeze for a millisecond before turning around. He sneered at the sight of the woman with ivory skin, sleek black hair and violet eyes in a red dress that draped from her shoulders, hugging her figure.

"Oh, don't give me that, sweetness." Eris pushed herself off the column, moving toward him suggestively. "I heard your pleas, and who am I not to oblige?"

"Have you?" Joseph responded icily. "What do you want?"

She laughed. "Oh, I'm just here to see you." She traced a spindly finger over his shoulder, clicking her tongue at his lack of comment. "Hmm... you're lucky you're gorgeous." Her hands picked up the picture frame, tracing her index finger over it.

The action made him shudder as if her pointy nails were tracing down his own spine. "What does *he* want now?"

"A sacrifice." Her eyes remained on the frame, voice softly taunting.

"I already gave him one this past month." He said through clenched teeth, attempting to stay as neutral as possible.

"He requires another one," she shrugged nonchalantly.

"Awfully demanding, isn't he?" Joseph hissed. "To only give me mere crumbs in return."

"He gives what he wants you to get. Not what you want." She released the frame, placing it back at the base. "You want more? Do better."

"Do fucking better?" Joseph scoffed. "I—"

"I'd choose my next words carefully, if I were you." Her gaze swept over the statue and then the tombstone bearing Quinn's name. "I'm not the one with something to lose."

Anger simmered through him as pain spread over his palms. He opened his fists. "What does he want now?" He asked again disdainfully.

"Three hearts." Her gaze finally met his.

"Fine," he said dryly, aiming for the door. *I'll just give him the hearts of pigs and be done with it.*

"But not just any."

He stopped, scoffing as he looked over his shoulder. "Of course not."

"He wants the hearts of the people who pledged fealty to—"

"My men did not pledge to him," Joseph shook his head. "And I swore to protect their integrity and wellbeing."

"You are keeping their integrity intact—so to speak." Her lips curled into a mischievous smirk. "You just have to carve their hearts out; everything else can remain intact."

"I won't kill my people." Joseph moved to the arched exit.

"As if you have a choice."

Heat prickled Joseph's scar, making him stop merely inches away from the door. *Fucking bitch.* Shoving away the reminder of what they took from him—*who* they took from him. He took a deep breath. "No need." He sneered without looking back. "When does he want this done?"

Eris let out a sly laugh and slithered back into his field of vision. "So eager. I knew I liked you."

Joseph resisted the urge to scowl. *Not only does he want me to do this, but he is not one to be merciful for a quick death. No. He wants them to be terrified. Wants them to plead. Wants them in agony when the sacrifice is given. I should be used to this bullshit by now. I don't know how Quinn did it. Perhaps they took something from him too; I don't know. But for her sake...*

"Dusk," she said suggestively, eyes lingering up and down his body and glinting gold.

"What do *you* want, Eris?" His eyes meet hers, and her lips curve upward.

"Must you think everything is transactional?" She teased.

"Everything *is* transactional, especially with you." He countered. "What do you want?"

Her icy fingers trailed up his arm and caressed the back of his neck, fingers playing with the bottom of his dark hair. His body tensed under her touch. "You'll find out once the tides have stilled. In the meantime, focus on retrieving the sickle. Also, this should serve as a pleasant reminder next time you decide to question him."

He peered down at his hands. *Fuck.* Just as he was about to call her out, she vanished, blowing a kiss goodbye. Joseph looked down at his hands again, where a silver ring rested, gleaming under the moonlight. *She's still alive...*

He turned to the tilted frame. *Fucking mess you've gotten me into.*

General Vivek dumped scrolls, coins, jewels, and crumpled parchment on top of Joseph's cherry desk. "Let's just say they won't be meeting again anytime soon."

Joseph scanned through the contents. He picked up a blue coin, slightly split in the middle, pale blue powder smeared over the metal. With a huff, he placed it aside and plucked a sheet of parchment from the pile and examined it carefully. Word had gotten to him that the mayor of Pathos was supposedly conspiring against him by meeting with rebel leaders and planning a strike against the Fortress. Joseph found the idea to be ridiculous and futile. Once they stepped inside Caverest, it would've been over for them in an instant. But he decided to surprise them.

Joseph's brows furrowed upon realizing the contents of the parchment. "How did they get the layout of the Fortress?"

Vivek chuckled. "About that." He snapped his fingers, and two soldiers entered, pulling a balding man by his chained fat arms and torn clothing.

Joseph straightened, clicking his tongue as the man's eyes darted at him, widening in terror.

"I swear I didn't know they would do this!"

Pathetic. Joseph stood.

"Please, I truly had no idea. Those animals raided my home and took everything I own!" The mayor pled on his knees as Joseph towered over him. "Please, you have to believe me. I told them not to do it. I told you would come for them. They didn't believe me. Please, I mean no harm."

"Strap him to the seat," Joseph ordered.

"Please! I had nothing to do with it!" the mayor screeched as his body got shoved onto a seat, back pressed tightly against the backrest. His arms and legs got fastened tightly with leather straps.

"I've been patient with you, Randal." Joseph removed his jacket and reached into the drawer, pulling out a leather whip.

"I swear!" He yells frantically, jerking his body in all directions. "Please!"

"Make sure we don't have any eavesdroppers." Joseph addressed his men, running the whip's smooth tail through his free hand.

Randal frowned as his eyes followed Vivek; horror washed over his face once he saw him nod in Joseph's direction.

"I'm going to make this simple." Joseph tightened his grip around the whip's base. "I—"

"Aren't you going to ask them to leave?" Randal's eyes scanned the room at Joseph's men.

Crack.

Screams filled the room as blood trailed from his chubby cheek.

"Don't interrupt me," Joseph said calmly. "It's considered rude."

His gaze seared into Joseph with clear, unrelenting loathing. But Joseph didn't waver. He had a job to do and answers to get.

"Besides, I don't care if they watch." *And Voilá. That loathing just morphed into panic. Hilarious.* "Since I am not a brute and have manners, I will tell you the rules of the game. Stray from the rules and—well, you'll find out soon enough." Joseph's lips curled upward.

"This is a game to you? You sick—"

Crack.

"Fucking—"

Crack.

"Heretic—"

Crack.

"Bastard!"

Crack. Crack.

Randal's face was now drenched in blood and covered in cuts. *So much for not knowing anything about it.*

"How did you get a copy of the Fortress' layout?" Joseph asked, brushing off dust from his dark shirt.

"I took no such thing." Randal sneered.

A quick glance from Joseph made Vivek bury his fist into Randal's stomach.

"I...I swe—" Randal heaved. "Swear."

"See... one of the conditions behind your appointment as mayor was that we would not lie to each other. So, we're going to try this again. How did you get a copy of the Fortress' layout?"

"I give you my word..."

"Your word means nothing to me." Joseph released the whip

onto his desk. "I am a... *heretic bastard* after all." He gave Randal a sly smile.

"You know I didn't mean that; we're on the same side." He cowered. "And truly, I have no idea how they got the floor plans."

"If that's the case, then what were you doing with this?" Joseph held up the bent coin, and Randal's face paled for an instant.

"It's just a standard coin."

"Is it?" Joseph shook it gently onto his open palm. Small, pale blue particles fell from it, piling in his hand. He brought it close to him. "Taste it."

"What?"

"You heard me."

Randal's eyes darted everywhere. *Calling for help?*

Joseph pressed his open hand onto Randal's face, smearing its contents on his cheeks, nose, mouth. "It's considered impolite to avoid looking at the person talking to you, even after your failed attempt to poison me."

"I didn't!" Randal went into a trembling frenzy.

"If this is as *standard* as you claim, you'll live." Joseph dusted off his hands. "I do have the antidote."

Randal's lips quivered.

"You think I can't recognize my own stash?" Joseph grabbed his face. "Who gave this to you?"

"Just kill me if that's what you want." Randal hissed through gritted teeth.

"No," Joseph said softly. "Death would be too kind. Besides, who better than you to let them know what will happen if they double-cross me."

"They won't believe me. I already tried to warn them—"

"What did I say about interrupting me?" Joseph took a step back, re-grasping the whip. "I swear we have to teach you some manners." *Crack.* "Let's try this again."

CHAPTER
SIX
ZEUS

"So, to hell with the law, huh?" Themis snapped from her encircled golden podium adorned with a scale symbol in its center, referring to the attack Zeus and Ares sent to Brienne.

"We tried it your way, and it didn't work." Ares retorted nonchalantly. "Imbeciles like those need to be dealt with differently. It's a bit out of your depth, so I don't expect you to understand."

"You expect me to believe you held judgment over these people?" She sneered. "*Proper* judgement."

"Oh, we held Judgment alright." Zeus snickered.

"Innocent people died. People who pledged to you died." She emphasized. "Don't you have any regard for their lives?"

"It's an unfortunate consequence of war." Ares shrugged. "Besides, I was about to kill the remaining two until Zeus stopped me. If that's not mercy, or... what did you call it? *proper judgement*, I don't know what to tell you."

"They had plenty of time to right their wrongs." Zeus stated, but he could sense that the comment only seemed to aggravate Themis further. "If they decide to stay and fight against us, then they will deal with the consequences."

"Their precious fucking Sovereign couldn't save them this time." Ares mocked.

Nothing but rubble and ash remained after Ares and I tore the place apart. What makes them think that they could vandalize my temple, my statues, blaspheme against me and not suffer the consequences? But he was curious... what did the people do to be hanged in full display? What was considered treachery in the eyes of the Sovereign? Group assemblies that pled to the Olympians? Just mentioning their names out loud? Refusing to follow this... *savior?*

"I've stood by you, council partners no less. But this, I cannot support." Themis addressed Zeus.

"And yet, you summoned me here to waste my time?"

"I summoned you here because you seem to forget we have a Divine Law to uphold."

"You forget, I am the Law."

"You are the enforcer, not the lawmaker." She sneered. "Divine Wrath shall be withheld unless sacred law is defiled." She quoted.

"No mortal shall desecrate a temple, slay a priestess, or bear false witness under divine name." Zeus quoted back. "Earth is granted to humankind for stewardship, not *sovereignty.* I may not be the law in your eyes, but I am the wielder of judgment and have the final word. So, I implore you to choose your next words wisely." Zeus leaned against his thunderbolt-adorned podium.

Her eyes blazed with contempt. *Did she truly believe that I was going to sit back and let them commit treacherous acts against me? Against us? Which included her, but I doubt she is level-headed enough to comprehend. The pure irony of it is interesting, to say the least.*

"If the villages have renounced their fealty to us, they should just be left without support." Athena said, her rich brown hair braided to her head.

"That's just the thing," Ares began, turning to Themis. "They renounced their fealty by destroying everything we made and represent. I'm not one to abide by rules, but who am *I*? Who are *you* to withhold judgment? The Sovereign sure as hell doesn't seem to shy away from it, so why should we? You do remember the Punishment Scale, yes?"

"Then let them suffer in their own mortal way." Hestia chimed in. "I'm not fond of having families suffer, but there are consequences, Themis."

"Precisely." Ares jeered. "This begs for Level 3 judgment."

"Yet, both of you brought down Level 4." Themis pushed back. "You could've done a plague, famine, storms for all I care, but—"

"But nothing." Zeus raised a hand, growing tired of this back and forth. "What kind of message does it send if we condone this behavior?" Silence fell, and only the crackling of the torches beneath their statues around the room could be heard.

"We're already dealing with his threat in Eseron, and he is expanding his hold to displace everything that we are. These attacks were not simple renunciations. It was a provocation."

"A provocation you impulsively answered." Themis jabbed. "There were other ways to deal with this."

"And what is that?" Ares defended, and Themis gave him a look of indignation. "You've been boasting about how we need to do things differently in how we deal with treachery. So, please, go right ahead."

All eyes fell upon her... at the seriousness of her stance, her hands rested atop her podium, how elegantly she looked with the thin spectacles that matched the brown accessories she wore with her navy dress... at the curves of her body, her full lips. Zeus tightened his grip on the edge of the podium.

"We cannot allow this." Themis broke the silence.

"I don't regret it one bit, if that's what you're asking." Zeus said.

"I'm still waiting to see what *justice* she has in mind as an alternative." Ares taunted.

"You could've spoken to the leaders in their community.

Advise them to avoid mass destruction. But no. Both of you had to destroy an entire town just to prove a point." She looked around, gaze stopping at Poseidon and Artemis. "They hung the dead for all to see. As if they were nothing but rags left to dry."

"As much as I want to take credit for the hangings, it wasn't us." Ares threw her a wicked grin, and her face blanched. But it wasn't until Ares gave her a cocky wink that she scowled and tore her gaze away.

"Is no one here going to say anything?" She surveyed the room.

Judging by the rampant silence, no one seemed to agree with her. The corners of Zeus' mouth curled upward. Her stunt had backfired. Who in their right mind would consider her stance to begin with? The war was a clear indicator of who was in charge and who the supreme ruler was. The death of Quinn was the end... until Joseph came around.

The time for talking was over, and everyone knew it.

"What does Apollo have to say about this?" Poseidon asked, tapping his tan fingers a top the podium.

"He denies all involvement. Yet, the Heretic, along with the regular folk, have named him their Savior and the one spear-heading this." Ares answered. "Well, it's been like that since the war, anyway."

"It doesn't make any sense, because how can he bless the country and give his power to the... Sovereign if he has been locked up in Tartarus for all these years?" Athena pointed out. "The chains that bind him prohibit the use of power."

"What are you suggesting?" Artemis asked, her tone hopeful.

"Perhaps, we might have to look deeper into who or what is the driving force behind Castelencia's insubordination."

"What if Apollo is working with someone? To cover for him while and when he got captured?" Hestia suggested.

"My brother is not the kind of male you are painting him to be." Artemis sneered. "He is not one to cause this sort of thing, and for you to think he is—"

"It's no coincidence that *he* was the one claimed by them."
Ares eyed his small blade, picking away any lint that lingered on it.

"Isn't their symbol a sun?" Hephaestus asked.

"Exactly, so instead of looking at Apollo—whose symbol is a
lyre, maybe take a look at Helios. He is the one who presides over
the sun." Artemis jerked her face toward Zeus.

"Helios was with me, fighting in the war." Zeus answered.
"All his time was accounted for. He is as innocent as they come.
Apollo is involved in it. He was claimed by them. Not Helios."
Not to mention that the group explicitly called him by his name.

Artemis shook her head. "I refuse to sit idly by while my
brother rots."

"You're free to join him." Ares offered, making Artemis sneer
his way before turning to Zeus.

"What about what happened at the training grounds?" All
eyes fell on Poseidon.

"What about it?" Zeus asked with feigned interest.

"The body of a nymph was found dead near the training
grounds. Aren't you at least curious given the timing?"

Navaiah's body was found dead near the training grounds by
one of Zeus' scouts. Most likely at the hands of his wife, no
doubt.

"There is nothing to be done. My wife has jealousy issues,
nothing new." He waved a dismissive hand.

"I wish I could take credit. But I am grateful to whoever did
me the favor." She smiled.

"Are you going to consider Athena's suggestion?" Artemis
asked.

Diving deeper into his son's treachery was not something he
wanted to do, but he'd be lying if he said that he was not curious
about how Joseph had maintained his *strength* despite Apollo's
confinement in Tartarus.

Earlier in the day, Argus had told him about the rising
tensions on the continent, and how insiders noted that the
Governor of Windermere, Lazaros Tatiades, had tried to send

correspondence to the Sovereign, but he hadn't received a response for months. It was rumored that Lazaros was trying to tighten or solidify his position with the Sovereign, but they've yet to know how.

Zeus had also looked into Joseph's *power,* and he didn't use anything that gave Apollo credit or any hint of his power source: light, music, archery... nothing. But why claim him?

Why claim him as their *Savior?*

CHAPTER
SEVEN
KATERINA

Darkness.

Silence.

Each step resounded far and wide into the abyss. I walked and walked and walked until a sliver of moonlight cascaded upon a small inky box.

Come to me.

My body halted, eyes fixed on it.

Come to me.

Heaviness weighed on my shoulder as I hesitantly approached it. Even when every inch of my body screamed not to.

"Katerina!" a woman called behind me. Her voice was distraught and urgent.

I turned to the source.

Nothing.

My heart raced, and with a shaky breath, I turned back only to find that the surrounding space had transformed into an endless, humid hall with countless skulls covering the walls and partially caved ceiling, with no real end in sight.

"Katerina!" the voice now echoed from the end of the hall.

Hesitantly, I moved toward it as if my body had a mind of its own. The chill air bit into my exposed skin.

Come to me.

My heart dropped, and an unwanted feeling lunged down my spine. I closed my eyes and focused on my breath.

In... out... in... out...

Upon opening them, two onyx doors stood before me, one with a golden handle and the other with a silver.

"Katerina!" the voice was near, almost as if it was coming from behind one door.

Come to me.

I outstretched a hand, opening the silver door and seeing the inky box on the other side. With trembling hands, I picked it up and almost vomited at the sight of what was inside. I tossed it away, and a single human heart slipped from it.

Still beating.

LUNGING UPRIGHT, KATERINA TAPPED HER CHEST repeatedly. *Still there. Still beating. It was just a weird dream.* She took a deep breath, attempting to bring her heart down to its normal tempo. Ten years after the trials and she still had nightmares... She rubbed her eyes forcefully and glanced at the clock atop her dresser. Merely half past dusk. She didn't remember how she had gone to sleep so early; usually, she'd stay up past midnight because of the nightmares.

Maybe some light reading could help me ease my mind.

She stood from the bed, grabbing the book on her nightstand, and took a seat on the arched, cushioned windowsill. The sheer curtains danced in the cool breeze that caressed her exposed arms. She soaked in the moonlight and allowed her body to relax.

Katerina opened her book, eyes skimming the page.

"To taste Castelencia's harvest is to taste the land itself: honest, living, and vibrant, a testament to a people who believe their prosperity grows only as deeply as their roots sink into the ear—"

What would life look like once I become a Re'Veillite? Would I be given the privilege of going outside without facing my father's wrath? Or will I be confined to the Acrailerion as I am here?

The induction ceremony was still two weeks away, and a lot could happen in two weeks... she put the book down, running her hands through her face.

She didn't need to worry about any of that now. She needed to get some rest. She needed sleep. She—her eyes landed on an orange glow in the horizon as faint music played. She could hardly make out anything that was happening, but judging by the lively music and the tiny figures moving around, she was sure that this was a celebration of sorts.

Odd. There weren't any events scheduled for this week the last time she checked. *You should go.* She shoved the thought away. *No, I shouldn't.* She glanced at the celebration again. *It didn't seem to be that far from here. Perhaps a twenty-minute walk?*

She pushed the thought away, picking up her book once again.

"As their roots sink into the earth."

You wanted excitement, didn't you? She moved away from the windowsill. *I'm going to town tomorrow anyway—but with the Re'Veillites to work—no, stop. Go to sleep. You know damn well that if word gets to father about you leaving again. Shit.* The sound of shackles and chains slithered into her mind. *No, I don't need a reminder.*

A tug in her chest screamed at her to go. She had to. *Father is most likely asleep... I'll be able to check it out and come back before sunrise... Savior help me.* Who knew when she'd had the opportunity again?

Her stomach turned, and the heaviness in her chest increased.

"Shit..." she didn't know why, but she had to go.

Knocks followed by the opening of her bedchamber's door revealed a housemaid with a silver tray in hand, filled with an assortment of fruits and a decanter.

"Good evening, miss." She bowed her head. "May I?"

Katerina nodded, unfazed by the sudden opening of her door. She was used to this. The only real privacy she'd gotten was when she was in the bathroom.

"Is there anything else you wish for before I retire for the evening?" She asked after placing the tray down atop the cream table near the bed.

"No, but thank you." There wasn't anything she could help with, anyway.

The housemaid nodded and strode toward the door.

"Wait."

She stopped, turning to meet her gaze.

"Just out of curiosity, what's that?" Katerina gestured to the orange glow and faint music.

The housemaid approached the windowsill. "What exactly are you referring to, miss?"

Confusion washed over Katerina's face. "That." She pointed at the only sliver of light in the distance. "Can't you see the light or hear the music?"

The housemaid scanned the area out the window before turning back at Katerina. "Are you feeling alright, miss?"

Katerina opened her mouth to ask her what she saw, but she knew it was futile. The housemaid may think of her as going insane or falling ill. Her face said it all, and this would just raise more questions than answers.

"I think I'm just exhausted." Katerina lied. "I may just need to lie down."

"Shall I fetch the House's Naturopath?"

"No," Katerina smiled politely. "Thank you, you may go."

The housemaid bowed her head and left. Once the door shut, Katerina looked out the window again. The orange glow grew brighter, and the music louder. How was she able to see this while the housemaid couldn't? Was she truly starting to go insane?

She rubbed her eyes. She knew she had to go, especially after this. She had to find out what it was; but she just had to find a way out first.

Katerina changed into one of her spare running outfits: a loosened, hooded cream top with a fitted darker brown leather belt at the waist for mobility; dark long pants and light running boots. Her onyx locks were bunched and secured with hairpins.

Cracking open the door, she slipped out of the room and stealthily maneuvered her way through the dim, decorated halls and toward the back room. To her surprise, there weren't any guards nearby, which was a surprise considering how her father was often paranoid of an attack. The challenge itself would be in actually leaving the grounds, but she couldn't get complacent. She hurried down the grand stairs, scanning for any passersby, but so far, the coast was clear.

Careful not to make any unnecessary noise, Katerina scurried to the left wing corridor and slithered into the backroom, where she was instantly greeted by pure darkness as soon as she closed the door behind her. Turning on the lights would be a dead giveaway. She couldn't use a candle; that would leave evidence. Her mind trickled back to this morning, envisioning the layout.

I entered the room from the back door... in front of me there was a hall slightly offset to the right when looking from the exit. Therefore, its going to be to my left. She took a sidestep and walked forward using her arms as barriers in front of her. *Near the hall, there was a... a...* her legs crashed against a hard box, making her lose balance. *Shit. So much for stealthiness.*

Blindly tapping the box, she managed to find a clear path and moved with her arms outstretched until her hands pressed against a rough surface. Her breath caught as her hand moved down, and cold metal bit her skin. *The door.* She turned the handle. *Why is it unlocked?* She stowed away the question, focusing on the task at hand.

With the door slightly ajar, she ensured no guards were within sight before slipping out and dashing toward the gates. Her gaze swept every which way, yet not a single guard was on patrol. She should worry... but, she was already out. Screw it. She reached the gates only to find them locked. *Seriously?* She looked at the top of the gate. *You are not jumping that. Well... am I? I could. No, you can't.*

"Out on another run?"

Johan's voice startled her. His dark curls barely fell over his eyes.

She turned. *Well...* "Can you blame me?" She shrugged bashfully.

"You're lucky the Sovereign reduced manpower for tonight," he laughed, approaching the lock. "Go, but be careful out there."

"Savior bless you!" She said, dashing out through the gates.

Trees upon trees and branches surrounded her, and she didn't stop running until she was a decent distance away from the Fortress. She pressed a hand against a tree, catching her breath. She might've overexerted herself in that sprint. But she made it out.

Focus. Where is this? There was a bonfire, and—distant drumming turned her attention west and without much forethought, she moved in its direction. *Leaving felt easy. No, it was easy.* It wasn't normal for the Fortress to be so... empty. Not a single housemaid or guard in sight. No guards...well, save for Johan. *Better him than anyone else.*

The tug in her chest returned, more intense with each stride, and her shoulders suddenly felt heavy, as if she'd been carrying a heavy bag for miles. *What is going on?* The surrounding air thickened as lively cheers and slurred conversations were able to be heard amidst the rhythmic sounds of tambourines and other melodies.

Bodies shoved past her, and she missed them by an inch. Her jaw clenched, and unease stirred in her stomach. She'd never seen so many people out at night. Most of the permitted gatherings were held during the day. *Why did I come here again?* Every muscle in her body tensed the closer she got to the sea of people.

Men scurried past her without a second glance as their bodies tumbled through, spilling the liquid in their cups.

On one side of the open field, women danced around the flame, while on the other, a large group knelt on the grassy surface, pressing their foreheads to the ground, in front of three large statues.

One of them wore a sleeveless black and grey tunic that showed off powerful arms, which held on to... a bident? A real one, from the looks of it, shining against the flames and moonlight. Her mouth dried as her eyes drifted to the one opposite him, who had a blue tunic that only covered the bottom half of his muscular body. He held on to a trident.

Her throat tightened as she finally laid eyes on the one in the center. Locks of white covered his face that matched the tunic, fastened with a golden brooch, covering half of his body as well as showcasing muscles beyond compare.

She blinked, and she could've sworn she saw a flicker of electricity emerge from his palms. *No, no. My mind is playing tricks on me.* She shook her head. *So help me, Savior. What did I get myself into?*

Katerina continued to move, evading the drunken men with women in their arms, charging toward the wood line. Some didn't have the decency to wait since they got it on near the fire. *Vulgar. Disgusting. Imbeciles. I've seen enough. I need to go home.* Her body shimmied past a group of people, surveying how they moved toward the fire. She cocked her head and noticed a dais in front of the large open flame.

"Oh," a deep male voice said with amusement. "I've never seen *you* here before."

She kept walking; it was more likely for someone else. *Just don't stop. Don't acknowledge.*

A strong hand grabbed her arm, flinging her around until her gaze locked with icy-blue eyes, blonde hair, and a wicked smile with light stubble on his strong jaw.

I am fucked. Her body trembled, but she did her best to remain calm.

"Where did you come from, sweet thing?"

"None of your business." Her hair fell loose as she jerked her body away from his grasp, but he held her in place. "If you don't wipe that smug smile off your face..."

"Oh." He cocked a brow. "Princess has a temper. Indulge me."

She gritted her teeth. "You haven't *seen* temper. Let me go."

His smile only grew more wicked, and he gripped her chin. She jerked away.

"The gods would love a sassy little princess like yourself." He lowered to her ear. "Not after I have my fun with you first."

"Fuck off." She pushed him away, but her body remained under his hold.

"Quite the foul mouth you have, don't you?"

Her body tensed as he dragged a sharpened tip along her jaw and down her throat. *Where did you pull that from? Oh, I'm dying tonight. That's what happens when I leave when I'm not supposed to.*

"You done playing, Nik?" Someone yelled in the distance, but his eyes remained on her, flashing an amused grin and resting the tip below her chin.

"Don't stray too far." He secured the blade. "A princess like yourself shouldn't be venturing into this part of town alone."

I have to go. Now. I'm done playing this game. I've seen enough. I've had enough.

She yanked her arm and walked away. She could feel his gaze pinned on her, but she didn't look back. The heaviness in her shoulders increased as she scooted past a couple kissing. She picked up her pace.

The tug in her chest intensified to the point she felt she was about to have a heart attack. She stopped, her sight becoming blurry at the edges. *What is happening to me?* She tried not to stumble as her head thundered against her temples.

"First time?"

Her eyes drifted to a redhead in a deep green dress. She was behind a table with an assortment of intriguing liquids.

"Let's see, a thundering headache and a foggy vision?"

"How'd you—"

"I'm a healer; it's what I do." She smiled. "Here." She slid a cup of turquoise liquid across the table.

"What's this?" Katerina managed to ask.

"An Ameliorate Tonic. It'll make you feel better."

She picked up the cup and twirled it lightly. *What if it's poisoned?* The redhead didn't seem to recognize her, and if she did; she was doing a hell of a great job in pretending she didn't.

"Don't worry, we have a lot of newcomers this year. It's pretty normal to feel a bit apprehensive; and with the big shift in energy with the Olympians." She fanned her face with her hand. "It can take a toll on the body."

I knew it. I knew it. I knew it. She kept her face neutral. She knew this was orchestrated by the rebels, but having someone say it out loud, just confirmed her unease.

"So, what's all this for?" Katerina brought the cup to her lips. Hints of blueberry, mint and other tangy scents filled her nostrils.

"Let me guess, Windermerian?"

"What gave it away?" Katerina lied, scarily easily.

"How lost and terrified you look. Typically, Windermerian refugees are the most frightened and the slowest to adapt to our ways. Mainly because of your Governor's rule and alliance with the heretic we have for a Sovereign."

Windermerian refugees? Heretic... Katerina resisted the urge to scowl at the insult. No matter how much she desp—disliked her father. "Yeah, it's crazy."

"I'm Chryssa." She shouted over the music.

"Rhea." Katerina peered down at the liquid, head slamming against her temples. "Aren't you all worried the Sovereign might attack with all this being out in the open?"

"Nah," she waved dismissively. "Whenever we do this, the

Olympians put a barrier around us so that we're not seen by the naked eye or heard by anyone not affiliated with us—better yet, we're not seen by the heretic's people. So, that's why we're able to be out in the open. Don't worry, we're safe."

But that made little sense for Katerina because how the hell was she—*how could I see you from my window?* But then again, the housemaid didn't. If this place cannot be seen by the naked eye, how was she here? Why was she drawn here? There was something here that was pulling her in; locking her in place. She should've been halfway home already, if not already in the Fortress.

Her head thundered ferociously as she gazed down at the turquoise drink in her hands. *If I die, I die.* She took a sip. Notes of blueberry and mint coated her tongue as it washed smoothly down her throat.

"So," Chryssa mixed different liquids. "What's your story? What made you leave?"

Shit. Think, think, think. She is a rebel who hates your family. Choose your words wisely.

"I guess I wanted to do something different for myself. I'm a bit tired of having others dictate my life, to be honest, so I came here of my own accord."

"A rebel." She smiled, and Katerina almost grimaced at the word. "I knew I liked you. You're not like other Windermerians I've met."

"How so?"

"Bah, too whiny. Too fragile. Pessimists. The works." Chryssa's gaze trailed behind her. "Looks like I'm not the only one who finds you interesting."

Katerina looked back, finding Nik with his eyes glued to her before turning away. "Do you know him?"

Chryssa let out a sigh. "Yeah... That's Nik Baratos, a soldier of the Olympian Army. He's a bit of a brute."

"You don't say." Katerina's words were bitter as she turned back to face Chryssa.

"I see you've made his acquaintance." She laughed. "Don't worry. He's harmless. He may be part of the Blood Legion, but he is harmless. Unlike those over there." She nodded to the group a few paces behind him.

"Blood Legion?" Katerina's eyebrows furrowed.

"Ares's division. Don't they teach you anything over at—nevermind, I already know how they're hounding everyone down there. I can't blame you for not knowing." Chryssa wiped down her table. "But yeah, the Olympian Army is divided into twelve divisions. As you can guess, one is for each Olympian."

Oh my... in a split second, Katerina's mind drifted back to the men her father had in the Light Militia... not that many when compared to twelve divisions....

"What about them?" Katerina gestured at the men behind Nik. "Are they part of the Olympian Army too?"

"Nah, they're just a group of imbeciles who don't have anything better to do." She downed the contents in her cup. "The one in the far right though, Thyrion, is the one you should stray away from."

Katerina's eyes fell upon the man with short, snow-white hair and a scar across his face.

"He's ruthless and trying to regain his position in the Army."

"What'd he do?"

"Betrayed his men during the war. That's all I know." She picked up a piece of something off her garment. "Apparently, he has a *special surprise* for the gods tonight in an attempt to get into their good graces."

"What's tonight, anyway? I see people doing all sorts of *things* here."

"I'm only going to answer because I like you. After this, go enjoy the night, love."

Katerina nodded, grateful for her willingness to share information, even though things would've gone very differently if she'd known who she truly was.

"This is Veneration Night. Every year, we summon or pledge

fealty to the big three. Sometimes they come to Eseron to bless the ones who worship them post-war and have lived a righteous life through devotion. If they don't show up, we use statues blessed in their name. The blessings look different depending on the collective's intentions and how strong their fealty is to them. People from all over bring offerings to them. Last year, we did it in Aeshelyn, and the blessing was incomprehensible." Chryssa smiled. "I've never known joy as pure."

"I'm guessing the offering is the special surprise these guys have for tonight?"

"Could be," she shrugged. "But I wouldn't be surprised if it's just another feigned attempt to get into their good graces after they betrayed them."

Intrigue blossomed within Katerina, but if she kept asking questions, it'll bring unnecessary attention to herself and potentially blow her cover.

"But enough history. Let's see what's happening over there." She gestured Katerina to follow as she stepped away from the table.

Katerina followed her to the back of the group, and the tambourines slowed down their tempo. A silver-haired man in a dusty cream tunic stepped onto the dais, bowing toward the statues of the Big Three before turning to the crowd.

"It is with great honor and pride that I commend you all on this blessed Veneration Night." He outstretched his arms, and the crowd erupted in a cheering frenzy. "We are survivors, and we will not be silenced. I don't care how many times the heretic's soldiers raid our homes and destroy our belongings. We are backed by the real. By the most powerful! I don't see this other blasphemous entity backing him! Blessing him! The City! NOTHING!"

Katerina's stomach hollowed. *I feel like I'm going to be sick.* She needed to leave, but something pinned her in place. She couldn't move. *Don't panic. Breathe.*

"Of course, it wouldn't be Veneration Night if offerings

weren't presented to our very special guests." He signaled to the crowd, and they immediately split in the middle.

Katerina found herself moving to the split, stopping on the first row of spectators.

"First Offering." The man announced.

A woman stepped forward with a basket in hand, the stench of fish invading Katerina's senses. She bowed and paid reverence to Poseidon for blessing their rivers by providing him with the first catch of the season.

People slowly lined themselves to present their gifts. *I've never seen them leaving them as piles... usually we burn them for cleansing. Do they take the items with them?* Katerina turned to leave, but her feet remained in place. It was getting late, and she'd already exposed herself enough.

A man stepped forward with a grin so sinister it stirred unease within her. He bowed slowly before turning his attention to the crowd. Katerina instantly recognized Thyrion.

"Fellow brothers and sisters, today is a blessed night indeed. It's not everyday we get valuable offerings in our midst. My chest swells with pride as I present to you, my offering." He extended a hand to the back of the split.

A wave of ice-cold chills ran down Katerina's bones as she laid eyes on a bound, small, delicate woman with golden brown hair and warm ivory skin in a celeste-colored dress.

Jezebelle.

Her body was being pulled forward by the chains binding her hands. Nothing but pure horror was plastered over her face.

"I present to you the daughter of the Heretic."

CHAPTER
EIGHT
JOSEPH

FLAMES DANCED INSIDE THE HEARTH AS THREE members of Joseph's council raised their palms to it—Vern, Fotis, and Ermis. They chanted in unison the blessing to be placed upon the Fortress, the Acrailerion, and Caverest. Joseph clasped onto the ceramic bowl and drank the blessed water.

"Accept this sacrifice," Joseph muttered in the ancient Calastalli tongue as he placed the bowl atop the black marble altar and grabbed the small Damascus dagger a top it.

He turned to his men, dressed in deep red robes with black trim. The sun medallion that hung from their necks glimmered under the firelight, the only light in the dark, humid crypt.

"May we take this blessing and provide to those in need," approaching the hearth, Joseph presented the blade. "May he grant us strength. May he make us fruitful." He cut into his palm, resisting the urge to wince. Sharp pain radiated through his hand, slithering up his arm as he hovered the wound over the flames. Droplets of blood trickled slowly. "May these offerings to you serve as reverence and *proof* of our unyielding devotion to you." Joseph closed his throbbing fist, letting the blood stream increase from it. "Praise be to our Savior."

"Praise be to our Savior." They echoed and bowed.

Removing his fist, Joseph instantly wrapped it in a cloth near the stone altar. His palm pulsed steadily. *Too deep.* He turned away from them, eyes still on the crimson-stained wrap.

He whispered in the ancient Calastalli tongue, and guards emerged from the shadows. Confusion painted his men's faces as the guards encircled them. Some asked questions. Others tried to pull themselves away from their hold. A part of Joseph wanted to stop this, but she had to come first. *If she wasn't at stake...* he drew in a sharp breath.

Joseph uttered some additional chants in the ancient tongue, and chains slithered through the ground, and shackles clamped onto their limbs. Screams rippled as their bodies slammed against the skull-laced wall. He ignored the urgency in their voices as he ordered his guards to leave but to keep the exit sealed.

He closed his eyes, reciting the remaining parts of the ritual. Ice-cold heaviness crept into him. Bracing his body against the stone altar, darkness slithered into his vision and claws sank deep into his throbbing mind. **Well, oh, well.** His breath turned heavy as he steadied himself as best he could. His limbs fell numb, his chest heavy, and his mind...

CHAINS RATTLED AGAINST THE BONES AS THEY PLEADED how they had been faithful to the Paragons of Light. How they never betrayed him. One even mentioned how he left his family to join their cause. Regardless of their beliefs and devotion throughout the years, this was a necessary action.

Joseph's back straightened, and he tilted his head upon noticing the tear-stained face of Ermis. The corners of his mouth curled upward as he reached for the blade and approached him.

Ermis' body trembled as he pathetically tried to reach the ground with his feet. "Please!"

Joseph traced the tip of the blade from his bald head down to his cheek and then down to his jaw.

He sobbed uncontrollably while the others, frozen in fear, watched carefully from the corners of their eyes. **Humor me.**

Joseph chuckled, scraping the tear streaming down Ermis' face with the blade.

"Y-your eyes..." He quivered.

Joseph smiled wickedly, lips stretching unnaturally wide and eyes growing darker, pupils dilating to the point they swallowed the iris entirely.

"Wha-what do yo-you want from me? I've been loyal. Been on your council for ye-years. Please Joseph. Please."

Joseph bared his teeth, keeping his eyes locked on his prey.

Ermis stuttered, clearing his throat. "I—" Blood poured out of his mouth, barely registering what just happened until Joseph brought the crimson-covered blade into view.

The color vanished from Ermis' face as pure horror washed over him. "Why?" he whispered as the life drained from his miserable eyes.

Joseph couldn't help but smile, but then his attention drifted to the next. **I'm getting bored.** He clicked his tongue disapprovingly and brought his blade to the next victim, not bothering to clean the gunk that coated his hand.

"No. Wait. Please. I'll give you anything!" Vern shrieked. His brown hair matted to his shiny forehead.

Joseph dragged his tongue through his sharp canines and raised a brow. **Let's make this fun.** With a snap of his fingers, the three bodies slammed against the uneven ground, covered in moss and scattered bones. Blood oozed out of Ermis' corpse, saturating the dusty concrete.

Vern sprinted as if there were no tomorrow. **As if he could go anywhere.** While Fotis remained frozen in place, eyes as wide as boulders. **I'll deal with you later.** Claws sank deeper into Joseph's mind and strode after Vern.

He tossed and flipped the blade over and over again, catching it by the hilt every time, casually moving through the crypt's tunnels. Torches lined the walls, barely illuminating the space.

*Hurried footsteps turn left, distancing themselves from him. Even though the place was vast, there was only so far you could go. Besides, with there being only one entry and one exit, Vern will soon find himself coming back to where he was. **But where's the fun in that?***

Joseph strode further and further into the darkened crypt. Rows of ancient, weathered skulls were arranged neatly in niches carved into the stone walls, their hollow eyes glowing faintly with an eerie light. Cobwebs and dust covered the corners, and a faint mist lingered in the air. Dim light filtered in through cracks in the ceiling, casting long shadows.

*He stilled between two massive vaulted arches, carefully listening to Vern's hurried footsteps. **Left, then right, then up...** His lips curl upward at the rattling sound of Vern trying to open the door atop the stairs. **Gotcha.***

*Like a predator hunting its prey, Joseph ran and stalked up the stone spiral staircase. The rattling and banging sounds grew louder and louder. Vern pleaded for help, for someone to let him out. For anyone to come to his aid. **Pity.** Joseph clicked his tongue and Vern's body froze, finally registering Joseph's presence behind him.*

Joseph smiled, eyes gleaming with malice. "Let's give them a show, shall we?" he said in a voice not entirely his own as he grabbed onto the back of Vern's collar before he could meet his gaze, and dragged his body down.

Vern thrashed against the musty ground, unable to stand. He screamed, pleading again and again as debris poked and scraped his exposed flesh and fabric. He even tried to grab onto Joseph's feet, but a swift kick to his face made him start behaving.

Joseph tossed his body next to Ermis' as if he were nothing but a dusty rag.

Vern struggled to his feet, barely able to hold himself up as rage filled those blue eyes. Absolute and utter regret glinted for a second, but he sized himself up as if telling Joseph that he was not going down without a fight.

Baring his teeth again, Joseph tightened the grip around his blade and offered a taunting smile. "Finally grew the balls I cut off ya'?" He tossed the blade.

Vern charged toward him and, in a swift movement, Joseph's hands wrapped around his head, snapping his neck. Vern's body dropped in an instant. **I'm getting tired of this shit.**

Joseph's eyes fell on Fotis, whose body hung from the ceiling. He'd made a noose out of the scattered fabric on the altar. Joseph cut the noose, letting Fotis' corpse drop, skull cracking upon impact.

The hearth still burned mightily as he carved and pulled the hearts out of all the bodies. Joseph's hands and clothes were drenched in blood and guts as he tossed the corpses into the fire, leaving the hearts on a silver platter.

He watched as the flames consumed every inch of flesh and fabric, stinking up the crypt. His head spun as the claws released their hold. He tumbled over to the altar, using it to steady himself. The heaviness in his chest ceased, replaced by a hollow sensation.

A CHILL WENT DOWN HIS SPINE AS HE PEERED DOWN AT his blood-stained hands. *What have I done?* He gritted his teeth, suppressing the urge to vomit. All he wanted to do was throw the hearts into the fire. *Deal be damned. But my wife... I can't just abandon her. My daughters already think I let her die.* Joseph pushed the thought away before he spiraled.

"I have to say, each time you put on a better show than the last." Eris emerged from the shadows, and he didn't hide his displeased expression. "Oh, come on," she pouted, gracefully moving toward the hearts. "Your debt is paid, and with an hour to spare."

I didn't realize you were keeping a timer on me. Joseph remained silent. All he wanted was to take a shower and get all of this gunk out.

She crushed one of the hearts in her hand, vanishing into thin air. "It'll all be worth it in the end, don't you worry."

Doubtful.

"Rena thanks you for your contributions."

"Don't you speak her name." Joseph snapped.

A smirk crept onto her lips. "Or what?" she crushed the last heart. "You'll carve *my* heart too?" she laughed.

I can sure fucking try. "As if you'll complain if I put my hands on you."

"Don't tease me; I might just take yours instead." She glanced over his disgusting ensemble and smiled wickedly. "I'll be back soon. In the meantime, keep working on getting Aeshelyn's buy-in. You have a country to rule, after all."

"They've pledged to Zeus."

"Then un-pledge them, stir conflict, get them to be distrustful. You humans are too easy to rile up; it shouldn't be hard for you to get this done."

"When will he let me see Rena?"

"Get Aeshelyn." She vanished into the darkness.

A non-answer.

FOR MANY YEARS, JOSEPH HAD ENSURED PEACE WITHIN his own country. He remembered it vividly. How he fought in the front lines. How Rena escaped. How a family begged for mercy as he tried to stop the blood from spilling out of a kid's stomach. How the Naturopaths exhausted themselves trying to save people's lives, yet there were not enough to get to the others in time. How men said goodbye to their families. The loud cries that rippled through the—he shook his head.

Countless lives of allies and innocents were lost. They defended they're grounds and fought against the Olympians with everything they had, and it wasn't until Zeus landed that destructive fucking blow that life as they knew it ceased to exist.

He was merely thirty-five, and he had to—Joseph took a breath. He'd never forgive Zeus for what he did to them. He scanned the marked map of Eseron, checking which villages had been targeted thus far. Red *X*s covered almost all of Castelencia, save the capital, where they lay.

"What's the status of the shipment to Windermere?" Joseph asked Sebastian, keeping his gaze on the lands.

"It arrived this morning. I received word once it docked. Governor Lazaros sends his regards and wants to schedule some time to speak with you."

"About?"

"The suggestions he made about the alliance. He didn't specify which one in particular."

The alliance between Castelencia and Windermere was one of the longest standing, dating back to when Quinn's father, Marcus, was in power. Joseph was brought up to speed on the conditions of said alliance, but the changes proposed by Lazaros aren't ones he was fond of, starting off with updates to weaponry shipment. He wouldn't be surprised if Lazaros inquired into why Joseph hadn't responded or paid a visit to his manor. Lazaros had been sending word, but in between Joseph's obligations, he never got a chance to read any of it.

"Send word to the leaders of Eseron that I am to hold a banquet in a week's time. I am to expect everyone's attendance, including Aeshelyn's. Have the housemaids prepare a feast for them—a special platter from each country to show our... consideration."

"Aeshelyn barely responds to any of our correspondence."

"Make sure they are in attendance." Joseph said, voice cold, threatening even. They almost had an alliance with Aeshelyn a long time ago, but... things happen.

Sebastian nodded once. "I will do my best."

"No. You will make it happen."

He gulped and nodded again. "I will make it happen, don't you worry."

Joseph turned back to the map in silent dismissal, surveying it once again. Yet, Sebastian's presence lingered like a putrid smell. "Is there anything else you need?"

"The people want to know who is to host this evening's mass."

I had forgotten about that. Shit. Joseph looked up at him, keeping his face unreadable. Vern usually was the one that covered for him whenever he was occupied. *Fuck.*

"I'll be there momentarily."

CHAPTER
NINE
KATERINA

KATERINA'S GAZE REMAINED GLUED ON HER SISTER AS the final offerings were presented to the gods. *How the hell are you here? Why? Just fucking why?*

She resisted the urge to run toward her. That would be a dead giveaway and not only put her in even more danger but also drag herself into it. *Oh, who am I fucking kidding? I am already in the middle of it.*

The tambourines played once again, and everyone slowly dispersed to different areas of the field, but Katerina remained in place, despite the bodies imploring her to move out of the way.

Chryssa appeared next to her, handing her a cup and tapping it lightly with hers. "To another year full of blessings."

Katerina forced a smile as they both brought the cups to their lips. *To another year...* "I think I'm going to call it a night."

"You've got somewhere to stay?" She asked over the sudden loud rhythm.

"Yeah... I've got extended family nearby." It wasn't technically a lie, but enough to cover herself.

"Alright! Hope to see you again soon. It was really great meeting you, Rhea!" Chryssa pulled her into a hug before trotting away and disappearing into the crowd.

Katerina turned back to Jezebelle, but she was nowhere in sight. Panic stirred within her. *Remain calm.* She trotted forward, scanning her surroundings. *Remain calm. I won't be able to get her out of here if I lose my mind.* She slowed her pace as she scooted by the sea of people dancing, laughing, kissing, and mingling.

A stark contrast to how she was feeling. How Jezebelle might have felt, too. *Savior help her. She must be so scared.* Katerina's mouth dried, throat clenched shut. *Who did this to her?* She suppressed every single urge to cry, to scream, to—she stopped.

There she was in the distance. Sitting as she hugged her knees with her head resting on top of them. The glint of silver chains around her waist made her skin crawl. She was bound to a damn tree like some animal. Rage boiled within her. Who cared about the outrageous piles of offerings that surrounded her? Who cared about any of this? She would burn this place to the ground if it was the last thing she'd do. She just wanted her sister safe and away from these lunatics.

Katerina's hardened gaze trailed back to the controlled flames behind the dais, and a smirk crept onto her lips as she turned back to her sister. Careful not to draw attention, she hurried toward her.

Jezebelle's head tilted upward, and Katerina's heart shattered at the sight of her crystal eyes and tear-stained cheeks.

She knelt beside her, cupping her face. "Are you hurt? Who did this to you?" Katerina's eyes searched hers for answers, but Jezebelle only blinked in return, each time slower.

"I'm... ffff... fine..."

Shit. Her heart leaped to her throat. *Don't panic.* Katerina raised her arms, eyeing the chains and looking for the lock. She'd been around chains long enough to maneuver around one. *Guess I have him to thank for that.* She rolled her eyes at the reminder, shoving the unease intensifying inside her core.

She examined the lock in her hands, tugging it. The rattle of the partially loose shackle made relief wash through her. But she couldn't get complacent. Her heart hammered against her ribs as she scanned her surroundings again. Everyone was still dancing around. Their attention locked on the celebrations and the sounds of tambourines. *I got to hurry.* She tightened her grip on the lock, attempting to stop the violent trembling of her hands.

"I'm almost done, okay, Jezy. Stay with me."

"O-o… okay…" Jezebelle's voice was breathy.

The lock shook uncontrollably. *Breathe. Breathe.* Katerina's mind raced a thousand miles per second. She ran a hand through her hair, and her breath caught upon feeling a hairpin.

This will have to do.

With a shaky breath, she pulled it out, opened and twisted it just enough. She hovered over the small keyhole. *Savior help me.* She jammed the pin inside, frantically shaking and twisting it again and again.

"Come on…" she said through gritted teeth.

Snap.

Her blood ran cold, burning her eyes as she stared at the half of the pin still encrusted inside the keyhole and then at the other half in her hand.

Leaf-crunching footsteps neared. Her throat tightened once again. *Fuck it.* She frantically pulled on the lock again and again and again.

The footsteps grew nearer, but she didn't stop. She tugged as hard as she possibly could, heat radiated through her hands. A pulse of energy jolted her palms.

Then the lock gave in, opening completely. She stilled, eyeing it in her hands. The shackle and the locking mechanism had melted… how—she stopped, remembering where she was.

She tossed it and quickly helped her sister stand, propping one of her arms over her shoulders as Katerina held her tightly around the waist, making Jezebelle lean against her for support.

"You know it's against the Olympian law to steal an offering for the gods, right?"

Katerina's body stiffened, and chills ran down her spine. A middle-aged man painted by the faint glow of the distant flames surveyed her and then Jezebelle. He wore a white and gold chiton made of fine linen, with intricate embroidery of symbolic patterns like olive branches and laurel leaves along the hem. Over the chiton, he had a gold-draped himation that cascaded over his shoulders and a scepter in his hands. *You have to be kidding.*

"And since when do I care about what your gods want?" Katerina hissed at the Olympian High Priest, readjusting her hold on Jezebelle, whose body became heavier by the second.

His lips curled upward. "This is a blessed night indeed." Surprise laced his words. "Both of the Heretic's daughters in attendance tonight."

Katerina scowled. "So you can give us both? I don't think so."

"Are you even aware of how valuable the both of you are to us —to the gods?" He motioned upward.

"I hope you burn in whatever hellhole it is you believe in." She hissed, tightening her slipping grip.

"I would rather send you in my stead." He took a step toward them, determination in his eyes.

Katerina clutched onto Jezebelle. *Like hell I'm going to let him take her.* Her throat clenched. *I don't have much time. Think.*

"I wouldn't." She warned. *Seriously? Was that the best you could do?*

He laughed but kept walking their way.

Her stomach turned as she carefully moved away from him without tearing her gaze away. She felt cowardly. She needed to fight. *If it weren't for Jezebelle's frailness right now... So, fucking be it. He wants us, he'll have to fucking drag us.*

"Hold yourself up for a moment." Katerina whispered as she released her sister carefully, and squared myself to fight.

He let out a sly laugh and released his scepter, letting it fall on the grass.

She didn't know what she was thinking. She'd never fought a day in her life, but she couldn't just... *breathe. Think. Think.* Her thunderous heartbeat drowned out the music. Her eyes scanned his body, searching for any weak spots. She could barely see anything; his tunic was too loose. *Shit.* Her heart leaped faster as she clenched her fists. Her body slammed against the ground, ripping the air out of her aching lungs.

He wrapped his veiny hands around her throat, applying just enough to cut off her air supply. She thrashed, reaching for the fabric along his neck. She couldn't reach. She gasped for air, but was futile. Her lungs burned, eyes watering in response. *THINK DAMMIT!*

She kneed his lower back again and again, making him release her. She pushed him off and slithered out from beneath him. She kicked his face, sending him tumbling back. Katerina welcomed the fresh air that filled her starved lungs, struggling to her feet.

He wiped the blood from his nose, a murderous look plastered over his face as he got to his feet.

Savior help me. Katerina looked around, grabbing the biggest rock she could find. *Please help me.* Pain seared into her palms as the rock dug into her flesh.

He rushed toward her, and Katerina raised her armed hand, ready to strike. He stopped. Confusion washed over her. His eyes widened as his body pleaded for air and clutched onto his chest.

Is he trying to get my guard down?

He gasped again and again.

"What... what are you... doing to me?" He asked between intense breaths. Shadows crept from behind him.

I'm not doing anything, but I sure as shit like to be.

He fell to his knees, one hand bracing the ground while the other frantically tugged on his tunic. He took one last breath before completely collapsing as the darkness consumed him whole.

Her body flinched at the distant screams of horror, pulling her out of her frozen state. Flames scattered, consuming everything in their path as people ran in all directions.

What... the... fuck?

She lunged over to Jezebelle, propping her up. Her body

leaned against her, eyes barely open as they maneuvered to escape the fiery night.

Jezebelle's eyes fluttered open as Katerina waited next to her bed with a small plate of cheese and bread and a glass of water. Flashes from last night slammed into Katerina's mind as she stared at her sister's moving body. It felt surreal. One moment she was in her room looking out the window; the next, she was saving the life of her sister. Katerina rubbed her eyes, while shaky breaths slithered out of her lips.

She couldn't shake it. How everything went down. How her sister was there trembling with fear. The horror in her eyes... she wanted to ask, *how did she even get there? What happened? Who brought her there?* She had so many fucking questions, but she needed to wait until... until she could make sure that she was okay before she started bombarding her with questions and potentially overwhelming her.

Jezebelle's eyes met her sister's, and the corners of her mouth curled. She slowly sat herself up, wincing and propping her hands beside her for stability.

"Hey, how are you feeling?" Katerina asked softly, eyes scanning for any other signs of trauma.

Jezebelle opened her mouth, and Katerina could've sworn she saw her eyes crystallize. *What happened to you? I swear I will fucking kill whoever did this to you.* She used to be full of light. Full of warmth, and Katerina hated whoever did this to her. She would find them, and she would make them regret making her sister go through this.

"I'm alright." She winced as she adjusted herself in the bed.

"Here, I brought you some water, figured you might need it."

She took the glass, bringing it to her lips.

"Do you remember what happened last night?"

Jezebelle's eyes surveyed the room slowly, and silent tears

traced her cheeks. She sobbed quietly before turning back to Katerina. "I... I remember... I remember just... very faintly..." her eyes darted around the room. "I don't know..."

"It's okay, just try. Anything that comes to mind. Just try, please."

"Well, I... all I know is that I... I was out, and we went to the... no, we haven't gone to the Acrailerion..."

Shit, this was worse than I thought. "It's okay, Jezy," Katerina whispered. "Drink some water and here." She passed the plate of bread and cheese, which Jezebelle placed on her lap.

Jezebelle scanned it carefully, playing with the small slices of graviera. She buried her face in her hands.

What soulless shit...? Katerina kept asking herself the same fucking question, yet she didn't want to push her; but she needed to fucking know what the fuck happened.

Her heart dropped. Everything made sense now... why she felt an intense pull to be there. It makes sense why the tug in her chest was so aggravatingly heavy. Why she couldn't sleep. Why she couldn't leave... Everything made fucking sense, but... *Savior please, what fucking happened?* Katerina grabbed her sister's hands gently.

"Hey... It's okay. It's okay. You're safe now. I am here now. I'm going to get Jasmine, so that she can take a look at you."

"Please don't, I don't want her to see me like this, please. She's most likely gonna send me to the Acrailerion and make me see the Naturopaths."

"I mean... it's not a bad idea."

Jezebelle glared at Katerina, indignation lining her features.

"If you think about it—come on. I hate seeing you like this. It's a good idea for you to actually go get help. You're lucky that it was me who found you..."

"I said, I'm fine. I just don't want to be her charity case."

"Don't worry, I won't make you see her." Katerina reassured. "Would you rather talk to me instead?"

Jezebelle nodded.

"Okay," Katerina breathed. "Please tell me what you remember. I don't wanna push you, but I really got to know who did this to you, please."

"Fine." She let out an exasperated sigh as her eyes scanned the room once more as if she were digging through her mind, shuffling through the plethora of memories until she opened her mouth. "Alright... I... I was... I was in the Rena Gardens... I was walking with Rhei, and we were just having a really nice time because he brought me flowers... He went all out, the whole nine yards. He was very attentive, and then all the sudden, you know... we went for a walk...? Yeah, we went for a walk and all of a sudden, we started to hear music. The people around us... we don't know why... but they could not hear the music."

"Whenever we do this, the Olympians put a barrier around us so that we're not seen by the naked eye or heard by anyone not affiliated with us—better yet, we're not seen by the heretic's people. So, that's why we're able to be out in the open." Chryssa's words slammed into Katerina. But weren't they considered part of the *heretic's people*? How did she even...?

"I know that the tambourines played, and it was a really nice melody. So, we just followed the music and... just a handful of the few people that were gathered around the Plaza *actually* went in that direction, the rest didn't move... it was *odd*, but, you know, people here have all sorts of abilities... I guess, but I—I don't know... I... I just know that I went there and that was it. I don't... I don't remember what happened after. Everything is just *blank* after that point if I'm being honest. But I know that once I try to remember something..." her eyes crystallized once more, tears threatening to spill. "A deep sense of fear just takes over me. My body shivers. My body freaking aches. My body hurts everywhere. I—"

Katerina's eyes scanned her sister's body, finally registering all the bruises around her arms, her legs... her neck. Rage boiled inside her even further. *I am going to kill whoever fucking did this to you.* Her eyes water. *No, death would be too kind.* She allowed herself to envision every possible thing she could do to make them suffer, to make every single one who laid a hand on her suffer.

Jezebelle hasn't even seen herself yet. But Katerina was sure she'd already seen the bruises on her legs and the ones on her arms, but she doubted she'd seen the ones on her neck and the nicks on her face. She was afraid to—afraid to even think of the bruises she might have under the dress she's wearing. *I hate this.*

Yet, I am the one who worries too much. The one that worries too fucking much and just because she went outside and trusted—Katerina breathed. A part of her was certain that Rhei was behind this because what are the fucking odds this happens what she was with him? *I should've known. I should've fucking known. I should've pressed. I should've told father. I should've stopped this from the very beginning. I should've protected. I should've been there to protect her. To stop her from going. I should've been... I should've been a better sister. I should've protected her. I should've—*

"It's okay." Jezebelle's gentle touch broke her sister's spiral. "I can see that you're beating yourself up over this. This is not your fault."

"It's not my fault, but it is. I should've known, but I should've protected you. I am...I am your sister, Jezy. I told you that I'd die if anything were to happen to you."

"I know..." she smiled timidly. "Where's Rhei?"

Katerina's face fell. "I don't know. I don't care; my only concern here is you. Why do you want him, anyway?"

"I vaguely remember that he said something along the lines of *I will find you again.* But I don't know what he meant by it."

"That *he will find you again*? That's what he said? I will fucking find you again?" *If that's not incriminating enough.* She didn't have the heart to tell her that she was about to be sacrificed, most likely by the hands of him—well, about to be given to the gods of Olympus as a token of their loyalty. *Not yet, anyway.*

Rhei was a rebel, and the fucker infiltrated our home and took advantage of her sister. Of her kindness. He took advantage of her kindness just because he could.

It took a lot of effort for Katerina not to break everything in the room. Yes, she had a problem with her temper, but she was doing an outstanding fucking job of keeping her shit composed not to send her sister over the edge.

Jezebelle was in a delicate place right now. Katerina needed to be the one levelheaded. She needed to be the strong one. For her sister's sake.

What they did to Jezebelle made her loathe their kind even more. Just because they followed the Olympian Grand laws. Laws that defile. Laws that threaten. Laws that destroy everything from the very core.

She desperately hoped Rhei would vanish and never return. Because if he stepped foot near her or inside the Fortress or the Acrailerion again, she would fucking destroy him.

The marks on her sister's body made her realize he did not work alone.

Katerina's stomach turned. *I've done so much protecting her, I am not stopping that today. Not ever. I will protect her until my dying breath.*

CHAPTER
TEN
ZEUS

Apollo's gasps echoed in the humid air as Ares tore the wet cloth from his flushed face. The cloth landed with a dull thud on the damp ground, its scent of mildew lingering. His body was obscenely thin, barely able to hold himself up, and his once radiant golden hair was now dark and matted to his dulled skin.

"What do you want?" He gasped, trying to pull himself together.

Zeus sat on the wooden chair near the entryway, examining his son's nervous yet enraged demeanor.

Apollo rolled his eyes. "I'm surprised you didn't come here with your pet."

Ares buried his fist into the side of his face, making him spit out blood.

Zeus chuckled at the comment. "How'd you do it?"

"You still believe I did this?" Rage ignited behind his hollow caramel eyes.

"I've been patient." Zeus responded icily. "You brought this upon yourself."

"Like hell I did," Apollo argued. "Might as well commit real fucking treason if this is how the innocent are treated based on mere speculation."

Ares laughed, earning him a sharp glare from Apollo.

It's been years since the attack. Years since the Paragons of Light took control of Castelencia. Years since they declared *Apollo* as their Savior. When confronted, Apollo was none the wiser and denied all claims made. He swore he was being set up. Yet, he didn't care that he stood in the presence of the Olympians, in the presence of his father, when he cursed the day judgment was bestowed upon him. If that was not an obvious display of his disdainful nature toward Zeus, he didn't know what was.

THEMIS STOOD AT THE CENTER OF THE COUNCIL HALL, surveying Apollo as he stood before her. He was strong, his face unwavering as he held her gaze. Nothing but unrelenting focus lingered behind his eyes.

I, enraged by this sudden turn of events, grasped the sides of the podium in an attempt to stop myself from lunging at him. The utter disgrace that it was to call Apollo my son was unfathomable.

Themis drew in a sharp breath as the Moirai spawned next to her. "Your name is to be struck from the sanctified rolls of Olympus. The Council of Judgement, now joined by the Moirai, has rendered its verdict." She glanced toward me; pity washed over her face.

How can she feel pity for this bastard? I shook my head lightly, and she proceeded.

"You shall be cast from the heavens, stripped of dominion, and chained in Tartarus until the stars cease."

Chaos broke out in the room as Apollo gaped at the words.

"Your powers of shapeshifting, prophecy, healing, and light will be stripped effective immediately. You will retain your eternal life, but every wound you get will take eons to heal. Your lyre will be destroyed—"

"Please don't." Apollo pleaded. *"I'll take anything, just don't destroy it."*

"So you admit liability..." I narrowed my gaze.

"I don't. I just don't want my lyre to be destroyed."

"Yet, you're being awfully accepting of your fate." I tapped the sides of the podium. *"Since you'll take* anything.*"*

"It's not my fate. It's just a recommendation being made."

I chuckled. *"That* is *your fate."*

Apollo's bronze face blanched. *"You cannot be serious."*

"I am." I gestured to Themis to continue, ignoring the undoubted rage boiling behind Apollo's glare.

―――――

"The *INNOCENT* ARE NOT SENT TO TARTARUS. THE *innocent* are not harshly judged. She must've seen something of you for her to place this judgement." Zeus said, standing from the seat.

"Surprised your little foresight didn't see this coming." Ares mocked.

"That's not how it works, and something *of* me does not necessarily mean that it is *by* me," Apollo retorted.

"I don't understand why you keep denying it, even after this long." Ares played with the small blade in his hands.

"I'll deny it till' the day I die."

"So you say..." Zeus trickled around him. "Yet, these heretics have shrines dedicated to you. Temples dedicated to you. They pray to you. Sacrifice for *you*." His gaze hardened. "You can't fucking blame it on mere speculation or mundane confusion." Repulsion filled every inch of Zeus' body. *How fucking dare you? How dare you go up against me?* Now the fucker sat there, not a hint of regret on his face. *I'll fucking give you something to regret.*

"This could've been worse." Ares lifted his gaze back to his half-brother, still testing the blade for sharpness.

"Doubtful." Apollo met his stare. "I'm confined for eternity in this hellhole."

"Perhaps," Ares shrugged. "But, you could've been bound to a fiery spinning wheel for eternity. Maybe stretched out and tormented by vultures who could devour your regenerating liver, condemning you to eternal torture; or perhaps getting shoved into a sealed coffin and dumped into the depths of the Styx doesn't sound as bad. With your great gift of eternal life and all, you won't die. No, you'd just drown and die and drown and die. But no. Sitting in a cell, unbothered with your precious fucking lyre, is so hellish and cruel." Ares mocked. "Looks like being the favorite son does have its perks, don't you think?"

"Enough," Zeus said, gaze falling on Apollo once again. For someone who kept proclaiming their innocence, Apollo didn't seem willing to yield any pertinent information. Even after all these years, Zeus suspected Apollo knew something, but he was so dead set he didn't, that Zeus didn't pry, especially after seeing how the Paragons of Light changed from Apollo to the *Savior*... perhaps that was the mistake. "You will regret crossing me."

"Do your worst," Apollo sneered.

Zeus's face turned stone cold as rage crept onto his skin, crawling its way around his boiling body. "As you wish." He gestured to Ares.

"Father's second pet wants to play..." Apollo taunted. "Aren't you tired of being his little bi—"

Ares shoved a piece of cloth down his throat.

Grabbing the binding chains, he unlocked the anchor and pulled his body out of the cell with the excess chain. The more they walked, the stronger the scent of burning flesh seemed to get. Ares stopped abruptly, making Apollo almost crash into him.

"That's right..." he turned to face him. "You think you're fucking walking?"

Apollo's eyes widened, and an inexplicable sound escaped his gagged mouth. With the excess chain, Ares bound Apollo's feet together, making the chain smaller and more restrictive to movement.

Ares tugged, and Apollo refused to move. But a quick, forceful pull made Apollo crash against the uneven ground, scraping his face and breaking his nose. Ares took hold of the chains again, ensuring Apollo's feet remained secured, and dragged his semi-bare body across the grounds of Tartarus and past the sea of entrapped monsters.

They roared for Zeus' blood, but he only heard music. With every step he took through this prison, the ground cracked in reverence, trembling beneath his heels. The air, thick with sulfur and the stench of ancient failure, parted like a curtain. Shadows clung to the jagged stone-like frightened vermin, and even the darkness knew its place in his presence. Unlike Zeus's piss-poor excuse of a son.

From behind their iron-barred prisons and shackled pits, they hissed, growled, and howled with rabid hunger.

"Let us out!" one spat, voice rasping like rusted chains dragged across bone.

"Come to grace us with your presence?" another shrieked.

"We will tear you limb from limb. We will *feed* on your arrogance!"

Zeus paused, letting their venomous threats wash over him as if they were nothing but scum. The weak always barked when they remembered what power tasted like. These were not rulers. They were the failures of countless futile rebellions, broken tools rusting in the pit of creation.

He turned his gaze toward one of the monsters. A mass of scaled limbs and writhing mouths, buried beneath chains engraved with divine script.

"You'll die waiting," Zeus hissed. "And when your cell cracks, it won't be freedom you find... you'll beg for me to kill you."

"So you say." It replied smugly. "Your time is coming; don't get too comfortable."

Zeus moved through the corridor, searching for Ares, who

seemed to have disappeared. The beasts still rattled their chains behind him, but their howls were softer now, like wounded animals.

The corridor opened onto a vast circular chamber. New, sterile, and humming with a colder kind of dread. The walls gleamed with obsidian, veined in celestial silver and lined with holding cells unlike the old worn cages in the chamber before. No screams. Just *silence*—the silence of precision, of inevitable judgment.

His gaze swept over one door. Slightly ajar. Not wide. Not blown open. Just... ajar. No alarms. No scorch marks. No blood. No broken chains. Just a sliver of darkness peeking through a seam that should not exist.

He stopped, eyes narrowed. There was no scent of escape, no hint of violence. No disturbance in the arcane lattice that should have flared with violation.

It was *undisturbed.*

A lesser warden might have panicked and left the cell open. They knew better than to linger near the cells. But it was still odd. Even if this chamber held no prisoners, the cells were to remain closed, regardless. He eyed it carefully; but nothing had emerged. Nothing lingered.

Zeus approached the cell only to be stopped by distant screams, which were unmistakably Apollo's. *What the hell is Ares doing?* He bolted toward the source.

Stepping outside, the sky, if it could be called that, was a churning bruise of smog and dying light, casting no warmth, only a flickering, ashen glow that pulsed like a final heartbeat. An oppressive haze turned shadows into long, twisted figures that stretched and coiled unnaturally across the open, desolate space, cracked and broken like a dried-out ocean bed.

Jagged stones stuck out from the ground, and veins of molten fire pulsed beneath the surface, occasionally splitting the ground open in brief, breathless quakes. Smoke seeped from the fissures in lazy spirals, carrying the faint stench of scorched bone and sulfur, with thorn-ridden stalks of obsidian, sharp enough to draw blood from the air itself.

In the distance, Ares's silhouette shifted, holding Apollo up, feet dangling several inches from the ground. Before he knew it, Zeus found himself standing next to Apollo as Ares tossed his body onto the ground as if he were nothing but scraps.

Heaving, Apollo struggled to his feet.

"He keeps denying involvement." Ares said, a smug smile creeping up his lips. "But he did manage to give me a name."

"Who?"

"Darius Andretzis."

For someone who wasn't involved, how come he is just spitting out this name? After all these years. He could deny all he wanted, but he knew more than he let on—hence the name. Perhaps this was something Mnemosyne could help with.

"Make sure no one harms him. We might need to pull more information soon."

Zeus braced himself over the throne, fingers tapping lightly atop it. The marble and golden doors swung open as Mnemosyne strode inside.

Her snow hair was half-braided to her head, while her cocoa skin glistened under the brightness of the Throne Room.

"You summoned me?" She uttered, holding her hands and placing them in front of her silken, silver gown.

After an excruciatingly long time in Tartarus, he needed to distract himself from all the horseshit and brace himself for whatever new information Argus could gather. But he couldn't stop now, not when he needed to know who the man was...

"Darius Andretzis. Heard of him?"

Her silver eyes narrowed. "I can't say I've made his acquaintance. But I'm sure the archives can trace his lineage. What do you need?"

CHAPTER
ELEVEN
JOSEPH

T<small>EN YEARS BEFORE THE</small> W<small>AR.</small>

Quinn slumped into his seat, carefully surveying the woman scowling before him. Delicate sapphire-embellished chains adorned her waist-long golden hair, matching her refined gown. She was almost an exact replica of her mother, Cynthia DeMarque, may she rest in peace, save for the poutier lips and freckled face.

"This is not up for debate, dear sister."

"I don't care if it isn't." She hissed. "You're not selling me off to be a pawn. I do plenty as a Denai. I help women across the continent. I advise the—"

"You could save the most helpless victim for all I care, donate to the poorest villages outside Caverest, Belsir—be a saint that crossed their paths, but my decision is final."

Not a flash of sympathy washed over Quinn's face. Bernadette was a sweetheart. All the time I've known her, she'd never led anyone astray and always found herself helping those in need. She even sold some of her most precious jewels and gave the money to an orphanage in one of the struggling villages near the coast. She was beautiful inside and out. But today, she was a completely different person: sharp tongued, swift to anger, and filled with utter disdain *behind those eyes. Today, it was evident that she was Quinn's sister, through and through.*

"And I suppose you had a say in this?" She glared at me, carefully studying my reaction, which I refrained from giving. It would just make the problem worse if I gave my two cents, for all parties involved.

"It doesn't matter if he had a say in this or not, Bernadette." Quinn stood, his tone aggravated.

But she didn't take her amber eyes off mine, with a silent plea reflected in her gaze. 'Help me. Do something. Don't let him do this.' But this was out of my hands. Quinn had already made up his mind, and knowing him, my interjecting was not going to make a difference.

No matter how much I loved her.

"Tomorrow, you will meet with Governor Orestis and his son, Malakai. If you do not, I'll consider it treason." Quinn added.

"Treason?" She snapped, finally tearing her gaze away.. "Have you lost your mind?"

My thought's the same.

"You've been warned." He shrugged. "And you know what happens to those who commit treason against me."

Her delicate hands curled into fists and took a breath before opening her palms again. "And who is to take my stead? I have to notify the Verenna of my change in position."

"Joseph will deliver the information." Quinn filled a chalice with amber liquid.

Was I? I stopped myself from looking confused and taken aback by the sudden assignment. Usually, he'd have me with him, advising on things around the Fortress, especially after Marcus's unfortunate passing. He'd never let me set foot inside the Acrailerion.

"And what role am I to play once I... marry?" she scowled at the last word.

"We'll discuss it tomorrow. You just make sure to be on time and on your best behavior."

"Believe me, I will." She said bitterly, and I could sense her mind doing something I knew all too well, before snapping back to the Bernadette we all know and love.

But Quinn was too involved in his drink to notice her sudden shift.

Her gaze softened as she looked back at me and gave a kind smile, perhaps a pitiful one. At least, that's the one I gave her before she left the room. The scent of honeydew trailed behind her.

Oh, how I wanted to kiss her... if it weren't for Quinn being in this very room... I would've done it. Should I risk it? Reach for her arm, twirl her around, until she was in my arms and savoring a tender kiss... I pushed the thought away. Quinn was about to marry her off. I hated it, yes. But us having a future was futile. Wishful thinking, if that.

As long as Quinn or Malakai was still in the picture, I couldn't dream of a future with her.

Quinn handed me a chalice of amber liquid, saving me from my spiral. "Joseph, you and I have been friends since childhood, which is why I'm extending the courtesy."

My brows furrowed.

"You can be with whomever you please. But if you don't stop making eyes at my sister, you and I are going to have a problem."

"I—"

"Don't bother." He downed the rest of his drink. "I see the way you look at her and the way she looks at you whenever both are in the same room. I'm not stupid."

My heart dropped. I never thought it would be so obvious. Bernadette was a beautiful woman, and yes, I was in love with her. But I knew better than to give in to it, especially with how Quinn was when it came to her.

"I'm just being friendly." I lied. "Bernadette is a good woman, and we've never had any issues with each other. So whenever she smiles, I smile back. I'm just extending the courtesy."

"Good." He said, keeping his eyes on me. "That's why I'm marrying her off, anyway. I can't have her becoming tainted goods,

especially when an alliance with Aeshelyn is already hanging by a thread."

I resisted the urge to scowl at the way he called her tainted goods. She was more than that. But I couldn't show any signs of bitterness. "Are you sure Governor Orestis will agree?"

"He has no other choice but to." Quinn poured himself another glass. "Unless he wants to see his precious country destroyed from within."

"And are you sure marriage is what they require?" I asked with feigned indifference. "Have you considered any alternative methods of securing the alliance? Yes, marital ties are... certainly the most traditional route. But perhaps not the only one. Perhaps by offering them a generous sum to fund their trade concessions, shared military defense pacts, or joint governance of contested borders—these could all prove persuasive."

Quinn studied me for a moment before knocking back the liquid and setting the glass down.. "You're suggesting I abandon the betrothal entirely?"

My heart gave a quiet, involuntary twist. I couldn't watch her be given away like a pawn on a board. I wanted to be with her, and I knew it since the day we ran into each other at the coast. But I knew the cost. The consequences that followed if I were to indeed intervene in this union. She told me once that she wished for a secluded life away from Belsir and Caverest and start anew with me. We knew better, and I couldn't allow myself to feel this—he'd kill me.

"I am merely suggesting," I said evenly, "that a stronger alliance may be forged through mutual interest rather than through the sacrifice of bloodlines. Marriage is binding, yes—but so is shared prosperity."

Quinn crossed his arms over his chest, sharp eyes searching for something beneath my words. I held my breath, keeping my face as composed as stone.

THAT EVENING, I HURRIED TO THE PIER. IT WAS A *struggle to leave without raising suspicions but I managed to sneak out the back door. Guards hardly ever patrol that area anyway, too many riots near the entrance. Waves crashed against the dock and salty air filled my lungs.*

Upon opening the wooden doors to the cottage, Bernadette greeted me with a tender kiss as she wrapped her arms around my neck. Sneaking my hands around her waist, I pulled her closer, deepening the kiss. The sweetness of honeysuckle filled my nose as I savored her. Fuck. Get it together. But... first things first.

I picked her up, making her wrap her legs around me, and walked toward the table in the center of the room.

"Joseph," she breathed. "We need to... we need to talk."

"Okay," I replied, setting her down atop the table. "Talk." I pushed a waft of hair out of the way, exposing her neck and kissing her gently.

Melting under my touch, she stammered as she tried to speak. Something about the entire ordeal with Quinn and the nuisance of Malakai. I want her to forget about him. Trailing from her mouth to her neck, I sank my teeth gently onto her.

"Please..." she panted. "Oh, Joseph..."

I claimed her mouth with mine, making her mold with my body. "Didn't you want to talk?" I teased.

"You're making it difficult." She breathed, pushing the clothes off my body. "Quinn's gonna kill you."

"Let him." I slipped a hand in between her warm legs and massaged her gently.

She tipped her head back, sneaking her hands into my hair.

"Talk to me, baby." I muttered inches away from her lips.

She moaned my name in response, which I took as a satisfied plea and a request for something more.

"Tell me what you want." I whispered, sliding two fingers inside her.

She writhed under my rhythmic tempo to sink deeper. But I

don't allow her, I pulled back slightly. "Come on, princess. Use your words."

"Please..." She whimpers.

"Please, what?" I slowed down and pulled my fingers out, showing her the delicious mess she made.

Her eyes darkened as she brought my fingers to her mouth.

My lips curled. "Show me how badly you want it." I placed myself in her warm entrance, teasing her just enough to make her melt.

"Please," she whimpered, and I was more than happy to oblige.

Just when I was about to slide in, she pressed a hand against my bare chest. "Please... we need to talk." She breathed.

Pulling back, I kissed her temple and cupped her cheek. "What's on your mind?"

"I think he knows..."

"I thought so too, but I brushed it off as mere politeness."

"And you think he bought it?" She said in disbelief. "He knows. He had no reason to pull me out of the Acrailerion, save for this."

"Princess, everything will be okay." I whispered. "I will fight for you until the end, I promise."

"Don't make promises you can't keep, Joseph..." she pulled my hands away from her face. "I think it's best if we end this now."

"You really think I'd give up on you?"

"It's not what I think..." she countered. "It's what's right."

CHAPTER
TWELVE
KATERINA

GOLDEN DECOR, SUN MOTIFS, AND MEMORABILIA OF THE most influential Castelenians, including Quinn and his lineage dating back to their founder, Weston Petrakis, adorned the Caverest Plaza. Lively music spread through every nook and cranny as children played around the blessed fountain without a care of the scorching sun. It was a refreshing sight after another nightmare-ridden night and Jezebelle's *situation* the night prior.

Castelencia was Katerina's home—*Caverest* was her home.

She'd joined the Re'Veillite Sisters on their monthly volunteer service as a *Sister-Initiate*. Katerina wore a cream gown tied at the waist with a silken rope, while they wore their signature white and dark red embroidered robes. Wide sleeves reached her hands, and a loose hood partially covered her hair because she draped part of it over her shoulders and chest.

She was surprised when Sebastian, her father's advisor, first notified her that she would have the opportunity to go to the Helios Agora with the Sisters without an escort. She usually had to beg and be on her best behavior, only for her father to say no under the guise of *safety*. Mainly because the agoras were located just outside the capital.

She didn't argue. This was the first and only real chance she'd gotten after her mother's passing.

I miss you; she thought. *I miss you so much.* A tear trailed down her cheek, and she immediately wiped it away. *Get yourself together.*

"A beautiful necklace for a beautiful lady."

Katerina smiled at the merchant and politely refused. Right before they left the grounds of the Acrailerion, she was strictly instructed not to take anything from the merchants or grab anything, even if looking, as they consider it sold and payment would be required.

She found it absurd. How was it that merely looking at an item would automatically mean that someone would buy it? If she was just looking, there wasn't a guarantee that she would purchase it. What if she found a dent, scratch, or mold some-where? Would she still be subjected to the obligation of providing payment? No, but regardless, she made a point to herself not to linger too long and potentially be hounded and pressured into purchasing something she didn't truly need.

"A lady should not go hungry." Another merchant approached. "Meats, fresh fish. Come see what my shop can offer."

Another polite decline. Massive arches slid into view with shades of grey, brown, and bright gold. *Here goes nothing.*

One of the Sisters linked her arm to Katerina's as they entered the Helios Agora. It was interesting that in their country, the worship of the Olympians waned over the years, yet they kept the agora named after their Titan of the Sun... most agoras got renamed after the war. Yet this one—

"Have they assigned you a merchant yet?" Sister Gaia asked, eyes scanning the crowded market.

"No," Katerina replied. "I was told that it'd be assigned upon arrival."

Stalls filled with muted-color fabrics, pottery, fresh fruits, and spices line the bustling marketplace. People from different walks of life were bartering, conversing, and walking. They looked so different from the ones in Caverest... more bitter, thinner—dare she say, malnourished. Not a single child in sight, either. In the back, buildings with tall Ionic columns and marble statues of their Savior were on full display. Despite the somber expressions around her, the place was lively, if it could be considered that. Bright daylight cast soft shadows, and a handful of trees provided shade near some stalls.

Sister Gaia gave the morning greeting to the merchants as they walked by. *Blessed Day*. Only to be sneered at in return. However, she didn't seem to care, while Katerina was taken aback by the disrespect, wondering how she was able to keep her normalcy, despite being blamed for the people's circumstances in life?

"Aren't you the tiniest bit worried about what people might do?"

"In what sense?" The Sister glanced at her, brows furrowed slightly. *Did she truly didn't notice?*

"Clearly, you've seen how the reb—how *they* look at you."

"Oh, that." She waved her hand. "We're all used to it. We receive hate no matter where we go, but the amount of women we're able to help outweighs the cost." They stopped walking. "Once you are inducted, you will understand so much about us and how we are the blessing so many of these people need. It just takes time to adjust to everything."

Katerina remained silent, unsure of what to say. The Re'Veil-lites had such a natural ease to them, unlike Katerina with her temper and judgmental ease. This further proved that her position inside the Acrailerion could not be solely because of her performance in the Trials. Her father must've used his influence with the Verenna or the Denai to be sure.

THE CEILING SEEMED TO TEAR INTO FRACTIONS; THE

ice-cold rain seeping through the cracks. The ground shook beneath my feet.

"We don't have much time." I whispered, looking around and trying to stop my heart from leaping out of my chest.

Three options lay before me: save the wounded children and bear the responsibility for their growth without knowing if any had a terminal illness; save the elders and gain access to the continent's archives; or save myself and forfeit all access to Eseron, save for the Fortress.

Can't I just save them all? How was I going to take the children and the elderly? What if I saved the children and then they died on me? Would I have saved them for nothing? But then, if I saved the elderly... everything I've wanted to know about the continent, all the knowledge would be at my disposal.

I looked at their expectant faces. The ground beneath me shook again, more violently than before. Think, Kate. Think.

"Katerina!" someone yelled in the distance. But I needed to make a choice.

"Katerina!" The voice grew louder, and pieces of the ceiling began to fall upon us.

"Katerina!" Strong hands grabbed my shoulders, pulling me out of the caving room.

"Wait!" I yelled. "I haven't chosen! Please! Don't leave them!"

"KATERINA," THE SISTER CALLED, SHAKING KATERINA gently by her shoulders and searching her eyes.

"I'm sorry," Katerina blinked, getting her sight back into focus. They had stopped almost near the end of the Agora. "You were saying?"

"Are you alright?"

Katerina nodded, rubbing her eyes. "Yes..."

"Are you sure? You dozed off for a good moment. If you're

not feeling well, it's completely alright. We could reschedule for—"

"No need." Katerina reassured instantly. She didn't know when *next time* would be, and she wasn't going to throw away the chance, anyway. She was already out here. "I'm alright, truly."

The sister's brows furrowed for a split second before returning to normal. "You'll be with Mrs. Dhalia. She's the textile merchant around the corner. I'll be with the spice merchant that's in the upper left section. Let me know if you need anything. Good luck." She gave her a smile and strode off before Katerina could ask questions.

"Alright," Katerina muttered.

As she passed the countless merchants and the powerful scents of cinnamon and citrus, she arrived at the textile shop. Compared to the other merchants, who solely had stalls, Mrs. Dhalia had an actual space indoors with colorful woven fabric hanging outside that displayed the delicate and dedicated work put into them. Some had a mix of colors, while others showed off intricate designs.

Was she capital-born or just lucky?

Upon entering, she saw an array of fabrics, woven and unwoven, piles of yarn, silk, linen, and cotton that were respectively divided into their own sections.

If only I knew how to crochet or sew... Jezy would adore this place.

To her surprise, the shop was among the ones with the most customers. Her hands grazed over the silken texture and then the linen. *How much does a yard or two cost? Maybe I'll get some for Jezy before I leave. A good way to get her distracted.*

"Good morning, child." An elderly woman greeted. Her grey hair was loosely pinned back, and her warm-toned body was adorned with a red and orange dress and an assortment of beads around her neck.

Katerina offered a kind smile. *"Blessed day.* I'm looking for Mrs. Dhalia."

"It is I," she said gleefully. "Anything in particular you need help with?"

"I'm Katerina," she offered a hand, which her soft, wrinkly hands took. "I was assigned here to assist you for the day."

"Oh." Her eyes twinkled. "You don't look like the ones I've had before." She scanned Katerina's outfit.

Her cheeks flared. "I'm not in the sisterhood yet, but I will be. In the next coming days."

"Ah... my second initiate." She laughed lightly. "Come."

Katerina followed her through the crowd while Mrs. Dhalia gave her a quick snapshot of what was expected of her while in the shop. Of course, she had to assist indecisive clients with choosing fabric or any product the shop offers, while keeping an eye out for any thieves that may come. *Simple enough.*

Katerina walked around the space gracefully, giving nods and greetings. *I wonder what Jezy is doing?* She knew Jasmine had promised to look out for her, but she had also asked her to look into Rhei, and she hadn't heard anything yet. Katerina's stomach turned at the reminder of her sister's bruised limbs.

A tug on my dress brought her attention down to an adorable raven-haired boy who looked no more than seven. All her anger melted away in an instant as she crouched down. "How can I help you, darling?"

THE REST OF THE DAY WENT BY IN A BLUR, AND SHE helped a total of six clients. Mrs. Dhalia had to help the others due to her expertise, and Katerina's lack there of. But all in all, it felt good to do something different for a change. They still had about an hour before they officially had to close, so Katerina got a head start in folding the displaced woven fabric and tidying up the area for easier closing.

Storing the misplaced knitting or cutting tools, strong yet soft arms hugged Katerina from behind.

"Thank the gods you're alive!"

Katerina turned as Chryssa released her. Her red hair was tied up, falling down the center of her back.

Her stomach sank. "It's good to see you too, Chryssa."

"Good? It's a miracle we're both still standing!"

Lingering eyes land on them, ranging from confusion to outright disdain.

"I looked everywhere for you."

"You did?" Katerina placed the folded tapestry on the neatly stacked pile of woven yarn and turned to her.

"I know you said you were going home, but this being your first time in an *event* like this, people tend to get lost in finding a way out of the *bubble*, so to speak." She patted down her sage dress.

I managed to find the exit pretty quickly. A lot of things didn't make sense, but she wasn't going to dwell on that.

"I'm sad like... I'm surprised. I don't know how I should feel because a lot of people died that night."

Katerina's heart dropped. "What do you mean, a lot of people died?"

"Oh, Rhea... after you left about... perhaps half an hour after you left, maybe... I don't know what happened, but the flames went crazy, and when I mean crazy, it was insane. Usually, we have the flames contained somewhere. Well, out of the blue, the flame next to the dais lost control and just consumed everything and everyone. It looked like it was fueled by hatred."

That's one way to describe it. Katerina kept her face carefully neutral.

Chryssa leaned in, making sure they were relatively out of earshot.

"This has never happened before, you know?" she whispered. "I've been to many of these for years. Even before the war, my ancestors came to these events after we got rounded up like criminals. It was a prosecution, to say the least, and I absolutely hate it. We've done nothing wrong, and for years we've been meeting in secret just to get a semblance of normalcy. We've been in this bubble, protected by the gods. This was the first time—" Her eyes began to water. "This was the very first time that we were attacked in our own safe space."

"Are you sure it was an attack?" Katerina asked with feigned interest.

"It had to be." She ensured. "I am certain that it was because it makes absolutely no sense for us to be safe and, out of the blue, everything disrupts into utter chaos." She looked over her shoulder. "They didn't just consume the stands or people's stuff... it also followed us. It's like we were getting targeted by the flames; that's why I'm saying that it was fueled by hatred. Somewhere, somehow... maybe the Heretic is getting stronger or better at detecting us, which is absolutely insane to think because the gods have much more power than that imbecile of a man," she wiped the tears on her freckled cheeks.

Chills ran down Katerina's spine as memories of the flames rushed to the forefront. *How when I saw my sister coated in terror and wished I could burn it all down...* she suppressed a gasp. *Perhaps our Savior was looking after me—looking after us.* Yet, people still doubted their kind. Katerina didn't see any of the Olympians putting out the fire, regardless if that was their worship night.

"Anyway, I am glad that you're alive. I am glad that you didn't have to endure this."

"Thank you for that," Katerina smiled kindly. "Now I'm curious, how did you manage to escape those rogue flames?"

"I have no idea. Somehow, the flames didn't attack me at all. It actually spared some people, but it looked like the flames were going after a specific set." She shook her head. "I don't know. I don't know the criteria for getting attacked or not by a flame. All I know is that it was absolute madness. Absolute chaos. But again, I am just glad and grateful that you're here and alive." Chryssa smiled, and her eyes drifted behind Katerina. "Oh, that's a gorgeous color." She hurried to the silken emerald fabric.

Katerina surveyed the shop. There was no sign of Mrs. Dhalia. But she couldn't get too comfortable. She needed to get rid of Chryssa before she returned. "So, what brings you around?"

"My brother is doing a small gathering, and I'm on the hunt for a gift."

"Anything in particular?"

"Not really." She examined the emerald fabric and then moved to the scarlet.

Katerina caught a glimpse of Mrs. Dhalia hovering around the customers. Her heart leaped. "Well, I doubt you'll find anything here... unless you want to sew or crochet something together."

She laughed. "I suppose you're right." She released the scarlet fabric and turned to her. "Want to join me on the search?"

"I wish I could, but I'm kind of tied up at the moment."

As if on cue, Mrs. Dhalia approached them. *Shit.* "How is everything over here?"

Chryssa smiled, tucking a rogue strand of red hair behind her ear. "Absolutely wonderful. You have such beautiful fabric here. I'm jealous."

"Hopefully, my *initiate* is being of great help, no doubt."

Katerina could've sworn her heart skipped several beats at the word *initiate.*

Chryssa's eyes furrow in confusion but didn't dwell on it for long. "She certainly is."

"Well, honey, let me know if you need anything else." Mrs. Dhalia walked away to assist another customer.

Katerina prepared herself for the array of questions about what she meant by *initiate.* But the questions never came.

"I didn't know you worked here."

"It's just my first day." She said innocently.

"I see... but you're quick." She folded her arms. "How long have you been out of Windermere?"

"Maybe about a week or so... I haven't been here long."

"And you managed to find a job this quickly? You better teach me your tricks because you know how long it took me to get a job? Especially since people don't hire *us* that easily because we didn't study at the Institute or take the stupid trials they boast about."

So, you're not Castelenian... Katerina shrugged with a laugh, attempting to be casual. "I guess it's just mere luck, I'm afraid."

"Perhaps," Chryssa laughed. "I won't hold you up cause I don't want to get in trouble, but if you ever need anything, I work at the Roselle Inn. That's about... I don't know, maybe a 10-15-minute walk from here. It's right outside Caverest. I know you're living with family, but if you need a place to stay on your own or somewhere to crash for a few days, just let me know. I'll hook you up with one of the rooms that we have over here. It's safe, so you don't have to deal with the haters around."

"Thank you." Katerina gave her a warm smile.

"Don't be a stranger! I'll see you soon."

With that, Chryssa left and once her figure was out of ear shot and out of the door, Katerina finally let out a breath she didn't realize she was holding.

She was playing with fire. If she were to find out who Katerina truly was, she would get blamed for what happened on Veneration Night and the things that happened after the fact. Chryssa may even set her up, turn her in—who knew? Give her as a sacrifice, maybe, or perhaps tell the soldiers and wait for her inevitable death. Chryssa only trusted her because she thought they were allies.

Katerina kept folding the clothes, and glanced at the clock once again. *Five minutes to closing. Finally.* She carried on cleaning and sorting out everything.

Mrs. Dhalia escorted the last few customers out the door with their bags in hand ready to finally close up shop.

"Blessed day. Unfortunately, we've closed for the evening." Mrs. Dhalia said. "You're more than welcome to come tomorrow. We open at dawn"

Katerina lifted her gaze to the customer with a thin face and ragged peppery hair and her blood ran cold upon recognizing him.

MY ATTENTION DRIFTED TO A MAN WHO YELLED obscenities to and about the Sovereign as he got dragged out by two soldiers. He looked feral and ready to kill anyone he got his hands on. His clothes were torn in all places, peppery hair ragged and falling across his bony face. A lost soul.

HER GAZE TRAILED DOWN TO THE CURVED BLADE IN HIS hand.

"I'm just having a look around." He hovered through the tables, eyeing its contents for anything he might consider of value.

"You think you're the first thief to come into my store?" she laughed. "I suggest you leave before we have to take other measures."

The man laughed but kept moving. "Quick with accusations." He stopped at a table, touching the fabric and examining the handcrafted jewelry. "As I said, I'm just having a look around."

Katerina's eyes landed on a pair of knitting needles on top of a partially woven tapestry just two tables away from him. *Just when I thought I could relax...*

"Is there anything in particular you are looking for?" Katerina approached the man as calmly as she could.

Mrs. Dhalia glared at her as if Katerina had grown three heads.

The man ignored her; his thin, calloused hands continued to rake through the bowl of necklaces and bracelets.

"What are you doing?" Mrs. Dhalia mouthed, but Katerina

dismissed her question, casually resting her hands behind her back.

Cool.

Calm.

Composed.

No sudden movements.

"Perhaps, it'll be easier to find whatever it is you're looking for if we help." Katerina stopped in front of the partially woven tapestry, waiting for him to meet her expectant gaze.

"I know what you can help me out with, sweetheart." A suggestive smile crept onto his crooked lips as he scanned her.

Pig.

His eyes narrowed at her. "Where do I know you from?"

Katerina's blood ran cold as she resisted the urge to scowl. Her heart thundered against her ears.

Mrs. Dhalia sneaked to the entrance, and the man threw the blade in her direction, stopping her with a jolt. The blade embedded itself into the wall, merely inches away from her wrinkled face.

He clicked his tongue disapprovingly, eyeing the elderly woman. "You're not going anywhere."

"And you're going to stop me?" She challenged.

Katerina blindly reached for the knitting needle. Relief settled in her body as her fingers traced the long, sleek feel of her now weapon and wrapped her fingers around it.

"I have men standing outside this place. If you or even princess here step outside—" he laughed again. "Go and find out."

A glint of light made her eyes drift to the pin on his cloak—an encircled cloud with a lightning bolt. Katerina's blood boiled, yet confusion stirred within her.

How did he manage to enter the Fortress? Was he a newly enlisted soldier?

"Oh, you're one of them." Katerina said in utter disgust.

"As if you're any better." He moved away from the jewelry,

eyes pinned on her. He tapped his head and then pointed at her with a malicious smile across his face. "Now I know you."

Katerina's stomach hollowed.

"Yes..." he snapped his fingers repeatedly. "I saw your face in one of the portraits inside the damn Fortress..." he gave a bitter laugh. "You think that your little Savior will spare you from Zeus' wrath when it comes down upon you, sweetheart?"

"So philosophical." She mocked, grip tightening around the needle. *Think of Jezy. No sudden movements. Not yet.*

He unsheathed a second curved blade up, merely at arms-length from her. "You come from filthy, disgusting blood. Your heretic father would not even shed a fucking tear for you, given that he has you so fucking hidden. Zeus will love when I send you directly to him." He inched closer to her.

He'd kill me once he has the chance. Katerina's jaw clenched. *Temper be dammed.* Her eyes remained on him. *Breathe.*

"No, not you." He tapped the pointed tip on his skull. "You have a sister, right? What's her name?" He moved the sharpened tip to his cheek. "Jezebelle?"

Katerina lunged at him, aiming the needle at his face. Without considerable effort, he held her arms and tossed the needle across the room. *Shit.* An amusing laugh escaped his lips as she thrashed against his hold. *I need to go back. I need to go back.* In a blink of an eye, her back slammed against the concrete floor, pushing the air out of her lungs. She tossed and kicked. White hot rage spread through her. How the hell was she back in this predicament so damn quickly? Her throat tightened, cold, sharp steel pressed against the underside of her chin. She went still. *I want to kill him. Just for saying my sister's name. Just for suggesting killing her in my stead.* Her hands trembled, eyes searing into him as he pressed the blade further against her flesh.

"I've never seen a princess with quite the temper." He mocked. "Maybe they'll spare your life and toss you around for us to use."

"I would rather die than be with your kind." She spat, trying to use her legs the same way as she did before, but it was futile. Quick, distancing footsteps turned her attention to the entrance. She saw Mrs. Dhalia dashing out of the corner of her eye. *At least one of us got out.*

"As you wish." He sneered.

Sharp, stinging pain spread through her chin as he slowly grazed the weapon against her neck. She gritted her teeth, trying to stifle her screams, and a treacherous tear fell down her cheek. *Jezebelle. Shit. How will she survive without me?* Thick, warm liquid trickled down her neck. How was she being so accepting of her fate? Was she truly going to die at the hands of a rebel?

Her heart slammed forcefully against her chest as the blood increased, covering the floor. *How am I still alive?* She blinked repeatedly, focusing on the man atop her. His eyes were almost bulging out, his face as red as a tomato. Her breath quickened. A thin onyx rope was wrapped around his neck. She tilted her head slightly. Someone stood above them. Suddenly, silver flashed before her eyes. The body holding her in place went limp, falling on top of her.

Katerina's breath stilled. *Get him off me. Get him off me. Get him off me.* She pushed the corpse off, skidding back. Blood smeared all over the floor the more she moved. *I'm alive.* A breath escaped her parted lips as she slowly got up. *Oh, thank our Savior.*

Her gaze trailed over to the man who saved her, and relief washed through her upon recognizing the Light Militia uniform.

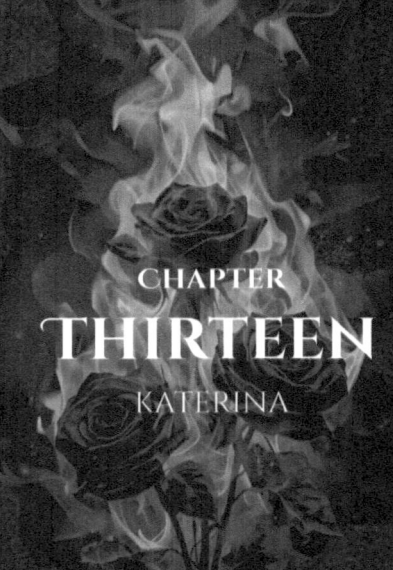

CHAPTER
THIRTEEN
KATERINA

Blood dripped from Katerina's clothing as she strode off and out of the textile shop. Hues of purple, orange, red painted the skies, and it seemed that most of the shops had closed for the day.

Fury coursed through her veins. *All I want is peace, is it too much to ask?* Steps followed closely behind her, so she quickened her pace. *I need to be alone. I do not want to deal with any of this.* Ignoring the lingering stares, she reached the entrance of the Helios Agora.

"I must take you home." The soldier implored, grabbing Katerina's arm.

"I wish to be alone. I'll go home, eventually." She said through gritted teeth, jerking her arm away. "Don't get me wrong, I am grateful that you saved me. But I just..." she breathed in. "I just need a minute alone."

She knew that if she went back to the Fortress in her current state of anger and distress, questions would arise and word would get back to her father. Not to mention the state of her dress would be topic of conversation enough.

"I'm afraid I must oblige, per orders of your father."

"You can tell my father—" she stopped, eyes surveying him closely. None of the soldiers, regardless of position or title, referred to Joseph as *her father*, only *sovereign*.

"Why did my father send you?"

"To ensure your safety, princess."

They never called her princess either. "Of course," Katerina remained composed, but she knew she needed to be smart. "I need another set of clothes first."

"Your father wants you back as soon as possible."

"My *father* would understand if I stopped to change what could clearly cause a scandal." Katerina gestured at the bloodstains along her dress. "It'll just be a minute."

He pressed his lips into a thin line and followed her back to the Helios Agora.

Katerina's eyes darted from stall to stall. Blood rushing through her, burning through her, screaming at her to keep moving.

Get away. Get away. If you stop, he'll know that you know.

Frustration grew within her at the sight of the continuously closed shops. She hurried back to the textile shop. The last remaining hope she had.

She slipped inside and tried her best to ignore the lingering scent of copper and the pool of crimson smeared all over the floor. The corpse still lay there, clothes saturated from beneath.

The shop was eerily quiet, each step unnecessarily loud.

Katerina's fingers sorted through the woven fabric, feigning a search as her mind drifted back and forth between her narrowing options and time. Her breath caught. There wasn't anything here she could use. It was all blankets and tapestry... no dresses or shirts or pants she could slip into. *Shit*. She felt the blood drain from her face.

"Let's go." He ordered, seizing her arm.

Stupid, stupid, stupid. No, wait... she pulled her arm out of his grasp. "I can walk myself."

He eyed her carefully, then nodded, guiding her out of the

agora. She wondered where he might lead her. Perhaps she could gather some information she could find valuable to bring to her father, in proof of her usefulness. But then again, by blindly following him, she was putting herself in danger. What if she didn't come back?

They passed the agora's entrance and went straight to a rubble passage within the wood line. Her brows furrowed, heaviness sinking in her chest as it screamed at her to run. But she wanted to know where she was being taken.

Run.

Kate.

Run.

Don't be stupid.

Run.

Her eyes drifted slightly to the soldier, sword glinting in his back. *How did he get the uniform?* She caught him looking at her out of the corner of his eye.

"Isn't Caverest in the opposite direction?" She asked.

"Filled with rebels. I'm taking you through another route."

"I think we should use the standard route." She said, keeping her voice level despite the unease in her body. "Usually, we remain on course regardless if there's a surge of people."

He remained silent, but his body tensed.

They were going deeper and deeper into the woods. If she kept following him, she wouldn't know how to go back. But if she ran, she'd die.

She shortened her stride, falling slightly further behind him.

He stopped and turned to look at her.

"Princess..." he warned.

Katerina's heart threatened to burst out, the beats possessing her ears, drowning the birds above her and the rustling of leaves.

"Who are you?" She asked outright.

"I'm not wasting my time on this nonsense," he reached for her arm but she backed away just in time.

"Who are you?" She glared at him.

"I'm not your enemy." He cautioned, taking a step.

"What is the Oath of Enlightenment?"

He snorted as he reached for the sword on his back. "Looks like you're not as stupid as they painted you to be."

"Who are you? Answer me!" She demanded, stepping back with each step he took her direction.

"There's a bounty on your head. Two million coin."

Run.

"My family suffered greatly at the hands of yours." He inched closer to her, but she didn't stop walking back.

Run.

"I'm going to give your father a taste of what he did to me."

Fucking run.

Katerina bolted, quick steps following dangerously close. Trees upon trees surrounded her, the canopy blocking the sky. She turned left. Then right. She kept going, jumping and ducking through everything that got in her path.

Branches and thorns nicked her arms. Her chest contracted, lungs burned. But she didn't stop running. It was like sprinting through an endless void. She needed to stop. But she couldn't afford to.

Her body crashed against the dirt, ankle searing in pain. *Shit. Shit.* Distanced footsteps neared. She pushed herself against a tree. She breathed as quietly as she could, yet the thundering against her ears made it difficult for her to listen to her surroundings. *Savior help me. Just let me go home.*

Her gaze drifted to her right, hand clasping over her mouth to stifle the sound threatening to come out. Johan's body lay sprawled against a tree, stripped from his uniform.

What would her father do once he'd been told that his daughter was kidnapped? Or worse, dead? Would he blame himself for allowing her to leave, or would he blame her for not taking the proper *precautions*?

Her sight blurred at the edges, body trembling violently. *Breathe. Breathe.* Strong hands grabbed her limbs.

"It's alright, princess, it'll all be over so—" A whooshing sound passed by her, followed by a loud thunk. His grip slackened, allowing her to slip away before his body collapsed against the ground.

Katerina blinked, unable to understand what just happened until her eyes focused on the arrow buried in her captor's head.

"Didn't I warn you not to venture this part of town alone, princess?"

Her eyes darted to Nik, who stored the bow on his back with a smug smile across his face. He moved toward them and plucked out the tip of the spear, wiping the blood with his pants.

"Just leave me alone. Please." She struggled to her feet and walked past him.

She needed to shower, get out of these clothes, get into bed and just lay there. Usually, running would help her manage the chaotic emotions, but she *did* run. A quiet evening was all she needed. Just a quiet evening.

Evening...

Shit. Soon she'd be summoned to her father's study, if it hadn't happened already. *Shit. Shit. Shit.* She quickened her stride.

"Hold on." He hurried to her side. "I didn't just save you for nothing."

"If you were expecting me to swoon over you or give you coin, you're sadly mistaken." She hissed, lengthening her stride.

"I know what you did on Veneration Night."

The comment made her stomach hollow, but she didn't stop walking. Stopping would be a dead giveaway.

"Just let me go home. I've had a rough day, and I'm in no mood to be entertaining nonsensical accusations. So, please." She shooed him off with a hand.

He grabbed her and pinned her to a tree.

"Get off me!" She pushed him off, but he remained still, his arms caging her inside. *I just want to go home.* Her eyes burned.

His blue eyes glared at her. "I'm talking to you."

"Me walking away is a clear indication that I do not want to speak to you." She hissed.

"Like I give a fuck about what you want, right now."

"Excuse me?" Her blood simmered.

"You heard me."

"Get off me." She said through gritted teeth.

"Why? So you can try to run away?" He scoffed. "Judging by how you almost died as a helpless victim, go. Run away. We both know I can have you pinned again, just as easily."

"Fuck off." She spat. "Are you following me?"

"There's a bounty on your head. Word spread that you were in the vicinity, so naturally..."

"You must have me confused with someone else."

"Horseshit," he spat. "You don't think a handful of us don't know who you really are?"

"And who am I?"

"This stunt may fool others, *Rhea*, but not me."

"Hmm, because you know me so well and can see right through me." She mocked. "Well tell me, if I am who you say I am, why are you so damn concerned for my safety? Why not let him take me?"

"And let him take the credit for bringing you back to the Citadel?" His brows raised as he examined her for a moment, then chuckled. "You're much move valuable alive than dead, and he–" Nik pointed somewhere in the distance. "–was going to take you to the Eyross Citadel to get you killed."

"And you know this how?"

"As if I'm just going to spoil the plans."

"You kind of did by killing him."

"Keep thinking you're safe with me." He taunted.

"I don't." Katerina hissed, pushing him back.

He released her and stood at arm's length. His dark blonde hair was tousled, falling over his temples and eyes. *He looked like an Olympian warrior alright.* His body was covered in leather armor, but she could see the strength beneath it all.

Fear stirred within her. *Go home.* Her eyes fell on the scar on his face that reached from his right brow to his lower cheek, barely missing his eye.

"It's an eye-catcher, I know."

Her cheeks warmed. "What do you want?"

"I know you killed the High Priest."

"Bold of you to assume this." Her stomach turned, palms clammy. But she kept a stoic expression, nonetheless. *He doesn't have any proof. It was only me and Jezebelle and the High Priest, but Jezebelle was half unconscious, and he died of natural causes; it wasn't anything I did.* "Especially after I almost died today as a helpless victim."

"Don't be a smartass." He warned. "How'd you do it?"

"I didn't. So are you going to let me go home or waste my time further?" She said coldly. "Besides, I left early."

"Don't lie to me." He inched closer, towering over her. She didn't cower. "What are the odds of his dying after you *vanish*?"

"Shit luck." She retorted. "Again, I left way before the fire broke out."

"And how do you know about the fire?" he cocked a brow.

"I ran into Chryssa, the healer, at the textile shop. She told me all about it."

He blinked, perhaps unsure of how to respond. She couldn't tell.

"You met Chryssa?"

She nodded. "That night."

"Does she know who you are?"

"Yes," she lied. "Perhaps I should jog your memory of who I am."

"I know exactly who you are."

She could feel the color drain from her face as a chill ran down her spine. "Pray tell."

The air around them thickened and her chest contracted as if the oxygen was getting sucked out of her lungs as he leaned in to her ear.

"The Heretic may not let you out often, but there's a handful of us who know how you look like. We're not stupid."

"Again, you're mistaken."

"You want to play this game, baby girl?" He stepped back, unsheathed a blade, and pinned her against the tree, tracing the sharp tip across her face, then neck. Like a cat playing with its mouse before demise.

"You think I'm afraid of you?" She sneered, despite the metal caressing her skin. "Just do it and get on with it." Her throat bobbed, but she refused to tear her gaze away.

"I could take you right here and kill you right now."

Rage boiled through her. "Then do it. You're not the first and won't be the last to try."

Nik applied pressure to the blade, scraping her skin. Mild pain spread from her neck to her face. "What if I take you now? Better me than any other."

"You're not taking me anywhere, and you're not my type."

He snorted, moving the tip of the blade to her chin, holding it up with the flat side. "You'd be lucky if I ever looked at you with that intent."

"Doubtful. You just look like any other brute."

"You wound me." He mocked, removing the blade and spinning her around until her face was pressed against the gritty surface. "You were almost killed. So, you should be thanking me for killing his ass."

His hot breath against her neck sent shivers down her spine. Revulsion consumed her.

"Oh, my darling Savior." Sarcasm coated her bitter tongue. "How would I ever repay you for this heroic gesture?"

Heat spread through her as he traced the sharp tip of the blade down her neck, arms, back...

"Judging by how your body is reacting to me, I may have a few ideas."

White hot rage erupted within her, and she used all the

strength she could muster to push herself off the tree and face him, not caring about the position of the blade.

He stepped away. "Oh, baby girl, you want me."

"You disgust me." She hissed. "Just because you killed him doesn't mean I'm going to sleep with you."

"I'd be surprised if you did." He put the blade away. "Not that I'd complain."

She rolled her eyes. "I'm going home."

He chuckles. "Don't get too comfortable, though. I may not have killed you now, but you will see me again and, believe me when I tell you, I will relish the day I send your soul to the depths of the Underworld."

"I'd like to see you try." She squeezed past him, not bothering to look back.

Night had already fallen when she managed to find her way out of the woods and into Caverest. She wasn't able to breathe until she was back in her room.

Curious eyes landed on her. On the blood in her body. On her hurried pace. On her furious, flushed face. *I need a cold shower. I want to get out of here. Stop looking at me.* She scanned her surroundings. Not a single Sister in sight. Her head thundered against her temples. Did they just leave her? Keeping a comfortable pace, she ignored her aching feet.

So much for sisterhood...

She reached the back entrance. An unknown guard greeted her instantly. Her shoulders slumped. She'd forgotten about Johan...

"Miss Argyros." He bowed his head lightly before unlocking the gates and letting her in.

"I know it's late." She headed to the mahogany door. "He knew I was out."

"The Sovereign expects a word with you."

She stopped before heading up the stairs. "I'll see him after I've showered."

The day just keeps getting better and better.

THE SCENT OF TOBACCO AND CITRUS FILLED HER NOSE as she entered the darkened study, led by a soldier. Warm candle-light illuminated a dated, yet polished wooden desk covered with scrolls, old books, and ink pots. The walls were lined with columns, and the faint glow from the candles cast shadows on the statue of their Savior. A large bookshelf with leather-bound tomes lined one wall, and a large window displayed the darkened silhou-ette of olive trees outside.

Katerina's eyes fell upon her father in a black ensemble with gold trims, sitting patiently behind his desk. Chills slithered down her spine.

"You wanted to see me?"

He kept his attention on the document in front of him. "Hours ago."

She stiffened. *Breathe.*

"Where were you?" He asked, signing the document.

"I was with...with um..." she cleared her throat. "I was with the sisters at the Helios Agora, per your authorization."

"They returned to the Acrailerion hours ago." He looked up from the parchment. "I thought I could trust you. I gave you the privilege of doing this volunteer service unescorted because you've been behaving yourself as well as your sister. I thought you would have the sense to come back with the Re'Veillites. But no, you decided to go into your own adventurous spree and comeback here near midnight. Do you realize what could've happened if any of them had gotten their hands on you?"

"I'm surprised you care so much after what happened to Mom." She cupped a hand over her mouth. *Shit.* "I'm sorry, I didn't mean that..." *Think of Jezy. Think of Jezy.*

Ever since her mother's passing, her father became an icy shell of a man. Not an ounce of sorrow glinted in his eyes when Katerina pleaded for his help at merely fifteen years old as she clung to her frail body, life slowly draining from her eyes.

"After everything I did to rectify your indecency, this is how you thank me."

"My... my..." she breathed, unable to finish.

"Your privilege to leave the Fortress is terminated, effective immediately, with the exception of the Acrailerion for mass and preparations needed for your Induction. If you are going to the Acrailerion, you will do so with my approval and escorted. Do I make myself clear?"

Katerina looked back at her escort, his face unwavering. *He can't be serious.* "What will happen after I move to the Re'Veillite Wing?"

"That's for us to discuss when the time is near." He took a swig of the drink on his desk. "If I hear that you disobeyed any of my orders again." He hesitated, his brown eyes cold and unfeeling. "You know good and damn well the consequences that follow."

The hair on the back of her neck stood. *The darkness, the shackles... the torture...* she lowered her head. "I understand." She turned to leave.

"I expect your attendance at the banquet."

Why? she wanted to ask, but it was futile to even try.

"We need to show a united front to secure our alliance with Aeshelyn."

"I'll tell Jezebelle." She nodded.

"No. Just you."

She arched an eyebrow. "You don't want her there?"

"I have no need for her there."

"And what do you need me for?" she retorted.

"Doesn't matter." He turned his attention back to the papers on the desk.

"I think it does considering you want an alliance and the display of a unified family."

"Katerina," he warned.

There it was. The end of their conversation. It wouldn't be wise to push the limits, no matter how much she wanted to. But the pain... the pain that shrieked through her body as she remembered the shackles that bound her. *Breathe.* "I'll be there." She muttered, bringing her eyes to the floor and dismissing the horrid memory. "Is there anything else?"

Silence.

Her official dismissal.

My eyes jumped from one door to the other. Beads of sweat trickled down my forehead as the key danced between my fingers, toying with my mind. Whether silver or gold, the unknown fate behind those doors made my skin crawl and mouth dry.

Surrounded by nothing but skulls and debris, I surveyed the cloaked figure between both entrances, urging me to choose.

Silver.

Gold.

Silver.

Gold.

Time seemed to slip from my grasp while the taste of iron filled my mouth. My heart sank as I peered at my bloodied hands.

"Choose, dammit." Taking another look at the unmoving figure, shadows rippled from beneath it, creeping into my sight. "Fuck..."

I lunged for the golden handle, and my body was plunged into darkness.

Puddles of water scattered throughout the space as my body crashed against the coarse, stony ground. Cursing under my breath, I slowly lifted myself. Sharp pain radiated through my limbs, urging me to stop. I placed a hand on the mildew-scabbed wall and balanced myself as my sight adjusted to the dim surroundings.

Screams echoed in the distance, and the smell of sulfur flooded my nostrils. I winced at the odor, but that didn't compare to the unnerving feeling inside me once I registered where I was.

I hurried to the iron bars in front of me only to be halted midway. My mouth went dry upon laying eyes on the shackles around my feet.

I opened my mouth to scream. Silence. My throat tightened as if the air was getting ripped out of my burning lungs. Eyes wide and crystalline, I lunged down and tugged on the chains as hard as I could.

"Come on." I tugged and tugged, my breath shaky and unstable. "Please."

Distant footsteps caught my attention, making me freeze. Scanning for anything I could use to free myself, I stood. But there was nothing. Absolutely nothing, save for the shackles and chains that bound me to the wall.

"Savior help me…" I frantically pulled on the chains, again and again until the footsteps neared and stopped.

The iron bars creaked. Turning ever so slowly, my eyes fell upon the man who would torture me forever.

"Again covering for your sister…" he grumbled, whip in hand.

My body cowered, making me back to the wall. "Jezebelle doesn't deserve this."

I wanted to fight, to stop this. I don't want to go through this. But if I don't, Jezebelle would be the one to pay the price, and I'd be damned if she ever has to endure this.

I'd rather go through it a thousand times if that meant that she would be spared.

"She must've done something terrible if you're taking her stead." He fixed the grip around the base of the whip.

"You can stop this, you know?" I said through gritted teeth, biting back the tears that threatened to spill.

"Orders are orders." He said, his gaze flitting away, the room's hum a dull thrum in his ears, a nervous sweat prickling his skin. "Better me than your father."

My throat tightened, and I just turned, bracing myself for impact.

GASPING FOR AIR, KATERINA WOKE, FRANTICALLY reaching for her back. *I'm alive. I'm okay.* Her gaze fell on Jezebelle, who slept soundly in the bed beside hers. At least she was getting some rest. Earlier in the night, Jezebelle couldn't sleep. She was screaming constantly. Katerina had to get the House Naturopaths to give her a calming tonic. The best thing she did was tell Jezebelle to stay here, at least until she felt better and the nightmares ceased.

Katerina rested a hand on her chest, feeling her racing heart slowly return to its normal tempo. *In... out... in... out... breathe in... out...* Climbing out of bed, she approached the dresser and poured herself some water, savoring the cool feeling down her throat.

She wondered how her decision to become a Re'Veillite would affect Jezebelle, especially after everything. Katerina was *happy* and doing the best she could within her limits, but... what would happen once she was officially gone? Who would protect her?

But she also wanted freedom. *Needed* freedom, and if the closest thing she could get to it was through becoming a Re'Veillite, then so be it. *Will I be protected once I leave?* She almost died yesterday and the night before then...

Her heart sank at the utter guilt that lingered inside her. *How could you be so selfish?* Her eyes burned. *She is at peace because of you. Now she is. Once you leave, she'll have to endure all of this alone. Imagine if it were her, the one who had to deal with the attacker at the Agora, and the fake soldier, and Nik...* she couldn't be the cause of her pain. But constantly having to suffer, having to deal with the pain, with the lashes. She bit back a cry.

I take on father's wrath because I have no other choice. Jezebelle is my world. I'd die if I ever saw her in the same condition as me: with a lashed up and bruised back. At least no one gets to see what a real monster he is and how broken I am.

"*We need to show a united front to secure our alliance with Aeshelyn.*" Her father's voice echoed in her mind.

A unified front.

A happy family.

To keep up the façade of the *brave Sovereign,* who lost his wife and raised his two daughters alone. Katerina seethed. Day and night, she had to live with the reminder that she was not her own. That if she stepped out of line, she would be lashed until her back bled. If she stepped out of here, she would be threatened, kidnapped or killed by Olympian rebels. If Jezebelle stepped out of line, she'd have to correct her, or else she would be lashed again.

And again.

And again.

Because it was her damn responsibility. Because their mother was no longer here.

Katerina wiped her damp cheeks. It's been a long time since the last lashing... but it was only a matter of time. As long as she made it to the ceremony, she wouldn't be subjected to lashings anymore. But she had to find an alternative for her sister.

Her head pounded, and she took another sip of water, her sight falling on the folded piece of parchment next to her hairbrush.

I did some digging and found several things about Rhei. But, lucky for you, it's not anything that you should be concerned about. So, relax. I can't give you all the details here, but overall, he comes from a family of healers in Upper Sylene.

Oddly enough, he's been the easiest person to research, which is not usually the norm. There's one thing tho that I want to discuss with you in person.

And yes, I know, I know. I can't be just dropping notes out in the open but, lucky for you, summoned it while you and Jezy were asleep.

Love you. See you tomorrow.

Jasmine

Katerina ripped the parchment, tossed it into the trash, and took one last look at her sister. *I will protect you always. Even if it makes you hate me.*

FOURTEEN

THE SCENT OF AGED PARCHMENT, BURNT WAX, AND THE faint musk of sweat filled the War Room. The flicker of oil lamps strained to illuminate the sea of scrolls that had claimed the room. They spilled across the long oak table like a flood, some unrolling onto the floor, others stacked in precarious towers that leaned like broken pillars. A few looked like they had been hastily pinned to the walls with blades and nails, maps inked with thick strokes, and strange symbols Zeus couldn't recognize.

At the center of the chaos, Argus was hunched over a parchment with a quill clenched in his ink-stained fingers. He didn't even look up when Zeus entered. He moved his lips silently, and had cast aside his usual armor in a heap near the fire, replacing it with a robe heavy with dust and fraying thread.

Zeus stepped carefully between the parchment on the floor, catching a glimpse of hand-written notes: numbers, tallies, enemy formations sketched with sharp angles and brutal clarity. On one sheet, there was a map. Not of Mount Olympus, but of Castelencia.

Just Castelencia and upon further inspection, he noticed that there was a bit of the Aesthite-Castelenian front. Red ink marked two places: the Hearten Citadel and Nanneau Cove—all of them connected by thin, zigzagging lines.

"I've been trying to piece everything together since I got back from Sylene." Argus scrambled through the papers, quill still in his hands. "And now, just now, everything is starting to make some fucking sense."

He released the quill and bolted to Zeus's side with his arm outstretched and a piece of paper in hand. "Read this."

Zeus took the parchment. It bore a smudged symbol he couldn't recognize, scorched black with what looked like a coal brand. Argus had circled it repeatedly until the parchment tore. It didn't seem to come from their archives... usually, those bore a stamp from Mnemosyne, and the script looked and felt different. Scanning over the paper, Zeus read the partially smudged passages.

> When the Sea of Shadows yields its iron fang, and the sickle of the Devourer is torn from its bed of brine, the veil between ages shall fray. From the Euxine's abyssal throat, silence will crawl ashore, for the blade that unmade kings shall taste the breath of mortal land once more.
>
> If it is brought to the altar of the Darkest Point, where no sun dares to trespass, then the cycle shall quiver, and the chains of time may uncoil and rouse the sleeper beneath the bones of the earth. His name is not to be spoken, for the wind itself withers at its sound.
>
> The sea shall turn upon itself, and the tide shall roll in without taste. Fish will rise belly-up, singing silence with mouths agape, and no net shall catch what drifts ashore. When brine becomes bland and the waves forget their sting, the blade shall stir beneath

the water's sleep.

The sky will blacken, and the stars will bleed in their places. They shall not fall, but drip slowly across the heavens, leaving a smear no hand can scrub. And those who dream beneath its light will wake with ash upon their tongues.

A flower shall rise where none should grow, blooming black beneath a dying tree. It will bear no thorns, for all defense will flee its beauty.

The earth will remember the weight of his wrath, and from that memory, a shadow crowned in ruin shall rise. He shall come not with armies, but with hunger for what was, what is, and what will be. Thus, starting the Dark One's hour.

When the blade's edge is wet with night, the earth shall bare unending respite.

Zeus's heart sank upon recognizing the handwriting. A handwriting he hadn't seen in a very, very long time.

"Where did you get this?" Zeus asked, keeping his eyes on the prophecy.

"You know where," Argus replied, marking more areas on the map on the wall.

"I thought she died after the war."

"She went into hiding. She is currently in Sylene under sanctuary since no one wants her lingering in the other countries."

How did he find her? How can I be certain that this is real? That her word is valid? "And she just gave this to you? No questions asked?" Zeus asked in disbelief.

"It took some convincing, but that's what I got." Argus finally turned to Zeus. "Don't you think is oddly fitting that the one person who can accurately prophesize our current standing and what's to come was cursed by the very one who sits in Tartarus for treason?"

Oddly fitting, indeed. "When did she write this?"

"Supposedly, thirty years before the war, when Harrison was still in power."

Zeus's jaw clenched, hands tightening into fists. *Thirty years before the war...* frustration and anger spread through him.

Her name wasn't brought up thirty years ago. He would've remembered. But it was brought up ten years before.

I SPOKE WITH THE LEADERS OF ESERON WHILE SEATED upon my throne. Each brought a significant concern for each of their countries, thus asking for support to keep their people fed and well cared for. Nothing out of the ordinary was mentioned until it was time for the Governess of Castelencia to brief.

Juliette McClaren squared her shoulders and tapped her fingers atop the circular table. "Currently, Castelencia is thriving in its agricultural production, thanks to the blessings bestowed upon us. Imports from Windermere, Sylene, and Aeshelyn have been nothing but stellar. Therefore, in that regard, I have nothing significant to report. However, there's a matter we've tried to handle at our level—your sovereignty—but it hasn't worked."

My ears perked up and, with a wave of a hand, I implored her to continue.

"The locals have been complaining about this woman. She stands at the capital, mainly near the fountain we have in the Caverest Plaza, to speak... what she calls prophesies. *But in reality, she's just spewing nonsense and telling people to flee the country and seek asylum in nearby countries because, supposedly, Castelencia will crumble into nothing but rubble and ruin."*

"And you're bringing this up because?" I asked nonchalantly. "It seems to me that you have a lunatic in your streets whom you're afraid to exile and deal with."

"*Here's the thing, your sovereignty. We have exiled her, but she keeps coming back, each time more intense than the last and somehow bypassing all of my soldiers.*" She ran a caramel hand through her neat black hair while drawing in a sharp breath. Her monolid, almond eyes danced around the room as if she were weighing her next words. "*Besides, not only did she mention that Castelencia will be reduced to nothing but ash, but she is very adamant that Mount Olympus is to fall as well.*"

I scoffed at the utter nonsense.

"*My thoughts exactly.*" She concurred. "*She is a pain to deal with. I tried the gentle approach, didn't work. I tried the forceful approach, didn't work either. I sent men to escort her out of the country and into Aeshelyn, where she could get the help she desperately needs. But she escaped the country and was back at the Caverest Plaza by dawn. All I ask is if you could place some wards around our country to keep her out.*"

"*I have something better for you.*" I adjusted myself on the throne. "*If she really is a nuisance, kill her and be done with it.*"

"*I say this with the utmost respect, that's not going to work.*"

"*And why is that?*"

"*We've tried, and she manages to cheat death every time.*"

"*Who is this woman?*"

"*She goes by the name Cassandra.*"

"Who else knows about this?" Zeus asked Argus.

"Just you."

"I'm still hung up on the fact that you managed to get this." Zeus raised the parchment.

"I have my ways." He turned back to the map.

"How are you certain that this is talking about now and not the actual war that happened?"

"I'm not. But I don't remember stars bleeding from the sky, or a plethora of fish floating on the surface of the sea." He turned. "It would've been something both of us would remember."

"Go over your notes," Zeus ordered.

Argus implored Zeus to take a seat and plunged into his research. After Argus had received an anonymous letter, asking for an audience with Zeus in a day's time at dusk at the Roselle Inn, he did some research and found that the letter came from the outskirts of Castelencia, near the border with Aeshelyn and Sylene.

Argus volunteered to go in Zeus' stead to ensure that it wasn't an ambush of any kind and to allow Zeus time to keep looking into their situation.

When he departed, he sought lodging at the Roselle Inn, where he met the one who requested the audience.

Frederick Gilderoy-McClaren.

"He is the only son of Juliette McClaren, daughter of Harrison. How is he alive? Don't know, don't care." Argus stated. "But he was quite forthcoming about his hatred toward Joseph and the things he learned while working in the Sorting Tower. Of course, he was willing to give me the information in exchange for protection."

The question lingered still. *How did he remain in hiding for so long? Even after Quinn had ordered the execution of his blood relatives? I guess it doesn't matter at this point.*

Quinn was no longer alive, and Joseph doesn't see him as a threat. Unless he found out about what he is doing.

"Frederick said that whenever he is delivering correspondence to the Fortress, which was hardly ever, he has seen Joseph talk to what seems to be a shadow figure. He even heard a few of the guards say that three council members *went missing* and that awfully young men had replaced them. How Joseph was becoming more and more unhinged and how he took the Mayor of Brienne and whipped him to the brink of death to use him as an example." Argus sifted through the papers on the table and uncrumpled one, holding it up. "He intercepted this from one of the letters leaving the Fortress, addressed to the Governess of Aeshelyn." He handed Zeus the paper. "In three day's time, he is to hold a banquet at the Fortress. Which means—"

"This is our opportunity to sneak in, get a good look at the layout, and identify vulnerable areas."

"Precisely." Argus snapped his fingers in agreement. "We have to be smart for this to work. I know Faviola loathes Joseph, but she's on our side, we can meet with her tomorrow and hatch a plan."

"This still doesn't answer the question of how you found Cassandra and got her to give you the prophecy."

Argus stilled briefly as if he's thinking about what to say. He drew a shallow breath. "Let's just say that I made a promise, and I hope I can keep it."

"What promise?"

Argus remained silent.

"Take me to her."

Starry night shone from above as the moon hid behind the darkened summit, *Mount Eventide*. Sylene was known for its reverence to the goddesses Selene and Nyx. While the country slept during the day, the high priestess along with the Governess would cleanse the territory and hold all necessary tribunals on the Sanctuary Sector—*Edus*.

Zeus entered the Governess' estate in his mortal form: shoulder-length, rich brown hair, muscular body and leather armor bearing his symbol. Whenever he traveled to the mortal lands, he'd morph into this version of himself, except when in war or casting judgement.

Argus led the way through the navy, silver, and white decorated estate.

The space was semi-open with large glass windows and access to balconies that overlooked the lavish capital.

"Evening," Argus stopped one of the passing staffers. "I'm looking for the Governess."

"I'm afraid you just missed her. She left for the Ortheaza not long ago."

"That's alright, thank you."

"Is there anything you need assistance with?"

"No," Argus shook his head. "Just let her know that we're here." Argus smiled, and she nodded, dismissing herself.

"Why do you need her?" Zeus asked, eyes trailing behind the woman.

"Just wanted to extend the courtesy of notifying our presence."

Argus led Zeus up the grand stairs and towards an onyx door with a golden handle.

Cassandra stood on the balcony that overlooked the mountain and the temple that lived atop it. Her dark auburn hair cascaded down her exposed back, adorned with dainty lines of what seemed to be moonstone, reaching her waist. Her body was covered in a navy dress that clung to her shoulders.

She turned to Zeus and Argus as they entered the room. Her brown eyes widened slightly.

"I didn't expect you to return so quickly"

"Gracing you with my company twice in a day is not something you're used to, I don't blame you." Argus teased.

She waved a hand, laughing, before her sight landed on Zeus.

"Zeus," she said dryly, as if she hadn't been laughing seconds earlier.

"Cassandra."

"If you're expecting me to feel an ounce of sympathy for your son—"

"We're not here because of Apollo," Argus said.

We are, actually. But he knew better than to stir the pot with her.

Her eyes narrowed on Zeus. "You never come to me unless it's related to him in some way."

"I'm not expecting your sympathy, but I expect your coopera-tion." Zeus said, gesturing at her to take a seat.

Her feet remained planted in place; arms crossed over her chest.

"Cassandra, please." Argus says.

"I'm going to be clear. He can rot in Tartarus for all I care. He took my life from me." She scowled. "Thanks to him, I can't control when I get a vision. I can't control my mind, my body, my ramblings, and the worst thing is that no one believes me when-ever I warn them of something. Why do you think I'm here? So that I can feel normal. Now, if you don't mind." She gestured to the door.

"We'll leave after you tell me about this." Zeus pulled out the parchment containing the prophecy and handed it to her. "I have no interest in your union with my son. Frankly, I don't fucking care. If you enjoy your time here, I suggest you start by answering what war you're referring to in that."

Cassandra's gaze sharpened, turning to the paper in her hands. "This could be related to a myriad of wars. Unfortunately, my gift won't let me ask questions for clarity." She gave the paper back to Zeus, but Argus took it instead.

"You said you wrote this ten years before the war." Argus said.

"No." she shook her head. "I said, I wrote this thirty years before..."

"Where were you then?"

She glanced briefly at Zeus, then looked around the room, as if searching for answers.

"I believe I was still in Castelencia."

"Can you please give us some details? What triggered the vision? Anything." Argus asked, putting the paper away.

Zeus resisted the urge to berate her for her lack of coopera-tion because if she knew something or saw something that could help him figure out Joseph's power source, he'd need her alliance. Well, not needed. He could force the information out, but that's something he'd seriously consider if she continued with this attitude.

"What do you want me to tell you? That whenever I look at a crow, it triggers bad omen visions? That's not how it works." Cassandra paced around the room. "Believe me, if I would've figured out how to dissect my forsaken gift, I wouldn't be in this predicament to begin with."

"But there isn't a problem with your foresight. The mortals just don't believe you." Zeus said.

"In simple terms, yes." She rolled her eyes. "Look, I will tell you what I know in exchange for peace. I want to be left alone. Here." She turned to Argus. "I'll even forfeit your promise to me."

Argus blinked, his expression unreadable by Zeus.

"So long as you do not lie," Zeus said.

CASSANDRA ROAMED THE STREETS OF BELSIR UNDER *the blazing sun. Her sight was fixed on the Temple of Light ahead of her. A heaviness in her chest screamed at her to turn the other way, but her body seemed to move of its own accord. People glanced at her worriedly, while others hissed at her to get cleansed. She didn't know what they meant as she approached the open oak doors.*

Heaviness gripped her shoulders and thrust her inside, making her fall to her knees, hands on the ground as they braced the impact.

She looked up from the marble flooring.

Day had suddenly turned to night. Thunder roared overhead, lightning visible through the glass ceiling.

Corpses covered the massive space, even the second story overlooking the onyx altar. Her heart raced as she was propped up to her feet and taken toward the darkened altar. Where the body of a woman resided, bleeding all over the floor.

Her body turned. Terror filled her upon meeting deep red eyes and a horrid smile that displayed razor-sharp teeth. A fire broke out from behind the shadowed figure as the corpses stood from where they lay.

She screamed, cowering while covering her ears and shutting her eyes.

Someone grabbed her shoulders, shaking her body violently. She didn't want to open her eyes. She didn't want to meet his gaze again.

She was going to die. Her body shook again, and she obliged by opening her eyes.

Daylight filtered through the glass ceiling and people surrounded her, ensuring she was alright. Cassandra's body trembled and a sinister voice echoed through her head.

"Castelencia will be the first. Olympus will follow suit."

She got to her feet and dashed out of the temple.

"After I got home, I wrote everything down." She averted Zeus and Argus's gaze. "I haven't had a vision since." Her body shivered. "Perhaps I should be glad. I've been wanting some quiet."

Zeus glanced at Argus, who matched his own understanding expression as he pulled out the prophecy again.

"What did their temple look like before the war?" Argus asked.

"It didn't have two stories..." Zeus answered.

No more prophecies... red eyes... three omens... the Acrailerion. The prophecy referred to a new, coming war.

Zeus paced around the War room. The prophecy had already been set in motion.

"You don't know if it was set in motion." Argus said.

"No, I do." Zeus retorted. "The Acrailerion wasn't even built when she had that vision."

The door busted open and Ares, Mnemosyne, and Hera entered the room, dragging a man in. He had a scrawny face, scars throughout his body, blind left eye coated in white, dark bristling beard and pasty white skin with drops of sweat and debris stuck to it as his head clung from his shoulders.

Argus grabbed his body with force, pushing everyone out of the way as he pinned him against the wall. Arm to the throat.

"Woah!"

"Argus stop!"

"Wait!"

He didn't listen. "Where the fuck is she?" He pierced into the man's eyes, and all he gave was a heinous smile in response. "Tell me, you piece of shit!"

"Get him off him!" Hera demanded.

A few grabbed Argus by the shoulders, pulling him away; only for him to send their bodies across the room as if they weighed nothing. His hands visibly trembled as he continued to corner the man.

Argus reached into his waist belt and slammed the dagger into the wall, inches away from the man's upper cheek. The man gave him a devilish grin as his one golden eye turned dark.

Zeus pulled Argus away. *What the fuck happened here?*

"Good to know that I made a lasting impression." The man breathed. "She was a delight. I'll tell you that."

Zeus cocked his head. His grip did nothing to keep Argus from lunging at him once more and burying his fist into the man's face; blood seeped from his nose.

The man laughed as the blood trickled into his mouth like a fucking psychopath, falling to his knees.

"Anyone would like to explain?" Hera gaped, almost hysterically.

Argus's blinding rage had him unfolding a side of him Zeus had never seen. It made him wonder who this man was to him and what had he done to warrant such a reaction, when Argus was the diplomatic one.

Zeus turned to Mnemosyne, expecting a response. She stood frozen and, after a considerable moment of silence, she finally spoke.

"I am unsure of the past between Argus and him but... I brought him to you, Darius Andretzis, with the help of Ares, of course."

Zeus's eyebrows raised. Darius. In the flesh.

"He was one of the first to infiltrate Mount Olympus during the war." She added.

Crossing his arms, Argus smiled smugly at the sight of blood. Zeus's sight trailed to Darius. At his frail body. There was an air about him that was unsettling. Like an empty void that swallowed everything with no way of escaping.

"How is he here without dying?" Zeus asked.

"Based on his memories, he was given something that courses through his bloodstream, allowing him to become partially divine."

"And that is?" Hera asked.

"I do not know. Apparently, he was just given the liquid by some woman I couldn't seem to recognize."

"What did she look like?"

"She..." Mnemosyne's silver eyes danced around the room. "That's odd... I—I can't seem to remember..."

Zeus' hands trembled. *I need a drink.* Scratching his beard, he approached the table and reached for the decanter. A sigh slithered from his lips as the wine filled the chalice.

"Who knew he had it in him?" Ares muttered.

He downed the wine in a single gulp and poured himself another.

"Getting a good look, pretty boy?" Darius broke the imminent silence, making everyone turn to him and Argus. Darius could barely hold the weight of his head.

Argus's eyes grew darker by the second, hyper-fixated on him.

Placing the wine down, Zeus approached Argus, giving him a shoulder squeeze, but he didn't look away from Darius.

The reasoning behind his anger wasn't one Zeus was privy to, and jumping through hoops to figure it out wasn't something he was enjoying.

"Who is he?" Zeus whispered.

Argus stayed silent for a moment, eyes narrowing into slits. Zeus felt Argus's breath stiffen, and he couldn't help but tighten his grip on his arm.

"I didn't know his name... but he's the fucker who took my wife during the war." Argus confessed. "I was not expecting him to grace us with his presence today."

"She was a fiesty one, I'll tell you that." Darius's eyes narrowed on Argus, giving him a wicked, blood-covered grin.

Grabbing the nearest piece of cloth he could find, Argus shoved it into his mouth. "Don't talk about my wife." He seethed.

Zeus almost snorted at the faces of indignation around the room. He didn't know why they were acting like they were the most offended ones in the Divine Realm when they had done so much worse.

"If I would've known we would be in for a treat, I would've brought him here eons ago." Ares said.

"You knew his whereabouts?" Argus turned to Ares.

"My men kept him surveilled after the war." He shrugged.

"And you failed to mention this because?"

"Didn't seem to be of much importance, considering we *won*."

"You fucking knew that I was searching for him and yet—"

"It wasn't going to last anyway. She was a mortal, and you needed to let her go."

It was the truth. A relationship between a god and a mortal, even someone with Argus's unique nature, wasn't going to last.

When Argus was first created by Hephaestus, he was the sole guardian of Windermere's borders. Everyone knew him as Talos. But Zeus saw potential in him after several years, thus bringing him to Mount Olympus to advise the Olympian Army alongside Ares and Zeus.

The only thing he asked in return was to be renamed and to be given the appearance of a human, instead of remaining in the body of a bronzed humanoid made out of metal. His sole weakness, a single vein running from his neck to his ankle, sealed by a bronze nail, was turned into a vital artery, but it would cause immediate death if pierced. Regardless of the 12 divisions inside the Olympian Army, Talos took charge of most of the training to destroy enemy formations, among other areas. After proven worthy by Zeus, Talos was renamed to Argus, a name of his own choosing.

"And you suddenly care about me." Argus snorted in disbelief.

"I don't." Ares retorted. "But I do care about our grounds and our men. Your wife—well, *ex*-wife, made you weak. It's about time you grew a fucking backbone, halfbreed."

Zeus's gaze remained on Argus. On his murderous gaze. But Zeus couldn't help but agree with Ares.

When Argus's wife was here, he'd lost all sense of urgency. The cunning, strategic being he used to be was squashed after he met her in one of his excursions around Castelencia.

He fell in love and let everything else go.

After the war, he went into a deep search for her across the continent, Mount Olympus, the sea, and the Underworld. Only to come up fruitless.

"Lay off." Hera interjected. "The boy lost his wife. I know *others* in his position wouldn't bat an eye and have a replacement set by noon." She gave Zeus the nastiest side-eye she could.

Even though she was an insufferable pain in the ass, Zeus had to admit that she looked so good when she was being a bitch. He wanted to untame that neatly pinned brown hair while he made her foxy chocolate eyes roll to the back of her head. Fuck, she was stunning. But she was a fucking pain.

Soon after expressing her discontent, Hera approached Zeus, picking a piece of lint off his clothes. "What are you going to do about Apollo?" She caressed his arm. "Are you going to look into Helios?"

"Did Artemis send you? Is that why you're here?" Zeus asked dryly. "I'm surprised you're looking out for someone else's offspring."

"Apollo is a good boy."

"He endorsed and supplied power to a group of people whose sole goal is to destroy us. Not to mention that he already tried to usurp me once before." Zeus muttered. "Perhaps you'd like to join him, if you think he's so good."

Her jaw tightened. "What about *him*?" she gestured to the gagged man, his body still propped up by two soldiers.

"I'm sure Argus will be glad to take care of him." Zeus looked over at him, who paced around the room for the second time now, another dagger in hand.

Anyway, let's have some fun. Zeus grabbed Hera's arm gently, making her eyes meet his.

"Let's get out of here," Zeus whispered.

"After you just threatened to send me to Tartarus? You're out of your mind." She laughs.

Zeus clicked his tongue. "I beg to differ. You love it when I talk to you like that." Giving her a mischievous smile as her eyes trailed down his body.

She covered her mouth with her hand, her breath catching slightly.

"Try not to be so overt, sweetheart." Zeus whispered.

"There are more pressing matters than your uncontrollable sexual appetite," she hissed.

"I have a nymph already waiting for me. You're welcome to

join us." Zeus smirked at the indignation plastered across her face. "You didn't think I was alone, did you?"

She opened her mouth, surely to give me a smart-ass comment.

"Search through his memories," Argus demanded, looking at Mnemosyne and pulling Zeus's attention back on him.

"I will do what I can, but what exactly are you looking for?" Her eyes trace Darius.

"Anything that can pinpoint to my wife's whereabouts."

"You'll have to give me more detail. I'm not one to work with ambiguity."

Letting out an exasperated sigh, Argus ran his hand through his hair and mentioned what he could remember of the night she was taken. He was vague and still spared a lot of detail. But Zeus assumed it was to avoid any judgmental looks, mainly from Ares.

"Secure him to the chair," she ordered.

The soldiers moved quickly and fastened his arms and legs against it with rope. "I need the room. Too many bodies here can interfere with my work."

Argus kicked everyone out in an instant, including Zeus, until there was no one left except for Mnemosyne, Darius, and him.

"That includes you," Mnemosyne said.

Argus sneered as he exited the room and joined the rest, standing right next to the door.

Before the door shut, Zeus saw her kneel beside Darius, placing a hand on his temple.

"What is your name?" she asked, her voice as sweet as honey. It was all he was able to hear before the door shut everything out.

On a mortal body, looking into someone's memories was a torturous process that had only been attempted once on Olympian grounds, and the man in question died as a result of his body collapsing during the procedure.

Zeus's expectations were low, especially after seeing what they were dealing with.

He glanced at Hera, who looked like she was comforting

Argus. But he didn't look like he needed comfort. His hands were balled into fists, his gaze averting hers. He wasn't depressed; he just wanted answers.

Not my problem. Zeus dismissed the thought.

While everyone was preoccupied with their own business and sidebar banter, this was Zeus's opportunity to leave unnoticed and meet with the deliciousness that awaited him.

He walked in the opposite direction, gliding through the servants.

Ares stepped in his way. "You said it was a good idea to bring him in, and he is wasting our time with this stupid search."

"Perhaps," Zeus retorted. "But if looking into his memories gives us a clue as to who is behind this, kidnapping aside, then so be it."

"I can't believe he is still looking for her. He should lay this to rest and focus on finding the real threat in Eseron."

"Let him follow whatever fallacy he's believing. Soon, he'll reach a dead end and give up on this foolishness entirely." Zeus responded coolly. "I don't want to waste my time and energy on someone who refuses to listen to reason. She is not a goddess. She doesn't come from a divine lineage. She is as mortal as they come and is most likely dead in a ditch somewhere, but if Argus doesn't want to listen, then so fucking be it. Let him break his own heart."

"Maybe that's what he needs to grow a fucking backbone."

"Argus is in the position where there are plenty of goddesses and nymphs here he can betroth or fuck, if that's what he wants. Jasmine isn't and won't be the only woman he'll encounter."

Screams filtered out of the room until a loud thump lets Zeus know that they had a goner. Not even ten minutes in...Argus entered the room, despite everyone telling him to wait. Ares and Zeus followed suit.

The man laid on the ground, face planted against the damp carpet, and body still secured onto the seat. Zeus pushed his body with his foot. No reaction. Mnemosyne walked toward Argus, and Zeus found himself moving with morbid curiosity.

"What did you find?" Argus asked.

"He was a Castelenian native who cames from the poorest side of the country. He was employed by a soldier in the Light Militia, apparently an officer, though I'm not sure who, to steal items of value. Primarily a lyre and Python's fang... your wife was not a part of his original plan... she was just an unfortunate victim."

"Why'd he want Python's fang? And how come I don't remember any of that?"

"Python's fang was to be used in a poison meant to dispel, wound, and even kill a divine being. Someone, a woman, inside an apothecary was gathering the last ingredients to prepare some kind of poison. Darius was the one tasked to get the items needed since he knew Castelencia through and through and had connections across the continent."

"Was she able to do it?" Zeus asked.

"Hard to tell, considering that he went into hiding during the war and hasn't spoken to her since." She paused, pursing her lips before continuing. "I also saw both of you... in the dungeon here... such vile things..." She shook her head.

"What did you see?" Zeus asked, side-glancing at Argus.

"We don't need to get into that." Argus interjected.

"Show me," Zeus ordered.

Her eyes jumped from Zeus to Argus and vice versa. *Had she forgotten that I have the final say? I am the Sovereign among the gods. She reports to me.*

Mnemosyne nodded once and placed a hand on Zeus's cheek.

Hidden in the depths of Olympus, Argus hung from the ceiling alongside his wife. The steel chains bit their skin every time they fought against the restraints. Their bare feet barely touched the cold concrete floor, and the cool air pierced their exposed skin.

"Shit," Argus whispered as he attempted to break the shackles with his strength or at least reach her.

"You were right," Darius said, scoffing in disbelief and surprise at the sight of him.

"No need to tell me what I already know, Darius." A man answered as he searched through the confined space, until finding a bag amidst the debris..

Darius approached the blonde woman. Her ivory face, flushed with a crimson hue, scowled at him. He grabbed her chin, moving her face gently but with enough force to do with it as he pleased. Her blue eyes narrowed as they met his golden ones. A mischievous smile crept onto his face as he looked at her hungrily.

She spat at him, leaving a trail of saliva on his bristling beard. "You foul, sick man." She hissed as her body began to lose sensation and feel heavy.

Darius tightened his grip. "You can't do anything about it, sweetheart. You're mine now." His calloused hands caressed her golden locks.

"Don't fucking touch her." Argus spat, continuing to tug on the shackles.

Darius moved away from her, directing his attention to him. "Or what, pretty boy? You have no power here." His eyes drifted to the restraints as his mouth curled up into a wicked grin.

"Fuck! Finally!" the man said, overjoyed as he placed a golden lyre into his worn leather bag and stood. "We have to go now."

"What about the fang, Eustin? We can't go back without it."

"You think I don't have it?" Eustin gave a cocky smile as he pulled it out of his bag. "They make things way too easy here."

"We're taking her." Darius pointed at her.

"Like hell you are!" she barked as she fought off the overwhelming weakness that consumed her body. Her eyes became heavier by the second.

Darius scoffed amusingly at her response. His accomplice pursed his lips, his mind racing a thousand thoughts per second. "You'll get half of the fun, Eustin." He pushed, insinuating the defiling things they could do to her once she was entirely in their possession.

"I don't know, man. We've already ruffled some feathers, and I don't want to risk anymore than what we already have." Eustin scratched his scrawny head as he clutched onto his bag tightly. Droplets of sweat fell down his face, and time was running out.

"Fuck it. I'm taking her." Darius snapped, storming toward her now unconscious body.

"Fine, but hurry." Eustin dashed to the exit, cracking it. An array of soldiers fought right outside the door. He shut it almost immediately.

"S-st-stop." Argus stuttered as the numbness overtook him. "D-don't touch..." His body succumbed to the heaviness of the poison as Darius took Jasmine away in his arms and disappeared into thin air.

THE TINGLING SENSATION IN ZEUS'S HEAD CEASED AS the war room focused back into view. Mnemosyne was now two steps away from him, and Argus was glaring again at Ares.

"I get that you're angry at the lack of information. But—"

"Lack of information?" Argus scoffed. "He deliberately hid this from me. I don't know his motives for doing so. I don't care to know either. He knew I was searching for him. Yet he kept it from me. I could've found her already. She could've been here where it's safe."

The question stirred inside Zeus. *Why did Ares keep this from him? Better yet, from me? I had given an order to find her and any information regarding her disappearance, mainly for show, but the order was given, nonetheless.*

"My *wife* was taken by those miscreants, and you've done *nothing* to get her back!"

"What have *you* done, huh? Aside from bitching and

complaining about what we fail to do or haven't done. How do *you* plan on getting her back? How do you even know she is still alive?" Ares retorted.

"I've done plenty, despite you and Zeus telling me to sit and wait until we get more *information*."

Zeus turned to Argus, who still stood at arm's length from him, but Argus's eyes were laser-focused on Ares, despite Zeus looking in his direction. He resisted the urge to chuckle and masterfully kept a straight face.

"You need to calm down." Ares said, putting his palms up.

"Don't you dare tell me to calm down," Argus hissed. "War itself may bow to you, yet you lost your lover to a smith. I suppose not every victory can be won with a sword... though you seem to lose those too, considering your end state during the war."

In a blink of an eye, Ares buried his fist into Argus's face. "You listen to me, you ungrateful little shit." Blood dripped from his fist, yet he delivered another blow. "Everything that you *have*. Everything that you *are* is nothing but a lie. You can change your name, wrap yourself in flesh like a coward, but no skin can hide the stench of what you really are, Talos." He punched again, but Argus blocked his fist. "You call yourself forged of bronze and legend, yet I've seen rust with more purpose. You and I are not equals. You'll never measure up to me." Ares seethed, pushing off him. "I almost pity you, Talos, hiding in a human shell. It must be exhausting pretending you're anything but a relic running from your own fucking shadow."

I FOUND MYSELF STANDING IN THE MIDDLE OF THE *Assembly Hall, where colorful patterns painted the marble flooring due to the stained-glass windows. Quinn perched on his throne, and Bernadette stood beside him in an opaque white robe with golden accessories and a cerulean belt at the waist that matched the designs along her robe. Her hair was sleek, half of it pinned to her head. Allowing everyone to bask in her beauty.*

My oh my, she was stunning, and she was all mine, even if no one else knew it yet.

"Governor Orestis, welcome." Quinn announced as the governor entered the room in his classic deep green ensemble.

A tall, robust man with slicked-back bronze hair walked behind him wearing the Aeshite colors. The son.

"Sovereign. Your Gracefulness." The governor bowed slightly. "May I present my son? Malakai Orestis."

Malakai bowed, making lustful eyes at Bernadette.

My blood simmered, but I kept my face neutral at the sight. Whether or not I risked it, Quinn was most likely watching my reactions to solidify his suspicions. I highly doubt my justification of being friendly was enough to sway him; therefore, I couldn't be too forthcoming with my sentiments about this imbecile.

Besides, how can he accept another man looking at her like she was nothing but a conquest, a piece of meat? Was it truly so terrible for him to know about our love? I looked back at Quinn, who stared right at me with murderous intent, confirming my suspicions with this betrothal. As long as you don't show anything, he won't have a reason to do anything.

"The comments about your beauty don't seem to do you justice, your Gracefulness. You're much enticing in person."

Give me a fucking break. *I swallowed down the scoff that threatened to escape my lips.*

Bernadette smiled kindly. "And I suppose you're here to revel in my beauty like everyone else?"

"On the contrary," Malakai stepped forward. "I intend to make you my governess, not just for your breathtaking beauty but for the intellect your brother praises you for."

Since when was Quinn this... generous?

Malakai, the Governor, and Quinn divert the conversation to the ramifications of their union and as much as I tried to pay attention, my mind and focus drifted back to Bernadette and how I'm losing her to another man, thanks to her fucking brother.

"Congratulations on your new *promotions*." Kalio, the elder counselor, said, pulling Joseph back to the present. The condescension was palpable in his sun-kissed face and tone.

"What happened to Fotis, Vern, and Ermis?" Khir, the eldest counselor, asked outright, uncaring if the newcomers felt uncomfortable.

Joseph traced his finger along the rim of the empty glass on the table. He knew was only a matter of time before someone inquired.

"New opportunities across the continent." He answered dryly, not bothering to hide his bitterness.

"I thought that as members of this Council, no other endeavors may be pursuit." Khir said. Yet, Joseph was unsure if he meant it as a question or a statement.

"New council members are to be treated to the highest standard and with the same respect as *seasoned* council members." Joseph dismissed Khir's words, which only made him turn his thin, wrinkled face to them.

His almond eyes sliced into Dremian first, who met his gaze head-on and unrelenting. "Tell me, what is the treaty that binds Castelencia to adjacent countries?"

Joseph rolled his eyes at the question. He knew precisely the intention behind it. Gesturing at the servants to fetch another decanter of amber ambrosia, he studied Dremian carefully.

"In what sense?" Dremian countered, making Khir scoff.

"The question is straightforward."

"Castelencia has three treaties with the neighboring countries. Therefore, you have to be more specific."

Khir jerked a brow at the challenge. "Name them—no, don't just name them. Tell me what they are for. Why they were established in the first place, since you want to be a wiseacre."

Dremian squared his shoulders and proceeded to mention the treaties, starting with the Treaty of Trade; which ensured that Castelencia supplied Sylene and Windermere with fresh produce, since our lands were the most fertile. In exchange, Windermere would supply them with weapons and tools, while Sylene provided medicinal goods.

The servant filled Joseph's glass with a hefty dose of amber liquid; but his attention remained on unrelenting Dremian, then at Khir's sour expression.

Joseph had picked Dremian after he scored exceptionally high on the Trials. Not only was he all brains, but Joseph also considered him to be a great asset to have when it came to infiltrating certain areas in the country since Dremian's boyish features would not be directly associated with the Sovereign's council. Not to mention that women tended to swoon over him just by his diamond-blonde hair and honey eyes; and women who swooned, were women who talked.

Dremian proceeded to explain the Justice Protocol and how it has kept the peace among their people. Joseph was even surprised that Dremian mentioned the Sanctuary Clause imposed by Sylene: *If a criminal enters their country, and somehow makes it to Edus, the sanctuary city, then the person cannot be extradited and a tribunal must be held.* Rumor had it that those who attempted to find this place rarely ever did, since it only appeared to those Edus considered to be wrongfully charged.

Joseph almost laughed at Mare and Kalio's shocked faces. *Did they think I would bring unprepared people here?* Aside from them being extremely young, despite the norm, they are also very... malleable.

Dremian concluded with the Union Convention and how it was specifically designed as a last resort, only to be invoked in dire situations. If either country needed a show of strength or was at the brink of ruin, two countries would find a member of their immediate family within the lines of succession, and they would be joined in marriage, and nothing could absolve it, save for death.

None of the countries invoked the convention after the Great War. However, Sylene proposed revisiting this and potentially be included in the accord.

Mare, the second elder with silver hair and olive skin, addressed Xaden, the youngest of the newcomers, commending him for his efforts during last night's mass and his support to the Sovereign. To which he gave him a humble nod and smile. Apparently, he'd done such a great job that the people wanted to see him more often; thus making Joseph consider him to be the one to lead the upcoming masses.

Better for me. The less I have to deal with the wretched sham of a mass, the better.

Mare then proceeded to speak to Julius. "What happened to your eye?" gesturing to the black eyepatch that bore a sun.

Joseph could've sworn he saw Julius tense slightly, but his face remained stoic as he answered. "Life."

Mare took the hint and returned to his notes. Joseph had been curious as well, but he knew better than to pry. That would open the door for them to do the same, and he couldn't have that. *Not right now. Not after what I'd done.*

Khir sat back in his seat, his spine stiff as he turned his attention back to Joseph. "What role will they assume? Our former companions had special duties assigned to them, based on their... background and expertise."

Of course, you've always been a greedy bastard. Joseph reached for the glass, lightly stirring it. *As if I can't see through your bullshit.* "That's currently under review. However, preliminarily, Xaden will be hosting the evening masses during my absence. Julius will be overseeing the Chroniclers, and Dremian will work alongside Sebastian."

"Aren't you concerned about what others may think if you stop leading mass?" Mare asked.

"I'm still sovereign," Joseph answered. *It doesn't fucking matter who leads it.* "He'll be covering down while I secure the alliance with Aeshelyn."

"What about the Denai position?" Khir finally showed his hand. "It cannot go unfulfilled."

Joseph suppressed a scoff. *I'm not selecting you, if that's what you're thinking.*

"The Verenna is taking over as interim for the moment." Mare answered. "It's not ideal, but it is currently being managed."

"She cannot assume both roles. It's a conflict of interest." Kalio retorted.

"That is precisely why I'm bringing this up." Khir turned to Joseph again. "Pardon my bluntness, but I am the eldest council member, and after the passing of Vern—may his soul rest with our Savior—I believe I am qualified to cover in his stead."

"Khir, there are protocols in place." Mare interjected.

"I believe protocol is something we stopped considering, based on *recent* developments."

A low blow. "And you expect me to place you in such a coveted position of trust after you overtly disrespected me? Your Sovereign."

His jaw tightened. "Pardon my bluntness."

"No, don't apologize now." A wicked grin crept onto Joseph's lips.

"Perhaps we can table this conversation and divert our attention to more pressing issues." Kalio suggested.

I should've killed you instead of Vern. Joseph's eyes slowly trailed from Khir to him. "Such as?"

Mare opened a scroll of parchment and dragged his finger down it, as if looking for something.

Kalio surveyed the room before falling onto Joseph. "There was an attack at the Helios Agora, and a poor woman died of a heart attack during the chaos."

Joseph rolled his eyes. "And I should know this because?"

"Rumor has it that it was your daughter who caused the bloodshed."

Joseph's body ran cold. "People often craft accusations about us to discredit who we are and what we do." *It wouldn't be the first time.*

"We can't have this sort of situation be linked to our image with the neighboring countries. Aeshelyn is already working overtime to get the Windermere and Sylene to abandon their alliances with us. This only adds fuel to the fire." Kalio stated.

"Who's to say this hasn't already reached the other countries?" Dremian stated.

"Who do you think provided me with the insight?" Kalio leaned in.

"Windermere reached out to you?" Khir arched an eyebrow.

Kalio nodded. "Let's just say that I was able to sway them into believing that this situation was caused by an Olympian radicalist who claimed to be your offspring in order to cause an uproar."

His lips curled upward, his sense of accomplishment in full display. "I'm sure Lazaros will sway Sylene as well. But there's only so much I am able to do. You need to speak to your daughter about this. Make sure she does not do anything of this sort again."

Joseph's mind juggled back and forth between who was responsible. Jezebelle was out at the same time as Katerina.

"Not only that, but we have to think about what Aeshelyn might do with this information." Julius added in his somber voice.

"How are you certain that it was one of my daughters and not some radicalist like you claimed?" *As I said, it wouldn't be the first time someone claimed to be mine. I've had lovers, yes; but no other offspring were sired.*

Last time something like this happened was several months ago, when a guy broke into the Acrailerion to *free those who were being led astray.* The man made a complete fool of himself when Joseph's men took him in; saying he was there under strict guidance from Joseph and that he was his son, when everyone knew Joseph only had two daughters.

"Some servants claimed they saw her get escorted here by one of our guards." Khir added.

"Apparently, her clothes were covered in blood too." Mare threw Joseph a worried glance.

She wouldn't... heat slithered down his spine.

"Katerina or Jezebelle?"

CHAPTER
SEVENTEEN
KATERINA

"Belsir was located in the northeast region of Caverest—the biggest town inside Castelencia, and it became the most secure area in the country. The grounds extended to just over a thousand acres of land, becoming the home for 5,000 people with only one entry/exit point."

KATERINA CLOSED THE BOOK, DREW A BREATH AND rubbed her eyes.

Without Johan around, she was forced to remain inside the grounds until she could identify someone she could trust not to tell her father about her runs. She'd been wanting to go, but then again, things were tense. If she were to go on a short run, it'd most likely be inside the capital.

Katerina stood, putting the book on the shelf. *I know I said I wanted to lay in bed all day, but I... I can't*—firm hands kept her from thrashing as someone carried her out of the library.

Nothing but pure darkness flooded her sight, and the only things she could pick up were the turns they took and the noises of doors shutting one after the other.

Her body ran cold upon hearing the unlocking and movement of chains let loose. She continued to fight her way to release, each movement more frantic that the last. *They've come to get me. She felt* the blood drain from her face. *They found me. They found away to break into my home...*

"*Don't get too comfortable. You will see me again and, believe me when I tell you, I will relish the day I send your soul to the depths of the Underworld.*" Nik's words hurried to the forefront of her mind.

I shouldn't have been a damn brat. Her body trembled. *I'm going to be sick.*

Cool air bit her skin as they descended lower and lower in a circular motion. Heavy footsteps echoed loudly around her, telling her they were in a confined space.

Her stomach turned. *No. No. No. No. No.* She thrashed as hard as she could; not caring if she fell to the ground.

Katerina plunged her bound hands into the solid back of her abductor again and again. *Fucking let me go!* She hit them again.

She fell, crashing against a hard, dusty surface.

The rattling of chains made the color drain from her face. *No. No. Please. No.* She did her best to slither back and out. But she couldn't see. Calloused hands grabbed her legs and pulled her forward.

"Please don't!" She yelled; and it wasn't until the blindfold was pulled off that her face paled completely upon laying eyes on her father, casually leaning against the mildew-scabbed wall.

She didn't know who she feared the most... him or the abductors she had imagined. The iron gates were open next to him. *I could make a run for it once my feet get unbound.* It always took them a minute to get the shackles secured, anyway.

His face was stone-cold as he surveyed her, and Katerina suppressed the urge to tell him to fuck off. To release her. To stop this. To avoid this. But even as she opened her mouth, nothing came out. Only a shallow breath.

The soldiers released her feet and almost instantly locked the shackles in place, barely allowing her time to register the change. One of them took her hand and raised her to her feet.

He unbound her wrists and, just as she mustered the courage to swing—another guard took hold of them overhead, stopping her strike. *I am dead. He just saw me. My temper. My intentions. Shit. I am dead.* The lashings hadn't even begun, and her back was already aching.

The soldiers stepped away after finishing securing her hands. Katerina's ankles were bound to the wall, merely a foot or two of chain from it, and her hands were bound to each other with barely an inch of chain in between them.

A silent nod from her father was all it took for them to leave. Her heart sank, and stomach hollowed at the sight of him.

"You just don't learn, do you?" He finally said.

"I don't know what you're talking about." She stammered. "Truly."

He scoffed, trailing his tongue along his lower lip as he ran a hand through his chin.

Irritation? Anger? Rage? Indignation? What was it?

She clasped her hands together to stop the rattling of the chains while her gaze landed on the item in his other hand. What haunted her nightmares—an ebony whip.

"Truly!" she cried out. "I don't know what I did! I've been focused on my duties. I haven't gone outside. I've kept an eye on Jezy." Her lips quaked. "I've been good."

"Have you?" He cocked a brow, tightening his grip on her torturer. "I will only ask you once. You know how this goes."

Simple yes or no questions. Her mind raced with the many things he could ask about. *Jezebelle and Rhei? My induction? Me asking Jasmine to sneak into the Chronicler Wing to find out about Rhei? What happened at the Helios Agora? Shit. Shit. What?*

"Did you kill a man in the Helios Agora?"

I'm going to faint. "No." *I was not the one who killed him. But he was going to kill me.*

He looked down at the whip. "Turn around, hands against the wall."

"I didn't!"

He gave her a warning glare that immediately sent her body cowering as she turned. Silent tears sprang out of her eyes. *I didn't do it.*

"I always knew you had a temper, Katerina. But never had I thought that you would go so far as to kill a man, particularly in enemy territory, of all places. We're already on the cusp of war."

"He was going to kill—"

A crack against her back had her arching as burning pain spread through her. She clenched her teeth, but she couldn't stop the cry from escaping her lips.

"Don't interrupt me." He said calmly. "Word of this got to Windermere. If it weren't for one of my council members intervening," he hesitated. "This stunt could've cost me."

Another lick of the whip. She bit her lip as hard as she could, the taste of iron coating her tongue. Burning, sharp pain rippled through her again.

"You want to become a Re'Veillite, don't you?"

Crack.

"Yes." She croaked.

"That is hanging by a thin thread. Don't think for a second that I can't pull away the induction. I don't care if it's the day of, or if you are standing at the fucking altar. One more stunt and you can kiss that dream goodbye. In fact, next time, it'll be Jezebelle taking your place while you watch."

No! She wanted to yell; but every ounce of her aching body stopped her.

"Do you understand?"

"Yes." Tears drenched her cheeks.

Another crack.

"Yes, what?"

To an extent, she was grateful that he couldn't see the hatred in her eyes. "Yes...I understand...and will not step out of line again."

"Good." He said. "Bring the dress down to your hips. Keep your eyes on the wall."

She obeyed. With trembling hands, she slid the top part of her dress down to her wrists. Cool air caressed her exposed skin. She knew this part would come. This was the end of the punishment. But it was the worst part of it.

"Three. That is all you are getting, since your situation was able to be... handled."

How considerate. She rolled her eyes, and then it began.

One.

Two.

Then three.

Warm, thick liquid trailed down her numb, exposed back.

"Get dressed." He ordered before striding out.

Distant doors slammed and, as if on cue, her hands cupped her face, suppressing the cries, as she fell to her knees.

The thief was right... I could've died, and he wouldn't even have shed a tear.

Stinging pain spread through her body as Jasmine gently cleaned Katerina's raw back with a cold, dampened cloth.

She managed to hurry to her room before the blood saturated the back of the dress. But it was already stained and sticking to her skin when Jasmine showed up.

"You really need to see the Nautorpaths, Kate. This could get infected."

Katerina winced at the burning sensation as she slowly dabbed again and again. "If I set foot inside the Healer Wing, questions will be asked. Besides, I've dealt with it before here."

"Let them ask." She dunked the cloth into the bowl next to her, wringing the water out and dabbing again. "You're under no obligation to respond, but you need to get this healed."

"I am getting it healed."

"Properly healed, Kate." Jasmine glared.

"Anyway, I *do* have to answer questions. You think they're not going to ask questions when they see the daughter of the Sovereign with a lashed back?"

"Blame it on a rebel for all I care. Just go. My powers cannot heal you." She wiped the cool cloth against her throbbing back. "Your back is completely covered, Kate. Between old and fresh..." She hesitated, fingers tracing the array of scars.

Katerina winced, drawing a sharp breath. "I just don't want anybody inquiring about what happened. Once father gets told about my condition, he'll take it out on Jezy because I was disobedient and aired out our problems. I'd rather deal with this than put my sister in the middle of this mess."

Images of the chains and shackles flooded her mind. *I didn't deserve any of it. I didn't kill a man. I don't know why he would think I did. Maybe... because I was covered in blood? But I showered before he saw me in the office.*

"Then think of something to say." Jasmine imposed. "You can't keep trying to heal yourself alone in your room."

Katerina snorted, sharp pain radiated through her back while adjusting herself. *I've been self-aiding ever since the lashes began. 10 years ago... at merely 18 years old. I'm lucky it hasn't gotten infected at this rate.*

"Please tell me you'll let it go." Jasmine asked.

"I—"

"Please."

"Fine," Katerina said in defeat. "But don't tell Jezy. She has a lot on her plate right now."

"I know... she told me."

"She did?" Katerina turned to her, ignoring her stinging back.

Jasmine nodded, her eyes still fixed on Katerina's wounds. "I saw her this morning going to the Acrailerion's Worship Hall. She seemed distraught, so I extended a helping hand."

A wave of relief washed through Katerina. *At least she is getting the help she needs.*

"Did she say what she'd do after?" She winced at the wipe Jasmine did across her back.

"All done. Be careful with the bandages as you get dressed." She cleaned the blood-stained cloth in the now murky water. "I believe she was going to take a walk around the Rena Gardens."

Good. "So, what was the thing you wanted to tell me?" Katerina asked, remembering the note while carefully fixing her dress.

"Oh, yes... Rhei has an interesting background, to say the least." She dried her hands with a dry cloth. "Apparently, there's no record of his family past his immediate relatives."

"But you said he came from a family of well-known healers..." Katerina arched an eyebrow.

"Yes, but..." She hesitated and placed the bowl of murky water on the table next to the dresser. "You know that in the Chronicler Wing, they have an archive where every lineage known to man is listed, aside from other information I'm not privy to. Well, when I looked for the Khol lineage, I only seemed to find his father and mother, Hendrix and Genevieve Khol. *That's* the odd thing. I'm used to seeing countless pages of parchment related to one lineage alone. And to be fair, I thought maybe someone had misplaced the rest of the documents." She shook her head. "Nope. I asked my boy—I mean, *friend* there, and he didn't seem to find anything either."

"Perhaps his father adopted a new name? People tend to do that when they want to cut ties with their relatives."

"A family line doesn't just vanish." She retorted. "Even if you change your name, the Chronicler's magic can still trace it, especially if the family and their offspring registered in the census."

The Chroniclers inside the Acrailerion were one of the four types of Re'Veillites and the only one that included men. They were in charge of the record-keeping of the entire continent, no matter how big or small. It was highly guarded, and only Chroniclers, the Verenna and the Denai were allowed entry.

"Is that the only thing you found? I can't do much based on this alone."

She nodded, but in a split second her eyes widened. "Oh, yes, I almost forgot. Did you know that Rhei also has a sister?"

"Who?"

"Chryssa Khol, if I'm not mistaken."

Katerina froze. *What are the damn odds?*

"Do you know her?"

"We met briefly when I... when I saved Jezy." Katerina responded hesitantly and prepared for the slew of questions. "Needless to say, the resemblance is uncanny now that you mention it."

"I also wanted to ask... How did you know that Jezebelle was in danger?"

There goes the first. "That's something I've been wondering myself. I just woke up and felt a tug in my chest that I just couldn't ignore, and before I knew it, I was heading out to some place, and I managed to come across her."

"None of the guards saw you leave?" she asked in utter disbelief.

"There weren't any in sight, which was odd to begin with. Except for Johan, who let me out."

Jasmine's eyes narrowed as if analyzing her every word. "How'd you know where to go?"

Katerina shrugged. "I just followed a hunch. Besides, I wholeheartedly believe that Rhei is behind what happened to her."

"You really have quite the vendetta against him. You can give him the benefit of the doubt, you know?"

"He doesn't *deserve* the benefit of the doubt." Katerina hissed. "I am convinced that his lying-deceiving ass took advantage of Jezy's kindness." Her throat clenched. "If I hadn't been there when I did—"

"Don't think of the worst. You *were* there, and she *is* safe. That's all that matters," Jasmine said, taking a seat next to Katerina. "Don't you think you being overly concerned about Rhei is somehow influenced by your own experiences?"

"No." Katerina shook her head. "And there is nothing wrong with looking out for her."

Even though she admired the Re'Veillites, there were times

when she'd wonder what it would be like to fall in love again, get married and have a family of her own. She almost had it once until her father destroyed her relationship at its very core. Sometimes, she'd think about how he was or where he could be more often than she cared to admit. But the thought of him and what happened made her skin crawl and eyes burn.

"TELL ME IT ISN'T TRUE...." I SOBBED, CLASPING A HAND over my mouth.

Byorn met my stare, cold and unfeeling. "If you already know, why ask?"

"Because, for—shit... for a moment, I want to believe that you thought about me, about us..."

He shook his head lightly, yet his face remained stone cold. "Don't pry, Katerina. You won't like it."

Katerina.

Not Kate. Not my love. Not—I sobbed. I was simply Katerina.

SHE WAS SO HARD ON JEZEBELLE, BUT RHEI NEVER SAT right with Katerina. *Could it be paranoia? Maybe.* But that's the type of betrayal Katerina knew her sister couldn't recover from. The type of betrayal Byorn did to her. The type of betrayal Rhei did to her younger sister by putting her out as an offering.

"I'm not saying that you're wrong. But don't think about that." Jasmine placed a gentle hand on Katerina's tender shoulder. "Let your sister experience this. Even if it's just for a little while."

"I could've lost her, Jas..." Katerina croaked.

"But you didn't."

"If I see that bastard here or anywhere near her—" she took a breath. "Is there any way we or your *friend* can find out more about him without depending on the archives?"

"Aside from straight-up asking him? I don't know, but please let it go."

"Fine, I will." She lied. *If Rhei was just a mere healer, then it shouldn't be an issue to get rid of him with the right approach...*

Jasmine tilted her head. "Care to share what you're planning?"

"I'm not planning anything." *Yet.*

"Kate... what's it going to take for you to let this be?"

"If you can prove to me that he poses no threat to her. I'll let it go."

"Didn't you say you met his sister?"

Katerina nodded.

"Leverage it. Try to see what she knows."

"What if she already knows who I am? I'm sure that's not something her brother would keep quiet."

"Gage it. Take advantage of your secret runs to get information. While you work on that, I'll do some digging over here."

"I can't go on runs. Father has me on a tight leash."

"Don't worry about it. I'll take care of that."

"How?"

"Do you want to lay this to rest or not?"

"Yes, but—"

"But nothing, let me do my thing." Jasmine reassured. "Besides, aren't you supposed to be preparing for the banquet your father's hosting?"

Katerina let out an exasperated sigh. "Supposed to be."

"Well, let's just say that I heard he invited the governess of Aeshelyn."

Katerina snorted. "She won't come."

"I don't know... your father was pretty adamant about securing an alliance with her."

"You're not suggesting...." Katerina's brows furrowed, stomach hollowing in the process.

Jasmine shook her head. "The governess would rather die

than agree to the Union Convention. But don't get complacent either. Anything can happen. I'm just preparing you..."

"I hate this." Katerina let out. "I'm going to see what I can find about Rhei on my end." *And try not to bash my head against a wall.*

"Alright, but go see the Naturopaths first."

CHAPTER
EIGHTEEN
JOSEPH

"WHEN CAN I SEE RENA?" JOSEPH ASKED ERIS, WHO leaned against the vine-covered statue, tracing a spindly finger down it.

It was close to midnight, yet Joseph was wide awake. The mausoleum reeked of the stench of humidity and decay, but he was too exhausted to pay any mind to it.

"So impatient." She teased.

"I'm not in the mood for games."

Eris laughed, pushing herself off the statue. "The lashing session took a toll on you?"

His stomach lurched, and all he wanted was to find whatever weapon possible and kill her where she stood. But he knew better.

"Rena is fine." She finally said.

"Show her to me."

"Anything you want, sweetness." She gazed into his darkened eyes, and a piercing sensation sank deep claws into his mind.

And there she was.

His wife... in some unknown place, sleeping soundly in a maroon dress. Her dark golden-brown hair rested beautifully atop her chest. *What I'd give to see her honey eyes*—Eris pulled out, taking the image of Rena with her.

"My job is done; let her go." He said through clenched teeth, blood simmering beneath. "There's no point in keeping her captive. You have what you wanted."

She laughed so loudly it bounced off the walls around them. "Pray tell, what makes you think you're done?"

"What else is there?" He stalked toward her. "I sacrificed three of my men. Men who trusted me. Men with families—"

"You have your own family to worry about." A mischievous smirk slithered onto her lips. "Besides, I'm surprised you care this much about darling Rena, considering you never loved her in the first place."

I couldn't love her for this same fucking reason. Breathe. She knows that I am barely holding on by a fucking thread. He was already being haunted by what he had done to Katerina. He couldn't let her get under his skin.

"Well... with an absent wife, a daughter that hates you, and another whose freedom you're bargaining... it doesn't seem you have a family left to begin with, now that I think about it."

Joseph pushed Eris against a column, pressing his forearm against her throat.

Rage flowed through him as her wicked eyes met his murderous ones and grinned, showing off her perfectly white teeth. "You're so easy to rile up. Now, I see where Katerina gets her temper."

"What the fuck else do you want?" His body almost crashed against the marble stone, bracing himself with his arm as she spawned behind him.

"If you wanted to get close to me that badly, all you had to do was ask." She teased.

He kept his eyes on the floor, his pulse hammering against his skull, and tasted the iron on his tongue. Not from blood, but from biting down so hard his jaw ached.

Eris's voice snaked through the air, slow and deliberate. "You still see her in your dreams, don't you? Bernadette... the way her hand lingered in yours, the way her eyes pulled you in. You still cling to the story that she was stolen from you. That you were betrayed. But..." She leaned close, her lips almost brushing his ear. "What if she let it happen?"

The heat rose instantly in his chest. Joseph's head jerked up, locking eyes with that slow, knowing smile that made him want to wipe it from her face.

"When the chance came to run? To fight for you? She didn't. She took his hand, wore his ring, and went to his estate. And when the sentence came..." Eris tilted her head in mock pity. "She didn't call your name. She went quietly. Like she wanted to."

His fists curled tight enough for his nails to bite deep into his palms. "Shut your mouth."

Bernadette's words echoed in his head, taking him back to their last moments together.

"I think it's best if we end this now."

"You really think I'd give up on you? On us?" I asked, searching her eyes for a semblance of hope.

"It's not what I think..." she countered. "It's what's right."

"Why?" Eris' tone was velvet over steel. "Because it cuts too deep to imagine that she chose the ax over you? That she'd rather be dead than yours?"

The rage was molten, flooding his veins, but he buried it under layers of discipline. He met her eyes, voice low, steady. "You do not know what we were to each other."

Her laugh was quiet, but sharp enough to draw blood and grind his gears.

"I know exactly what you were: the reason she's dead. And

now…" Her eyes flickered, a golden flash in the dark, "…the reason Rena will be too."

Something cold settled in his gut.

"She *is* something," Eris purred, "very lovely. Soft. Loyal. Still hopeful enough to believe you'll keep her safe. But you and I both know she's only breathing because *He* wants her to be. Fail, and she will share Bernadette's fate. The only difference is that she will die in a never-ending abyss instead of by a blade in front of a crowd."

His nails bit deeper. *Don't speak.*

"So," she continued, her smile widening, "you'll do what you were brought here to do. Get Kronos' Sickle. Then perhaps your precious Rena will return to you. Fail…" She shrugged, the gesture almost playful. "And you'll watch her die knowing it was because of you… again."

The air felt heavier, as though the walls were pressing in. Every instinct screamed to rip her apart, but he knew he couldn't, not yet. Not until Rena was safe. Because now wasn't just about the past. It was about keeping Rena out of death's grip.

"Remember, it's not only Rena's life in the balance, it's also your daughters—well, *daughter*…"

His stomach twisted, and Eris trailed a finger along the edges of the statue, eyes glinting in the moonlight.

"Katerina has such… striking features," she said, her tone light, almost absentminded. "Beautiful deep green eyes. You rarely see that shade of green in your bloodline, do you?"

Joseph stiffened, but she only smiled.

"Ah, but I'm sure it's nothing," she added, with the kind of softness meant to feel harmless. "Genetics do work in mysterious ways, don't you think?"

"Whatever you're suggesting, stop." He said coldly. "Katerina is as much mine as Jezebelle."

"I'm sure." She disappeared before he was able to respond.

Katerina is mine.

Jezebelle is mine.

THE CANDLE BETWEEN US BURNED LOW AND STEADY, throwing shadows across her face as Rena sat on the edge of the bed, fingers playing in the hem of her nightdress. I watched her hands instead of her eyes, since it was easier than seeing whatever truth waited there.

"I need you to answer me," I said, my voice low, steady. "And I don't want the half-truths you're so good at."

Her lips pressed together, then parted just enough for a breath to slip through. "About what?"

"You know what." My chest felt tight, the words clawing their way out. "Katerina."

Rena's eyes flickered up to mine, then away. She smoothed the fabric in her lap as if the creases mattered more than my question. "What makes you ask? She is you in female form."

"That's not what I asked." I leaned forward, elbows on my knees. "Don't hide in pleasantries, Rena. I've lived with that girl for fourteen years. I've taught her everything she knows. I've kissed her goodnight more times than I can count. But when I look at her..." My voice caught. "When I look at her eyes..." I shook my head. "Tell me the truth, Rena."

Her shoulders tensed, but she didn't look up. "Genetics are a mystery. What if you or I have a distant relative in our bloodlines with green eyes? Will she be condemned because she doesn't bear your black or my brown?"

"Rena..." Her name was a bitter laugh in my throat. "You better not lie to me."

She was quiet for a long moment, and the silence pressed against me like a closing door. Until finally, she said, "How or why would I? She was conceived soon after we married."

"Yes," I said, sharper than intended. "I remember it vividly..."

Her hands stilled in her lap. She drew a slow breath, still avoiding my gaze. "You are her father." Rena's eyes finally met *mine, glistening in the candlelight, but there was no confession there. Only a sadness that felt like an apology without the words.*

"You asked for the truth," she whispered, "yet, when I give it, you refuse to believe me..."

The candle guttered between us, and I realized she utter sadness and mistrust she must feel at my accusations. Did I step too far? Katerina was a remarkable young lady. Yet, she looked so different when compared to Jezebelle. But did she really? Katerina bore my black hair and her mother's skin. Jezebelle was almost an exact copy of Rena...

But those eyes... where did she get those emerald eyes?

THE CROWDED STONE HALLS OF THE HEARTFEN Citadel parted as Argus and Zeus walked down and past the sea of Olympian soldiers, who bowed their heads in respect and acknowledgement. Despite Zeus being in his mortal form, his soldiers were still able to recognize him.

"Make way." One of them shouted, opening the doors to the room that sat at the heart of the citadel—*the Command Room.*

An expansive circular chamber built from smooth-cut ash-grey stone materialized, with its surface veined with faint traces of quartz that caught the light like frozen lightning. The walls were decorated with bronze reliefs depicting past campaigns of the gods, each scene hammered in meticulous detail.

The vaulted ceiling rose high overhead, crowned with a central dome painted in deep lapis blue, constellations picked out in hammered gold leaf so that the heavens seemed to shimmer in torchlight.

Around the perimeter, twelve pillars shaped like spears hold the structure, each wrapped with banners bearing each of the Olympian Army Division crests, hanging in perfect order: silver for Zeus, sea-green for Poseidon, blood red for Ares, and so on.

Governess Faviola Kiarelli stood at the far end of the war

table, a great slab of obsidian edged in gold. Its surface was carved with a relief of current battlefronts, troop positions marked by miniature bronze platoon-sized elements and carved ship figurines. She moved several pieces around and talked to the officers present; her long chocolate curls bounced with every movement. Symbols of the twelve Olympians glowed faintly along the edges, allowing commanders to shift and update the map as needed.

The air carried the faint tang of bronze and parchment, mixed with the distant thud of war drums from the training yards.

A soldier grabbed her attention, then pointed over at Zeus and Argus. She excused herself before departing the table.

"Zeus," she bowed. "I'm surprised to see you in mortal form. Argus, is great to see you as well."

"Every once in a while it's good to blend in. Let's me go by undetected." Zeus winked.

"Well, you are just in time. We just received confirmation that our men located the Light Militia's outpost deep inside the Belsir Ruins. Apparently, Joseph intends to attack one of our northern villages to hold captive in exchange for our alliance. So, we have a surprise in store for them later tonight. We also just finished reviewing the security protocol for Blossom Peak, which we are happy and looking forward to Hera and Hestia's company during this auspicious time. I'd be happy to go over this with both of you, if you'd like."

"Some other time. We need to discuss an urgent matter. If you may," Argus gestured to an empty chamber.

Her brows furrowed, confusion and concern washed over her face. But she moved toward it, closing the crystal doors once they all entered. At the far end of the chamber, a towering window of clear quartz looked out over the citadel's parade grounds, offering an unbroken view of the army's training below.

"I suppose you are familiar with the rising tensions in Castelencia." Argus began.

She nodded. "They tried attacking our borders not long

ago, and the imbecile has the audacity to invite me to a *banquet*." She repulsed at the last word, "to win my alliance, no doubt."

"Have you confirmed your attendance?" Argus asked.

"I wasn't planning on gracing him with my presence, so no." Her eyes studied Argus, then Zeus. "What's going on?"

"You are to confirm your attendance and take soldiers of our choosing to escort you." Zeus ordered.

She hesitated for a moment, then nodded. "Anything in particular you're looking for?"

Argus turned to Zeus as if waiting for his permission to speak about it.

"It would be beneficial for me to be in the know, considering that I can control how slowly or quickly I leave the event."

We need all the time we can get inside the Fortress. But telling her would also implicate her and the entire plan if she talks or someone overhears. She has to keep the group tight, only those with a need to know.

"Take the Oath and you'll know." Zeus said.

"And here I thought that after years of allegiance you trusted me." She mocked.

"It's not personal." Zeus retorted. "You should know this after years of allegiance."

She snorted but laughed. "Alright." She extended a hand.

Argus pulled out a dagger and sliced her palm, allowing her blood to fall to the ground.

Zeus took her hand in his, and she closed her eyes. Electrifying heat radiated through his palm, engulfing her flesh.

"By the Will of the Immortals and the Scales of Themis, I bind my breath, my tongue, and my thought." She recited. "Let no secret pass my lips unless freed by the One who holds my Oath. Should I betray, let my name be erased from the mortal realm and my soul chained in silence beyond death."

One last pulse of electricity bolted through them, sealing her wound and evaporating her blood from the ground. A thin lightning bolt marked her palm, only able to be seen by her, Zeus, and Argus.

She stepped back, balancing herself against the weight placed on her soul. Faviola blinked repeatedly, and when Zeus ensured she was back with them, he proceeded to go over the plan, starting with the departure from the Citadel.

While she and a handful of men travel to the Fortress, a squad-sized element would be sent to a separate location to serve as a distraction. They won't go into the Fortress, but stop at a considerable distance to garner just enough attention not to pose a direct threat but to notify Joseph and keep his mind distracted from what's happening in his own home.

The soldiers with Governess Kiarelli will assess the area accordingly and dissipate to find the apothecary where the poison was being made or at least find anything that could be useful.

"You've known Joseph ever since he stepped into power, correct?" Argus asked.

"Yes." Faviola nodded.

"Then, you are fully aware of his desires and motivations. So, you have to balance your approach out." Zeus advised. "Don't be too forthcoming, but at the same time don't be too stubborn for him to raise suspicions or kick you out earlier than intended. You have to be astute because, right now, your entire country and everything you hold dear is relying on you."

"We should bring them in." Argus suggested, turning his attention over to the group of soldiers that just entered the Command Room.

"Who?" Faviola followed Hough's gaze.

Zeus nodded, prompting him to leave the room. *Might as well complete the planning with the key players. I know that Argus had sent a few men to infiltrate the Fortress. But that's the extent of my knowledge. Supposedly, they've made significant progress in their mission. Mainly with those with direct ties to Joseph. I absolutely loathe being in the dark. But it has allowed me to focus on other matters while he and Ares spearhead this whole process.*

"Who is he bringing in?"

In a matter of seconds, Argus entered the room followed by four men.

"These are the men I've chosen to enter the Fortress with you. We're going to add about 3 more to stay with you, so we can avert suspicion when they move out." Argus gestured them forward. "This is Dremian, Westley, Rhei, and Nik. They are well acquainted with the Fortress."

BACK AT OLYMPUS, SERVANTS GREETED ZEUS AS HE strolled down the lavish corridor lined with landscape paintings and golden embellishments, some of them more cheerful than others. *They should be grateful to be here. Many would kill to be in their position and not be scraping the streets for a semblance of food or shelter.*

The majority of his staff were women with the occasional men, but he had them working within the Olympian Army. He preferred to have women around him, since they served as a pleasant presence, and they often worked harder to impress him in many ways than one.

His gaze trailed one of the servants, who gave him a sensuous look and a hint for him to follow. Zeus obliged and found himself almost crashing into Poseidon when he turned.

"What do you want?" annoyance laced Zeus' tongue.

"I can't control the tides." Poseidon said outright.

Zeus blinked. "What?"

"I *can't*. Control. The tides." He repeated slowly, emphasizing the word *can't*.

"Explain."

He proceeded to go into detail about what precisely happened several hours ago.

POSEIDON STOOD WITH HIS TRIDENT RAISED HIGH against the horizon as the evening sky bled crimson into a darkening sea. The air trembled with the low, guttural growl of a coming storm. His voice rolled over the waters, carrying the weight of countless tides before, where he commanded the tides to rise and unfold with fury to punish those who sailed the Euxine Sea, but cursed his name.

The wind surged in answer, whipping salt spray into his beard, bending the black kelp that clung to the rocks. Clouds churned overhead, eager to unleash their rain. Yet below, the ocean did not move.

The water lay flat as a sheet of polished benitoite, the foam retreating, the rhythmic breath of the waves silenced. The scent of brine hung stagnant in the air. Poseidon frowned, tightening his grip on the trident until the gold groaned under his strength. Again, he pushed his will outward, like an invisible pressure meant to stir the sleeping depths. He felt the vast weight of the sea, but now it was not pliant.

It was cold and unyielding. He commanded the tides again. But the water did not so much as tremble.

"IT SPOKE TO ME." POSEIDON'S GAZE DARKENED, searing into Zeus. "Claiming that I do not command it anymore."

Zeus shook his head. "Impossible." *But, was it?* His stomach plummeted as the realization hit him. *It's too soon.* He countered to himself. *Or are we just too late or too slow?* He kept a straight face despite his burning worry. "Check with any of your offspring; perhaps they are messing with the sea just to get a rise out of you."

"I think it's more than that."

"You're just paranoid." Zeus walked past him. "You're the god of the sea, for fuck's sake, fix it."

CHAPTER
TWENTY
KATERINA

Footsteps echoed through the ethereal foyer as Jezebelle, Jasmine, and Katerina entered the Acrailerion. Large, refined Ionic marble columns and delicate gold accents, with graceful arches and elegant ceilings, embellished the space. The walls were lined with sophisticated sun motifs and gold leaf detailing. In the center of the foyer, a stunning statue of their Savior, cast in gold, stood with an aura of calm reverence in the middle of double grand staircases.

Beams of morning sunlight filtered through the large, clear windows, creating a serene atmosphere of grace, peace, and devotion, blending elegance with divine majesty. Katerina's eyes glowed at the sight of it all. She'd never get tired of it.

The Sisters walked around in their signature white and dark red robes, with their heads held high, adorned by the sheer white veil. Some have candles in their hands, while others moved gracefully, consoling other women not part of the sisterhood.

She caught a glimpse of the Naturopaths in their sage-colored, long, hooded robes walking on the second floor through the mezzanine, with vials and herbs in their hands and waist-belt pouches.

Katerina thought it was incredible that such a select few from the Institute are chosen to serve here. But it still raised the question: how was *she* allowed to join? The Verenna was adamant that all inductees must comply with the basic requirements before the official sorting.

They had to be women between the ages of 18 and 25, and their virtue must be untouched. Katerina had neither... she was 28 and... but then, how come the placement here, even if it was based on her scores of the trials, came so late? Katerina graduated from the Institute at 21, thus completing the trials at the same age. Why was she getting sorted so late? What was her true score? What was her original placement? This has her father's money and ink written all over it. Then again, she could use what she learns with the naturopaths to heal and erase the scars on her back...

"We may have to wait for the Verenna; she's the only one that can do the initial interview." Jasmine said, pulling Katerina out of her thoughts.

"Do I have to talk to someone beforehand or—"

"No," Jasmine confirmed. "Normally, a High Re'Veillite will see you and she will escort you once the Verenna is ready for you."

"I'm so happy you're doing this, Kate." Jezebelle offered a heaping smile. "Father is going to be so proud."

Katerina suppressed the scowl inching toward the surface and gave her a polite smile of appreciation instead. "Are you sure you don't want to join me?"

Jezebelle waved a hand in dismissal. "As lavish and beautiful as all of this is, this life isn't for me."

"Who knows? With all of that reading you do, you could be an Adept Chronicler." Jasmine gestured to the vast mahogany arched doors to the left—*the Chronicler Wing*. "Perhaps even become a Master Scholar."

"Perhaps," she laughed, casually glancing back at the main entrance. "That's *if* I ever decide to venture this route. I do have to admit that light blue robe looks gorgeous." Her eyes followed a female Chronicler, books in hand, heading for the mahogany doors.

The robe was long and silken, with silver embroidery along the hems and the cuffs, resembling ancient script. It seemed lightweight and semi-transparent, with a soft, ethereal quality. The robe had a high collar, adding an air of modesty. The elegant dark blue sash around her waist let Katerina know instantly what rank she was. *A Scholar.*

"I'm sure you'd fit right in." Katerina gave her sister a reassuring smile. *Besides, having her here would ease my worry about how father would deal with her once I'm gone.*

Jezebelle glanced back at the open entrance, her eyes widening and lips curling upwards. "I will not deter you from this, Kate. I'll be back. Best of luck." She kissed Katerina's cheek and hurried out before her or Jasmine could utter a word.

Katerina's blood ran cold as Jezebelle wrapped her arms around Rhei and he pulled her in for a tender kiss. She strode toward them, eyes focused on him, rage boiling inside her. A hand on her shoulder stopped her. She jerked her shoulder away, but the hand tightened its grip.

She turned, and Jasmine gave her a warning glare.

"Why?"

"You can't be causing a scene out in the open. Especially when you're on thin ice with your father." Jasmine said.

"I'm sure he'll be happy to know that we have a traitor in our midst." Katerina's heart beat faster. "Mainly one that almost killed one of his daughters."

"You don't have proof, Kate." She pointed out. "And frankly, this is getting old. We made an agreement, yes?"

Katerina sighed. "I'll give her space."

"No," Jasmine's scolded. "Don't just say that. Actually, do it."

Katerina's gaze followed his movements. From the way he caressed her sister's blushing face to the way he held her hands. *How can she trust him?*

"What if someone sees them? At this rate, it's only a matter of time before father hears about it."

"Jezebelle is an adult. She should bear responsibility over her own actions."

The problem is she won't. I will bear the consequences. I will be lashed. I will be scolded. "I'm still curious though." Katerina said, her eyes still focused on her sister.

"Of?"

"How they came to be." She drifted back to Jasmine. "Yes, they talked with each other through regular correspondence, but I've never seen her receive a letter once."

"Maybe she had the letters go somewhere else inside the Fortress? Remember, the Sovereign is not a fan of you two dating people outside the community."

"No," Katerina shook her head. "We don't get correspondence at all here. Safety procedures and whatnot."

After receiving so many death threats and poisoned parchment, the rebels got creative in claiming their lives that her father banned all correspondence from arriving at the Fortress. There's a team, curated by the Sovereign, to sort any correspondence and bring only the ones of absolute necessity to him. Neither Jezebelle nor Katerina were allowed to receive anything, which begged the question, how did she get the letters? How did she send them?

"Perhaps a visit to the Sorting Tower?"

"It's like you're reading my mind." Katerina laughed.

The Sorting Tower was almost an hour away from both the Fortress and Acrailerion. Going there would require that both Jasmine and Katerina leave at a time they were not needed for an extended period, including a time her father wouldn't summon Katerina, which was difficult to pinpoint. *Unless I leave at night... he usually doesn't call me once the sun goes down.*

"Tonight?" Katerina suggested.

"How am I surprised?" Jasmine gave her an incredulous look.

"Princess Argyros."

Katerina turned her attention to the tall raven-haired woman in a deep-red velvet floor-length robe with golden accents that matched the sash cinching her waist. A matching hood draped over her head, lined with delicate golden trim. *A High Re'Veillite.*

"*Se're vosto.*" Katerina quickly greeted, feeling her face turning a light shade of red.

Jasmine followed suit, bowing her head.

"*Blessed day to you as well.* I'm Destiny." Her eyes trailed over to Jasmine in what seemed to be in a condescending manner. "*Trepidavi, Caosen.*"

Jasmine only smiled and nodded once. Katerina didn't understand what was said, but judging by Destiny's expressions; it wasn't a warm welcome. Jasmine was graceful nonetheless, holding her head high and shoulders back.

Destiny's eyes moved back to Katerina, softening and smiling lightly. "The Verenna is ready to see you."

Jasmine instantly excused herself, wishing her the best of luck before parting ways.

CHAPTER
TWENTY-ONE
JOSEPH

LEAVES DANCED AROUND THE CAVEREST PLAZA AS THE cool breeze slithered through the stiffened crowd. Before him, a Castelenian male pleaded on his knees for mercy with his forehead pressed against the rubble. Two guards stood behind him, hands resting on the hilts of their blades.

"Please, I humbly ask you—"

"Silence," Joseph ordered, tapping his fingers atop the armrests of his throne.

"The Sovereign has heard your pleas and will make an effort to ensure that your family receives the food you seek," Sebastian told the man.

"Thank you, thank you, Your Gracefulness." He said as he got to his feet, tears streaming down his face.

"You may retreat."

The guards escorted the man out and back to the crowd.

"You shouldn't be making promises you can't keep," Joseph whispered to him. "It's above your station."

"My apologies, Sovereign." He bowed his head. "I had understood that after being placed in a position of trust, you'd want me to advise in certain—"

"Advise," he cut him off. "Not promise."

Sebastian nodded quietly and turned his attention towards the chattering crowd as a tall, malnourished-looking man stepped forward.

"Sovereign," he bowed. "I come humbly toward you asking for mercy. My family hasn't been able to eat in days... I've combed the streets, tried to grow crops of my own, yet... as you can see, my efforts have been fruitless." He dropped to his knees. "Please, I beg you..." he crawled over to the dais until stopped by soldiers. "Please! I have a son. I have a wife." Tears streamed down his sunburnt face. "I will do anything, devote to you for the rest of my life, serve in your military if that is what it takes to take care of them."

He bowed again, pressing his head against the scorching concrete. Joseph could sense the desperation that reeked from him as the midday sun seared his arched back. The man's shoulders shook; whether from fear or hunger, Joseph couldn't tell. Around them, the Plaza had gone silent save for the dry rustle of banners and the faint creak of leather as his soldiers shifted in place. Every eye in the crowd—from merchants, farmers, beggars to old hags—was fixed on him, anticipation lingering in the air like a putrid smell.

"I beg you, Sovereign," he rasped, his voice carrying just enough to reach him over the space between. "My son... he'll starve. My wife—" He croaked to the ground, as though the earth might pity him.

Joseph remained still, letting the weight of his gaze press down upon him.

The man was gaunt, clothes faded to the color of ash, yet his posture, even in supplication, spoke of a stubborn thread of pride not yet broken.

A thread he could pull.

An opening.

Even though the crowd saw only a miserable man pleading for mercy, Joseph saw a man shaped perfectly for what he needed. With a face so common, he could slip into any market, any tavern, even in the heart of enemy territory. A man with nothing to lose but the hollow shells of those he loved.

Joseph suppressed a laugh.

Some may call it cruelty if Joseph sent him to the wolves. But was it truly cruel if it kept their mouths fed and their borders protected? An entire country protected at the expense of one feeble man desperate to take care of his family. And, as shown before him, hunger and desperation make even the most wavering of hearts.

"What is your name?" Sebastian broke through the silence.

"Thiseas," he raised his gaze slowly.

"How old is your son, Thiseas?"

"He's two, your Gracefulness."

"Is your wife here with you?"

Joseph rolled his eyes. *What's with this line of questioning?*

"No, she's at home taking care of him as best she can." His eyes briefly drifted to Joseph and, judging by how quickly he looked away, Joseph could deduce that his annoyance was as visible as it was palpable.

"How long have you been together?"

Muffled chatter turned Joseph's attention to the crowd, who were... pitying him? Some women held their hands in what seemed to be in silent prayer. Their once selfish expression turned sympathetic in less than five minutes.

"Almost half my life.... twenty-five years."

He turned back to the Sebastian, who eyed the man in a soft and kind way. He was making him humane. Thus, making him look a savior for his family. If Joseph tore him from his family, they'd see him as a heartless dictator. He suppressed a scoff. *As if I care what they think.*

"But you do." The voice invaded his mind. **"Letting a worthless waste of space dictate your actions not only makes you weak, but it proves my point when Quinn made you his successor. I always knew you were useless and softhearted."**

"You speak of useless yet you depend on my useless ass for you to come to full strength."Joseph retorted.

"As if you had a choice in the matter. Remember, I hold power over your wife and daughters' lives."

Barely audible gasps tore from the crowd. Nowadays, it was difficult to last with someone that long. Usually they'd die from some strange illness, famine, the war, treason, you name it. Let's see how strong this *love* is.

"Your wife and son will be cared for," Joseph said reassuringly.

"Thank you. Thank you. Thank—"

Joseph raised a hand, making him quiet as he stepped forward to the edge of the platform, his shadow falling upon Thiseas.

Thiseas lowered his head. Murmurs rippled through the onlookers.

"However, this comes at a price. You will work for me here. Once you do, your family will be protected and provided for."

"Will I be able to see them, Sovereign?" He asked, raising his head just enough for Joseph to see the raw, unguarded vulnerability there.

"So long as you uphold your duties," he responded, his voice carrying over the stilled plaza.

The silence that followed was thick, heavy, broken only by the caw of a distant crow. Then he saw it in his eyes, the precise moment when desperation swallowed fear. When Thiseas knew he had no choice but to agree.

"You have my word and allegiance, Sovereign." He bowed his head again. "Thank you." He stood and walked back to the crowd.

"Wait." Joseph laughed. "Where do you think you're going?"

Thiseas eyebrows joined in confusion, then fear. "I...um...I was going to...um—"

"You are not going back today." Joseph gestured to his soldiers.

Panic settled in Thiseas' eyes, but every time he tried to speak, nothing came out.

"Take him to the Fortress."

Soldiers dragged his trembling body out of the open space as he screamed for an opportunity to say goodbye to his family, over and over again.

Joseph sat back on the throne, ignoring Sebastian's look of indignation directed his way. *Could I have taken him away quietly? Perhaps. Could I have let him say goodbye to his wife and son before pulling him into service? Sure. But not everyone has the luxury of saying goodbye to the one they love before they're stripped away from you.*

"It's happening!" A ragged man burst through the crowd and into the open space, his balding hair wild and eyes blazing like burning coals. His voice cracked the air, sharp and frantic, slicing through the murmurs. "I warned all of you, and no one listened!"

The crowd parted, moving out of his reach in what looked to be fear. Joseph remained in his seat, but his attention was on the lunatic.

"They're here!" he bellowed, spittle catching in his beard. "The first signs! You think you can still pretend it is all a lie? You think you can *hide* from it?!"

Women grabbed onto their children. Men shooed him away as if he were nothing but a nuisance, which, in the eyes of Joseph, he was.

Two soldiers stepped forward, moving slowly, cautiously, like handlers with a feral animal.

"We're all going to die because all of you prefer to serve false deities!" He added, getting close to anyone who'd listen, but they all stepped away.

"You still don't believe me..." He scanned the crowd until his eyes landed on Joseph. "The fish..." he jabbed a filthy finger toward the direction of the pier, "Dead. Their bellies white in the sun, floating in their own graves! And the sea..." he clutched his head as if trying to stifle a piercing headache. "The tides... still as a corpse's breath!"

The crowd murmured, some scoffing, others glancing

nervously toward the crazed man, but Joseph's stomach plummeted. *Is it really time?*

He lurched away from the grasping hands, pointing wildly at the crowd. "You all heard it! You all saw it! The sky will blacken, the bones will rise, the rivers will choke on ash, and the stars will *bleed* upon us. This is just the *beginning*! The seals have broken. Oh, Zeus, have mercy on us. The seals have BROKEN."

One of the soldiers caught his arm, but he thrashed, voice rising to a ragged shriek. "Don't you take me away! I'm the only one telling the truth! They'll come for you all when the black tide rolls in. The Dark One will rise, and it'll be too late when he does!"

A chill rushed down Joseph's spine. *Fuck. Fuck. Fuck. Fuck.* He stood as they dragged the man away, his voice bleeding into a hoarse, almost giddy laugh. "Dead fish, stilled tides... yet you still believe this heretic will save you?"

WHITE HOT RAGE BOILED WITHIN HIM AS JOSEPH entered the study, slamming the door behind him, rattling the gold-framed landscapes on the walls. He hadn't meant to shut them so hard, but the restraint he'd shown in the Plaza had to give way somewhere. He forced his tight fists open.

The study smelled of parchment and ink. Normally, this space was his sanctuary. A place to think, to plot, to breathe away from everyone's vulture eyes. But tonight it felt smaller, almost predatory.

His sight fell on Thiseas alongside four men and the company of two soldiers with their hands placed atop their swords.

Joseph moved over to his desk. His reflection in the polished wood stared back at him, wearing the same perfect mask he had worn minutes ago: poised, unshaken, untouchable.

Except he wasn't.

He stowed away his pathetic feelings and opened the cabinet, pulling out the wooden box with a sun carved atop.

"Arms out." He took the black and gold dagger out of its cushioned space.

They hesitated, but his men were quick enough to pull their arms out forcefully, exposing their palms and forearms. Fear was plastered over their faces as Joseph approached and traced the dagger over each of their flesh. Drawing a sun and snake with the sharp tip. Blood trickled down their arms, staining the floor.

"Vow." Joseph cleaned the blade with the nearest cloth he could find.

A heavy silence followed, and Joseph turned his attention to the men, pointing the blade at them.

"Before the eyes of the eternal," one of the men elbows the other to repeat after him. "I pledge my spirit and steel to secrecy. I will guard what is veiled by oath and blood, and if betrayal stains my name, may the savior himself cast me into everlasting silence."

Storing the blade away, Joseph locked the cabinet and turned his attention to the bleeding men, who winced at the burning sensation of the oath beneath their flesh. A sensation Joseph knew all too well.

"You are to go to the apothecary inside the Acrailerion's Naturopath Wing after you're done here. They will hand you a package." He turned to the largest map in the room. "You will deliver it to the Belsir Outpost inside the Belsir Ruins. It's about half a day's walk from here."

"If I may, Sovereign?" The raven-haired man next to Thiseas spoke.

"You may not." Joseph threw a piece of cloth at them. "Clean yourselves."

A hint of indignation flickered across their faces, save for Thiseas, who looked like he was about to cry at any second. Only one picked up the cloth.

"You will meet with Dremian and hand it to him." Joseph scanned the row of men as he moved back to his desk. "You will do anything and everything to make sure he receives it. I don't care if you get ambushed. I don't care if you injure yourselves on the way there. I don't want to hear excuses. If I hear you failed to deliver, might as well not come back."

Their eyes widened with fear.

"And don't think for a second that death awaits you."

Joseph turned his attention to the parchment atop the desk, prompting them to leave. As soon as the door closed, he sat back in his chair.

The raving follower of Zeus still haunted his ears. His voice was loud and shameless, echoing with the aura of one who had nothing to lose. *He stormed the Plaza as if Olympus had hurled him into my territory, asking Zeus to have mercy. Even though the soldiers seized him, the damage was already done.* The people saw Joseph standing there, still as a statue. They saw him refuse to silence the lunatic with blood or chains. He had smiled instead— that perfect, measured fucking smile he'd mastered over the years.

But what they hadn't seen—what no one *could* see, was the moment his hand twitched toward the hilt at his side. The moment the image nearly cracked.

A low, rolling hiss cut through his thoughts.

Joseph turned toward the shadowed corner of the room, and the air thickened. The scent of ash and sulfur filled his lungs.

"You let him speak." The voice was not loud, yet it pressed on him like the weight of a mountain.

"I maintained composure before the people," Joseph countered, though the words felt like a poor excuse. "I showed them I am unshaken by crazed brutes." His eyes fell upon two distant embers in the middle of the dark.

"You showed them you can be mocked without consequence." His tone lowered, the weight now pressing against Joseph's shoulders and chest. **"You showed them *mercy* they did not deserve."**

"It was not mercy," Joseph said quickly. "It was strategy."

"*Strategy* is a blade, and yet you dull it with pride."

Joseph swallowed. "I almost struck him down."

"Almost," he said, the word curling with contempt. **"The people saw restraint where they should have felt fear. The next fool who does this will not care, especially after today. They will care only if their bones are still intact after the words leave their mouths."**

Joseph's jaw tightened, bitterness searing his tongue. "I will not fail you again."

"See that you don't."

The weight lifted from his shoulders, the scent of scorched earth lingered in his wake.

Joseph sat alone in his chair, staring at the sun-serpent sigil carved into the desk. His mask of the mighty sovereign was still intact, but now it felt less like armor and more like a noose waiting for him to slip.

KATERINA RESISTED THE URGE TO TWIDDLE HER thumbs by smoothing the fabric over her thighs. *This is protocol. You'll be alright.* Her eyes analyzed the High Priestess. She'd never seen her this close.

The Verenna shuffled through the pages in front of her until plucking one out. Her silver hair was neatly pinned in a perfect bun, and despite her elder age, her skin didn't appear to be wrinkled to the same extent as other women. Her maturity was noticeable in her sharp and striking features, yet there was an ethereal, youthful aura around her. *Well, she's a high priestess. She has to keep up appearances of grace and mystique, so I wouldn't be surprised if she drank a tonic or used magic to counteract the effects of old age.*

"Katerina Faye Argyros..." She mumbled. "You were a stellar individual at the Institute of Enlightenment."

Katerina bowed her head. "Thank you, I strived to do my best."

"Well, your hard work clearly paid off." The Verenna smiled. "However, I am intrigued by your scores on the trials."

Katerina's heart sank. "Oh?"

"You scored as a high performant in several categories like

cunning, knowledge, and critical thinking, yet in other areas you scored average. However, my intrigue is with your score in trauma response."

Katerina's eyes swept the floor as if searching for her score between the tiles. *Trauma response? What was the challenge for that?* Her mind flipped through her memories like an open book, sorting through years of recollections.

"Your score was inconclusive." The Verenna's eyes met hers.

"I am unsure of what you'd like me to say." Katerina responded gingerly.

The Verenna analyzed her for a long moment.

Katerina remained still even though her insides felt like they wanted to spring out of her. She focused on the scent of cinnamon and frankincense emanating from the small altar on the left side of the room, bearing a small statue of their Savior.

"Katerina Faye, you are aware that the Re'Veillites are a symbol of purity, *untainted* before the eyes of our Savior, yes?"

Katerina's breath caught. Yet, she nodded calmly.

"Sister Gaia brought to my attention the incident at the Helios Agora. It is my understanding that she was the one who assigned you to the textile merchant." The Verenna held up a hand at the sight of Katerina about to interject. "As a Re'Veillite, you must not give in to these earthly impulses. Did he attack you?"

"Not at first but—"

"But nothing, my child." She countered. "He posed no threat, and yet you attacked based on mundane assumptions."

So, was I just supposed to let him hurt me? Katerina remained silent as her nails bit into her palms. *He threatened me. He threatened my sister. I wasn't going to let that go easily.*

"Your initiation is in a week, and it would be a shame to inform the Sovereign that his eldest daughter lost her position in the sisterhood because of her disruptive behavior."

He would end me. "Please, I did not intend to cause any problems.

"I will not tolerate any smears to the Acrailerion or the Re'Veillite title. Consider this your first and only warning." She stood, revealing the deep red floor-length robe she wore, flowing elegantly with intricate gold embroidery featuring sun and celestial patterns; the sleeves were wide and bell-shaped with a golden trim.

Katerina instantly stood out of respect and bowed her head. "I understand."

"You may be the Sovereign's daughter and you may have been placed here per his guidance, but that doesn't guarantee your place here nor gives you special treatment. Once you join the sisterhood, your title and your connection to your family will be stripped." The Verenna approached her until they were at arm's length from each other. She stood with an air of supreme reverence. "It'd be wise to remain composed for the next few days."

I knew he meddled in this. Katerina lowered her gaze. "Of course." She smiled politely. "I appreciate your time."

"May the Savior bless you, my child."

Katerina smiled and left the room. To be stripped of her title and connections to her family was not something she had considered. Yes, her father may have secured her position but if her connection to the Argyros lineage was to be erased, where would she stand with her sister? How would things change?

She walked out of the Acrailerion, wiping her clammy hands. *It was almost here.* Even though she was nervous about what could happen in the coming days, she couldn't hold back a smile from plastering her face. She was finally getting something she'd wanted, regardless if her father had involved himself in her slotting.

But, was it selfish? Was it selfish to want this for myself? Was it selfish to want this despite what would happen to Jezy? By renouncing everything, would I be doing a disservice to my sister?

Jasmine's words came to the forefront of Katerina's mind, reminding her that whatever Jezebelle did or would do, it was no longer her burden to carry. Jezebelle was a grown woman, twenty-four, but still an adult in the eyes of the world. But what she did wasn't the issue or concern; it was what her father might do. Would he lash her the same way he did to Katerina?

Joyous laughter pulled her out of her somber thoughts. Children played among themselves, running, jumping, and some hide and seek. A smile tugged at her lips, erasing every worry in her mind. *This. This was priceless.*

Katerina took a moment to sit by the fountain. She still had a couple of minutes to spare before her father would inquire about her extended absence. She closed her eyes, basking in the tolerable heat of the sun. Breathing in the refreshing misty air, she tilted her head toward the sky. *How I've missed this. Mom would've loved for us to sit here and just decompress. Store our worries away until it was time to go back to reality.* Her lashes dampened. *Don't cry.* Heaviness sank into her chest. Her mother would want her to be happy.

Katerina wondered what she'd say about all of this. Rena would scold her, there's no doubt about that, but she'd listen. *Actually* listen and not assume that her daughter attacked the man just because she wanted to... besides, Katerina wasn't the one who gave the killing blow. She wiped her damp cheeks.

The faint memory of Katerina and her mother painting in the garden bloomed in her mind. Rena used to love to paint. That was her way of escaping reality. Katerina wasn't particularly gifted in that regard, but she enjoyed the peace it brought her and how it became a quiet moment for her and her mother.

At the time, Jezebelle used to spend her free time with her teeth sinked in books. That was *her* escape.

Katerina cherished those days deeply. *I think that's my only real connection with her now that she's gone.* She hasn't painted since her mother's death, hence why she diverted to running.

She would want me to be happy. I'm so close to getting what I want. I should be happy. I have to be happy.

"Penny for your thoughts?" An all-too familiar male voice said to her.

"It'll take a lot more than pennies to get me talking." She looked down at the blonde man who landed one of the killing blows. "A bit out of your territory, aren't you?"

Nik chuckled. "Good to see you too, baby girl."

"Are you following me?"

"Is it so wrong for a man to admire beauty?"

Katerina snorted. "Sure, first you threaten to kill me, then you claim I'm just a bounty, and now you want to bask in my beauty? You must drive women crazy."

"I have my ways." He winked.

"What are you really doing here?"

"Just in the area on business."

Katerina's brows joined slightly as she finally noticed his ensemble. A dark grey and white nobleman's attire, his hair was neatly combed. "Aren't you one of their brutes?"

"Brute?" He placed a hand over his heart mockingly. "You wound me."

"Yet, you haven't answered my question."

"You don't have to know everything, princess." He clicked his tongue. "Although based on the fine commentary, I take Chryssa spoke to you about me?"

Katerina's face blanched. "She may have mentioned some things."

"Such as?"

"You don't have to know everything, Baratos." She sneered, standing up from the fountain.

"Baratos?" He sounded surprised. "The conversation went more personal than I expected."

Shit, did I say too much? "I should get going."

"Don't want the heretic to catch you talking to a brute, *Rhea*?"

"Actually, I'm going to the Acrailerion." She lied, noticing his brows raise slightly. "Didn't think I was a respectable lady?"

"I have no doubt that you are a respectable lady, but I didn't take you for the type to seek divine guidance."

"Well, looks can be deceiving."

"They sure can." He said, eyes softening upon locking his gaze with hers.

Katerina's cheeks warmed, but she couldn't look away from his icy eyes; both seemed to study each other. Nik reached out, sneaking his hand through the base of her neck.

"What are you doing?" Katerina muttered as he placed just enough force to tilt her head back.

Her emerald eyes trailed down his scar... merely inches away from his partially parted lips. *If it weren't for the scar on his face— no, even with the scar, he was a handsome man.* He traced a gentle finger beneath her jaw.

"I didn't think he'd left a mark on you."

"What?" Katerina blinked, jerking her body away, brows furrowed and eyes scanning him.

"The attacker. He left you a scar." He pointed beneath his chin. "Right here."

"It's not a big deal." Katerina traced her fingers along it, feeling the scab. It was longer than she had thought. "Just focus on your own life, alright?"

"But promise me one thing."

She scowled. "What's that?"

"Try not to stress yourself too much; the greys are starting to come." He laughed.

"Fuck off." She hissed, turning away from him.

He grabbed her arm, making her turn to him. Nik drew a sharp breath, rubbing his temples.

"Tonight, Chryssa is hosting a celebration at the inn where she works. She couldn't find you after the day she saw you at the textile shop." He breathed deeply, annoyance radiating through him. "So, she asked me to invite you if I saw you again, and here you are."

And here I am. "So you *were* following me? You were hoping to see me..."

"I'm only doing Chryssa a favor." He sneered.

"Pass. But thanks for the invite."

"I snuck in here trying to find you." He stated, giving her an incredulous look.

"I thought you were in the area on business." Katerina arched a brow.

"Don't start with me."

"Don't start what?" she eyed him innocently. "I'm just reiterating what you said."

"I am, not that it is any of your concern. My being here is simply for Chryssa. Don't get it twisted."

"I'm sure it is." *What are you to her, anyway? If they are together, I'm sure she wouldn't be happy if she were to know how he treats other women.* She squared her shoulders. "Again, thanks for the invite. But I'm going to have to pass."

"The heretic won't let you out after dark?"

"I have plans. Otherwise..."

"Sure." His tone disbelieving. "Again, I'm doing Chryssa a favor."

"So you keep saying... if I'd known any better, I'd say you want me there for yourself." She hissed, striding off.

He grabbed her arm. "If you'd known any better, you wouldn't have gone to Veneration Night."

"If you have any sense of yourself, you'd let me go." She bickered, and he slackened his grip. "If *Chryssa* wants me there so badly, tell her to come get me herself." She turned and headed home.

Each stride felt like a ticking bomb as she rushed to the Fortress. *Why did I entertain him? He's going to kill me.* Even with her aspirations to explore the continent, she had to focus on getting home. She'd been lucky. Lucky she hadn't been caught on her previous runs. But it wasn't just her father keeping an eye on her now; it was also the Verenna. She needed to find a way to quiet her mind from the constant reminders of her past. But what? *How am I going to keep my mind from spiraling? Doesn't matter. Just get home.*

Controlling her breath, she quickened her pace until she reached the back of the Plaza. The streets were almost ghostly with a handful of townsfolk roaming around or closing up shop as the scent of citrus and spice filled her nostrils. She'd lost count of the amount of times she'd looked over her shoulder as if it was only a matter of time before her father would send a fleet to come get her and chain her up once more. She shuddered.

Soldiers opened the golden gates of the Fortress and rendered their daily greeting as she stormed past them.

SHE LEANED BACK AGAINST THE DOOR OF HER bedchamber. Katerina exhaled, closing her eyes. *I can't live like this.*

"Rough day?" A male voice asked, making her bolt upright.

"Yes, so please—" She stilled, blood boiling at the sight of Rhei.

He stood in front of her dresser with his hands in his pockets. His fiery hair was combed, and a smug smile stretched across his freckled face.

Katerina's jaw clenched as images of her sister, bound and horrified, flooded her mind. *You did this.* She balled her hands into fists. *I almost lost her because of you.* She should ask him to leave. Ignore him. But every inch of her body wanted to wipe that smugness off his face.

"Easy now. I don't want you exploding on me." He laughed.

The Verenna's words rushed to the surface, urging Katerina to stop; to rethink her next actions, her next few words. The urge to bury her fist into his face for causing pain to her sister was almost unbearable, and his nonchalant demeanor only fueled her fire.

"If you don't wipe that grin off your face. I swear—"

"You have quite the temper, has anybody told you that? Besides, it's not like I haven't heard those words before. Yours are just empty threats."

"Want me to show you how empty they are?"

"As long as they are as empty as the ones you gave Nik, go for it."

You know Nik?

Jasmine's warning flashed before her eyes. *Jezebelle is an adult. She should bear responsibility over her own actions.*

"What do you want with my sister, anyway?"

"Same as you protect her from the *rebels*, and whatnot." He said casually.

"Sure."

"Not what you expected?"

"You know precisely what I meant. Stay the fuck away from my sister."

"Oh, it's little sovereign going to stop me? Or will you?" He laughed. "I pegged you for a much more daring sort of woman. Not one with empty threats."

If my Re'Veillite position wasn't hanging over my head... "You haven't *seen* daring. You don't even know me."

He cocked an eyebrow. "I know enough."

"Stay away from my sister and go back to the hellhole it is you came from. Why are you in my room?"

"See... I'm not the monster you paint me to be. So, I'm here for us to have a conversation."

"I have nothing—"

"You might want to hear this or don't; anyway, your sister will give you the details soon, I presume."

"What are you talking about?" Her stomach hollowed.

He chuckled. "I'll let your sister do the honors, then."

"You snuck into my room to tell me nothing?"

"I thought she already told you about our plans, but who am I to hinder some sisterly bonding time?"

What fucking plans? "If you don't stay the fuck away from her."

"Again with the empty threats." He closed the distance between them, stopping a little less that arm's length away.

Her blood boils as he grabbed her chin. She jerked out of his grasp and punched his face. "Don't fucking touch me."

"You're much feistier than your sister, I'll give you that." He wiped the blood from his lip. "No wonder you get along so well with Chryssa."

She scowled. "Get out."

"She told me all about you, *Rhea*. How she finally made a friend after so long... I haven't seen my sister this happy since her friend passed, and I am not gonna be the one to ruin that for her." He walked closer to her, yet Katerina stood her ground, ready to land another blow. "I know that once Chryssa finds out who you are..." he clicked his tongue repeatedly. "Let's just say it wouldn't be a pleasant experience... for you at least."

"Why haven't you told her?"

"I'm not going to break my sister's heart." He shrugged.

"Now look at it this way from a *brotherly* sense. If you find your sister in pain. Horrified at whatever she's going through. Wouldn't you want to kill whoever caused her pain?"

"I would kill whomever."

"Precisely my point. So what makes you think I wouldn't do the same to you?" Katerina pushed him away.

"I wasn't the one responsible for what happened to her," he countered, "But you'll find out about that soon enough. I'm not the enemy here, even though you don't wanna believe it. I'm actually your ally."

"You're not my ally. You're not my fucking ally. My sister may forgive you for what you did. May forgive you for everything, for all I fucking care, but that doesn't mean I will. I won't, and I'll be damned if I see you near her again."

"See, you're quick with threats, but I don't see anything to back up any of the claims you're making. Maybe you and your father are more alike than you think."

A chill crept through her arms. The lights snuffed out, plunging them into utter darkness, despite the nonexistent daylight from moments before. She lunged at him. Her vision blackened. *All I want is to destroy him.* The air gets pulled out of her lungs as her body crashed against the ground. Her arms became bound over her head. Her weakened breath caught. *The chains. The shackles. No. No. No.* She thrashed and kicked, but it was no use. *I'm trapped.*

"She would be better if she were with me." Rhei's words pulled her into reality. "You know it."

"You're not taking her anywhere." Katerina raised her torso, but his body pinned her down.

"Anywhere is better than here. I've seen how you guys operate, how your *father* operates inside the Fortress. Your sister is not safe."

"She is safe with me."

"Safe with an erratic sister who can't keep her temper in check? I don't think so."

"*I* actually had to save her. You were nowhere in fucking sight."

"I was, you just didn't see me."

"Yet you allowed her to be a spectacle. You fucking allowed it. You saw her terrified, yet you didn't stop it."

"I had to prove a point."

"You had to prove a fucking point?" Disbelief coated her bitter tongue. "At the expense of her safety?"

He got off her and propped her upright. "Like I said, I will let your sister to the honors. I'm seeing her this evening anyway, so I'd hurry before she leaves again."

"You're full of shit..."

"Rest easy."

TWENTY-THREE

ZEUS TOWERED OVER THE BODIES, SCANNING THEIR rotting flesh. Pieces of skin were being gradually consumed by whatever infection coursed through their veins. Repulsed by their putrid stench, his nose wrinkled.

"Someone better start talking."

He looked at Asclepius, who tended to someone with a severed leg. His melanin-rich hands were covered in dried blood and unknown gunk.

Rows of cots lined the stone hall, each one groaning beneath the broken forms of soldiers. Some writhed in fevered pain, their bandaged limbs trembling with every breath, while others lied silent, their chests unmoving, eyes glazed over in an eternal stare.

Zeus forced himself to walk slowly, each step heavy with the weight of unknown worry. The wounded reached out, hands calloused, bloodied fingers clutching at the hem of his clothes, whispering pleas for strength, for salvation. Zeus clasped them one by one, but he could feel how frail they had become, how close they lingered to the edge of life.

How the fuck?

The healers in Asclepius' division moved like shadows,

pressing herbs to wounds that no longer bled, murmuring prayers that drowned in the silence of death.

His gaze fell on a young warrior. His chest was split by an enemy blade, and though the healers did their best to keep him tethered, he was certain that his soul was already walking the Elysian Fields.

The soldier's lips parted, and with what breath remained, he whispered Zeus' name—not in accusation, but in faith. That single word broke something in him more than the thunder of battle ever could.

Rage simmered through him, electrifying every inch of his body. *How was this possible? His men drank his blessed ambrosia; they had the gift of immortal life. They couldn't just die.*

Lined against the far wall, a sheet had been drawn over a dozen soldiers. For the first time, Zeus' hand trembled.

He was no stranger to death, nor had he shied away from bringing down to those who turned against him. But seeing his men in such heinous conditions without knowing the reason behind it, irritates him.

Zeus' attention drew back to Asclepius. He scraped pieces of flesh with thin tweezers and placed them inside a glass jar. Zeus' eyes focused on the smaller piece inside it.

The skin disintegrated.

"Remarkable..." Asclepius whispered, his voice riddled with what seemed to be awe.

Zeus cleared his throat, and Asclepius raised his eyes for a moment before turning back to the jar. "As terrible as this is for us, I have to admit, whoever did this is devious. I've never seen flesh decompose in this manner, much less coming from your soldiers." His attention didn't stray from the jar, as the largest part of flesh was halfway through becoming dust.

"You better be quick if you want to autopsy the bodies, then." Zeus suggested, while Asclepius placed the jar on another table, next to an array of papers, which Zeus assumed was his research.

"Is it contagious?" Argus asked, stepping away from the infested corpses.

"I'm not sure. I've never seen anything like it," Asclepius replied, his hands scrambling through the mountain of sheets. "They shouldn't be able to die at the hands of any mortal weapon..." he muttered, frustration lingering in his tongue. "I personally crafted the elixir with Hecate, you blessed it..."

Zeus turned to Argus, both looked at each other, brows raised.

"The ambush to the Outpost..." Argus muttered, eyes scanning over the bodies, unbothered by the stench.

"I wouldn't even call it a fucking ambush. They were waiting for us. Somehow, their defenses were up, and they decided to give the *poison* a try." Zeus added.

"No mortal poison shouldn't even have this effect." Asclepius retorted.

"There are a lot of things that shouldn't have fucking happened." Zeus looked closely at the bodies, unable to process what the fuck he was looking at.

Zeus blessed every single one of his soldiers upon joining his ranks, which meant that he granted them the gift of immortality once they drank the elixir. They could bleed, endure mortal wounds and go through whatever a mortal can, but their bodies regenerated at a rapid pace.

His soldiers didn't have any weaknesses, thus giving them the upper hand in combat. They should've healed long before they became putrid mush.

"What is this disease, anyway?" Ares moved through the array of healers.

"It looks like an egregious form of necrotising fasciitis. It's rare but—"

"I asked one question. Not a biology lesson." Ares stopped him. "No need to get into the nitty-gritty."

"Actually, it's—"

"I don't give a fuck." He interrupted.

Asclepius cleared his throat, turning to Zeus. "I don't know if this is from a mortal disease." He said coolly, attempting to hide the discomfort seeping out of his skin. "I don't have any information yet. They haven't been here long." He examined the discolored, chapped lips of one of the corpses. "Perhaps a poison of some kind... or a combination of divinely crafted weaponry...I don't know," he muttered irritably. "I'm fairly certain that one of those two is the cause."

"How can you tell?" Argus asked.

Asclepius snapped his fingers, and a healer materialized almost instantly at his side.

"Bring me the prongs and vial with myrrh."

She nodded and hurried off.

"If we *were* able to secure the poison, can you trace what's made out of?" Argus asked, unbothered by the foul smell.

"Do you?" Asclepius asked, ears perked in interest.

"Not yet, but I have my ways."

"And how are you planning to do that?" Asclepius asked, disbelief coating his tongue.

"Like I said, I have my ways." He shrugged off the disbelief.

"How long would it take you to find out what this is?" Zeus asked, swatting away the surrounding flies.

The healer returned and handed Asclepius the vial and metal prongs.

"I can't give an exact time frame. It's going to take me a while to fully understand what's happening here." He picked a piece of partially detached flesh from the body and dropped it in the myrrh-filled vial. "And perhaps fashion an antidote... you're seeing the bodies. Their condition is horrendous." His nose wrinkled. "I hope that this holds up long enough for me to examine it. It's going to take me a while."

"We don't have a while," Zeus hissed. "Can we give them some elixir? That's supposed to counteract this."

"Don't you think I've tried, Zeus?" Asclepius rubbed his face with his hands. "They'll die quicker if they do."

What the fuck? Irritation prickled Zeus's skin.

"What I'd like to know is what made them lose their immunity?" Ares poked parts of their flesh that had yet to rot with a stick. "There's divine work involved, no doubt about it."

"Oh really?" Asclepius mocked. "I wish you would've been here sooner to solve all our problems with your keen observation."

Ares snickered.

"Where were you anyway?" Argus asked, turning to Ares.

"Mind your business." He sneered.

Zeus glanced at the apothecary located at the very end of the infirmary. The glass door was open, displaying partially spilled jars and overgrown flora with dirt and insects, commanding the space. Not to mention the array of parchment and tomes on the floor. Asclepius had been busy indeed.

Three men stood near the entrance of the Apothecary, bound by their hands and mouths gagged, and each had a soldier standing behind them, like an owner walking his dog.

"Who are they?" Zeus asked Asclepius just before he left to tend to another.

Asclepius looked at them briefly. "Ah..." He inhaled sharply, turning his attention to his next patient. "They were found fleeing the outpost during the attack."

Judging by their worn attire and the severe thinness of one of them, Zeus knew for a fact that they were not soldiers.

"Do you know how long they were at the outpost?"

Asclepius shrugged, wiping the face of the now-deceased soldier with a wet rag. "Hard to tell. That's why I told Talos—I mean, Argus, to summon three from the Blood Legion. Which explains why Ares showed up here not long after they got summoned."

"Has anyone interrogated them yet?"

"With the amount of wounded my branch has, I couldn't spare any of my personnel. So, no." He took a step back to examine the body. Clicking his tongue repeatedly, he shook his head. "If Argus can get so much as a drop of the poison, it would save me a great deal of time."

Zeus' eyes traced back to the terrified men. Time to get answers himself. "Send the men to the dungeons."

Chapter
TWENTY-FOUR
KATERINA

Low classical melodies filled the space as Katerina entered Jezebelle's lilac-colored room. Her sister continuously tapped the brush onto the wet canvas. Shades of blue, brown, and yellow had already stained her ochre dress, but she didn't seem to care.

For a moment, Katerina's anger washed away. It was like she was watching their mother painting, venturing into whatever world she desired without thinking of stupid duties and responsibilities. Katerina's chest caved.

Wiping her forehead, Jezebelle added the finishing touches to the painting and took a step back. "Do you like it?"

Strokes of green contrasted with the brown, detailing the trees that stretched for miles upon miles. The delicate light blue sweeps added depth to the river coming from the waterfall, cascading through the mountains on the far-right edge as birds fly over the clear skies.

Freedom. Peace.

She placed the brush inside a cup filled with green water.

"Since when did you start painting?" She managed to say, searching inside her mind for how she was going to ask her what her plans were with Rhei.

"I don't know... I was just missing mom, and I remembered how you and her used to paint, and I decided to try it out..."

"Well, it's beautiful..."

"It's alright, and I must admit, it was refreshing..." She admired her work with a wide smile adorning her face. "Besides, I have great news to share with you as well. The most absolutely beautiful thing just happened to me." She said gleefully.

"Oh?" Katerina just braced herself for whatever it was, ignoring the heaviness that clung to her chest.

"My stars, Kate!" She plopped onto the bed, her paint-stained dress flowing at her legs. "I know you're not fond of Rhei... but—"

"It's fine." Katerina assured her. *It's not. But I can't give her any reason to keep certain things from me.*

Jezebelle sat up and stared at her in confusion, perhaps surprise; Katerina couldn't precisely tell.

"You're happy, and that's all that matters," Katerina added, offering a kind smile.

"Oh, I knew you'd come around!" Jezebelle leaped from the bed and wrapped her arms around Katerina.

Not my burden to carry... not my burden to carry...

"What made you change your mind? You know what? It doesn't matter." Jezebelle beamed. "I have to tell you the news." She sat on the bed once more, barely able to contain her excitement.

I don't know whether to be happy or worried.

"Rhei and I were walking around the Caverest Plaza, and he took me to the most beautiful shop. You know, all sorts of flowers —you'd love it. Um... while I was looking at the peonies, the merchant called my name and asked me to go around back for a moment." She took a breath and grinned. "Ah! Okay, so I went out back, right? And I walked into this absolutely gorgeous space with tons of torches, greenery, ugh the ambiance was to die for—"

"Get to the point, Jezy," Katerina let out, more harshly than intended.

"He asked me to marry him!"

I'm about to have a heart attack. "He what?" *I'll let your sister do the honors.* His words haunted her thoughts.

"He did and, of course, I said yes—"

Happiness be damned. Temper be dammed. "You can't marry him, Jezy."

Jezebelle glared. "Yes, I can, and you can't stop me."

"Fine, I can't." *I sure damn hope I could.* "But that doesn't negate the fact that you can't marry him. You don't know him. He's been here for a total of what? 5 maybe 6 days?"

Jezebelle grimaced and opened her mouth to respond, but Katerina stopped her.

"Correspondence alone is not enough for you to know someone, Jezebelle. Don't be rash. Think this through."

"Oh yeah. Just because your love life failed doesn't mean that mine is going to. It's not my fault that father stopped you from being with the man you loved, and I am sorry for that. My heartbreaks for you. I sympathize with you. You may be my sister, but you can't get in the way of my life."

Low fucking blow. "If you do marry him," Katerina muttered, biting back the venom threatening to spill from her mouth. "Are you staying here, or is he expecting you to move to Sylene?"

"For now, here... but we will move to Sylene, eventually."

"You know damn well that father won't allow you to travel to another country."

"I don't have the same restrictions you do."

"And that's supposed to be—wait." Katerina's body went rigid. "What are you talking about?

"Huh?" Jezebelle crossed her arms over her chest.

"You know precisely what I'm talking about." Katerina's eyes locked on her sister, like a predator stalking its prey.

Jezebelle shuddered as she fidgeted with her fingers. "I-I'm not allowed to—"

"Jezebelle Delí... you are walking a very fine line right now."

Katerina's voice ran cold, calculated. Pain radiated through her palms as nails dug into them. "Talk."

Jezebelle's lips quivered and let out a defeated sigh. "Father made an agreement with me... He swore he would let me keep my freedom, in exchange for... information..."

Katerina's mouth dried. "What *kind* of information?"

"Nothing crazy." Her gaze remained on the ground. "Just about the people outside. The... you know... *them*." Her voice cracked. "The staff... *you*."

Katerina's muscles tightened, and her heart plummeted. *My own sister... He is using my own sister and used her freedom as leverage... sick... fucking... bastard.* Her clenched and blood boiled as she shook her head slowly. *What has she told him? Does she know about my runs? Was she responsible for what happened to Byorn? My own fucking sister. The one I saved a few nights ago...*

In a cautious manner, Jezebelle approached Katerina, reaching for her hand. "I haven't told him anything about y—"

And how am I supposed to believe that? Katerina slithered out of her sister's reach. "I need a moment alone, Jezebelle." Katerina stood.

Jezebelle grabbed her wrist. "Please, I—"

"Let me go." *Or else I will not be able to stop myself from spewing nothing but pure venom.*

She paled and frowned at Katerina's icy rejection.

"I'm sorry." Jezebelle croaked before releasing her.

Katerina stormed out of the room. *What the actual fuck?* Her head pounded ferociously, threatening to explode. *What had she told him? All this time, I've been trying to protect her from his nefarious schemes, only for it all to be in vain. She had a lifeline of her own. Free to do as she pleased... all because she kept him informed.* She scoffed.

Jezebelle was able to roam freely, in and out of the Fortress, while I had to stay here, sneak my way out, subjected to whatever duty father deemed fit. Subjected to torture... If I were to leave the grounds, I would be locked up, chained, berated, defiled... tears threatened to spill. *I don't know what I'd done to deserve this... I've done nothing but be the exemplary daughter—highly educated in the Castelenian culture, about to assume one of the coveted positions on the Continent, yet... it wasn't enough.* Katerina's eyes burned. *No matter what I did, it wasn't enough. What does she have?* The question lingered in her mind longer than desired. *Yes, I might've been the temperamental sister, but that doesn't justify the horrid things I endured. Savior be my witness, if I will be penalized for doing what Jezebelle does on the regular*—her body froze and she shook her head, realization slamming into her. *The Sorting Tower.* She had forgotten.

Katerina ventured into her room and locked herself inside. *Get yourself together.* She turned on the bath, letting the water rise to her desired level.

"He asked me to marry him!" Jezebelle's voice echoed in her mind.

She's most likely going to get the chance to... Katerina wiped her wet cheeks. *While he tore my chance away...how is it that she gets everything she desires while I am stuck here to rot?*

Prisoner over my dead body.

TWENTY-FIVE

ENTERING THE DUNGEONS UNDER THE TRAINING grounds, Zeus stumbled upon a pondering Ares and a frustrated Argus in front of the three men. One blonde, one redhead, and one raven-haired. All three sat on the dirty ground, bound to one another. Each looked in a different direction, and their backs were used for support.

"I hope you have something worth my while," Zeus said.

"They won't talk," Ares responded. "And since you told us not to do anything until you got here, we haven't been able to get much out of them, anyway."

"Most we've gotten are their names." Argus said, pointing at each one. "Blonde one's Alexis, thin one's Thiseas, and red hair is—"

"I don't care. Just get to it."Zeus watched as Ares unbound Alexis and pulled him by the shirt, tossing his body to the center of the room.

Alexis didn't seem fazed by the roughness or the fact that his death might be near. Zeus guessed that he had made peace with his miserable life. Sweat matted Alexis' hair to his forehead, and he looked at all of them with a brooding expression between his lashes. Yet, he refused to stand. *The eyes of a man who's got nothing to lose.*

"This is how it's going to go. I'm going to ask you a series of questions, and you will answer me. If at any given point you don't answer, you will lose a part of your body. Of my choosing, of course. Are we understood?" Ares pulled a blade from one of his many pockets.

Why is he giving him the rundown? Just fucking do it.

The man nodded as sweat trickled down his reddened face.

"How did you know about the ambush?" Ares asked.

"We didn't."

"Bullshit." Ares slammed the blade into Alexis' thigh.

Loud cries filled the space.

"Either you start talking or I'm just going to enjoy myself right..." Ares pushed the blade further down. "Here."

Alexis cried through gritted teeth.

"I'm just going to keep this here. Should serve as a proper reminder of what to do." Ares stepped back.

"How did you know about the ambush?" Zeus asked calmly.

Silence.

Ares pulled the blade from the thigh and slammed it onto the opposite one. His cries did little to sway him to take it easy.

I'm fucking tired. Tired of the fucking stalling. Tired of being undermined. Zeus' skin tingled with electrifying heat. He grabbed Alexis' face forcefully. "How long have you been working for your Sovereign?"

Alexis opened his mouth to speak, yet nothing came out. His face reddened, veins popping out of his neck and face the more he attempted to speak.

Was he making a show of effort? Zeus doubted Alexis could bargain out of this one, but if he were to tell Zeus something of value, perhaps he would be merciful enough to give him a quick death.

Alexis opened his mouth again, and only an incomprehensible sound came out. Panic settled on his face, sweat dripping onto stone like a second confession. His lips trembled, his voice cracked as he drew the courage to speak.

"I-I" he stammered. "I wa-was with—"

A curved blade flew right into his face, landing between his eyes. The crack of bone echoed against the dungeon walls as blood saturated the coarse ground.

He collapsed backward, eyes wide, his truth silenced.

Zeus turned, eyes blazing.

Ares leaned against the wall with nothing but a bored expression. Zeus jaw tightened. A storm rumbled far above Olympus, the ceiling itself trembling at Zeus' wrath. Before he could utter a word, Argus stepped forward, his voice sharp and edged with fury.

"What the fuck is wrong with you?" Argus exploded. "He was just about to tell the truth."

"The truth?" Ares responded, his voice even, measured. "This waste of space has been talking in circles, wasting our time with half-words and fucking cowardice. He had nothing more to give. His silence, his fear, all spoke a lot louder. I ended his fucking charade."

Argus's nostrils flared, fists tightening, but Ares pressed on, his tone shifting to that of a strategist delivering reason rather than violence.

"Every wasted breath from imbeciles like him delays answers, and our time is not an endless river to be wasted on coward tongues. So don't mourn his fucking death. It was a judgment rendered for squandering patience. I'm surprised you weren't seeing through his bullshit." He pushed off the wall. "How convenient that he only seems to be able to speak except when asked a question related to the sovereign. Seems oddly fitting." He pulled the blade from the corpse and wiped the blood off with Alexis' clothes.

Ares' words were crafted with such ruthless logic that it struck Zeus for a moment. Ares didn't falter. He didn't bow or stammer.

Instead, he straightened and fixed Argus with a look of cool disdain.

"What I find oddly fitting is your deciding to kill him just when he was about to speak." Argus said.

"And waste even more time in potential speculation? Be my guest," he gestured at the remaining two.

Ares unbound and pushed the redhead forward, making him stand next to Alexis' bleeding corpse with trembling legs. Argus hesitated for a moment.

Zeus knew that suspicion meant little without proof, and Ares had made his justification ironclad. Brazen, yes, but still...

Argus pulled Alexis' corpse by the top of his shirt. Stopping in his tracks, he grabbed his arm. Argus tilted his head, muttered something under his breath in what looked to be frustration.

"Come look at this," he said to Zeus, keeping a firm grip on the corpse.

Zeus approached him, his eyes falling on the smoky sun in his forearm. *Fucking bastard.*

"Check the other two," Zeus ordered, clenching his jaw.

Argus and Ares moved quickly and checked the remaining men.

The redhead had nothing to show for himself, and a quick blow to the head, courtesy of Ares, had his body dropping next to Alexis.

The last remaining man—Thiseas—trembled, eyes bulging with tears, and incomprehensible mumbles left his lips. Zeus knew he couldn't survive even the lightest of tortures. His skin clung to his bones as if he hadn't eaten a day in his miserable life. Yet this fucker knew something, and the mark on his forearm was evidence enough.

Contrary to Alexis and the other one whose name mattered little, Thiseas silently pleaded for mercy.

Zeus suppressed a snort.

"What do you want to do?" Ares asked, as if he'd just read Zeus' mind.

"Get creative." Zeus answered dryly. "He knows something."

"Try not to kill him this time." Argus warned nastily to Ares.

Ares smiled as he threw a knife in the air, catching it by the hilt.

Long ago, Zeus was the only one with the power to *claim* the price whenever someone broke the vow. But now, it seemed that things had changed. *Who was claiming the lifeline?*

Zeus pulled Thiseas' gag down. "Name."

"Thiseas." He stammered. "Please, I-I mean n-no harm."

"As if you could," Ares snickered.

"What was your position at the Outpost?" Zeus asked.

"I didn't ha-have any."

Zeus examined his body language. No noticeable life-threatening injuries had spawned. *Not the topic of interest.*

"I'm just a man trying to take care of his family." Thiseas added.

"Ah..." Ares approached him. "Then you'd better cooperate if you want to see them again."

"If you didn't have a position, why were you there to begin with?" Zeus asked, eyes scanning his body carefully.

Thiseas opened his mouth, a silent gasp escaping, while his eyes widened, reflecting the harsh light. The sudden tension made the veins on his neck stand out, pulsing visibly against his skin.

There it was. The invisible gag that prevented him from speaking. *I got you now.*

Zeus extended a hand to Argus, keeping his eyes on Thiseas. He closed his palm around the hilt of a blade and brought the sharp tip to his sweat-covered face.

"Why were you at the Outpost?" Zeus asked again, slowly.

Silence.

Electricity trickled from his hands to the blade as Zeus pressed the tip against his exposed shoulder. His flesh trembled of its own accord. Thiseas gritted his teeth, fighting back the urge to scream.

"You know, metal is an excellent conductor, don't you think?" Zeus pushed a surge of his power through the blade, intensifying

Thiseas' shocks. "One last chance. Why were you at the Outpost?"

Silence again. But Zeus didn't pull out the blade; he buried it further, laced with electrifying heat.

"That's alright." Ares said. "We'll send Jerica your regards."

Thiseas eyes widened. "Leave her out of this!"

"Then speak." Argus ordered.

Thiseas gaze darted all around the room as if looking for answers or an escape of some sort.

"My turn." Ares took Zeus' place.

Zeus stood back, examining Thiseas' every move. A loud crunch turned his attention to Ares, who had broken one of Thiseas' fingers. His lips quiver, struggling to breathe. Thiseas' eyes jumped from Ares to Zeus, whimpering as the pain radiated through his body. He was on the cusp of hyperventilating but gritted his teeth to stop himself from giving in to the fiery agony coursing through his veins.

"Don't look at him. Look at me, you had your chance." Ares ordered, breaking another finger. "I have men near your pesky village at my beck and call. So, you either start talking or we'll pay a visit to darling Jerica and little Thomas. "

Fear laced Thiseas' face. "Please, you must understand! Please!" he cried, his eyes darting to Zeus, pleading for him to intervene.

"Send them." Zeus ordered, not bothering to waste his time further.

Ares stepped back and aimed toward the exit.

"No! I was delivering a package!" He confessed. "He made me swear. I didn't have any choice! I—" His eyes bulged as he gasped for air. Biting his now-bruised lip, he begged again and again for mercy. Rambling about he was just following orders and how he didn't have any choice as he fought off the pain consuming him from within.

"What did you deliver?" Zeus asked point-blank.

"He-e didn't tell us." He stammered. "He only ordered us to

pick it from the Acrailerion's Apothecary... Ahhhhh." His body contorted in different directions. The sound of breaking bones was drowned by his screams. He was so close to joining the rest of the men.

"He made you vow and not dare to tell you what you were delivering?" Argus scoffed in disbelief.

"I was just trying to—pro-protect m-my family. He told us to deliver it to someone na-named Drem-mian." A single tear fell down Thiseas' cheek, taking with it his last breath.

"It's pretty obvious that they were delivering the poison to the outpost." Zeus commented, moving away from the bodies. "Find Dremian and a way into this *Acrailerion.*"

"I may have someone who could help." Argus said. "He could sneak in, get what we need, and sneak out."

"And you think it'll be that simple?" Ares snorted. "It is common knowledge that the Acrailerion is a women's-only temple, so whoever it is you're thinking of won't be able to move past the foyer if he's lucky."

"You seem to forget my *wife* used to be one of them." Argus retorted. "I'm *very* familiar with the place."

"If Dremian has the poison, we might've just saved us ample time." Zeus said.

"I'll talk to him, see what he has." Argus said. "I need to know what other ingredients it has to make it extremely lethal to our kind. Maybe with a blood sample I could trace something..."

"*Our kind.*" Ares muttered mockingly.

"Talk to Asclepius to see if it's not too late to get the blood sample." Zeus said, then turned to Ares. "You and I are going to pay another visit to your brother."

THE DESCENT INTO TARTARUS WAS NEVER GENTLE. The air grew heavier with each step, pressing down on Zeus' chest. The stones hummed with the cries of those bound here, though their voices remained muffled, wary in the presence of Zeus.

Ares walked beside him, his steps measured, his face calm. He noticed that Ares didn't wear his usual edge of impatience, nor the wolfish grin he bore when blood was near. He was subdued, his gaze steady, almost indifferent to the shadows that clawed at the iron bars around them.

"What else do we have to find out?" Ares asked, his tone unbothered. "We got what we needed last time, did we not?"

"He knows more than the name he gave us."

Ares snorted. "Or maybe he'll just waste our time once again with yet another lie."

They pressed deeper, and the cells grew darker, colder. The whispers rose around them, yet they sounded different. It wasn't their usual curses but something else Zeus couldn't quite decipher. Perhaps warnings? Then again, why would these monsters warn their captor? His skin prickled as the weight in the air thickened. A chill ran down his spine, but Zeus remained neutral and composed. The rough, cold stones pulsed with a slow, heavy rhythm. A subtle tremor vibrated underfoot, like a held breath escaping, making the air in the pit feel thick and expectant.

And then he saw him.

Lying in his cell, sprawled against the stone, with his golden hair dulled, his body motionless save for the shallow rise of his chest. His lyre rested near his limp hand, its strings torn as though by unseen claws.

Zeus stopped, lightning bristling along his shoulders and trailing down to his fingertips. "Apollo..."

The dark pressure around him clung to his body, wrapping tight around his throat. Yet it wasn't familiar. His mind raced through the endless possibilities. *It is not from Hades. Not of Nyx. Not Hecate. Not Erebus.* It was something else...

Ares stepped forward, his brows drawing together. "What the hell?" His voice, though still low, carried the weight of unease. "He wasn't supposed to die..."

Zeus gripped the bars, sparks flaring beneath his fingers. "The seal is broken." Zeus hurried inside.

"What?" Ares asked.

"I put a seal over his cell," Zeus replied. "Just in case any of the vermin here decided to pay him a visit."

"Even when committing treason, he still gets preferential treatment." Ares kicked Apollo's foot lightly.

"You'd rather he die than find out the truth behind this?"

"For fuck's sake, Zeus." Ares hurried to his side. "We've been going in circles. We've been trying to find answers for fucking years, and yet we always come back with absolutely fucking nothing. He's been here. What? 28 fucking years now and we've got absolutely fucking nothing out of him except for one or two things—if we're lucky. I'm fucking annoyed, and I'm not surprised that his ass got killed because it was a matter of fucking time before someone did."

Zeus turned sharply, eyes narrowing. "And you knew *nothing*?"

Ares met his glare, steady at first, but then it flickered to hesitation or perhaps confusion. "Of?"

"I may not have asked for an update as of late, but you *were* tasked with his welfare here, which included that you periodically checked on him."

"I knew nothing." Ares' calm voice remained.

The darkness surged, pressing harder. Zeus kneeled, pressing his palm against Apollo's chest. His pulse was faint, his skin cold, but alive nonetheless. Shadows coiled through Zeus, striking memory like lightning. Ice prickled his fingertips, and a raging sensation of sorrow and despair overtook him.

I know you. Zeus said in his mind. *Don't I?* Vague snaps of an ancient clash forgotten by time sorted through his mind like flipping pages in a book.

Zeus pulled his hand back, thunder growling deep inside him. He knew it; the truth lay here, in the depths of Tartarus, as partial realization slithered in his throat.

"What do we know about The Paragons of Light?" Zeus asked as he rose, eyes locking with the darkened corner of Apollo's cell. Somewhere in the abyss, he felt it. Something lurked and waited patiently for him...

"That they're an extremist group led by a heretic with no true identity save from following in his predecessor's footsteps." Ares replied.

Zeus tore his gaze away from the corner, though the sight of it still gnawed at him. Ares lingered a step behind, unusually silent, his calm face hardened into something more wary. For once, his eagerness for violence seemed to have abandoned him.

Ares broke the silence. "What do you have in mind?"

That our enemy escaped. That the threat we've been battling for over twenty-eight years has been living amongst the mortals, leading the Paragons of Light and supplying Joseph with power. That Apollo is innocent. But who? Zeus looked back at the darkened corner. *I can feel you.*

Zeus' mind drew back to the open cell. Undisturbed. Ajar. No broken chains. Nothing that could've tampered—*fuck.* He shook his head, but remained silent. *I can't speak until I have some kind of confirmation. Besides, to admit that the memory evades me and that I didn't inquire further would be to reveal weakness, and weakness has no place in this abysmal place.*

The cell narrowed, the stone walls sweated with black ichor that trickled like veins. Zeus summoned lightning, illuminating the space, yet the darkness thickened until his light got swallowed whole.

Ares muttered under his breath with a warning tone, "Zeus."

"Wait," he commanded, though the words were for himself as much as for Ares.

The rattling of snakes echoed in the darkness before his body was plunged into an abyss. Zeus' body crashed against stone; Ares followed suit. Zeus blinked. He fell into a chamber he didn't recognize. That alone chilled him. *There should be no part of Tartarus unknown to me, yet this...*

The floor was carved with spirals of ash and bone, sigils that glowed red and shifted when he looked at them too long. At the center lay a crater. *It's here. Lingering.* Thick and intoxicating. Zeus' knees almost buckled beneath its weight, but he forced himself upright.

Then, a voice.

Not heard, but felt, coiled inside his skull, dragging against his thoughts.

"You remember me, scum?"

Zeus' blood roared, lightning flaring around him. The sound alone shook the chamber. "Show yourself!"

Ares stepped closer, bracing himself to fight whoever spawned. "Who speaks?"

The shadows rippled at the edges of the crater, swelling upward like a tide. They take no shape, no face, yet their presence alone was suffocating. The air burned cold.

"You caged me once," the voice murmured. *"But you did not destroy me. You could not."*

Memory clawed at Zeus. Fragments of a battle drowned in storms, of a figure born of night and ruin, of a war fought in silence because even to name this imbecile was to give it strength. Yet, he'd fought so many, he was unsure of who this rival was. His hand trembled at his side, but a quick tightening of his fists kept his rage under control.

"I should have ended you," Zeus snarled.

"And yet you did not." The shadows writhed, stretching toward him. *"So I waited. And now, I'll take what you hold dear."*

Zeus thought of Apollo, broken in his cell. He thought of the others—of Olympus itself.

Ares bared his teeth, drawing his blade. His stance was tight, defensive. "Name it. Who is this?"

He can't see it? Zeus remained silent. The name remained coiled, buried, forbidden in his mind. The shadows surged, and the chamber quaked. Chains rattled down the corridor, prisoners wailing in unison.

Ares tightened his grip; his calm shattered. "Stop playing games, Zeus. Either we fight it, or it takes us."

It can't take us. It's not strong enough to sustain itself. It lives in the shadows, yet has a way to move... Fucking bastard. As much as Zeus hated to admit it, Artemis was right. Apollo *was* innocent, and he needed to get him out of here.

The storm within him rose, crackling, furious. Yet beneath it all, the fear gnawed deeper. Because the truth was clear—this shadow was no stranger. Sinister laughter surrounded them as it disappeared back into the shadowy abyss and spat them back with Apollo.

The torches along the walls flickered, though no wind stirred. *Who are you?* The flames bend inward, pulled toward the black. *We're too late.*

"We're taking Apollo to Asclepius."

Damp air clung to Joseph's skin, heavy with the stench of mildew. Water dripped from the ceiling, each drop echoing loudly across the hollow chamber. The torchlight flickered against skulls stacked neatly in alcoves, silent witnesses to the words he dared to utter.

I'm desperate.

There were no other words to describe it.

He was able to defend the outpost. But what would've happened if the men hadn't gotten there in time? Or lost the poison? Or if they stopped somewhere? Even if it was for a mere second, it could've cost him. Word had already gotten to him about the potential alliance between Aeshelyn and Sylene, and he knew it was a matter of time before he lost Windermere and all three countries riled against him.

Kneeling within a circle etched into the stone floor, Joseph pressed the dagger's edge across his palm. Blood welled up, warm against the chill of the catacombs, and let it spill onto the snake sigils he had carved. The lines pulsed faintly, as though the catacombs came to life.

"My voice is the chain...my blood the key. By flesh, by death, by will—" he hesitated. *Fuck...* he exhaled sharply. "By will...I summon you."

Heaviness fell upon him, dragging on the silence and dreadful anticipation. *I need this. I fucking need this. I can't keep depending on others to do what I am supposed to do. Not when Rena's life hangs in the balance.*

The soft scraping of footsteps made the hairs at the back of his neck stand, but his eyes remained on the floor. *I must endure. I must endure. No matter the cost. I must endure.*

"You kneel in filth, begging like a child."

He blew out a breath and turned his sight to Eris emerging from the darkness; her smile luminous in the gloom. The torches sputtered at her arrival, shadows twisting unnaturally along the walls.

"Charming." She leaned casually against one of the stone pillars, arms crossed. "You weren't expecting me, huh?" She let out a breathy laugh.

"I suppose *he* sent you."

"Nothing gets past that smart brain of yours."

Joseph pressed his bloodied hand harder against the circle, bowing his head though his eyes were locked on her.

"He's not going to come to you just because you asked. What do you want?"

Joseph slammed his hand against the ground. "I want power. The kind only *he* can give." He felt pathetic doing this in her presence, but he had no choice. She was the tether, the direct line between him and the damned *Savior.*

Her head tilted, and ink hair gleaming in the firelight like the threads of fate. "And what would you give in return? What you're asking is perilous, and your trinkets won't buy his favor, and your wife is your only collateral."

"My life. My will. My soul. Whatever it takes." Joseph vowed.

Eris circled him, each footstep deliberate, echoing in the chamber like a drumbeat. Her presence felt suffocating—too close, too sharp.

"Not enough," she purred, leaning in so her breath ghosted against his ear. "He doesn't want your pitiful devotion."

"My men are close to finding the sickle—"

"That doesn't mean you *have it*." Eris knelt in front of him, leveling her eyes with his. "Tell you what. He'd be willing to bestow *some* power in exchange for a *lifeline*."

The word lanced through him, colder than the stone beneath his knees. He swallowed hard. "A... lifeline?"

Her lips curved into a grin both playful and cruel. "Yes. Yours, if you are foolish. Another's, if you are clever. A lifeline anchors his power to this realm. The more profound the loss, the stronger the anchor. The life of a loved one, freely given or brutally taken, is the firmest chain. Only then will his partial gift flow through you. Of course, after you get the sickle, he'll bestow the full power you seek. Do we have a deal?"

The shadows deepened, and for a heartbeat Joseph felt him looming behind her, vast and formless, pressing against the veil of mortality.

My heart hammered, not from fear, but from uncertainty. I knelt in the circle, blade in hand, blood dripping from my palm onto the symbols Quinn had carved into the stone.

He was waiting. I could feel him in the dark, vast and patient, the silence of the crypt stretched thin by his presence.

"My soul is yours," Quinn said, the words catching in his throat. "Take it. Bind me to your will. Give me strength to finish what no other dares. Bestow upon me the power only you can give."

The shadows stirred, answering, curling like smoke around his body. What role did he want me to play? Why am I here?

Whispers slithered against my ears, voices layered on voices, old as the bones around me. A lifeline, it hissed. Blood for blood. A tether, or nothing.

I faltered, breath shallow. A tether. He demanded more than Quinn.

"I will give it," Quinn rasped, lifting his eyes to the dark. "Take my soul. Bind me—" His voice cracked. "Bind me to him."

My heart dropped. What? His legacy was dying, and he knew it.

Shadows pressed closer, and the ground shuddered beneath my knees. My blood seared, veins alight with fire and shadow. The circle flared, and I felt the bond cinch, a thread yanked tight between us. My soul unraveled, pulled like silk into the hands of something immeasurable, and in the same breath it anchored itself inside him.

Pain ripped through me—then clarity. He wasn't sacrificing his soul to it... Quinn was tying his life to mine.

I glared at him. Indignation washed through me. He fucking knew he would die once he stepped onto the battlefield against Zeus. It was obvious to all of us with eyes. Fuck. My heart thundered against my chest. That's why he made me fucking vow.

First, he took Bernadette from me. Married her off to some stranger, and now he takes my life as if it were his to take and own.

I knew then that if he died, I would carry the legacy. The war would not end with his breath. His purpose would live on in my veins, my bones, my mind. If I didn't live up to the bargain, it'd ruin me.

The shadows coiled tighter, sealing the pact, and a deep, sinister voice shuddered through the chamber like thunder.

"It is done."

Quinn collapsed, bloodied hands pressed to the stone, tears burning down his face. Not from fear. Not from regret. But with certainty. I would finish what he had begun. Because I was his now. My lifeline. My purpose after his death.

Joseph's chest rose and fell in ragged breaths. The stones beneath him were cold, but sweat trickled down his spine as if he stood inside a furnace. *A lifeline.* The word gnawed at him, like a parasite burrowing into the marrow of his bones.

What would this mean? Would he have control over my mind? Over my body? Fuck. You wanted power. You wanted to be better than Quinn. This is your fucking chance.

Eris's face focused back into view, her eyes gleaming in the half-light of the torch. There was no pity in them, only delight, sharp as a blade. "Well?" She whispered. "Whose life would you sacrifice?"

Joseph swallowed, his throat dry... *she knew I had no other choice. She could sense my fucking desperation.* "Take mine. Bind me to him. Let my blood be the thread." *If I die, I die...*

Her smile widened. "Ah," she breathed, brushing her fingers against the circle's edge. "A sacrifice most noble. How fitting."

She stood and lifted her hand; the shadows thickened like storm clouds behind her. They writhed and pressed forward, coiling around the catacombs.

Joseph could feel him leaning into the catacombs as though the walls could no longer hold him back. *Show yourself, for fuck's sake. Stop being a coward.*

The circle flared with light. His blood boiled on the stones with something darker. It raced upward, crawling across his hand, his arm, and sinking into his chest. Joseph's heart seized as though gripped by an icy hand, then thundered so hard he thought his ribs would shatter.

Pain wrecked him, pushing him into the ground. He resisted the urge to scream. *I will not go down as a coward. I must endure.* His body contorted in different directions. Unbearable heat bloomed from his chest, expanding to his arms and legs. The taste of copper filled his mouth from the pressure. He screamed, and the crypt swallowed the sound whole. He fell forward onto his hands, gasping, and drenched in sweat. His vision swam with fractured light and shadow, and the pain in his chest dissolved into something else... something greater. Strength coursed through his veins, fire, thunder, and shadow mingling until he could barely tell where it ended and began.

Eris knelt beside him and touched his damp jaw with delicate fingers, tilting his head toward her. Every ounce of his being wanted to jerk away from her touch, but he was too fucking weak to even stand.

She clicked her tongue. "This bargain with Quinn really made you age deliciously." She huffed, tracing her thumb along his lower lip. "No one can even tell you're 62 with those muscles and strong jaw."

Joseph sneered, struggling to keep his eyes open.

"It's too bad that Rena can't enjoy the goods..."

He tore his face away from her touch in utter anger.

"There," she murmured, her smile radiant. "It's done. You are his now. Your lifeline is bound, as you offered."

Joseph staggered, clutching at his chest where the darkness had taken root. "I feel it... gods, I feel it." His voice shook with awe. "It's mine... mine," he muttered to himself.

"Yes," Eris purred, brushing a lock of hair from his forehead. "Yours. Every breath you take now is his *gift*. Every heartbeat, his echo. So long as you remain loyal to *him,* the power is yours."

TWENTY-SEVEN

MOONLIGHT FILTERED THROUGH THE LEAFY CANOPY. Leaves crunched beneath Katerina's running boots as she walked beside Jasmine to the Sorting Tower. Both took the long route instead of going through the Caverest Plaza to keep as much anonymity as possible.

Jezebelle's words still haunted her with each step.

"Just because your love life failed doesn't mean that mine is going to. It's not my fault that father stopped you from being with the man you loved... Father made an agreement with me. He swore he would let me keep my freedom in exchange for information."

That's what I get for saving her? That's what I get for being a protective sister. What did I—

"Do you really think she's in danger?" Jasmine asked.

"I don't know..." Katerina shook her head. "But if she's in danger, it's most likely of his doing."

"Um... perhaps, but he has no—it's odd because he had no reason to tell you."

"I just can't believe my sister actually forgave this man." Katerina grimaced. "No, not just forgive him. *Marry him*, Jas."

"I would like to understand that myself. He *did* mention that he had to prove a point."

"I don't know what kind of point he had to prove that merits putting her life at risk." Katerina pressed her lips into a hard line, eyes burning. "You didn't see her, Jas. You didn't see her petrified. It breaks—it *broke* me."

"I get that you're trying to understand why she wants to marry this man, why she said yes in the first place, everything that she is doing."

Katerina scowled.

"But, like it or not, *she* made this decision, and *she* has to live with the consequences that come with it."

Katerina's chest caved. "I just feel conflicted."

"Because she is with someone you don't like?"

"No—I mean yes, but conflicted because I wanted to protect her. I want to protect her from other people. I want to protect her from the world we live in, especially protect her from these rebels, but I don't know if her leaving with Rhei will give her the opportunity to slip off my fathers grasp, and not subject her to the lashings I've been receiving." Her back itched. "It could give her an opportunity at a different life..." she bit her lip, refusing to give Rhei the satisfaction of potentially being right.

"And how do you know your father hasn't been lashing her as well?"

"Because she told me that she doesn't have the same restrictions I do."

"Wait... what?"

"Mhm." Katerina's face soured. "I know, but you know what's the kicker? She kept her freedom only because she's been supplying him with information. Information about the staff, about me, about the rebels... I don't know how the hell she would even know about these people given that she barely leaves—wait a damn minute."

Jasmine gave her an incredulous look.

"She's using Rhei..." Katerina muttered. "Is this why father hasn't intervened in her union with him? Because she is his insider."

"I'd like to say that you sound ridiculous, but I wouldn't put it past your father."

What the fuck? I know I shouldn't be angry, because she is maybe doing her job. But... how did I not realize this sooner? With their overt public displays of affection, it's evident that word must've gotten to father about them, and now it made sense that he never intervened. How come—no wonder he said he had no need for her at the banquet. I'll be damned.

A flash of red and silver light captured her attention. She turned to the starry night only to witness a sea of stars cascading towards the earth, emitting a faint red hue that almost resembled blood.

"What are you going to do?" Jasmine asked, pulling her attention back.

I have no idea. She couldn't be rash, not yet anyway, but she needed to choose this battle carefully.

A massive eight-sided tower, perched on a rocky cliff, materialized in front of them with marble columns, a blue rooftop, ivy-covered walls and an arched bronze double-door entrance. Wide stone steps led to a triple-arch entrance, and the closer they got, the better Katerina could make out the detailed stone carvings along the sides of the tower.

The right side displayed a carving of their Savior with an aura of powerful reverence. He stood tall—face covered and unidentifiable. His body was concealed by a long, majestic drape. His hands, palms up, emitted powerful energy, symbolized by carved spirals trailing up and out. He looked calm but powerful, despite his unseen face. Katerina's gaze fixed on his hidden face, and an icy chill slithered through her spine. She bowed her head. *Praise be to our Savior.* She'd never dared to look him in the face until now. She ran a finger down the carvings emerging from his back that resembled shadows. Energy pulsed through her fingertips.

Katerina moved over to the left, where it showcased each of the Olympians alongside their symbols. Zeus with thunderbolts, Hera with a peacock, Poseidon with a trident, Demeter with a sheaf of wheat, Athena in armor with an owl, Apollo with a lyre and sun rays, Artemis with a bow, Ares in battle gear, Hephaestus with a hammer and forge, Aphrodite rising from the sea, Hermes with a caduceus, and Dionysus with grapes and a goblet.

The Sorting Tower seemed like the only place untainted by the feud of their people, like a neutral ground of some sort.

The lock rattled, and Katerina joined Jasmine at the entrance.

"I thought they were open all hours of the day." Katerina muttered.

"They should..." Jasmine's hands covered the lock as she closed her eyes, inhaling deeply. "Perhaps..."

Katerina leaned forward, trying to comprehend what Jasmine was attempting. Then again, she knew her all too well, and it was only a matter of time before—*click.*

Katerina laughed. "Those powers still come in handy, huh?"

"The best power I never asked for." Jasmine chuckled.

No wonder Jasmine was listed as one of the most valuable High Re'Veillites...

"Okay, before we go in. What are we even looking for?" She asked.

"Anything that may help us understand how the Jezebelle received and sent letters in and out of the Fortress." Katerina said. "Anything that could help us at all."

Jasmine nodded, and they entered the Sorting Tower.

Scrolls and folded parchment flew through the air, directed by small-pearl fleshed winged creatures. Dim, flickering orange and blue lights moved around the space. Piles of unsorted correspondence were scattered across the tiled floor.

Counter tables for messengers and citizens to submit letters were placed to the right, covered in wax stamps, ink pots. Carved plaques showed the postal codes of the continent.

Right next to the entrance, a list with all the levels of the tower hung from the wall.

Ground Floor — Registration Hall, Offices & Archives

Second Floor — Sorting Chamber
Third Floor — Scribe & Seal Room
Fourth Floor — Carrier Vale Loft
Fifth Floor — Messenger Quarter
Sixth Floor — Wind-Reading Room
Seventh Floor — Dispatch Hall
Roof Dome — Signal Platform

Jasmine slammed her palm onto Katerina's back, vibrating rapidly. Katerina opened her mouth to ask what she was doing, but Jasmine placed a finger to her lips.

The winged creatures swarmed toward the entrance, and past them. Up close, Katerina saw eyes like molten black glass reflecting the dim light. No lips, just razor-sharp teeth bared in a silent snarl. Their long fingers, though small, looked sharp enough to slice through flesh.

Confusion stirred within Katerina as they didn't seem to acknowledge their presence as the creatures closed the doors and carried on with the sorting and delivery of correspondence.

She raised an eyebrow. But Jasmine held a hand up, stopping Katerina from speaking as her eyes scanned the surroundings. She removed her hand from Katerina's back slowly.

"The Vales are sensitive to sound and light." She said through Katerina's mind. *"My power can only help so much. Let's stick to this type of communication until we're out of here."*

Katerina nodded. *"How come they can't see us?"*

"My power is focused on keeping us hidden and keeping this line of communication open. Our bodies are unable to be seen by anyone except each other. Plus, our movements are muffled, but not completely. So, be careful when moving things around."

"Got it."

They walked deeper into the main room. Gentle golden light streamed from the domed ceiling, faintly illuminating the glistening magenta, indigo, and golden Vales as they sorted piles of parchment into alcoves above.

Katerina found them intriguing, to say the least. She'd never seen anything like them. The Vales near the entrance were medium-sized with pearl-like skin and feathery wings. Yet the others were similar but with different kinds of wings.

She tapped Jasmine's shoulder. *"What are Vales? I've never seen anything like them around the Fortress or the Acrailerion."*

"Hermes created them," Jasmine began. *"They're dedicated to the Tower, sorting and delivering correspondence across Eseron. Pearls go to Windermere since their bodies are built for the cold and wind. Thus, the compact wings. Indigos deliver to Sylene, always at night, avoiding interception by anybody that may be a threat to the sanctuary country. Golds handle Castelencia's heat, hence why their wings are more spread. And Magentas deliver to Aeshelyn. If you look closely, their wings are much lighter compared to Castelencia or Windermere, but their frames are slightly smaller because they need to move quicker between territories since, with everything that's going on, correspondence flies in and out quicker than other countries."*

Katerina looked back at the Vales. They moved stealthily but gracefully all the same. Some carried packages while others moved bags full of parchment with ease, as if the weight didn't bother them despite their size.

Jasmine tapped her shoulder. *"What if your father allowed your sister to receive letters?"*

"Doubtful." Katerina shook her head. *"After the plethora of poisoned parchment, he wouldn't risk it. He might be cruel, but he's not stupid."*

The sharp scent of wax and the earthy perfume of ink made Katerina's nose wrinkle as they entered a hall. A single door stood on each side: to the left, a gleaming gold door with a stark black placard; to the right, a cool, silver door with a clean, white placard.

"I'll go left." Katerina said, and Jasmine nodded, trailing toward the silvery door.

She gazed up at the onyx placard.

<u>Quality Control Surveyor Office</u>

Without much hesitation, Katerina opened the door and slithered inside. The office was filled with a mix of artifacts, open-and-closed scrolls, scattered books, and ancient relics. Floating lanterns illuminated the room with a warm glow that contrasted with the coolness of the night filtering through the arched window behind the desk as she approached it.

I'm not sure what I should be looking for, but I am certain that I'll know it when I see it... I hope. The scent of burnt parchment made her wince. *Or it may just be wishful thinking.* The desk seemed to be made of twisted rosewood as she scattered through the mess atop it. *Letters to relatives. Letters to loved ones. Log of the deceased. Significant Notes?* She picked up the parchment, trying not to smudge the semi-fresh ink.

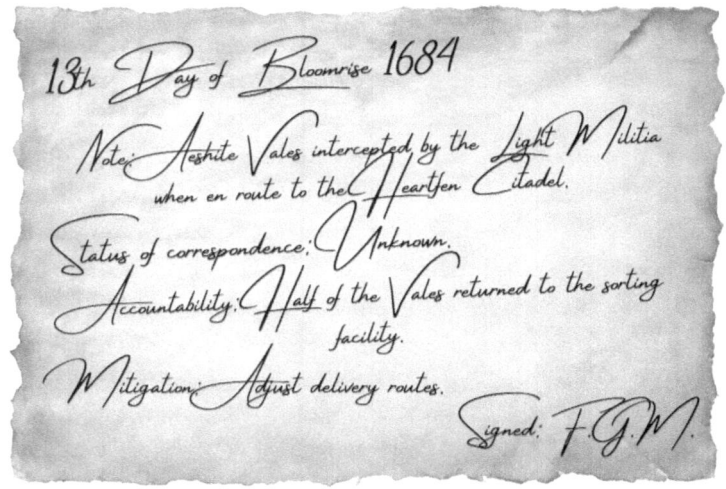

13*th* day of Bloomrise? *This was no less than five days ago... but why is the ink still partially fresh? My father is playing a dangerous game...* Katerina's eyes narrowed on the status of correspondence. *What do you want to know? Better yet, what are you hiding?* She continued to sort through the mess and picked up a sealed parchment.

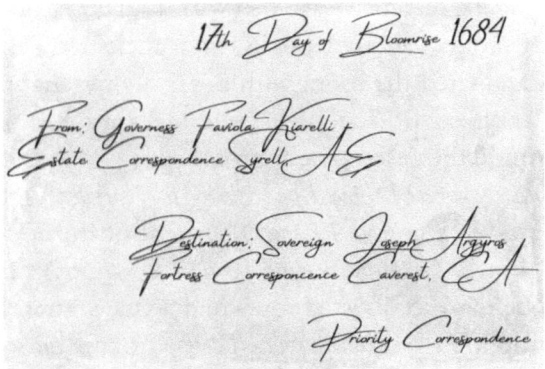

Is she really coming to the banquet? I heard father sent out the invitations, but I didn't think she'd respond. Perhaps she's rejecting his offer. She kept shuffling through the mess, growing increasingly annoyed. She peered down at the drawers and found nothing but torn-up parchment, several notes on new administration, and overall trash. Letting out an exasperated sigh, she continued searching throughout the room. Overly packed shelves lined the walls and—not that she was surprised—there was nothing of importance there either.

If I were to keep a log of correspondence pending to be dispatched or ones that have already been delivered, where would I store it to avoid others from finding it? Her feet tapped the tile repeatedly, then stopped herself, remembering Jasmine's warning about noise and the Vales.

She walked to the silver cabinet adjacent to the window. *If there's nothing here, let's just hope Jasmine had more luck.* She opened the first drawer. *Sheets of empty parchment.* Second drawer. *Address logs A-M, N-Z.* She pulled out the address log from A through M and traced a finger through the assortment of locations, found the letter F, and flipped through the pages until landing on The Fortress.

The Fortress

Information as of:
Serenith 1656

Current Address: 3726 Savior Street, Caverest, CA.

Authorized Pickup Personnel: Sebastian Briar
Dremian Solace.

Requests/Restrictions in Place: No delivery of correspondence unless pickup personnel provide the correspondence slip signed by the Sovereign. Requires a new slip for correspondence collection if an individual is not on the Authorized Personnel Roster.

Historical Data:
Former Reported Address: 3726 Olympian Street, Caverest, CA.

Former Reported Contacts: Harrison McClaren (Deceased)
Juliette McClaren (Deceased)
Quinn Petrakis (Deceased)

Katerina blinked. *Only two people are authorized to pick up corre-*

spondence? I recognize Sebastian, but Dremian... he's new. Is he one of the men my father included in his council? There were comments about his new counselors being awfully young... She then focused on the first sentence in the Request/Restrictions in Place. *So, Sebastian and Dremian are the ones authorized...* She clicked her tongue. *Father isn't going to be open with them if he is doing his own thing on the side. I doubt that they know about Jezebelle's detours... then again... no. It's not like him. He wouldn't jeopardize his plans by involving other people... no matter how high the position... I know him—well, I think I do.*

She shoved the address log back in the drawer and opened the last. Her throat tightened, and she shoved the drawer closed. *Breathe. That was just a nightmare. It wasn't real.* Katerina closed her eyes and shook her head, focusing on her breath.

Breathe in... breathe out... in... out...

Upon opening my eyes, two onyx doors lay before me, one with a golden handle and the other with a silver.

"Katerina!" the voice was near, almost as if it was coming from behind one of the doors.

Come to me.

I outstretched a hand, opening the silver door and seeing the inky box on the other side. With trembling hands, I pick it up and almost vomit at the sight of what was inside. I toss it away, and a single human heart slips from it.

Still beating.

She opened her eyes, stifling her racing heart. *You're okay. You won't find a heart. Just open it.* Her gaze drifted to the silver drawer. *You'll be fine.* With trembling hands, she opened it and picked up the velvety onyx box. It was small. Barely the size of her palm. *Highly doubtful I'll find a heart this size—*

well... she dismissed the inappropriate thought and opened the box.

An onyx 16-point star pendant rested in the center of a cushioned velvety support. The main points were slightly longer and pointier than the rest. *Stunning...* The pendant hung delicately on a thin silver chain as she removed it from the box. At its core, lay a partially translucent stone with a blue-like sheen that Katerina instantly recognized. *Moonstone.*

Her chest tugged, and an icy feeling prickled her fingertips, despite the humidity of the room.

"Come to me." A woman said from behind her.

Katerina turned.

Nothing. She was alone. Yet the tug in her chest only seemed to make her worry because last time it did, it brought her to her sister about to be offered to the Olympian gods. *Is Jezebelle alright?* She shook her head. *Focus. Focus.*

Turning the box, she searched for the owner's name or potential recipient, but there was nothing. The small box just sat at the bottom of a cabinet drawer, collecting dust, and there was no name attached to it.

"Take it."

Her eyes searched the room, heart thundering against her ears. "Get out of my head..." she whispered, the first time she'd spoken since stepping foot inside the Tower.

She put the necklace back in the box. *No one will miss it...* and place the box back on the drawer, prompting herself to close it. *But I can't just leave it... it's a beautiful piece.... Collecting dust... But someone will know if it goes missing.* Defeatedly, she aimed for the door.

Her stomach dropped. *Where is it?* Nothing but a blank wall lies in its stead. Her throat clenched. *Breathe. It's all in your head. Breathe.*

She looked around the room. The desk was gone. The window was gone. The shelves were gone. She turned back to the blank wall only to find iron bars that locked her inside. *But is it really all in my head?* Her eyes burned. *I can't breathe.* Katerina lunged toward the cell bars and rattled the iron door with all her strength. *Let me fucking go!* Tears streamed down her cheeks.

She turned back.

Stone walls surrounded her, screams echoing all around. She ran back to the iron bars. A forceful restraint around her legs stopped her body. She peered down. *I can't breathe.* She felt the air getting ripped out of her lungs as she pulled the shackles and chains that bound her to the wall.

The door unlocked.

A chill ran down her spine.

Her head turned ever so cautiously. "Please, I've been good." Her vision blurred. "I've done everything you asked me."

A man moved toward her, but she couldn't see his face. Her sight trickled down to the ebony whip in his hand. Her skin crawled at the sound of tightening leather.

"Please." She pleaded. "Don't do this. Please."

Her back ached. He hadn't even touched her, and her back fucking burned. *Fight. Fight back this time.*

He put a hand on her shoulder.

Savior help me. She swung, aiming for his face. He dodged. She swung again and again using both arms. "Leave me alone!" She fell to her knees.

He grabbed her arms. "Katerina."

"Let me go, please!" She shut her eyes.

"Katerina."

She focused on her breath. *You won't hurt me again.*

"Katerina." A familiar female voice called.

Stop playing games with me. She struggled to breathe.

"Kate. Open your eyes," Jasmine urged.

Katerina shook her head. *It's not real. It's not real. It's not real. It's not re*—she opened her eyes, blinking repeatedly as she pressed a hand to her warm, aching cheek. "Did you just fucking slap me?"

"Keep your voice down." She whisper-shouted. "Someone had to pull you out somehow."

"What happened?" Katerina whispered.

"You tell me." She urged. "One minute, I'm reading through a dispatch log and the next, I hear thrashing and screaming. And here you were cowering on the floor... I thought someone had found you."

So, it was all in my head... She removed her hand from her throbbing face. "What'd you find?" *I don't wish to retell this fucking nightmare.*

"Come see." Jasmine helped Katerina to her feet. "You and I need to talk about this."

No, we don't. Katerina shrugged and followed her out and into the room across the hall.

Dispatch Office

The room was brighter compared with the other one. Large arched windows lined the walls. Between each window lied a bookshelf filled with tomes and busts. Jasmine went around the desk and opened a large, overflowing book.

She flipped through the brittle pages. *"A few pages back... I saw a name."* Her voice echoed in Katerina's mind, stopping abruptly at a list. *"Not only did I find Jezebelle's name but also—"* She pressed a finger, a slight pressure, to the ink beside Jezebelle's.

Frederick Gilderoy-McClaren and Dremian Solace.

"Who's Frederick?" Katerina asked. *And what role are you playing, Dremian?*

"According to this..." she flipped over to the first few pages. *"He's one of the few human delivery men here and the only one allowed to deliver to the Acrailerion."*

"But the only ones allowed to receive correspondence there is the Verena and the Denai." Katerina pursed her lips. *I should've checked the Acrailerion's address logs.* *"And with the vacancy of the Denai position, I highly doubt the Verenna has taken the role of*

messenger." She looked back at the log. *So, Frederick had been receiving and delivering the letters since—*she ran a finger up the page. *Five months? Almost damn near last year's Vespera... Jezebelle has been doing this for five damned months? and Dremian. He started last month, on the 24th day of Seraphine. But he just showed up at father's council...*

Katerina glanced at Jasmine, who looked transfixed, and tapped on her shoulder. *"What is it?"*

Jasmine's gaze remained fixed on the parchment. *"That name... it just sounds familiar..."*

Katerina looked down at the name. *Frederick Gilderoy-McClaren.* She frowned. *It doesn't ring a bell.* *"Old relative of yours, perhaps?"*

She shook her head. *"No..."* and stepped away from the book. *"But I'm sure I'll remember at some point."*

"If he's been helping Jezebelle, how would she even know when new letters have come in? It's not like he can go into the Fortress without prior clearance." Katerina pointed out.

"Dremian, perhaps." Jasmine said, putting the tome back in place. *"Being a member of your father's council grants him access to a ton of information and places."*

And him being on the authorized personnel list, he's one of the people to get called when new correspondence arrives. Maybe he even has special instructions for letters addressed to Jezebelle. Who knows?

"Do you think father told him about Jezebelle and Rhei?"

"I'm fairly certain that he did." Jasmine dusted her hands off on her pants. *"We need to get out of here. We've talked too much, and it's only a matter of time before the Vales find us."*

"Fine," Katerina said. *"But we're stopping somewhere first before we head home."*

TWENTY-EIGHT

WARMTH FILLED KATERINA'S SHIVERING BODY AS SHE and Jasmine stepped inside the Roselle Inn. Lively music and conversations emerged from the countless patrons gathered in the taverna.

Wooden beams and brick walls with flickering candlelight cast a warm glow over the large oak tables scattered around, some with plates of fresh bread, olives, and wine decanters.

Katerina's nostrils welcomed the scent of roasted chicken and fresh herbs. A roaring fireplace sat at the end beneath decorative shields and weapons.

Jasmine pulled on Katerina's arm. "Explain to me why we are here?" she whispered

"Do you trust me?" Katerina asked, eyes scanning the inn.

"I do, but I'd like some context."

"I'll explain soon. I just need you to trust me."

"Fine..." Jasmine said skeptically. "By the way, I forgot to ask you. How did the meeting with the Verenna go?"

Katerina glanced down for a brief moment. "It went as expected." She met Jasmine's gaze. "I was blamed for what happened at the Helios Agora. But somehow I expected her to listen to me and believe my innocence."

"Did you lie at any point?"

Katerina's brow raised. "Why would I?"

"No reason, it's just that..." Jasmine leaned close. "She has a way of finding out things... we're not supposed to talk about it." Her eyes scanned the room for any within earshot. "She can see into other people's minds without so much as touching them... why do you think people are afraid of her?"

Katerina's stomach hollowed. *Does she know about the lashings? Did she look into my mind? What did she see?* They moved between the tables.

"How come I'm just finding this out?" Katerina whispered.

"All Re'Veillites are sworn to keep others' abilities a secret. For the sake of safeguarding the integrity of the Acrailerion."

"Yet you're—" Katerina's body got tackled, followed by loud squeals.

"I didn't think you'd make it!" Chryssa pulled out of the embrace. Her fiery hair was tied up in a loose bun. "Especially with how...*sunshine* the messenger can be."

Katerina laughed. "I wouldn't miss it."

"Hi, I'm Chryssa." She extended a hand to Jasmine, which she gracefully took.

"Jasmine." She smiled.

"My goodness, you're a delicate thing." Chryssa examined Jasmine's hand as it slipped from her grasp. "Oh darling, I don't mean it in a bad way."

Jasmine shot Katerina a subtle glance.

"I just don't come across a lot of women whose hands are this soft."

"Thank you." Jasmine replied with a smile.

"So, what are we celebrating?" Katerina asked, diverting the attention away from Jasmine, who clearly looked uncomfortable.

"My brother's engagement, of course." She beamed. "You didn't know? I swear, Nik can be such a—doesn't matter. I'm just happy you're here." Her eyes drifted to Katerina's hair. "Honey, that stress is really doing a number on your hair."

"What?" Katerina blinked.

"Here." Chryssa ran her hand over Katerina's hair, focusing on the top. "Stress can make your hair lose pigment quicker than normal."

"We should be expecting the guest of honor here anytime soon, right?" Jasmine asked.

"I hope so. I didn't go through all this trouble for him and his fiancée not to show."

"Who's the lucky girl?" Katerina asked, feigning obliviousness.

"Some girl he met while in the capital." Chryssa said. "He wouldn't give me details but—no! The drinks need to be stacked! I am so sorry. I'll be right back." She scurried off behind several assistants with trays.

Jasmine swatted Katerina's arm. "Is this why you wanted to come?"

"In my defense, I had no idea this was an engagement party." *I didn't know why the invite, if I'm honest.*

"So I'm supposed to think that you're not here to keep an eye on your sister?"

"Yes," she retorted. "I'm here because I knew Rhei was."

Jasmine pulled Katerina away from the array of people surrounding them. "And are you sure she doesn't know who you are?"

"After my conversation with Rhei, I'm certain she doesn't."

"And now you suddenly trust his word?"

"I don't. But if she knows, she's doing a great job of pretending she doesn't."

"Kate, you're testing your luck with these people..." Jasmine whispered. "Even though there aren't Olympian banners around, this place is packed with supporters." She gestured subtly to the people mingling around the place.

Some had Division patches on their shoulders, while others broadly displayed their hand-crafted weapons and boasted about the craftsmanship of their blades, courtesy of Hephaestus. Katerina's stomach turned. *Shit...*

"Did you consider how close this place is to the Heartfen Citadel?"

I did not. "I know what I'm doing. Trust me."

"Most of the people here would love to see your head on a spike. We should leave while we still can."

"I just need to—"

"You need *nothing*." She cut Katerina off. "We've been out for too long, and it's only a matter of time before your father finds out you're gone."

"And I'm supposed to cower while Jezebelle gets to roam freely without punishment?" Katerina scoffed. "While she has the liberty to be engaged?"

"Is that what this is about?" Jasmine's eyes softened.

Katerina kept her face neutral, but she felt the pit of her stomach lurching every which way.

"I'm not saying that you should just take it. I'm saying that you can't be this reckless." Jasmine added before Katerina could respond.

"So you keep saying, but you need to have some faith in me. There is something that Rhei didn't tell me, and getting the invitation to come here was no coincidence."

"What if you're just paranoid?"

"Excuse me?"

"Before you go all haywire on me. What if you just got invited because Chryssa genuinely considers you a friend?"

"That would be in an ideal world." *But I can't show my distrust here.*

"And what is it that you're hoping to find? Because clearly Rhei is nowhere to be seen; let alone your sister. Please, Kate, we have to go. Trust me. Believe me when I tell you we have to go."

"Is there something you're not telling me?" Katerina's eyes narrowed.

"I'm looking out for you, Kate—" she fell silent, gaze drifting behind Katerina.

"Some ambrosia for the ladies?"

They both smiled at the assistant and grabbed a drink from the tray.

"You asked me to trust you when we got here. I'm asking you to do the same."

"Fine." Katerina let out. "Let me go to the bathroom first."

"Just hurry."

Katerina moved through the cluster of people, careful not to push anyone. Conversations ranged from boasting of their latest conquests, to Rhei's engagement, to swordsmanship, to the citadel, to the casual hatred of her father. *Of course.*

She surveyed the space and caught a glimpse of the restroom sign on the other side of the taverna.

"Never in my life did I foresee that Rhei would be the one to marry."

"Right? My coin was always on Nik and Chryssa."

Nik and Chryssa? She stopped, dusting her pants and fixing some parts of her shirt that didn't need fixing.

"True. But I don't blame the bastard though for ending it."

"Perhaps. But Chryssa is a smoke show, it'd be hard for me to end a six-year relationship, especially with her."

Savior... I need to keep walking. Not my business...

"Yet you weren't the one to get humiliated."

A chill ran down as spine as she ran out of things to fix. She dropped down to wipe smudges off her boots.

"I might go for it, see if she likes a Scout rather than a Bowman."

Katerina resisted a snort and kept walking. *Not my problem to dwell on.*

Oddly enough, she found the people normal compared to how her father painted them during mass. *That's until they know who you are.* One of the things she was most grateful for was her father's adamancy in keeping her anonymity, to an extent.

The people here knew Jezebelle. She'd been paraded with her father when doing diplomatic events outside the capital territory. Katerina protested. She truly did. *How was it that the eldest child got to be hidden, while the youngest got to explore the world?* But now... she relished the partial anonymity. But then again, everyone here *knew* Jezebelle... *they knew Jezebelle.* Katerina's chest caved. *How would they react once Rhei walked through those doors with her in his arms?*

She reached the wooden entrance to the bathroom, only to find it locked. *Great.* Rubbing her temples, she turned back.

Her attention drifted to the man playing music on the stage. The way he poured his heart and soul into each beat, entranced by the rhythmic melodies, is one she envied. Katerina suppressed the feeling before it could rise to the surface and surveyed the room for Jasmine.

Her eyes fell on Chryssa in a corner of the taverna. Her attention fixed on a tall, blonde man with a face scar and a bow hanging from his back. *Not your problem. Keep walking.*

She does, but couldn't help glancing subtly in their direction.

Nik looked serious, even as she caressed his face. *Does the man even*—she dismissed the question, remembering the comments from earlier. *Six years... in the flesh.* Chryssa's lips reached up to meet his, kissing him. Yet, his eyes landed on Katerina.

She tore her gaze away, heat rushing up her cheeks, and rushed back to Jasmine.

"About time." Jasmine said. "Let's go."

Katerina followed her to the door, avoiding looking back at Nik or Chryssa.

"Jasmine?"

They turned. A strong, copper-haired man with a slight beard and an Olympian crest pinned to his chest stood before them, his steel-grey eyes pinned on Jasmine.

Jasmine's brows furrowed, eyeing Katerina for a brief moment before turning back to him. "I'm sorry. Do I know you?"

His brows rose, and a pained expression washed over him. "You don't remember me?"

Jasmine bit her lip, eyes narrowing on him. "I'm sorry." She shook her head. "Am I supposed to?"

"Jasmine... it's me. *Argus.*" His eyes searched hers rather urgently. "If you just give me a minute."

Jasmine shook her head again. "You must have me confused with someone else. I must be going, but I bid you good night."

"Please." He reached for her hand.

"She said good night." Katerina interjected.

"I just need a minute of your time," Argus insisted, ignoring Katerina completely.

"I suggest you entertain someone else," Katerina sneered.

He turned to Katerina, eyebrows raised.

"What do you want?" Katerina added before he could speak.

"I would like a moment with my *wife.*"

"Wife?" Jasmine laughed. "You surely have me mistaken, sir."

He grabbed her arms, eyes unrelenting as she drew a shallow breath. "Please." He whispered. "*Amoritzie*, please... surely you didn't forget about me. I searched for you for years... I am your husband."

"My husband is dead." She snapped, visible tears on the verge of spilling. "Good for you for reading the history scrolls and post-war memoriam."

Jasmine turned to Katerina, jerking her arm away from his grasp. "We're leaving, and that is the end of it."

Without any hesitation or further inquiry, Katerina followed her back to the Fortress.

Stone walls surrounded Katerina, decorated with ivy vines. The body of water in the middle of the bathhouse was massive and lit by blue orbs at the bottom with a clear view to the sky above. The place was empty. *Peaceful.* Cold stone pressed against her bare feet, sending shivers down her spine.

She let her nightgown fall at her feet and submerged her body into the warm waters. It'd been ages since she had mustered the courage to come here since her mother's passing. It was designed and built by her... *Don't mourn. She is with you always.*

Images from their walk back surfaced, focusing on the man... *Argus,* and how he called Jasmine his wife. She tilted her head back against the stone. *The audacity of people—taking advantage of a vulnerable situation. Makes me think of how Byorn took advantage of—this isn't about you.* She suppressed the thought. *I didn't come here to dwell.*

She didn't know if it was the man, the place or the combination of it all, but she couldn't go back, even if Chryssa asked her to. It was too risky. Besides, she didn't need to witness any public displays of affection if she could help it.

She closed her eyes, allowing her mind to wander into a peaceful abyss.

"My chest swells with pride as I present to you, my offering." He extended a hand to the back of the split.

A wave of ice-cold chills ran through my bones as I laid eyes on a bound, small, delicate woman with golden brown hair and warm ivory skin in a celeste-colored dress.

Jezebelle.

Her body pulled forward by the chains binding her hands. Nothing but pure horror was plastered over her face.

"The daughter of the Heretic."

Katerina opened her eyes. *Breathe.* She ran her hands through her face. *You're okay. Jezebelle is okay...* Frustration stirred within her. *You're home safe. You can relax.*

She looked down at the crystalline waters as crimson spread out of her, stinging her back. Her mouth dried.

"He was going to kill—"

A crack against my back had me arching as burning pain spread through me. I clenched my teeth but I couldn't stop the cry that escaped my lips.

"Don't interrupt me." He said calmly. "Word of this got to Windermere. If it weren't for one of my council members intervening," he hesitated. "This stunt could've cost me."

Another lick of the whip. I bit my lip as hard as I could to mask the pain but it was futile. The taste of iron coated my tongue.. Burning, sharp pain rippled through me again.

"You want to become a Re'Veillite, don't you?"

Crack.

"Yes," I croaked.

"That is hanging by a thin thread. Don't think for a second that I can't pull away the induction. I don't care if it's the day of, or if you are standing at the fucking altar. One more stunt and you can kiss that dream goodbye. In fact, next time, it'll be Jezebelle taking your place while you watch."

She rubbed her eyes as hard as she could. *Please. Just stop.* Tears sprung out as her eyes adjusted to the bathhouse, supporting herself on the edge of the pool. A cool breeze caressed her skin. *I need a way out.* She breathed. Ice gathered on her palms. The room around her darkened, and her vision blurred.

Savior help me...

TWENTY-NINE

"SURELY YOU UNDERSTAND THE PREDICAMENT THIS puts us in." Khir implored. "It was a miracle they arrived when they did but imagine if—"

"We don't have to go into none of that." Dremian waved him off. "It's great that our men were able to defend the Outpost. But we need to focus on developing a defense and offense strategy. It's only a matter of time before they strike again."

The six counselors sat around the table, while Joseph drummed his fingers atop it. All of them spoke at once, their voices an endless thrum that banged against his temples.

The morning light, no matter how gentle it filtered through the room, seared his eyes, intensifying the throbbing in his head. His hands felt rougher than usual, more calloused. He thought that even the lightest of touches could break the table in half. *And this was only part of the power?*

"You speak as if you know our modus operandi regarding these sorts of things." Khir sneered. "They are not the first to attack, nor will they be the last."

"Then what do you propose we do, Khir?" Joseph asked coldly, turning to him. "You did want Vern's position, did you not?"

"Yes, Sovereign." He gulped, evidently feigning confidence.

"Then speak."

"Sir, if I may," Mare interjected, and Joseph stared at him expectantly. "Our men got captured. The ones who delivered the package. Informants say that they are currently being held hostage by some Olympian soldiers or maybe even Zeus himself."

Joseph shrugged. "And?"

Mare blinked. "And... um, they are most likely being tortured for information as we speak."

"It's not like they know anything worthwhile," Joseph retorted, reaching for the decanter of water in front of him. "Besides, there's nothing left of the poison, anyway."

"You will just leave them to die?" Mare gaped.

"Shit luck to allow themselves to get captured." Joseph took a hefty sip. "Unless you rather volunteer yourself for the rescue mission. At this point, they are either dead or soon to be. I won't waste my time on them."

Mare fell silent.

The chamber smelled faintly of smoke and iron, as though the battle had followed them here in the folds of their cloaks.

"We need to return to more urgent matters." Kalio spoke loudest, garnering Joseph's fleeting attention. "The Outpost held, Sovereign. But at what cost? Half the garrison lies dead, and the rest bleed in their cots. This victory cost us greatly."

Joseph traced a crack in the armrest with his finger, feigning interest.

Julius' exposed eye glinted like a knife. "If this is victory, we cannot endure another. I did some research in the Chronicler Wing and it seems that this is their preparation tactic to divert our attention. I am unsure of where they plan to strike but I advise caution in the next few days, specially at the banquet."

"Their assault was probing, nothing more." Khir said. "If they attack with full force, which I don't doubt they will and it's only a matter of time when they do, we will not have enough men."

Xaden slammed his palm flat on the table. The sound reverberated, irritating in its insistence. "Then let us take the fight to them! Strike now, before they gather their strength again. We should not wait to be bled dry."

Always so eager. He should be tending to the evening mass, not intruding in this. Then again, I did appoint him as a council member. Joseph shook his head. *For some another time.*

Dremian's voice threaded between the clamor, softer, but weighted with thought. "Sovereign, the scouts say their banners still linger beyond the ridges. They test us, yes, but their losses were heavy as well. If we prepare wisely, we can choose the ground and bleed them further before they ever see our gates."

Kalio stroked his beard, as though the gesture alone added importance to his worthless words. "He speaks sense, Sovereign. Yet every drop of blood spilled at the outpost was the blood of our brethren. We cannot squander the lives left to us."

Julius leaned forward, his eye burning with the fire of the desperate. "Then let me go to the sister strongholds in Windermere and Sylene. Let me call their men. If each sends at least a battalion or a company, we can replace those lost and face them with unrelenting strength."

Their gazes slid toward Joseph again, expectantly.

Joseph sighed, slow, letting the weight of the silence hang until it frayed at the edges. "We defended the outpost, and yet you mourn as if we lost it. Raise your fucking companies, plan your damned counterstrikes. Do what makes you sleep easier. The dead will not return, and the living will only march to join them."

Their faces twisted with what Joseph presumed was offense, disbelief, or maybe even surprise. But he didn't care enough to read them clearly. "Victory, defeat," he waved a hand, dismissing both as though they were gnats. "It is all the same. One leaves us weaker, the other merely delays the inevitable."

The council fell back into argument, voices rising again in the hollow chamber. Joseph leaned against his hand, letting their words wash into nothing, already weary of the noise.

"Sovereign," the Verenna's voice cut through, moving toward Joseph.

Fuck. I forgot she was even in the fucking room.

The council's bickering dulled in his ears as he turned toward her. She stood apart, ruby robes heavy with gold thread, her presence carved from poise and reverence. "The Acrailerion cannot remain unattended. The Denai's seat is still empty. As you know, that is our Liaison in matters of faith and governance. The country trembles, Sovereign. Will you address this?"

"The Denai." Joseph leaned against the armrest, letting the word fall from his lips as if tasting something bland. "Another name, another face beside yours. What will it matter when the soil is painted in blood?"

Her gaze didn't shift. "It matters because absence breeds weakness. Without a Denai, the Acrailerion's will is fractured. Orders hesitate. Our hands falter. And when faith falters, Sovereign, so too does loyalty."

The council's voices rose behind him—Dremian urging a strategic approach, Mare mumbling of restraint—but he kept his eyes on the Verenna. She didn't waver in the slightest.

"You have candidates, I assume," he said at last. "Pick one. Wrap them in your silks, whisper your prayers, and call them Denai. It changes nothing."

Something hardened in her eyes. She stepped closer. "*Nothing.* Yes, that is the word you clung to when your predecessor ruled. You called every decree tyrannical, every command toxic, every law inhumane. You spat upon his name. Yet here you sit, weaving the same chains you so despised."

The council fell silent as her voice carried like judgment through the chamber.

"Do you think he lies restless in his grave? No, he welcomes you as his true successor, proud of the abomination you've become. You smear further filth upon what his grandfather carved in blood and—" Her voice broke. Not from hesitation, but because he willed it.

He hadn't raised a hand or spoken a word aloud, yet power rippled out like an uncalled storm. The torches along the walls guttered, and shadows stretched across the chamber.

Her lips moved, but no sound came. Her eyes widened, nothing but horror carved lines where composure once lived.

The councilors recoiled, some stiffened. Dremian's bravado shriveled. Even the eldest in council, braced for the earth to crack and swallow them whole.

Only Joseph remained calm. "From this moment forth, you will not speak unless *I* allow it. Not here. Not in your temple. Not even at my daughter's fucking ceremony. Your tongue belongs to me now." He said low and steady. Yet heavy with a weight his counselors had never heard before.

The silence that followed was absolute. The braziers hissed softly, but even flame seemed subdued.

The Verenna clutched her throat, trembling, fury smoldering in her eyes but trapped by his command.

Joseph saw the power coiled around her like unseen chains, bending even her will to silence.

He leaned forward slightly, letting his gaze sweep the room. "Do you understand now?" His voice sounded deeper than it should have. "Your treacherous faith does not command me. Tradition does not bind me. I am no man's heir. I am something greater. I am what Quinn *wished* he was."

None of them answered. None dared.

The Verenna bowed her head, stiff, humiliated—but bound. The council stared at him as though seeing him for the first time, their fear laid bare in their silence.

"And for you," he turned to Khir, eyes venomous. "Disrespect me again, and you'll meet a fate worse than death."

Khir's face drained of color, and bowed his head.

Joseph sat back, calm, almost bored. "Now," he murmured, dismissive, "continue your bickering. Let's see who dares to raise their voice again."

Yet, no one did. Seven sets of eyes remained fixed on him as if waiting for something more. As if scared he would unleash his wrath upon them. His turned to Dremian, singling him out.

"Tighten security around the Fortress. The night of the banquet will be their moment. Governess Kiarelli believes in spectacle. She will not waste the chance to strike when we gather, dressed in silks and drowning in cheap wine."

A ripple of unease spread among them, glancing at one another. All shifted in their seats.

"You will see it done. Double the guard at the gates. Search every servant, every guest, every crate that crosses the threshold. If she is as cunning as I know her to be, she will not strike with swords at the walls, but with daggers at our throats and perhaps poison in our drinks."

Dremian bowed his head, grave. "It will be done, Sovereign."

"She confirmed attendance?" Kalio asked, surprised.

Joseph nodded. "I received her correspondence this morning." He leaned back, resting his chin against his knuckles. "Let the banquet play its course. Let the governess come. We will toast in her honor while she tightens the noose around her own neck."

THE INFIRMARY'S SIGNATURE SCENT OF INCENSE AND burnt herbs was more intense than before, yet nothing could mask the unease that gnawed at Zeus as he stared at Apollo stretched upon a frail cot, his golden skin dulled to a pallor. His chest rose shallowly, each breath weaker than the last. Asclepius's hands trembled as he traced Apollo's pulse; his brow furrowed deeper with each silent moment of study.

"I don't understand," he murmured.

"Is this similar to what happened to the soldiers at the outpost?" Zeus asked.

He shook his head, pursing his lips. "The soldiers were poisoned; there's no doubt about it. Their flesh was actively and rapidly decaying. He, on the other hand, is still alive. Barely, but still alive."

Zeus' gaze flickered to Apollo's face, and a hint of regret stirred within him. *I caused this. If it weren't because I was so hell-bent on his culpability... on his involvement with the fucking Sovereign, he wouldn't be in this situation to begin with.* And admitting that Artemis was right was not something he wasn't keen on doing.

Asclepius's confusion burned through Zeus, feeding a fire he couldn't contain.

On the other side of Apollo, Ares stood rigid, arms folded, his eyes dark as storm clouds. He did not shift or blink, only watched with the intensity of a predator scenting blood.

"He fell like a worthless mortal and, even on his deathbed, he gets the favorite's special." Ares muttered.

Zeus' teeth ground at his remark, but he didn't scold him. Ares was right in a sense. Soldiers blessed by Zeus carried into war under the mantle of divinity, and yet still they fell broken, their cries no different from any man's.

Apollo was no shadow of divinity. Yet, he fucking fell. By whose hands? He's yet to know, but he was close. He could sense it.

Zeus drew closer, irritation clawing at his temples. "Then what does this mean? If only a god can deliver such harm, then who?" *I know the thing that revealed itself to me was responsible for Apollo, but I can't seem to recall its name nor origin...*

Asclepius dropped his gaze. His silence was answer enough.

Ares' voice broke the silence. "Or perhaps one of those monsters in Tartarus finally had enough of him playing his lyre."

The thought hit Zeus, chilling the fire in his veins.

"And where were *you*?" Zeus asked outright. "You were tasked with watching him in Tartarus, keeping note of his wellbeing. Is this what you call vigilance?"

Ares' gaze didn't waver, though his jaw tightened. "I watched," he said, voice clipped. "But Tartarus is no mere prison —it bends even gods. And I already told you, I knew nothing."

"Don't turn this back upon me," Zeus snapped, taking a step closer to him until the air vibrated with his anger. "You've always had a vendetta against him."

"You're saying I did this to him?" Ares cocked an eyebrow.

"I wouldn't put it past you. You said it yourself; even on his deathbed, he's still getting the favorite's special."

For a moment, a flicker of challenge crossed his war-hardened features. Or maybe Zeus was getting under his skin. Ares always wanted to be among Zeus' favorite offspring. But alas...

"As I said, I knew nothing. Perhaps, you should turn your attention to finding out who wanted him silenced."

"And who might that be?"

"The fuck should I know." Ares hissed. "I've been just as busy as you and Argus with the threat in the mortal lands to be wasting my time on babysitting duty."

Zeus loomed over him. "You failed in your duty, Ares, no matter how fucking basic it was. You're useless to me."

Ares' lips pressed into a thin line. The silence that followed was broken only by Apollo's shallow breaths, each one a reminder of the mystery that gnawed at them all. And still, Zeus' fury grew.

MOONLIGHT PRESIDED OVER THE CELESTIAL OLYMPIAN Archives as Zeus buried himself in piles upon piles of research tomes. The Archives wasn't a place he frequented, he never had a reason to. Yet, things change.

Mnemosyne provided everything she had of The Paragons of Light, including a sheet of her personal notes, in hopes that it would aid in his search.

He had asked her to keep quiet about his presence here; since he didn't want anyone inquiring about what he'd found and fueling potential theories that led nowhere and caused further delays. But one thing was certain, Ares knew more than he was letting on.

His demeanor alone was cause for concern. Yet, Zeus didn't have enough evidence or details as to Ares' intentions. He'd been aiding Zeus and Argus in their investigation, despite how Ares felt about Argus. He'd been there. He'd helped.

But then, how else would someone explain Apollo's state under his watch? Zeus flipped through some more pages. Tartarus was a ruthless place, even to the gods. Perhaps Apollo was just unlucky, and a monster did actually get to him, hence the state of distress... *someone did get to him. But fucking who? Who lurked in the shadows? Who called me scum? Who is able to jump back and forth between Tartarus and the mortal lands?*

An exasperated sigh escaped his lips. He picked up a parchment to suppress his thoughts and then considered all possible avenues to compare with Argus' information once he returned from meeting up with Dremian. Supposedly, it was regarding Joseph. Argus didn't go into details, but it seemed urgent.

Zeus focused on the parchment and researched as if he were back at square one.

A Detailed Account of The Paragons of Light, as recorded by Mnemosyne.

All events detailed in this record are based on compiled information from countless sources, including interviews, articles, and notable correspondence.

The Paragons of Light was founded by Weston McClaren, *the son of the late-Governor of Castelencia, Tomassec McClaren.*

Weston's aspiration was to continue his father's legacy; however, the role was given to Harrison, for reasons that have not been documented, despite Weston being the eldest. He consistently sought his father's approval, hoping to persuade him to acknowledge his claim to the governorship.

Weston believed he possessed superior mental acuity and charisma compared to Harrison; however, Tomassec was unconvinced due to his son's worrisome ambition for dominance and control, as well as his self-serving perspectives. Weston subsequently visited the Pantheon of Olympian Trifecta in Central Caverest, a local place of worship dedicated to Zeus, Poseidon, and Hades, and sought divine guidance due to his rage.

However, based on his statements and accusations later on, his prayers went unanswered. Following several days, he attained enlightenment from a divine entity during one of his nightly prayers, who offered him power and influence contingent upon his worship and unwavering loyalty.

Weston preached in the streets for days, subjected to public scrutiny and painted him as a fool. He was labeled as the deranged son of the Governor. Therefore, his father disinherited him because of the damage to his family name, which intensified his anger.

In Belsir, CA, he settled, impoverished and bitter, and during a moment of introspection, the same divine being materialized before him and beseeched him to persevere, to swear allegiance, and he would attain the power and influence he craved.

On the eve of Veneration Night (the 30th day of Seraphine), Weston renounced the McClaren surname and adopted the Petrakis surname.

Weston, resolute in his conviction to disprove his family's beliefs, returned to Central Caverest, where he delivered sermons continuously. Recognizing his relationship with the Governor, the public began to heed his critiques of the McClaren Government's corrupt practices. Gradually, the Castelenian populace started to accept his sermons, and they began to refer to him as the Seer of Light, given that all his prophecies appeared to be fulfilled.

Weston claimed that those who joined him would see the truth behind the corrupt curtains of the government, continuously kicking dirt toward his former family's name. Furthermore, Weston declared that those who join him will also see through the facade of following Olympian guidance, using his own unanswered prayers as leverage to lure them to his side.

Driven by ambition, he urged his followers to relocate to Belsir, seeking purification from perceived corruption and ultimately, spiritual redemption. Thus, sealing a faith to an unseen entity and creating the first divided faith in Eseron's history.

Historical accounts indicate that 200 individuals initially accompanied him, establishing a settlement in Belsir and forming the baseline of their community. They increased exponentially within a year, thereby attracting the attention of the McClaren government.

Community members were allowed to leave, with the understanding that such action constituted treason punishable by death, based on Weston's Solstice Sermon's statement: "Why would anyone rebel and act against the Seer of Light, the highest form of the Divine?" In that same sermon, he anointed his followers as The Paragons of Light, thus solidifying the name of the group.

Belsir was situated northeast of Castelencia and became the second most secure territory, trailing closely after the McClaren Estate. The territory encompassed slightly more than a thousand acres and accommodated 5,000 residents, accessible via a single point of entry and exit. Armed personnel were stationed in watchtowers at each corner of the compound, with others patrolling the perimeter. Belsir was self-sufficient with its internal security, agriculture, marketplaces, private homes, and government. The regulations enforced by the Governor were not effective within their enclave.

Weston created the Light Militia, composed of drafted men between the ages of 18 and 40. Their crest was designed based on the Paragons of Light's sun emblem. With the motto "Strength of the People" underneath.

At the heart of the grounds, they built the Temple of Light, an establishment made of volakas marble with glass vaulted ceilings and a large mahogany entrance, meant for the worship of their Savior.

The McClarens were prohibited from entering the premises without authorization and, if granted entry, were required to be accompanied by security personnel and remain on the designated route. Upon entering the compound, the McClarens were subjected to death threats, insults, and a barrage of hateful comments.

It is recorded that the McClarens never returned to the compound after their first visit.

With the passage of time, people met their demise, and others were swayed by his influence. He engaged in sexual relations with several women, and should a child not be perceived as the chosen one, he would order the women to terminate the pregnancies or face execution for violating divine decree.

It is recorded that Weston married a woman named Nulia Sue and had one offspring, <u>Marcus Petrakis</u>.

As Marcus matured, Weston commenced his instruction, initiating him into the practices of the Seer of Light and preparing him for his eventual role, which included allowing his son to participate in public ceremonies. The group members considered Weston, followed by Marcus, as figures of immense authority, divinely endowed with foresight and understanding.

Additional Notable Contributions:
The Institute of Enlightenment - an educational establishment for children ages 10 to 18 that lived in Belsir.

At the age of 87, Weston passed away, leaving Marcus the legacy and a mother to care for.
Marcus became the Sovereign of the Paragons of Light and,

based on what he learned from his father, refused to be in touch with his cousin, Governess Juliette McClaren (daughter of Harrison McClaren and Iliana Belvoir).

He wished to have a higher degree of structure and command over the area. Consequently, he implemented a curfew for his populace and dictated their attire and diet, cloaked in the guise of a divine revelation. Masses, which had been monthly, were then held weekly, and occasionally, he delivered sermons daily to influence his adherents further. At the time of a person's death, he would offer a blessing over the body before consigning it to flames for the purpose of cleansing.

Soon after implementing the new guidance, he met his wife, Cynthia DeMarque.

Marcus and Cynthia conceived four children: <u>Sebastian Petrakis, Theresa Petrakis, Quinn Petrakis, and Bernadette Petrakis</u>; and adopted one orphan: <u>Joseph Argyros.</u>

Out of the offspring, only Bernadette, Quinn and Joseph decided to follow in Marcus' footsteps. Upon being renounced by his two eldest children, Marcus ordered their incarceration and execution, even as Cynthia begged him to spare them, offering her own life in their stead. Marcus refused.

> Note: It is recorded that on the night of their incarceration, Cynthia snuck into the dungeons and set Sebastian and Theresa free, guiding them through the grounds toward a hidden passage on the outskirts of the compound. She warned them to disappear and never to come back.
>
> -Source requested to remain anonymous at the time of the chronicle.

Marcus executed Cynthia for treason, and he named Quinn his official successor. Joseph was to become Quinn's advisor, and

Bernadette would spend her time inside the Acrailerion to remain pure and uncorrupted as a Denai.

Notable Contributions:

Extension of the Institute of Enlightenment - allowed students to engage in higher education until graduating at age 21.

The Trials - a post-graduation requirement for all graduates of the Institute of Enlightenment for job assignment inside the compound.

Age Restrictions - for an individual to be considered an adult inside the compound, they must be 21 years of age. This guidance supersedes the guidance of 18 being the defining age of adulthood.

The Acrailerion - a convent dedicated to keeping women pure and sanctified and a place of worship for their Savior, located in a secluded location out of Belsir.

Marcus was killed at the age of 58 by order of the Governess, thus making Quinn the Sovereign at age 27.

When Quinn became the Sovereign, he decided to be more ambitious and, alongside Joseph, began planning for the downfall of the McClaren Government through the execution of their Governess and offspring, <u>Frederick Gilderoy-McClaren</u>.

Post-War Note: It is recorded that an entity had visited him and asked him to devote his life to it, and It'll grant him the power to control destructive winds and fire, with two conditions: <u>he must keep her identity a secret, and she warned him that his line may not die.</u>

With this newly acquired power, Quinn personally executed

Juliette McClaren and took control of Castelencia as a whole, establishing the Paragons of Light as the official government.

Following Bernadette's execution for treason, the people's fear of him resulted in their compliance with his every directive.

He ordered the destruction of the Olympian temples, statues, and agoras across Caverest and to only leave the Temple of Light untouched, under the guise of cleansing the world from the wicked. After the first temple went up in flames, an overwhelming sense of power engulfed his being. Feeling unstoppable, he planned and executed an attack on Mount Olympus.

War was officially declared.

ZEUS TOOK A MOMENT AND WENT BACK TO THE previous paragraphs. *It's evident that Eris had a hand in all of this. Based on her history, I wouldn't be surprised if she was the one crafting all this chaos. Most likely, she was the driving force. But the power Quinn was given didn't seem to be the same as Joseph's... or perhaps he hadn't gotten to that level yet?*

"The power to control destructive winds and fire..." Zeus muttered. *This was to Quinn. Not to Joseph. But I don't remember Quinn putting up a fight at all...*

Zeus kept reading.

Note: there are no official records of the war between the Paragons of Light and the Olympian Gods. Please read the following carefully, as it is a recount based on survivors of the war and former members of the Paragons of Light.

During a late-night mass, Quinn preached to the congregation inside the Temple of Light, when in the middle of a sermon, pieces of wood and metal flew across the room as the entrance blew off its hinges, making Quinn halt and the congregation freeze.

Ares, the Commander of the Blood Legion, stood in the doorway. An air of arrogance and superiority surrounded him as he walked through the fearful crowd, soldiers piling through behind him. His face was hidden behind a black Corinthian helmet that matched his cuirass.

Quinn addressed Ares, but the god of war implored him to continue with the sermon. The thunderous rain intensified, drowning the muffled screams coming from outside the palace of worship.

While Ares hovered around the altar, Quinn addressed the congregation, cautiously holding onto each other, tightening their grips. "May Apollo guide us in this uncertain time. May he grant us strength and light in the times of utter darkness... praise be to Apollo."

This was the first recorded time where Apollo's name was mentioned in their worship, according to validated sources.

Ares took hold of a young woman, pulling her out of her seat and using her as leverage to make Quinn succumb and surrender before bloodshed was ensued.

"Whatever it is you're looking for, you won't find it here," Quinn stated, attempting to bring the woman back to safety.

"Aren't I?" Ares taunted as he traced a dagger against the woman's face and neck. Tears streamed uncontrollably down her face. "You think you can force your way into our grounds and leave unscathed?"

Quinn froze and mumbled under his breath repeatedly, growing more irritated each time, only to find out that the power he was given had vanished entirely.

"I'm not one for diplomacy, so I will only ask you once." Ares said as tears streamed uncontrollably down the woman's face. "Where is Rena Vitalis?"

Quinn remained silent for a moment, eyes scanning the congregation. "Who?"

Ares scoffed, applying pressure onto the blade, warm blood trickling down the woman's neck, staining her dress. Her cries intensified.

"Alright! Enough! Please!" Quinn pleaded, but the Commander continued. "I don't know who that is! I swear it!"

"Pity." In a swift, practiced movement, Ares slashed her throat, covering his armor with blood. Dropping her limp body, he turned to his men.

Screams and gasps echoed from the crowd, while some prayed for their salvation in silence.

"Barricade the doors." He said, standing as the woman bled out behind him. They could not help but look over Ares' shoulder as they obeyed. Her body twitched sporadically.

Quinn drew in a sharp breath as his trembling hand sneaked into his pocket, securing a capsule in his palm. He muttered under his breath and popped the capsule into his mouth, crushing it with his teeth and sending him into instant shock. His body collapsed as foam pooled out of his mouth. The crowd went wild, and Ares remained unfazed.

"You're a Monster!"

"We're all going to die!"

"Where's Jenny?!"

"Murderer!"

"We need to get out of here!"

"Not so high and mighty now, are you?" Ares smirked, addressing the crowd. "Kill them all."

The crowd, consumed by fear, fled as he walked toward the exit, slashing anyone that got in his way. Screams of agony echoed; puddles of blood soaked the concrete pavement. Men revolted against the soldiers, causing bloodshed to increase as they collapsed and rogue flames ignited the Temple.

He lost his power... how? And who the hell is Rena and why was Ares after her? Zeus flipped back through the parchment, finding the vow Quinn had taken and the conditions.

"It is recorded that an entity had visited him and asked him to devote his life to it, and it'll grant him the power to control destructive winds and fire, with two conditions: <u>he must keep its identity a secret, and she warned him that his line may not die.</u>" He read. "But he never revealed it's identity..." he keep sorting through the text. *He didn't do anything to violate the—wait.*

"His line may not die..." He muttered as realization hit him. She wasn't warning him that his line would be immortal; she warned him that his line could not die, by his hand, or else he would lose his power... and Bernadette was publicly executed for treason. *Fucking Eris and her loopholes. This thing she is working for doesn't want him to keep his power for long, and it knew that Quinn would fall eventually... But how did Joseph get in power? How the hell...* Zeus flipped back to where he'd left off.

The Olympian Army scattered and seized each building, raiding everything they considered of value and burning the rest. Wild embers consumed everything in their path, building upon the sea of smoke and flame that threatened to devour a once sacred village rapidly being mutilated and warped into rubble and ruin.

Men, women, and children alike could be seen fleeing from all parts of the village. The Temple of Light, the town's eternal symbol of protection and hope, had succumbed to the raging fire. On the streets, a crazed fanatic ranted on about the end times, about a great uprising, a fallen kingdom. A New Order.

"Commander!" A soldier rushed toward Ares, wiping the water off his face. "One of our scouts spotted a woman with what appears

to be a baby in the Liverfront Forest. Do I give the order to kill on sight?"

"No." He smirked. "Let me have her." He jumped onto his horse and rode toward the Forest.

It is recorded that Belsir turned into ruins. Quinn and the Paragons of Light became a Castelenian myth, and since Quinn never married or had any children, his line died with him. However, sources state that before his death, Quinn made a pact with Joseph Argyros that in the event that he died, Argyros would carry on with the legacy and pledge fealty to the entity, who then would be granted the power of destructive winds and fire under the same conditions; but no official confirmation has been made at the time of this chronicle.

End of Account.

"DESTRUCTIVE WINDS AND FIRE..." ZEUS PICKED UP THE parchment displaying the symbol of the Paragons of Light.

A sun. At first glance it's just a sun. But upon closer inspection...

Two snakes atop.

A snake tail at the bottom.

A lightning bolt at the bottom right.

A spiral in its center, surrounded by spikes.

It's not a Gorgon... even if the presence of snakes is all too evident. What is the purpose behind the lightning bolt?

"Destructive winds and fire..." Zeus repeated, eyes focusing on the emblem. "Destructive winds and... fire... lightning bolts... open cell in Tartarus... divine entity... monsters..."

"I don't understand," Asclepius murmured.

"Is this similar to what happened to the soldiers at the outpost?" I asked.

He shook his head, pursing his lips. "The soldiers were poisoned; there's no doubt about it. Their flesh was actively and rapidly decaying. He, on the other hand, is still alive. Barely, but still alive."

"Snakes... lightning bolt... snakes... lightning bolt... spiral... darkness... monster...sna—" Zeus's stomach plummeted, ice slithered down his spine.

Typhon.

"Took you long enough."

Zeus bolted upright. *How are you in my head?*

CHAPTER
THIRTY-ONE
KATERINA

"MAYBE IT'LL BE SOMETHING TO LOOK INTO," JASMINE said as they moved through the array of people inside the Fortress' Great Hall.

White and amber hues emanated from the towering columns adorned with lavish décor and lanterns that hung from the high ceiling, along with a large, luxurious ruby carpet that led to the grand throne, bathed in warm light. *Father sure does like to be the center of attention...* harmonious melodies spread around the room along with the leaders of each of the countries and their respective guests in their respective colors, who mingled as they awaited the arrival of her father.

"Perhaps," Katerina replied, offering a smile to a passing Aeshite woman in a sage and amaranth gown, then addressed Jasmine again. "Have you talked to Jezy lately?"

Jasmine shook her head and then provided gentle nods of greeting as they passed the first batch of elaborate tapestries that depicted radiant suns and scenes of prosperity that lined the walls.

Heaviness sank into Katerina's chest as she replayed their last conversation and the absolute disappointment—no, *betrayal*—she felt.

"The last time I saw her was in the Rena Gardens," Jasmine added.

"Was she alone or with Rhei?" *I wouldn't want her to talk about this with him, of all people.*

"I couldn't tell. I just saw her in passing." Jasmine pursed her lips.

Katerina opened her mouth to ask about her looking into Rhei, but she couldn't help but ask in a hushed voice. "So... what's the story behind the guys from last night?"

"I am just as confused as you are," Jasmine admitted.

"You've never spoken about your husband or his passing..."

"It's not the kind of pain I wish to remember, and this is hardly the place for this kind of conversation."

"Would you rather mingle with the Aeshites, Sylenians, or Windermerians?"

"You know what I mean, Kate." Jasmine gave her a subtle nod.

Katerina looked around them, everyone was entangled in their own conversations. "I don't. It's not like anyone is paying attention to us."

Jasmine drew a sharp breath and patted down her ruby gown. "My husband died during the war. We met while I was still at the Acrailerion." She hesitated. "He sacrificed himself to save me, and the next thing I remember, he was gone, and I was back in the convent."

"But didn't you like being in the Acrailerion?" Katerina's eyebrows furrowed.

"I liked my freedom more. But that's a conversation for another time." Her gaze trailed behind Katerina.

She turned and noticed a snow-haired man in a refined white and black ensemble approaching them. His presence made her table the questions that still lingered.

"Katerina, you're a sight for sore eyes." He beamed, voice raspy.

"Governor Lazaros," Katerina bowed. "Indeed. It has been long since our last encounter."

He swatted at the air. "No need for such formalities, dear. Come here." He pulled her in for a warm embrace.

"My dear," he turned to Jasmine. His grey eyes fell on her exposed golden locks braided to her crown. "Aren't you supposed to be in your *special* attire?"

"I retired." Jasmine said. "My time as a High Re'Veillite is long over. Now, I have the pleasure of being a part of other pursuits."

"Ah. I have no doubt that you are excellent wherever you're serving now."

Jasmine smiled in gratitude.

"Would you mind giving us a moment, my dear?"

"Not at all, please." Jasmine bowed and dismissed herself.

Katerina glanced at her as she approached a group of people in indigo and silver attire—*Sylenians.*

"Walk with me, dear." The governor offered his arm, and they walked through the sea of people. "How have you been? How are things here with your father?"

Terrible. Disgusting. Atrocious. She kept her face gentle and unfeeling; remembering her role in these sorts of events. "Everything has been great. My sister is soon to be married, and I am to join the Re'Veillites. I couldn't ask for more, if I'm honest."

"Good. What about the incident? How are you feeling?"

Her brows furrowed, and the confusion must've been displayed clearly on Katerina's face since he immediately clarified. "I heard about what happened at the Helios Agora."

Her stomach twisted.

"It is absolutely preposterous that after all this time people still attempt to pass as either you or your sister, just to besmirch our faith and what we do."

That's what he meant about my situation being rectified. "It is a struggle, but we do our best not to entertain this sort of... situation." *What innocent life did he take in my stead?*

"Savior only knows what fate lies in their tainted lives." He shook his head lightly. "But enough of that; you are well, and that's what's important."

"I appreciate your concern." She smiled in an attempt to stop the guilt that bloomed in her chest.

"I'm going to be frank with you, my dear." They stopped far enough for them to be out of earshot. "I know you are aware of the alliance between our families, so I will spare you the historics. You mentioned that your sister is to be married. Have you ever considered the possibility of it for yourself?"

Once. "It's not something I've considered recently given my soon-to-be position at the Acrailerion."

"Of course, my dear." His calloused hands grasped her gently. "I truly believe that a union between our families ought to be of great benefit to you. Dare I say, *far* more beneficial than anything the Acrailerion might offer. Yes, a Re'Veillite position as a—which one are you aiming toward?"

She resisted the urge to roll her eyes and kept her face graceful, polite. "Naturopath..."

He surveyed her for a moment, unsure of what lingered behind his eyes. "I see," he smiled lightly, but his tone was wary, perhaps... disappointed? "As I was saying. A Re'Veillite position is highly coveted and respected. As a Naturopath, I'm sure you'll be able to heal those with black death, mend many wounds, and so on... but I fear that you might be limiting yourself to something greater."

As if I had another choice. "What are you proposing?"

"My son—a fine young man—has had his eyes on you for a very long time. Said it would be beneficial for both our families to solidify our relationship."

"You'd like to invoke the Union Convention?" *I'm going to faint.*

"It doesn't have to get to that, but it is currently on the table. I thought you ought to know."

"I believe that's something you should discuss with my father."

"I fully intend to." He clarified. "However, I want to know if *you* are open to the possibility prior to my conversation with him. I wouldn't want you to feel forced into accepting this."

If you invoke the convention, I will not have a choice at all. Goodbye to my Re'Veillite position. Goodbye to my freedom. Goodbye to the—wait a second. Her mind silenced. "I am grateful for your consideration, Governor, truly."

Perhaps the Union Convention can give me the freedom I seek. No more lashings. No more being under the control of him or the Verenna... I can be free of this place... Yes, it'll be an arranged marriage, but it can't be worse than what I've endured here. Though... I can't recall if I've met him before, it's been awfully long since I've seen the governor.

"Tell you what, my son is soon to arrive." He said, as if he read her mind. "Why don't you take a moment to talk to him? You know, get to know each other a bit, take advantage of the evening."

Maybe... "Of course." She smiled.

The sound of grandiose trumpets made everyone turn to the entrance as the guards announced the arrival of her father. His presence commanded the room, wearing a refined black, gold and red ensemble that showed off what people called his strong age-defiant body, that seemed to send the women here in a damn frenzy.

"I can't believe he is in his sixties."

"The rumors do him justice. He doesn't look a day over thirty."

"If I could just run my hands through that deep dark hair... and those muscles..."

"Even with that five o'clock shadow, he is a handsome man. Sovereign at last."

Katerina almost rolled her eyes at the slur of comments behind her.

"I heard his wife passed away."

Her blood ran cold at the mention of her mother, and it took her a monumental amount of effort not to curse them out. *Temper. Time and Place. Think of what may happen and who will be to blame.*

"Better catch him before he gets swarmed. It was great seeing you, my dear." Governor Lazaros patted her shoulder and left without looking back.

The comments behind her continued, along with silent— well, poor interpretations of silent—bets on who will be able to score her father tonight. *Gross.* Before she gave in to the temptation of telling them off, she left the Great Hall. *I need some air.*

CHAPTER
THIRTY-TWO
JOSEPH

THE HALL GLITTERED WITH LIGHT AND MUSIC DRIFTING from the minstrels, servants weaving between knots of guests, laughter rising like smoke toward the ceiling.

Joseph stood with the three other governors of Eseron in a small circle near the hearth.

"Blessed evening, Sovereign." A servant in a cream and golden robe handed him a goblet of wine.

He nodded in dismissal and brought it to his lips, savoring the tangy taste.

"Good to see you are well." Lazaros smiled.

"Likewise, old friend." Joseph raised the goblet slightly in acknowledgment. "How is everything in Windermere? I heard the Olympian army was establishing a stronghold near the border."

Lazaros leaned in, speaking low but wearing the grin of a man telling some clever jest. "They are... Joseph, times weigh heavy on my country. Famine is pressing us, merchants are muttering of leaving, mainly due to the militarization on every front. They believe we might get attacked..." He hesitated. "I must invoke the Union Convention."

The words were like a blade hidden behind his cordial tone. Joseph took a sip of his wine, feigning amusement. "The Union

Convention," he said as though recalling some old memory. "A matter of blood and legacy. You never expressed this... *difficulty* before, and now you propose joining our lines?"

"Can't blame an old man with pride. Especially one you've known almost all your life." Lazaros chuckled, lifting his cup toward Joseph as if in toast. "Your eldest, Katerina, and my son Byorn. I believe they used to work together at some point, so they should be well acquainted with each other."

Well acquainted is an understatement. Joseph kept his smile fixed, eyes sharp. Around us, a servant passed with a tray of honeyed fruits; he plucked one absently, chewing as though Lazaros' words were not a turning point in the fate of Eseron. But Joseph's chest tightened with an old memory.

Byorn.

And how years ago, when his daughter was still more girl than woman, he had caught them together in the gardens one summer evening. Hands and lips intertwined, voices hushed with that reckless sincerity only youth could conjure.

Byorn had been a fine lad even then, strong of build and steady of spirit, even if he came from a poor family. In the grounds, he was a fine shield-bearer, but Joseph couldn't allow Katerina to throw away her life this recklessly.

So, he ended it swiftly, without hesitation. A sovereign's heir could not squander her hand on sentiment, not when alliances and thrones depended on her future and *purity.* A future that could've easily been ruined by a child out of wedlock.

Joseph remembered the look in her eyes the night he forbade it: hurt, betrayal, the first *real* fracture between them— save for the loss of Rena. And he remembered the silent defiance in Byorn's stare, as though he swore to keep fighting for her.

But knowing people's weaknesses can serve as a great tool of persuasion, and I knew just the thing that would make him turn my way.

If he wanted his father to become governor, if he wanted to

get out of poverty and working as a pitiful shield-bearer... well, he had to do something for Joseph first.

Now, Lazaros spoke of them as if fate itself carved their path toward union. Little did he know that his own son was the sole reason he stood in my presence. *Funny how things play out when you shuffle the cards right.*

Lazaros leaned closer with the ease of an old friend. He gestured idly with his goblet. "You know," he said, his voice light and full of nostalgia, "I've always thought of your eldest as though she were my own daughter. I remember when she was no taller than my knee. Little Kate...chasing sparrows in my garden while you and I debated trade routes."

He laughed softly, a warm, fatherly sound that blends seamlessly into the banquet's din. But Joseph felt the weight of the memory, how neatly he tied the innocence of youth to the bonds he now sought to forge.

"To see her grown, strong and wise," he continued, smiling easily, "is a joy. To see her united with Byorn would not feel foreign—it would feel... *natural*. As though fate had meant it all along."

His words were polished, carrying both affection and the faint sting of claim. Governess Kiarelli arched an eyebrow, and Governess Verois' lips curved into a knowing smile. Looks like they also heard the governor's attempt to fold personal history into political leverage.

Joseph forced a chuckle, though his mind stirred. "And what?" He asked at last, keeping his voice light as though sharing in the amusement, "What would you place upon the table in return?"

Lazaros laughter carried easily, covering the gravity of his reply. "The Smiths. Every forge, every hand that bends steel in my lands. Your armies armed without delay, weapons at your command faster than any rival could dream."

Oh, he's desperate...

Both governesses in the circle nodded as though humored by

a pleasant anecdote, but their eyes betrayed their calculations. Music swelled behind us; dancers spun, oblivious.

Joseph swirled the wine and allowed a thin smile to curl his lips and a chuckle to slip out, and met Lazaros' eyes over the rim of his cup.

"Strange, is it not?" Joseph said lightly. "How paths we once closed find their way back to us again?"

"Can't mess with fate, I'm afraid. No matter how hard we try." Lazaros sipped his cup.

Joseph's fingers tightened around the goblet. *To refuse again would be easy, instinctual. Yet I could not ignore the bargain behind his offer. The Smiths—every forge, every hammer, every blade in Windermere at my beck and call. A river of steel pouring into my armies. With my power and his weapons at my disposal, I could stand unbroken against any enemy foolish enough to test me... I could take complete and utter control of Aeshelyn.*

Expand my will. My control. Then move to Sylene and Windermere.

Joseph could control the continent. Do what Quinn was never able to do.

"My will." His voice scratched against Joseph's temples. **"Remember your place."**

Remember my fucking place... he suppressed the scowl inching toward the surface, remembering where he was. *What is sentiment against steel? What is pride compared to the edge of a thousand blades ready at my beck and call?*

"It's a generous offer, Lazaros," Joseph said. "But generosity and wisdom don't always walk hand in hand. I'll consider it."

They clinked goblets, laughter mingling with the chatter around us.

The music shifted to a brighter tune, lutes and pipes blending as guests clap in rhythm. Their circle remained apart from the dancers, laughter stitched upon their faces like fine embroidery.

Governess Verois, sharp-eyed and lean under the navy and silver gown that shimmered like moonlight, raised her goblet as though in salute, her voice as smooth as honey. "An enticing thought, Governor—steel enough to arm an empire, and a marriage to quiet the restless. But tell me..." She sipped delicately, eyes flicking toward Joseph. "Would that not tilt the balance of this continent? One Sovereign with both the crown and the forges, while the rest of us wait, dependent?"

Lazaros' smile was light, though Joseph noticed the tightness in his knuckles around the cup. "Balance is found in stability, Governess. Better one strong arm holding the line than three weak ones fumbling to catch the blade. You should rethink your stance, considering that Sylene is the sanctuary country."

"Precisely why I bring this up to your attention. Being the sanctuary country, we must not be left defenseless."

Governess Kiarelli leaned, her green and amaranth embroidered gown glistening faintly. As expected, she carried the lightest smile of them all, her tone honeyed, but her brown eyes glittered sharp as gems. "Yet, Governor, too much strength in one hand makes the others tremble. And trembling hands... well, they tend to strike first."

The three of them laughed together as if sharing some harmless joke, but the sound pressed like stones against his ribs. *Was this jab directed to me?* Guests brushed past, servants offered trays of sugared figs and candied nuts.

Joseph raised his goblet, forcing the circle back into ease. "Friends," He said warmly, "let us not spoil a fine banquet with the language of suspicion. Governor Lazaros has offered much. The matter deserves consideration—deliberation, not whispers under music."

They nodded, smiling, each satisfied in their own way; Governess Verois with her point made, Governess Kiarelli with her warning laid, and Lazaros with his proposal set upon the table like a dagger among wine cups.

Joseph's gaze settled on Governess Kiarelli with her voluminous brown curls cascading down her back. Her poise was sharp as a blade at a duelist's hip. She carried herself with the practiced serenity of a woman who knew every eye in the hall was hers, if only she chose to claim it.

"Governess," Joseph said warmly, gesturing with his goblet. "Would you join me for a moment?"

She nodded and followed Joseph away from the hearth.

"I'm surprised you decided to grace us with your presence this evening."

"It would've been impolite to refuse such a generous invitation." She replied softly. "We must keep a cordial relationship with each other to ensure peace, don't we not?"

"Certainly." Joseph smiled as if finding her passive-agressiveness amusing. "It strikes me that in times such as these, strength lies not in solitude but in alliance. You and I have always respected one another's boundaries, but I believe the hour has come to weave those borders into something stronger." His words, clothed in charm, made her head tilt with grace, her smile as flawless as polished marble. But he felt the invisible threads tightening.

His men moved quietly at the edges of the hall, their steps masked by music and chatter. He had ordered them to watch for her soldiers, to count, to measure, to know if her strength this night was for pageantry or preparation.

"You honor me with such words," she replied, her voice carrying just enough sweetness. "But I have no son." She added curtly. "Surely, you don't mean the merging of our bloodlines."

"Would it be so terrible if I was?" Joseph laughed, bringing the goblet to his lips.

"I'm flattered, but my people have weathered storms alone for generations. We are stubborn, I fear. We know how to bend without breaking."

"Ah, but even the strongest oak splinters when the tempest grows wild enough. Together, you and I could plant a forest no storm could uproot."

She sipped her drink delicately as if weaving her answer in the space between them, her olive skin glistening under the lights. "Perhaps," she said, her eyes never leaving Joseph's, "but forests,

Sovereign, can also choke the ground until nothing else may grow. My people thrive because our roots are our own. To tangle them with yours would risk the soil itself, I'm afraid."

Clever. He pressed, leaning closer, voice soft enough to suggest intimacy while his smile suggested nothing more than amusement. "The merging of our bloodlines is out of the question, no doubt. But, your soil, Governess, would be well watered by the rivers of my realm through a well-formed alliance. Think of the prosperity. Of the *safety.*"

Her gaze hardened ever so slightly, though her lips never lost their curve. "And think of the cost. My people's freedom is no currency I am willing to trade, no matter how rich the purse."

Governess Kiarelli dipped her head, lowering her voice so it would sound to others like a playful aside. "You will forgive me, Sovereign, but I must refuse. My loyalty lies first with those who entrusted me with their fate. An alliance with you... would blur that sacred bond. Otherwise..."

Joseph forced a smile, though the steel beneath his ribs screamed with restrained frustration. He let a moment of silence hang between them, then laughed softly.

"Ah, but of course," he respond. "I shouldn't be surprised. Your steadfastness is famed across Eseron. Still, I wonder..." his smile widened, friendly enough to fool the passing nobles. "You place much faith in your friends across the heavens—the Olympians. But when the hour strikes, Governess, and the wolves are at your gates... do you truly believe they will answer?"

Her expression barely shifted, yet he caught the faint stiffening of her shoulders.

"They are gods of their own making," he continued, voice low but laced with cheer for the ears of any passersby. "High on their mountains, drowning in temples and prayer. They have little appetite for bleeding over mortal quarrels. And when your enemies march—when fire touches *your* walls—they will not descend. They will not fight your battles. They will leave you with nothing but hollow hymns and broken statues, as they have before." He finished his wine, savoring the moment. Then added with mock solemnity, "I fear your alliance, Governess, is but a painted shield. Lovely to display... but splinters at the first strike."

"That's where you're wrong." Kiarelli's smile didn't falter, though he could see the fire kindling in her eyes. "They've always listened and provided whenever my people are in need."

"Just because it rained in the middle of a pitiful drought, doesn't mean they're at your beck and call."

"And yet, better a painted shield that inspires faith in my people... than to bind myself in chains disguised as armor. If you'll excuse me." She headed back to Lazaros and Governess Verois.

The music swelled again, and the hall carried on none the wiser to the daggers traded in plain sight.

Still, as he raised his goblet once more, gesturing for more wine, he knew he had struck a nerve. And perhaps, in time, that nerve would unravel into something far more useful.

He saw Kiarelli's eyes burn beneath her polished smile, and though she stood her ground, he knew he had landed a cut deep enough to leave a mark. Or perhaps, plant the seed of doubt.

The music drowned the silence between us, a waltz of flutes and strings masking the storm of thought that churned behind his smile.

Olympians.

She draped herself in their shadow as though it could shield her. But he had seen enough of them and their games to know the truth: they meddled when it suited them, abandoned when it did not. She had no shield, only hope. And hope was the frailest of defenses.

A servant rushed to Joseph's side and filled his cup. She left without comment, and he drank slowly, letting the liquid coat his tongue as his gaze drifted over the hall.

His men were already returning from their quiet survey of her entourage, slipping through the crowd like wolves among sheep. A nod here, a glance there—messages enough to confirm what he had suspected. Her presence was not heavily guarded. Either she was arrogant, or she believed too much in the Olympians to send her champions in her stead.

Both were weaknesses he could use.

Joseph's thoughts slid back to Lazaros' offer.

Byorn.

Katerina.

The memory of their indecency in their youth still stung, yet now... it no longer seemed valid. If their union gave him the Smiths, then every weakness in Kiarelli's Olympian pact would matter little. Her painted shield would shatter the moment Joseph pressed with iron and his power, that not even her darling Olympians would arrive in time to bind it. And when her prayers went unanswered, she would kneel—not to her gods, but to him. And he could be *very* persuasive.

He moved back to the hearth.

The musicians softened their tune into something gentle, and guests trickled toward the doors in pairs and clusters, servants bowed with trays of fruit wine and sweetmeats, and laughter softened into the tired warmth of an evening well spent.

He stood among the three, the very picture of a gracious host. He clasped hands, shared shallow jokes, and smiled. Joseph was, in fact, Sovereign and friend alike, generous and welcoming.

Kiarelli lingered near Governess Verois, their conversation polished, rehearsed, perhaps meant to mask her earlier refusal. She laughed at some remark, though her eyes strayed once toward Joseph.

You'll be mine. Don't you worry. He returned her glance with the easy charm of a man who took no offense, letting her believe she had steadied herself and that the matter was closed.

"Friends," Joseph raised his chalice one final time, voice carrying over the softened music. "Your company has been a gift. May the night linger sweetly in memory, and may the bonds we share only grow stronger." He glanced briefly at Kiarelli, who only smiled curtly in return.

Polite cheers followed, and the circle dispersed into side

conversations with other patrons. Lazaros caught Joseph's eye as he departed, the faintest of nods passing between them. *A silent agreement. Katerina will marry his son.*

As the hall emptied, he let his expression fall into its truer shape, colder, sharper. He leaned toward one of his captains as he approached, his bow low, his voice low enough for none to overhear.

"Keep eyes on her men," Joseph murmured, his tone as even as the dimming notes of the music. "Mark their numbers, their routes home, their contacts in the city. I want to know who her allies are and how many there are here."

THIRTY-THREE

KATERINA

THE RENA GARDENS WERE LIT BEAUTIFULLY BY YELLOW and orange orbs that complemented the iridescent calm river that circled the greenery. Katerina's eyes soaked in the ethereal ambiance. The sharp pain on her palms made open the fists she didn't realize she was making.

I definitely have to get a grip on my temper... okay. She took a breath. *My life can take a completely different turn in a matter of minutes.* She kicked a rock, hating that her life was not her own. The only thing she could say was remotely *her* choice was the induction. They haven't taken that away from her yet. *I could weigh my options, not that it'll make a difference, but it'll at least prepare me mentally for whatever happens. It was the lesser evil—well, the one with the least amount of headache, as much as I hate to admit it—is the arranged marriage. That alone would stop my father in so many things relating to me...* She rubbed her temples. *Jezebelle... you're in for a rude awakening once I'm gone.*

"Hello Sunshine."

Her body stilled, and she could've sworn her chest hollowed.

"You look radiant this evening."

She lifted her gaze, landing on a man in an elegant black

ensemble with white trim that complemented his bronzed body and muscles. His black hair partially fell over his grey eyes.

Her throat clenched, disbelief rushing through her veins as she beheld Byorn's presence, who eyed her black and gold gown.

"I wasn't sure I'd see you this evening." He smiled, extending a hand. "You're still as beautiful as I remember."

"I'm sure." Her gaze seared into him, ignoring his offered hand. *How are you here?*

"I guess some things never change."

She forced a smile.

"Please," he offered his arm.

Walking past him, she strode down a paved trail surrounded by red roses and lilies until she reached a stone bridge. The tranquil waters flowed underneath, and she perched herself on the veranda.

"I'm aware that you are not fond of me or what I did. In fact, I know you are displeased about the fact that we're to be wed considering our past."

Her heart dropped. *Out of all the damn people...* "I'm glad to hear that you're aware of such and we're doing no such thing." She laughed bitterly as she tore her gaze away from the water. "How come I never knew you were Governor Lazaros' son?"

His gaze softened. "You met me when I was at odds with my father. He claimed he had no son for years. It was after he became governor that he claimed me once again..." he sighed heavily. "I'm not supposed to tell you this, but... I want us to start on the right foot this time." He walked closer to her. "Your father had... *someone* alter your memories of how we met... but kept the pain I caused you, in hopes that you'd forget about me."

"That's just doesn't make any sense, who would—" Her body ran cold.

JASMINE LEANED CLOSE. "SHE HAS A WAY OF FINDING out things... we're not supposed to talk about it." Her eyes scanned the room for any within earshot. *"She can see into other people's minds without so much as touching them... why do you think people are afraid of her?"*

CAN THE VERENNA ADJUST MEMORIES AS WELL? Her stomach lurched. *This changes everything... so much for the lesser evil. Both options are now equally bad.*

"My son—a fine young man—has set his eyes on you. Said it would be beneficial for both our families to solidify our relationship."

How could I have been so stupid to agree? Katerina shoved all emerging thoughts of their past down. *I feel like I'm going to be sick.*

"Katerina," he frowned. "The least we can do is put our past and differences aside, for the benefit of the people."

"For the benefit of the people?" She couldn't help laughing at the audacity. "Seriously?"

"Kate," his eyes softened, pain washing through them. "I know you have no reason to trust me, but I've changed and I've stayed true to the promise I made to you, despite how much time has passed. This is an unavoidable fate now. One we've wanted for a very long time."

"Wanted." She emphasized, glare blazing.

"Katerina, please." He warned.

"I want to make something extremely clear. I have no interest in entertaining any of this. I'm only here because I have a duty to fulfill." A lump formed in her throat. "Our time passed, and you made sure of it. So, *I'm sorry* if I'm not receiving you with open arms." *I can't cry. Not now. Calm down. Breathe.*

"What happened to us?" he muttered, not bothering to hide the pain that lingered in his eyes.

"You know exactly what happened, Byorn." Her eyes burned. Biting her lip, she suppressed the tears that were on the cusp of slipping free.

"I said I was sorry for how things played out."

"An *I'm sorry* is not going to bring our son back." She snapped, feeling a treacherous tear escape. *Fantastic.* She swatted it off and crossed her arms, turning away from him. *I can't.*

"Silas was a threat. I was only doing my job." He dared to justify.

"He was just a baby..." she croaked. "Baby... you're telling me that my father felt *threatened* by a damn infant?" She bit her quivering lip. "You and I had a great thing. I'm not denying that." *I Loved You.* "But killing our son is not something I'll ever be able to forgive."

"What did you want me to do, Kate? Tell your father to go fuck himself?" He barked, using his arms to emphasize his words. *As if that's reason enough to kill Silas.*

"Yes! I wanted you to protect our family! To tell my father that you would not sacrifice our only child just because of a stupid, pathetic, nonsensical hunch he had! Not condemn us. Not destroy us."

"Just because I did my job, I'm in a much more favorable position for us." He reached for her hands. "Remember when your father was against us because I wasn't one of you and because I was a Shield-bearer? After that... the sacrifice I had to make, my father brought me back home at the request of yours."

"Is your family on the brink of ruin?" Katerina's brows joined, but her discontent remained. "It makes no sense that your father, after all these years, coincidentally enough, brought this up to me tonight. Mind you, he denied that he wanted to invoke the convention." *Perhaps, shame? A once powerful lineage slowly reaching its end?*

He remained silent, and that was all the confirmation she needed.

She slipped out of his hold. "That still doesn't explain why you never told me you were his son? Even after all this time. How come you knew about what was done to me and your memories are still intact? You didn't even bother to reach out to me, just out of mere courtesy."

"It wouldn't have made any difference." He rubbed his temples. "Don't look at me like that."

Katerina didn't back down from her glare and display of utter repulsion.

"I remember the promise we made before we had Silas." He said softly, closing the gap between us.

She took a step back, but her body stopped against the veranda.

"Remember when we swore to each other that no matter what happens, we would find a way for us to be together? Despite what our families may think? Well, now we have the chance to do so without the fear of retribution."

She shook her head. *I can't just forget or even forgive the betrayal. The pain. The guilt. The... Loss.* "Well, I changed my mind." she slithered out of his closeness. "Can you even imagine the pain I felt? How agonizing it was to learn that your son died at the hands of the man who was supposed to protect him?" There it was again, the burning in her eyes, the tightness of her throat.

"You think I didn't suffer the loss too? He gave me an impossible choice, one that was very difficult to make. I was only doing my job."

"HE WAS A CHILD BYORN! A FUCKING CHILD! I can't bear to imagine that if you and I were... were to get married and have more children together—Savior help me—they would meet the same fate."

"They won't." He said firmly.

"How can you be so sure?" She croaked as she held back the second wave of tears threatening to break free. "If my father were to tell you that one of them was a threat—again, look me in the eye and tell me you would refuse the order." *Please say yes...*

"You know I can't guarantee that." His lips formed a thin line.

Her heart hardened as disappointment coated her words. "And you expect me to trust you in this marriage..."

"Your safety and your father's safety are part of my duties," Byorn retorted.

"My safety, nor my father's is no longer your priority. You're a titled man now, but I'm afraid your mindset hasn't changed." She softened her gaze, realization hitting her. "Thank you for this evening. I hope you find safe passage on your way back to Windermere."

She walked away, and the burning in her eyes didn't cease. *My father has been a part of this for so long. He punished me for not disciplining my sister, for falling in love, for having a son, for paving a life for myself—at what cost? To what end?*

"You think you can get out of this?" He gripped her arm. "We're bound under contract."

She turned stone-faced. "I haven't signed a damn thing."

"You didn't have to. Why did you think I came to find you? The Union Convention is getting invoked tonight. You belong to me now."

"I belong to no one." She spat, pulling her body away from his hold.

"You'll soon understand the importance of your people following orders and what's at stake." He released his grip.

"What was at stake for you, huh?" She hissed.

"You were!" He yelled, making another lump form in her throat. "I was faced with a choice, Silas or you. And, considering how everything was between us, I chose you."

"And you expect me to fall to my knees and worship the ground you walk on..." she sneered, heart aching.

I want to forgive him. Forget what happened and move on with our lives. We were truly happy despite Father's disapproval. We had to meet in secret for years. When he used to be in the Training grounds, I used to sneak in to watch him whenever our military had joint training and we would get together afterward. We enjoyed each other's company so much that we were each other's escape from the drama and politics of Eseron. When I was several months deep into the pregnancy, that's when my father found out about our relationship.

A film of crystal liquid coated Katerina's eyes. Losing their son broke every part of her, and she vowed never to return to Byorn. He wanted them to be like they were before, but she didn't see how. *I can't bring myself to do it. Union convention or not, I am not marrying the man who killed my son.*

"Goodbye, Byorn."

"My father and I will leave for Windermere tomorrow." He said cooly. "We have several things to sort with your father's council and the treaties in place between our countries. Depending on how things go, its how soon or late we leave."

"Don't waste your breath." She pulled herself together. "Treaty or not. Convention or not. Contract or not. I am not marrying you."

"You don't have a choice, sunshine." He grabbed her arm.

"Let me go."

Tightening his grip as she pulled away, the man she knew disappeared in seconds. "I'm not letting you keep my family in ruin."

"Stop. You're hurting me. Let me go." She jerked her body away, but he held tight.

"We could've done this the easy way." His grip tightened further, and he used his free hand to grab her chin and make her eyes meet his. "You belong to me."

"Fuck off." She kicked him in the crotch, sending him to his knees. She hurried off, her body crashing against another body that stopped her from falling.

Rapid footsteps made Katerina turn, bracing for impact. An impact that never came. She looked at Byorn who was stopped by —*Nik?*

"You lay a hand on her, I will kill you myself. I don't care who you are." Nik said in a cool tone.

Byorn laughed, his eyes falling on me. "No wonder you don't want to marry me. Too busy fucking your way around. I thought you were classier than that."

Byorn reeled as Nik's fist slammed into his face with a sickening thud. "You have two seconds to get out of my face."

He looked up, blood spilling from Byorn's nose. "You'll regret this." He strode off, leaving Katerina alone with Nik.

Tears streamed down her cheeks as rage boiled inside her. *How dare he? How fucking dare he? I should've done more than just kick him. I should've—*

"Are you okay?"

She looked at Nik; confusion washed over her. *How did you get through the gates?* "Why are you here?"

"Security detail for Governess Kiarelli."

"Aren't you supposed to be with her?"

"I am. But I wouldn't be doing my job if I didn't survey the area for any threats, wouldn't I?"

"You could've just left. This wasn't your problem to deal with."

"Judging by the punch I just gave, I'd say it was."

But why? He is so damn confusing.

"Perhaps a thank you should be in order?"

"Thanks." She let out.

"Do you want to talk about it?"

"So you can exploit my weaknesses? I'll pass but thanks for the offer."

He snorted. "Contrary to your belief, I'm not here to kill you. Besides, he seemed like a jackass. So, I figured—"

"I suggest you focus on your relationship instead of mine." She said coldly, reminding herself of the night at the inn.

"I don't have a—what did they say?"

"Nothing you don't already know."

Annoyance flashed in his eyes for a split second before softening again. "I don't have a relationship with Chryssa, if that's what you're referring to."

"She seems to think the opposite, considering how tenderly she kissed you."

"So you *were* looking at me." He smirked.

And you looked at me. Katerina scowled. "Don't flatter yourself."

He bit his lip and shook his head. "You should get inside."

"I'm just fine here."

"Go inside." His tone unrelenting.

Her chest tugged, and before she could form a response, she found herself doing as told.

"I'm telling you, I saw her." Argus said, standing in the middle of the War Room.

"And how are you sure it was her and not someone who looked like her?" Ares asked.

"You think I can't recognize my own wife?" Argus retorted.

"We don't have time for this," Zeus hissed, perched on his seat. "What did you find?"

"Apparently, the Sovereign used his power to assert dominance within his counsel. He silenced their High Priestess by removing her tongue, saying she would not speak unless he allowed her to do so."

"So he *was* given power?" Zeus said.

"I thought he already had it." Ares raised a brow.

"Not completely." Argus replied. "I don't know how Dremian is doing it, but he found the Catacombs where the Sovereign keeps the altar to this thing we're dealing with. He didn't see any signs of the sickle, so we might still have time, but he did see a circle with blood at the center."

Zeus shook his head. "He made a lifeline." *Fuck*. He slammed his hand on the table, burning it with lightning. "Does he have any idea of who the tether is?"

Argus shook his head. "He didn't mention anything about that. But we might just be able to get additional insight since one of our own is marrying."

Ares scoffed. "Marrying? We have to wait for someone to get married to get answers... fucking great."

"Think of long term." Argus implored.

"See what I mean?" Ares addressed Zeus. "We don't have long term, and it looks like I'm the only one here with his fucking head on his shoulders."

"Rhei is marrying one of the Sovereign's daughters."

"And that's supposed to make it better?" Ares huffed.

"That may give us insight into who the tether is. What if he notices something that Dremian doesn't?"

"What about Nik?" Ares asked.

"He's been working on earning the trust of the eldest; supposedly, it's been difficult."

Zeus rubbed his eyes. *Should I tell them I know who's behind this? If I do, more questions will arise, and that could open the possibility of them finding out that he somehow has a direct connection to my mind...*

"What about the poison?" Zeus asked, irritation gnawing on his chest.

"All of it was apparently lost during the attack. but I"m working with Asclepius on the blood sample, he should be done with it soon." Argus said.

"Fine," Zeus said. "Don't let this thing with you and Jasmine derail you from what's important."

Argus nodded, and Zeus dismissed both men. *I think I know who may have a better idea of how to deal with this.*

THE INFIRMARY WAS QUIETER THAN WHEN HE LEFT IT, though the air still stank of blood, herbs, and sweat. Zeus' footsteps were heavy enough that Asclepius glanced up from his work.

Most of the cots have been covered, their forms stiff beneath white shrouds. But one still lingered—one soul clinging to life with desperate, failing hands.

The soldier trembled, chest rising in shallow pulls. His skin had turned the shade of ash, his lips cracked, his veins crawling black up his throat like cursed rivers. Each breath he took felt like a theft, as though the Underworld already had its grip on him.

Asclepius bowed his head. "He's the only one who survived. I sent a vial of his blood to Hecate. She replied not long ago." His voice lowered, nearly reverent. "There are traces of serpent venom in his veins. But not just any... Python's."

Zeus' jaw clenched. *How the fuck did he get Python's venom? The war. Mnemosyne's vision. Python's fang. Fuck. More and more, everything kept falling into place. Shit, he even answered himself when I realized.* "That's why Apollo hasn't died?"

Asclepius nodded. "That and how I've been using everything at my disposal to keep him stable while I develop an antidote."

Zeus' eyes fell to the man, watching the strange shimmer beneath his skin as though something alive still slithered within him. The soldier stirred, lids fluttering. His eyes opened, clouded, lost, yet somehow he found Zeus. His hand rose weakly and began to fall. Zeus caught it before it struck the sheets, holding it tight.

"Zeus," he rasped, words breaking like shattered glass. "It... burned. The ground... alive. Teeth in the shadows..." His body shuddered violently, a cry escaping him as the pain surged.

Zeus felt it pulse against his hand. It mocked him, even through his skin. Zeus' nostrils flared, rage bubbling inside him.

"Enough," Asclepius said sharply. "He cannot endure much more."

The man's lips trembled as though pushing his final words out. Zeus crouched and leaned close.

"We... we fought *him*... we failed you..." Blood flecked his lips. One word tore free, broken and frail.

"You fought bravely." Zeus reassured, knowing he didn't have much left. "You and your brethren will rest in the Elysian Fields."

The soldier's body stiffened. His last breath rattled from him, leaving only silence.

Zeus straightened slowly, shadows breaking across his face. His hands curled into fists, and he left the infirmary without another word, despite Asclepius calling out to him.

His dying breath echoed in his head. *How dare he feel the need to apologize?*

He would pay for this. Typhon would pay for all of this. His stride cut through Olympus like a storm on its march, and the air around him grew restless, the clouds above answering my unspoken fury as he made his way to meet with Hecate.

HECATE'S DWELLING LAY DEEP IN THE DARKEST shadowed grove of the Underworld where three paths converged, each road leading in a different direction. Her home was a stone structure veiled in ivy and nightshade vines. The walls are blackened stone, shimmering faintly under the faux moonlight. Tall, narrow windows glowed with candlelight. An enclave of shadows and silver flame, standing apart from the temples of the others.

Three spectral hounds patrolled the grounds, their eyes ember-bright, ever watchful.

Zeus approached the heavy door carved with sigils and crescent moons, flanked by torches that never extinguished, even in rain. The flames guttered as he entered, though they never burn out in her presence.

She was waiting for him. Always waiting as if she had seen his steps before he took them.

Before him stood a beautiful maiden with long raven locks that reached to her waist, cloaked in violet and deep hues of blue, gold and black.

"You come with storm clouds in your eyes," she murmured, her three shadows bowing in silence behind her. "And blood still clinging to your hands."

Zeus didn't waste time on pleasantries. "You told Asclepius the truth—Python's venom ran through my soldier's veins. But we both know who's truly behind this."

Her lips curved, but it didn't seem to be in mockery, more like grim knowing. "There is no shadow of a doubt that it bears the scent of Typhon."

His teeth clenched, and a growl rose from his chest. "Typhon should lie bound in Tartarus. I cast him there myself."

"You did," she agreed softly. Her eyes, lantern-bright, held no comfort. "But Tartarus shifts, just as Olympus falters. You have felt it. The cracks are widening; the boundaries are thinning. And you know, when gods quarrel and mortals bleed, such bonds weaken."

Zeus stepped closer, his voice thunderous. "Did he escape? If so, how?"

She tilted her head, shadows shifting like serpents behind her. "Not fully. Not in flesh. His body is still bound to the shackles of Tartarus, but his essence stirs. I see him reaching through cracks, seeking vessels. And I have seen the Sovereign, your mortal king, walking with power that is not his own. Power that twists. Power that devours."

The air tightened around them, Zeus' chest heavy as if the very thought pressed down like chains.

"What are the chances that he became its vessel?" Zeus's mind raced back to every word laced with defiance, dating back to Joseph's predecessor, Quinn. The arrogance. The sudden strength.

Hecate's voice lowered, threading into the silence. "The question, Zeus, is whether you are strong enough to face him again. For if Typhon wears a mortal's flesh, he is free to walk where chains cannot bind him. There's no indication that the Sovereign is his vessel yet... but if he does, then the war you see brewing may only be the beginning. Olympus will crumble."

Her words coiled inside him like the venom he had seen in his soldier's veins.

"Look and see." She extended a hand. Fire flared, and against his will, the vision struck him.

THE SOVEREIGN STOOD TALL ON HIS OBSIDIAN DAIS, HIS eyes, once human, now molten red. Around him, men bow, not in loyalty but in terror. His shadow twisted on the walls, massive, winged, a serpent's coil spreading far beyond his mortal form. The air shivered as his mouth opened. Fire and venom laced his breath. Laughter, low and thunderous, a sound that shook Zeus to his bones.

"They will all bow to me," the voice hissed, split and many-tongued. "And Olympus will be mine."

THE VISION SNAPPED AWAY. ZEUS STAGGERED BACK, fury warring with the dread still clawing at his chest. His hand crackled with lightning. *I don't have much time.*

"How can I stop this?"

"So long as he does not retrieve Kronos' sickle from the depths of the Euxine Sea, you'll be able delay the prophecy and potentially stop it with the death of the Sovereign."

"Won't he just find another vessel?" Zeus retorted. "This will bring us back to where we are now, like what happened with his predecessor."

"He will try. But with the proper measures, we can prevent it from happening. Come."

Zeus followed her into another chamber, which had a cauldron in its center. The fire beneath it burned with three flames: gold, silver, and violet.

Each representing one aspect of her: Maiden, Mother, Crone. Around the room, offerings of grapes, garlic, honey, and wine are placed on three different altars.

She turned back to Zeus, now as the Mother with her hair equally as long, but half secured to her head. She had aged beautifully, with sharper cheekbones and thin, defined brows.

"You, as well as I, know that the prophecy cannot be stopped nor undone once it's set in motion. Therefore, we must stop the chain of events." She conjured a map of the Underworld, zooming in on a remote territory. "I, alongside Hades, prepared an area in the deepest parts of Tartarus. It is warded by me and him. No one will be able to leave unless I and Hades deem it so. Kill the Sovereign and send Typhon here. That may be our only chance to stop him."

"How are you certain the prophecy hasn't been set in motion? I've seen the omens."

"The omens are just to indicate the sickle is almost ready to be retrieved. How do you think Poseidon lost control of the tides? He was ensuring the sea kept the weapon on the bottom. But now you have a job to do."

"Where was this twenty-eight years ago?"

"Quinn made a bargain. Created a tether between him, Typhon, and Joseph." The map vanished. "Make sure Joseph didn't create a tether and then kill him. Once he dies, you'll have a window to trap both Typhon's soul and body and bind him to this prison. If he created a tether, be prepared..."

"Where is his soul now?"

"From what I found, his soul roams between Tartarus and the mortal lands. Perhaps because of the bargain Quinn made."

"Don't you have a way to track whenever someone crosses realms? Isn't that your job?" Zeus huffed.

"Careful." She warns, her three voices blending into one, her face contorting to the Crone, with untamed ashen hair. "You may command the skies, but here, I do."

"Fine." Zeus took a step back, and she turned to the three flames.

"If you're smart, you'd take this time to assess the mortal realm and develop a plan to take the Sovereign's life. Unless you want to find yourself crumbling at the hands of someone you thought you destroyed."

CHAPTER
THIRTY-FIVE
JOSEPH

ERIS LINGERED IN THE SHADOWS OF THE MAUSOLEUM before stepping into the light, her smile the same cruel slash that always threatened to unravel Joseph.

"You don't command respect." She circled him slowly, her voice gentle. "They bow, yes. But only because they fear what would happen if they don't. And fear fades, Joseph. The governess proved that. She stood before you and twisted your words into nothing. She made you look small, and you let her."

Joseph steadied himself, his arms folded across his chest. Her words were meant to wound, but he wouldn't give her the pleasure of seeing him bleed.

"I didn't let her." He retorted, each word measured. "She thinks she's safe behind her alliance, but I planted a seed of doubt within her. Doubt is patient. It festers and gnaws away at certainty. It is only a matter of time before she yields to me."

Eris threw her head back and laughed. "A seed? You speak of patience as if it makes you wise, but I see only a coward waiting for fortune to do the work he cannot. You're pathetic."

She leaned close, her lips near his ear, her whisper colder than steel.

"Do you know what's truly amusing? Rena is better off where she lies. She thrives without your shadow looming over her. She breathes and grows into something more than a tethered ornament at your side." She laughed. "Ironic, isn't it? That she is more at peace with us than she ever was with you. And deep down, you know it."

Her words struck harder than he cared to admit. A flicker of anger rose in him, but he held it, forced it into silence, refusing to give her the satisfaction of his rage. Joseph's jaw tightened, but he met her eyes with calm.

"Careful, Eris," he warned, his voice low. "Mockery may be your gift, but when the time comes, and doubt has rotted the governess' alliances from within, she will kneel. Willingly. And you will have to shove your mockery up your pretty ass."

Eris tilted her head, her smile widening, eyes gleaming with cruel delight. "We'll see," she purred. "But I think you're the only one still clinging to that fantasy and calling it strategy as you wait for others to break rather than daring to strike. And still, you pretend this is power."

"You forget yourself."

"No," she hissed, leaning in close, her breath a venomous whisper against his cheek. "*You* forget whose life hangs in the balance." She slithered back.

His vision blurred with fury, pulse thundering in his ears.

Eris only smiled wider, savoring it. "Look at you, so easy to unravel. And to think—" her tone turned mocking, "that all that power was *bestowed* upon you. What a waste. Power squandered on a man who cowers behind so-called patience. Quinn should have chosen better. He should have left you in the shadows where you belonged."

Something inside him snapped as the ground trembled. Power surged unbidden from him, rattling stone and iron alike. The torchlight bent, shadows writhed. His voice tore from his throat, raw and thunderous.

"Enough!"

The words shook the air, but Eris didn't flinch. She only laughed again, delighted, as if she had been waiting for this all along. She stepped closer; her smile widening. "No, not enough. Not ever. Look at you. Shaking like a child scolded by his mother. And you expect to wield *his* power and take control of the continent? Hilarious."

The last of his restraint shattered.

A roar thundered deep within him, shaking the air. Power surged, violent and unbound. Torches exploded in showers of sparks, shadows twisted like serpents across the walls, and the stone floor splintered beneath his feet.

His vision blazed with white fire, and he felt the energy tearing out of him, slamming against the walls, cracking them, shaking the very foundation of the sanctuary.

He hurled it at her.

The source of every wound she tore open with her tongue. A torrent of power, enough to reduce a foe to ash.

And yet—

She didn't move.

The force slammed toward her, but it broke as though striking an invisible wall. The blast shredded the floor around her, carved gaping cracks into the ceiling above, but she stood in the center untouched. Her gown fluttered in the tempest, her hair whipped by the violent wind. The vine-covered statue, now headless. Iron sconces screeched and twisted, torn from stone.

"You will not mock me." He threatened dangerously cold, his voice layered with something not entirely human. "I am the Sovereign."

For an instant, silence followed. Heavy and absolute. The sanctuary lay in ruin, smoke rising from shattered stone and burning remnants of plants.

Eris stood in the center of the devastation, her smile unchanged, her laughter quiet now but no less sharp. She brushed a strand of hair from her face and tilted her head, surveying him.

"There it is," she whispered, almost reverent. "How delicious." She grinned. "But remember, power unleashed is power wasted. And you, Joseph, are still nothing more than a child screaming at the dark."

Her words slithered through the silence like smoke, and even though everything lay broken by Joseph's wrath, he knew she'd won this exchange. Not with strength. Not with power. But with her fucking laughter still ringing in his ears.

"You know what has to be done."

Joseph pushed through the wreckage and out of the mausoleum. His head thundered against his temples. Her laughter clung to the marble, echoing through the crowded hall of the Fortress. His hands trembled with the fury that gnaws inside him as he ignored the ones calling him name.

Eris stood untouched, her words fucking sharp, her mockery seared into him deeper than fire. *I refuse to be humiliated. I refuse to be painted a fool.* Servants glanced at him warily, as if he were nothing but a rabid dog. *Did they hear it? The destruction? The roar? The laughter?*

I will not be remembered as the Sovereign who faltered beneath a worthless governess's defiance. No. I will make her choke on the smoke of her burning grounds. I will turn her laughter into screams.

He pushed past Sebastian, arms full of parchment. "Sovereign."

"Summon the council. Have Generals Lee, Veris, and Ware present." *No more patience. No more seeds to sow. The time for waiting is fucking finished.*

Silence simmered heavily inside the Council Chamber, the air thick with tension. His generals and counselors sat stiffly around the table, their faces pale in the flickering torchlight.

"We march on Aeshelyn," Joseph ordered.

A ripple of unease moved through the room as they shifted in their seats, seemingly hesitant to speak. *Were they truly still scared?*

General Veris, grizzled and broad-shouldered, leaned forward at once, the fire of battle clear in his eyes. "It couldn't have come at a better time, Sovereign. Aeshelyn is ripe. The Governess has grown arrogant, throwing open her gates for this convocation to honor Hera." He scowled in disgust. "Her guard is divided. If we strike now, we not only take the country, we humiliate her before her allies. A perfect blow to shatter their confidence."

Across the table, General Ware scowled, his weathered face carved with disapproval. "Sovereign, he doesn't speak reason. Aeshelyn is no mere country. It's Olympus's *stage*. Hera's name will sanctify every stone, and Olympian envoys will be present. An attack during such an event is not war; it's a defiance of the gods, and you risk drawing Olympus into open conflict with us, and we don't have the men to handle such a threat."

As if I fucking care. I've defied them ever since I joined Quinn in this fucking ordeal. Besides, they fail to realize that I have power beyond compare.

Veris slammed his fist against the table. "Fear-mongering, Ware! Have you grown so timid you would counsel our Sovereign to bow before a woman who dared to mock him? Shall we let Aeshelyn parade her insolence before Hera's chosen and do nothing?"

"Better to live to fight another day," Ware snapped back, "than to drag our legions into a slaughter we cannot win!"

"Whose side are you on, General?" Joseph turned to Ware.

"My apologies, but I would be doing a disservice to you and our men if I knowingly put them in a fight they cannot come back from."

"They're grown men. They knew the implications of joining. Danger is part of the job." Joseph retorted, his voice low, sharp. "What is this convocation, anyway?"

"It's some kind of celebration or ritual where Hera comes down from Olympus to bless women in childbearing years, pregnant women, and women who struggle with fertility. Supposedly, Hestia would be in attendance this year as well." Mare answered.

"Forgive me, Sovereign, but the coffers—supplies, coin, weapons—our campaigns these past seasons, not to mention the recent attack on the Belsir Outpost, have bled us lean. An attack now could drain us beyond recovery." Khir interjected.

"Recovery?" Joseph spat the word, the torches flaring with the heat on his chest. "Do you speak of recovery or cowardice?"

The council flinched as the table trembled beneath his hands. He forced himself to remain still, though the power inside him bucked and strained like a chained beast.

General Lee finally spoke, his tone cool and measured. "Sovereign, there is truth in both their words. A strike carries risk, but so too does hesitation. If you desire to break Aeshelyn, it must be done swiftly and decisively. Before the convocation is at its peak, when Hera's attention is on the blessings, capture the governess... alive. Display her *broken* before her guests. A living symbol of your dominion will speak louder than ashes. But delay..." He tapped the table with one gloved finger. "...and Olympus will have time to react. We will find ourselves not only besieging a country, but battling the divine."

Julius's eye studied Joseph. "He's right. You know that the Olympians will not ignore the smoke. Who knows, their banners may already be waiting."

"They're fractured," Joseph said. "Scattered. They squabble like children. And you want me to fear them?"

"You must measure the blade before the strike!" Dremian said. "A campaign of this scale, at this hour, risks our army as much as it risks theirs. If the Olympians move, our legions may not return."

His words fanned the storm inside Joseph. His fists clenched, sparks flaring at his fingertips. The torches guttered, shadows twisted across the walls. For a heartbeat, another voice surged through mine—deep, commanding.

"Enough." The word cracked like a whip from his tongue.

Everyone fell silent, though the fire still burned in their eyes. The council shifted uneasily. The clash of arguments hung heavy in the air.

Joseph rose, hands braced on the table, the torches flaring wildly in response. Shadows writhed across the walls, and the power inside him surged, restless, demanding.

"You speak of Hera as if I should tremble before her." His voice deepened, layered with something that was not wholly his. The table shuddered under his palms. "I will not tremble. I will not bow. Let her watch as her chosen country burns. Let her hear the screams of her devotees as they fall before me. Let the gods know their time of untouchable dominion is over."

The flames guttered low, and for a moment the chamber seemed to breathe with him—an unnatural pulse, a presence not his own pressing against the skin of every man present.

Veris bowed his head, fierce approval in his eyes. "It will be done."

Ware hesitated, his jaw tight. His gaze flickered to the cracked walls, the trembling shadows, and finally to Joseph. Reluctance warred with fear, and fear won. He lowered his head. "As you command, Sovereign."

Lee inclined his head, cautious but obedient. "We will leave at dusk."

One by one, the others murmured in agreement, though the room stank of unease. They didn't bend in conviction. They bent to the storm that seeped from him, to the realization that resistance here was not merely disobedience, but instant death.

You don't command respect. They bow, yes. But only because they fear what would happen if they don't. And fear fades, Joseph.

Joseph shoved Eris's words away. He surveyed them, chest heaving, the storm within him coiled and restless. It whispered, pressing against his heart, urging him on, feeding his rage. He clenched his fists to keep it caged, but he knew—*his* hand guided Joseph's, steering him toward this war.

The council had ended.

Aeshelyn's fate was sealed.

And the governess would bear witness to its ruin.

He just had to be prepared to do what it took in the aftermath.

THIRTY-SIX

A SEA OF SPECTATORS FILLED THE CAVEREST PLAZA AS Quinn sat atop an elevated dais with direct view of the crowd and stage. I stood several paces behind alongside Malakai.

People from all over continued to gather until the ground was hidden from view. The air became tense as members of the Light Militia placed a small wooden stand with a curve at the center of the stage, next to a noose.

Quinn stood and addressed the crowd, calling up the traitors subjected to judgment and punishment for their crimes. One by one, the criminals were pulled onto the stage in single file, and, depending on the severity of their crimes, Quinn would determine the type of punishment they'd receive.

It was rare to see someone walk out alive. He wasn't all that merciful to begin with.

Most of them aided the McClaren Government with intelligence and weapons from Quinn's arsenal and apothecary. All, save for one, were hung for all to see. Their bodies twitched over and over as the life and oxygen drained from their lungs. Decapitation gave one a quick death for stealing from the Acrailerion of all places.

Quinn called up the last criminal, and I leaned back against the column behind me. I could understand why Quinn would want us here. He'd want to show a united, unshakeable front; which explained why Malakai was here. Being recently married to Bernadette—fucking bastard—Malakai needed to showcase to the people that his loyalty stood with the Paragons of Light, who now run Castelencia. He'd be down there in a heartbeat if he showed any sort of inclination toward aiding Juliette McClaren before her death.

They way we won and successfully tore down the McClaren government was still beyond me, but that's something I'd dive into another day. I just want to be over this bullshit.

A soldier brought up a struggling blonde woman in an off-white dress. I pushed myself off the column, and my heart sank to the pit of my stomach as I laid eyes on Bernadette.

"Why is she down there?" I asked, not bothering to hide my panic.

"Traitors will be punished for their crimes against the law." Quinn replied, eyes still on his shock-ridden sister.

"What crime did she commit?" I countered. "You need to stop this."

"Why?"

Her eyes, steady and defiant, swept over the crowd, pausing for the briefest second on me. A single glance. Enough to shatter me. The executioner looked up at Quinn, waiting for his judgement.

"She's your fucking sister."

"Family doesn't go above the law."

I turned to Malakai, who gave me an unrelenting look of disgust. "You're going to let your wife be treated like a criminal? Slaughtered like an animal?"

"I suppose you care, considering that you're the reason she is up there."

"What the fuck are you talking about?" I dismissed his words as mere speculation and turned back to Quinn, who still had his eyes on her. "She is innocent. Whatever rumors have reached your ears, they're all lies. I beg you, do not—"

"Do not?" His voice carried easily over the hush and finally *turned to me. "Do not what, Joseph? Spare a woman who defiled her vows? Or spare you, the man who defiled her?"*

My stomach lurched. "I—"

"Do you deny it?" he pressed, voice like a blade against my throat. "Deny that you lay with my sister while she was bound in marriage to another? Better yet, do you deny you lied to me when I asked you about this and brushed it off as being friendly?"

I opened my mouth, but no words came. My silence was confession enough.

Quinn rose, his presence towering, damning. "Joseph, you were my trusted confidant... but now, you're my traitor." He lifted his hand, pointing not at me, but at her. "And your punishment shall not be death. No. Yours shall be worse. You will live—to watch her die."

The ground seemed to fall from beneath me. My knees weakened, but I forced myself upright. "Please," I choked, stepping forward. "Take me instead. She doesn't deserve this."

"She deserves everything she chose," Malakai cut in flatly, his voice devoid of warmth. He didn't even look at her.

You'll pay for this. Rest fucking assured.

Her gaze never left me. Calm. Unyielding. Silently pleading for me to save her. For me to stop this. A faint smile touched her lips, as though she wanted me *to be the last thing she carried with her into the dark. As if she knew that she wasn't coming out of this alive and was making peace.*

"I'm sorry," I mouthed to her.

The executioner stepped forward. Steel flashed in the dying sun.

I surged, but the soldiers held me in place. "No! Don't—please! For the love of everything, not her!"

And when the blade fell, it wasn't her scream I heard.

It was mine.

CHAPTER
THIRTY-SEVEN
KATERINA

Silence surrounded Katerina, with only the faintest chimes of the holy bell echoing down the Worship Hall as she propped herself onto one of the cushioned seats. Some sisters hovered around consoling other women inside, and others walked around with incense, cleansing the space.

So far, two sisters have approached her, asking if she needed some spiritual guidance; and as much as she did, she needed to venture this alone; especially if her last volunteer assignment was in a few hours.

She got to her knees, resting her hands on her lap, and bowed her head, closing her eyes. Five deep breaths send her deep into a peaceful abyss. The faint chatter faded. The chimes quiet. Her body loosened, and her mind went blank.

I stood at the center of nothingness. Bright white light surrounded me. The silence was deafening. The sound of my footsteps was absorbed by the void. I kept walking. But there was nothing. No horizon. No end point. Nothing.

I opened my mouth to speak, yet nothing came out. My thoughts were clear, as if I could hear them out loud. I kept walking.

My chest tugged, prompting me to turn left. Then right. Then forward. I didn't know how far I had walked or how much farther I had to keep moving, but my body didn't stop.

A figure materialized at a considerable distance. It wore a cream cloak, face hidden and fastened at the waist. It moved toward me, and the tug in my chest intensified, then it was replaced by a familiar warmth that spread through my body.

My throat clenched as it pulled back the hood, revealing its face.

Tears swelled in my eyes. "Mom?"

She smiled and pulled me in for a warm embrace.

My body melted under her hold. Every worry, every doubt, every moment of suffering. Gone in an instant. I tightened my hold. "I miss you."

She pulled away slightly, holding me at arm's length. "You are as beautiful as the day I saw you last."

"I need you home." I said..

Her eyes softened as her lips curled. "I am always with you." She cupped my cheek, wiping the tears. "My darling Kate, you're stronger than you believe. Don't let what's happening at the Fortress stop you from reaching your full potential."

"I'm trying..." I suppressed the next wave of tears. "I truly am. But I don't think I can hold on much longer..."

"You can, and you will." She placed her fingers on my temples. "You're close. The induction will open your eyes; make sure to stay grounded." She held my hand. "Regardless of what happens, don't allow yourself to be consumed by darkness. Control it. Don't let it control you."

"Darkness follows me like the plague." I countered. "Father is not the same. After you left he changed..."

"What the Sovereign does is not a reflection of the type of woman you are."

"You haven't see my back..." I croaked.

"I don't have to. I know what he's done. I may not be there in the flesh. But I am always with you. Even when you think you're utterly alone. I was with you the first time he lashed you. It broke my heart. It keeps breaking my heart because I'm not there to stop him. But... remember when you wanted to end it, all those years ago?"

I nodded.

"I felt your willingness to die. To stop the pain." She tightened her grip. *"I wasn't going to allow you to throw your life away..."*

Many years ago, after she passed, my father went into a fit of rage. He lashed me almost weekly. Threatened to do it to my sister if I uttered a word or risked staining his image. I endured it... I endured so much until I couldn't anymore. I was 22 at the time... I had snuck out of the Fortress and managed to find a cliff somewhere...

"It was you who talked me out of it?"

Mom nodded, tears lining her eyes. "I'm not denying that he is a monster. But you have something special in you. You can effect real change, Kate. I couldn't allow myself to let you end it. So, I gave you strength."

"What can I do? Neither of the options I have are... great. My life can change in an instant."

"Your life will *change in an instant."* She emphasised. *"All you have to do is make it to Induction."*

"But why?"

"Just trust. Everything will fall into place."

"I need—"

"I have to go." She interrupted. *"I'll leave something with you. It'll protect you so hold on to it. I Love You. Tell Jezebelle I love her."*

My chest caved, pulling the air out of my lungs.

KATERINA'S EYES DARTED OPEN AS SHE GASPED FOR AIR, clutching her chest. A sudden stabbing pain had her opening her clenched hand. She gasped. *I left this at the sorting tower...* she ogled the 16-point star pendant in her palm. *Was this hers?*

She looked around; the sun was beginning to set. *How long was I out?* She bolted upright, securing the necklace around her neck. *The festival!* She rushed out of the Worship Hall, careful not to crash into anyone. *The one damn chance I have after the agora situation, and I am going to be late.*

Katerina spotted Jasmine in the Grand Foyer, making her way into the Chronicler wing with a male Scholar. *Should I call her?* She shook her head. *Things to do, places to be.* She hurried to meet the sisters before they left for the festival.

As the sun descended on the horizon, the festival came to life with vibrant colors and pulsating energy. The sky transformed into a canvas painted in hues of orange, pink, and purple, promising a stunning backdrop to the lively scene below.

Men, women, and children danced to rhythmic beats, their silhouettes swaying against the twilight. Glowing lanterns and colorful decorations adorned the surroundings that cast a magical glow across the festivities. Laughter and cheers filled the air, creating an atmosphere of joy and celebration that mirrored the breathtaking sunset.

"Katerina!" a woman yelled.

She scanned her surroundings, but didn't see anyone. She quickly dismissed and followed the Sisters through the Caverest Plaza. She spotted a group of people holding candles and gifts in the distance as they walked over to the Acrailerion. The vibrant colors and bustling crowd instantly drew her in, igniting a sense of thrill and anticipation.

"Katerina!" a woman called again, and she just ignored it.

They wandered through the streets filled with tables adorned with an array of crafts. Mesmerized by the kaleidoscope of colors and textures, Katerina couldn't help but admire the dedication and talent. They stopped every so often, providing blessings to the people or even a listening ear to those in need of someone to talk to.

Amidst the sea of people, Katerina was able to find moments of tranquility in unexpected places—a quiet corner with flickering lanterns or a serene garden filled with fragrant flowers. These respites offered a chance to soak in the festival's essence and appreciate the small details that added to its charm. *This has been a different but good volunteer service.* Her mind flickered back to her first volunteer service with Mrs. Dhalia, *may her soul rest with our Savior.* She shoved the thought away. *Enjoy this.*

From trying exotic dishes to joining in communal dances, every moment felt like a celebration of life itself. As the evening progressed and night emerged, the festival transformed into a stunning scene, making her fall in love with the people and Castelencia even further. *I said it once and I'll say it again, Caverest is my home.*

She bought a cup of strawberry ambrosia from one of the merchants and savored its smooth and sweet taste.

"Now you can say that I am following you."

Katerina turned away from the people, glancing up at Nik. "You're lucky that I'm in a good mood."

"Well, that's a first." He laughed. "How are you enjoying the festival?"

"It's refreshing." She smiled lightly, heat blooming on her cheeks. "Let me guess, you're here for what? Security detail, bounty, or to bask in my beauty?"

"This might come as a surprise to you, but I'm just here to enjoy the festivities."

"You?"

He nodded. "Is it so hard to believe that I am?"

"Yes." She chuckled.

"You know, for someone with such a nasty temper, you have a beautiful smile. You should use it more often."

"Don't have any reason to use it often." She retorted.

"That could be arranged." Nik said, eyes flickering from her eyes to her lips.

Heat spread through her skin as she tore her gaze away. "I should find the Sisters. I'm supposed to be doing volunteer service."

"Will they miss you for five minutes?"

"I've already been gone for more than that." *And most likely, father is somewhere around here.*

"Come on," Nik tilted his head, icy blue eye glinting with the colorful light. "When was the last time you did something *you* wanted?"

"Don't do that." She shook her head, drinking some more strawberry ambrosia.

"What?"

"Don't use that to get me to break the rules."

"You mean the rules you've already broken just by talking to me?" He arched an eyebrow.

He's right. "Have a good night." She turned away, but he grabbed her hand.

"Let me show you something before you wander back to your *volunteer* work."

"What are you—"

"Trust me." He tilted his head, eyes locking onto hers.

"Poor choice of words," she said, finishing her drink. "Make it quick."

He smiled and guided her through the crowd. Katerina ignored the people who glanced at them as they passed, silently praying not to get caught by her father.

They passed the entrance to the plaza and onto a path in the middle of the wood line.

Katerina's mind swirled. "Where are you taking me?" *If I die, I deserve it. I should've never....* Her mind quieted.

Everything was so quiet it almost hurt. The music from the festival seemed far away. For the first time in what felt like forever, there was no shouting, no smoke, no chaos... only stillness.

The lake glowed, its crystalline surface catching the moonlight like shards of glass smoothed by time. She approached it, her steps careful and slow. She could see straight through it: pale stones, swaying reeds, the faint shadow of her own reflection trembling in the ripples.

Her eyes burned. *Don't cry, don't cry, don't cry.*

The air was cool and gentle as it caressed her skin. The smell of rain and growing things slithered into her nose. The trees around the water swayed, their leaves whispered like a language she once knew before fear made everything foreign. The greenery stretched endlessly, untamed but peaceful.

"How did you find this place?" Katerina said gently without looking at him, biting back the urge to cry. *Why are you feeling this? Why? Why? Get a grip on yourself.*

"I like to explore." Nik said.

"But why bring me here?" She asked.

"I figured you needed a moment of respite."

Katerina looked up at him, heat spreading from her hand. Her hand that still held onto his. She let go.

"But why?" She said, unable to control the tear that escaped her eye. "Why are you doing this? You wanted to kill me on Veneration Night, then you invited me to Chryssa's party, then you meddled in the fight between me and—"

He wiped a tear from her cheek. "Is it so hard for you to believe that not everyone is out to get you and accept genuine kindness?"

He cupped her face, and Katerina found herself leaning into his gentle touch.

"Kindness is almost never genuine... especially when it pertains to me." She looked away.

"Look at me," he said, eyes soft. "You can enjoy the small things in life. Sometimes you have to be selfish, and there's nothing wrong with that."

"What do you have to gain?"

"Nothing." He breathed, lips parting slightly. "I just couldn't let you go after I saw you at Veneration Night."

"Is that so?" she whispered, gaze drifting to his lips merely inches away from her.

He nodded slightly. "You're a phenomenal woman. Is that so hard to believe?"

"Maybe..." Katerina drew a shallow breath. Every inch of her body wanted to stop whatever came next, but she missed feeling like *this*. "Besides, Chryssa is my friend." She slipped away from his grasp and walked to the shore.

"Chryssa is nothing to me. We were just a fling."

"She didn't seem to think that."

"Chryssa expected a relationship. Others thought we had a relationship because we were having fun for six years."

"Mhm." She muttered. "Still, you don't know me, Nik."

"I know more than you think, baby girl."

She met his gaze. "Pray tell."

Nik closed the gap between them. "Do you push *everyone* away?"

"If it keeps them safe, yes."

He cocked an eyebrow. "So you're concerned about my safety?"

"You don't know my father." She said, eyes soft, pain washing over them. "He'll kill you, punish me, I-I can't handle another lashing. I can't."

"He lashes you?" Nik's face paled.

Shit. I shouldn't have said that. "Forget I said that."

He grabbed her hands. "Let him come for me; I don't care."

"You're not the one that lives with him." She croaked. *Stop crying.* "If it finds out I'm here with you—"

"He won't."

"He will, and this wouldn't have worked anyway—"

His lips crashed against hers, making all worry and guilt wash away from Katerina in an instant. His hand crept up the nape of her neck, tilting her head, and deepening the kiss.

Katerina melted in his arms, holding onto his biceps for stability. *I shouldn't enjoy this. I shouldn't. This is wrong. Father is going to kill him.* Nik's words came to the surface. *Sometimes you have to be selfish, and there's nothing wrong with that.* He was part of the Olympian Army. This was wrong, yet she couldn't let go. She didn't want the kiss to end; it had been so long.

Her hands slid up his body, running through his hair as he wrapped his arms around her waist, pressing her body to his.

Nik trailed down her neck, kissing and biting her sensitive skin. He pulled back slightly, meeting her green eyes as they fluttered open. "Let him come for me."

THE RHYTHMIC BEAT OF DRUMS GUIDED THEIR STEPS back to the festival. Nik subtly paved the way for her, the ghost of their kiss still lingering on her lips.

They followed the crowd to a makeshift stage where performers enthralled the audience with their dance routines.

A man with a full grey beard and a significantly receding hairline dressed in an off-white tunic took the stage. His presence was commanding, and the crowd instantly shushed themselves.

Who is this guy? A chill ran down her spine. *Is he one of the local priests?*

"I stand before you tonight to bring forth the offerings for our Savior. But first, I would like to give a warm welcome to our guests of honor." He gestured to a dais right across the stage, amidst the sea of people. "Sovereign Argyros and his daughter, Princess Jezebelle."

Katerina's heart sank at the sight of her sister all serious, her juvenile spark almost nonexistent.

"Praise be to our Savior." The crowd said in unison.

"May thy light cleanse us from the tainted. May these offerings be enough to lift the curse Zeus has imposed upon us!" the man said.

Boos resounded from the crowd, and the air around her began to shift. She noticed Nik's body tense.

"Families go hungry every day! *Children* go to sleep hungry every day! And he has done *nothing* to aid us or relieve us from this torment!" He continued. "We have done everything to correct the wrongs of our ancestors, but that merciless cunt doesn't give a shit about none of us! Our one true Savior will take us to where we need to be!" he preached.

Katerina's body trembled and her jaw clenched as the crowd ruptured into a cheering frenzy.

Nik leaned toward her. "Is this what your Savior advocates for?"

She opened her mouth to respond, but someone in the distance shouted

"What makes you believe He will save us? Every month we give offerings. Sacrifices!" He gets on top of the stage; he had rich tan skin, a worn shirt and shorts, sandals, and dark curly hair. "And we are still the same as we were ten, fifteen years ago!" He scowls. "None of the gods have proven themselves to be as righteous as we paint them to be!"

Does he want to get killed? Katerina's gaze trailed to her father, his face unreadable.

"Go back to the poor side of the country, you unbelieving fiend." The elderly man spat.

Darkness slithered through the crowd, extinguishing the lanterns and candlelight. Heat spread through Katerina's body as her glare locked in on the elderly man.

His eyes widened, almost protruding out of his head. Gasps and screams rippled through the crowd. Her heart pounded heavily. The man gasped for air and collapsed.

Katerina's breath caught. *Did I do that?* She thought back to the Olympian priest, how he had collapsed under similar circumstances.

The crowd dispersed, running away from the invisible threat.

Her breath quickened. Bodies crashed against her. She couldn't move. Her heart raced. Everything was dark.

Her arm got grabbed and pulled. Squinting, she looked at the shadowy figure taking hold of her body, and she immediately jerked her body away.

Again.

And again.

And again.

The pressure on her arm diminished, making her lose balance for half a second. Bodies crashed against her again, and she fought the urge not to push them out of existence.

A massive lightning bolt struck one of the establishments, sending it ablaze.

Katerina cowered, tears swelling at the back of her eyes, threatening to escape. Bodies lie on the ground, stretching as far as the eye could see.

People trampled over the bodies while others mourned their losses upon realizing it.

"Katerina!" a woman called.

She faced the fire, and all she saw was the silhouette of a woman. "Katerina!" she called again. A flicker of light illuminated her face momentarily, and an audible gasp escaped her lips.

Jezebelle!

Katerina's body got pulled in the opposite direction before she was able to run towards her. She glared at the one pulling her body, but the figure was unrelenting.

"Let me go!" She snarled, punching the figure. "I have to go see her!"

It didn't release her, and its grip tightened every time she pulled her body away.

People continued to run and consumed her surroundings as Jezebelle disappeared from view. *No.* A tear slipped from her eyes.

She kept pulling her body, but that only got her a scolding to keep quiet.

It was a man. But it wasn't Nik. *Where is he?* Panic settled in her stomach. She glared at him, and prayed that she her theory was right. He stopped, grabbing his head and wincing in agonizing pain.

She ran.

Shoving everyone out of her way, her throat clenched at the sight of the monstrosities attacking the people with their leathery wings, snake-like hair and bloodshot eyes. Clawing their victims, a sea of rich crimson saturated the plaza. She kept running. The gates to the Fortress, so close yet so far amidst the chaos.

Grunting, she jumped over everything that crossed her path, tossed anything she could get her hands on.

Then it hit her. *Jezebelle.* Her sister was alone. And she was not confident that her father would put her first instead of himself. Well, she was a valuable asset right now. *Shit. I can't stop.* She had no choice but to trust he had her best interests at heart.

Sharp pain radiated through her calves with each agonizing stride. Her body crashed against the gates as she screamed for the guards. Again. And again.

"You have to be fucking joking," she quavered, constantly looking back for any signs of potential attackers. She rattled the gates forcefully. "Open the gates!" She shrieked and then blinked at the sight of the soldier's bodies inside the gates.

Her heart dropped, then turned at the loud thud behind her.

A fury emerged from the plaza; eyes fixated on Katerina, flashing its blood-covered sharp teeth.

Her body trembled as her mind raced to make a choice. *Kill or be killed?* The fury's body was massive compared to Katerina. *It's now or never.* She tightened her fists.

If I die, I die.

The fury lunged at her, and Katerina swung with everything she could. The fury collapsed. Blood seeped out of its hideous skull. Katerina peered down at her hands. Her fists were intact. Confusion plagued her mind.

She turned at the sound of the creaking gates and saw her father, blood covered and livid, accompanied by two soldiers, and it was at this moment that she didn't know whether to be grateful or terrified once more.

CHAPTER
THIRTY-EIGHT
KATERINA

HER FATHER PACED FURIOUSLY UP AND DOWN THE SAFE room beneath the council chamber, blood still dripping from his clothes.

Katerina sat next to Jezebelle, holding her sister's trembling and cold hands tightly. She surveyed the room, looking for Jasmine, yet only her father's counselors and generals were here. *Where the hell are you? Surely she knows what happened.*

A loud bang made her jump upright and turn her attention to her father.

"I am glad to know that all of you are alright and that everyone is safe. But we need to discuss our next moves. The furies did not come here just because they wanted to; they were sent here."

"This was a provocation." Kalio said.

"A provocation that I fully intend to respond to."

"Aren't you afraid that this might unleash a war?" A guy with a black eyepatch asked.

"We're already at war," her father replied. "Some of you refuse to acknowledge it, but we've been in a war for a very, very long time. The unfortunate passing of Quinn did not put a stop to the terrorizing. First they attack Brienne, now they attack one of our sacred days, one of our celebrations, and they think that I am not going to respond? That I'm just going to let my people sit and be victims of their unrelenting vicious—"

"What would this mean for us?" General Vivek said. "We can mobilize soldiers out of the Stronghold and station them around the capital."

"If we retaliate, it's only a matter of time before this becomes a bloodbath, Vivek." General Ware responded.

"Which is why we must prepare both our offense and defense strategies now."

"What about the people?" The man with the eyepatch asked. Silence fell across the room and he stood. "Countless of people will die if we don't grant them safe passage out of the country."

"Julius, this is one of the many unfortunate consequences of war." Kalio responded.

"Can we invoke the Justice Protocol?" Xaden asked.

"We can." Father responded. "But, even though Sylene provides sanctuary, they will not be able to accommodate all of Caverest, let alone Castelencia." He paced again.

Katerina glanced at Jezebelle, who was getting paler by the minute. "Are you okay?" she whispered.

She smiled, but didn't speak.

"You're shivering." Katerina whispered. "Here." She removed her cloak, which had been placed on her by one of the housemaids, and wrapped it around her. *What's happening to you?*

"You must do your due diligence. Leverage our alliance with Windermere." Her father turned to one of the generals still sitting. "General Lee."

"Sovereign?" He stood.

"Gather your troops and ensure to evacuate our people by dusk. I will send correspondence to Lazaros about the influx of refugees. Go through the northern border, and avoid the Aeshite crossing. After this, any sort of movement near their territory will be one they'll monitor closely. Especially since the Heartfen Citadel is not far from it."

"It'll be done, Sir."

"General Vivek and General Ware, have your soldiers gather in the Stronghold right after this meeting."

Both generals nodded.

"We're not gonna have survivors. I would be lying to you if I said we would." Her father said grimly. "I will do my best to avoid mass casualties, but there's no guarantee that everyone will make it. You are dismissed."

They all stood in unison, and Katerina glanced over at her father again before she left the room. He seemed different, rougher around the edges. Something unnerving stirred within her. In plain sight, he looked like her father but... she couldn't tell what was different. Perhaps exhaustion was taking its toll on him.

"Do you think this was sent by Governess Kiarelli?" She whispered to Jezebelle before she left.

She shrugged. "If it was, she has a rude awakening coming."

"Aren't they in Blossom peak season?" Katerina kept the alarm in her voice at bay.

She pursed her lips and looked away. That's all the confirmation Katerina needed to understand her father's next move. "There are going to be children present." She whisper-shouted.

Jezebelle looked to the floor, and chills slithered down Katerina's spine. *Governess Kiarelli doesn't know what she just unleashed.* Her body trembled. *Nik will most likely be on the front lines.* Her stomach dropped. *What will happen to Chryssa? Oh, shit. Chryssa... Savior help me if he tells Chryssa...* She shook her head. *Where's Jasmine?*

She waited until the last of the council members filed out of the room. Jezebelle was about two steps ahead.

"Katerina."

She froze, hands still folded neatly in front of her, though her stomach twisted. Jezebelle looked back at her curiously, but with a silent shake of Katerina's head, her sister turned, shutting the door behind her.

She tightened the grip on her trembling hands, but her

father's eyes were sharper than knives and partially bloodshot as they surveyed her.

"Yes?" she asked, averting her gaze.

He sat back on a seat. A chill invaded her body. *Calm down. You haven't done anything wrong... no. You did. Did he see the kiss? Did he have me followed?*

"Looks like what you wanted all these years it's going to be yours after all." He said.

Her stomach fluttered. *I thought my position in the Acrailerion was already secured... well, this means that I am officially getting inducted then, but the wedding... did he cancel?* She tried to keep her face neutral, but it was hard to suppress the smile tugging at her lips.

"You are to marry Lazaros' son, Byorn," he said without much preamble.

Her breath caught. Ice spread through her limbs. "N-no." She suppressed the panic screaming to get out. "That marriage would take away my opportunity to become a Re'Veillite. Everything I've worked for—"

He waved her words away like smoke. "I thought I made it clear that the position is a *privilege*, not a duty."

Katerina stepped closer, her voice rising despite the weight of his stare. "You would take everything I have built, everything that defines me, and chain me to a man I do not love—"

"You've built nothing." He hissed. "I'm surprised you're so against this." He mocked. "Considering he was the man you loved."

"Loved." She reiterated bitterly. "You did a splendid job in that area."

His eyebrows rose.

Careful. Careful with your words. Now he knows that I know. Fucking great.

"You're marrying him. End of discussion."

"What will you get out of it?" She snapped, not caring about the consequences. "Why can't Jezebelle be the one to be married off?" *Not that I would like her to be married to that animal.*

"Windermere." He responded blankly. "And as far as your sister is concerned, she has her duty to fulfill. Besides, you wouldn't allow yourself to let Jezebelle marry him, anyway."

Her chest caved. *Can he listen to my thoughts? Or am I just so damn blatant about it?* Tears sprang out of her eyes, but she kept her face composed. *Poised. Calm. Fuck... my freedom...*

"He's a monster." She protested. "You expect me to deal with that imbecile?"

"Looks like it's time for you to find a way to tame that beast." He mocked again.

I hate you. I hate you. I fucking hate you.

"What will happen to my induction?" *Was this seriously the best I could come up with?* "Will you really make me give that up?"

He scoffed. His annoyance was evident, but she couldn't allow herself to go down without a fight. This was the only thing she wanted. The one thing she fucking wanted.

"You know what?" He stood with a wicked grin plastered on his face. "We'll do your precious initiation. It'll mean nothing, of course. You'll still be expected to marry and move to Windermere. But anything to make you happy."

Don't fucking patronize me. "How considerate..." she mumbled through gritted teeth. "You don't have to do all that."

"Oh, but I do." His grin dropped. "How else will I show the world that you're still *pure*?"

She blinked. "What?" The fire in her chest burned hotter.

"I'm not blind, Katerina. I know about you and the governess's dog being rather close. The lake was not as private as you believed."

Her blood drained from her face. *Shit... but we just kissed... nothing more.*

He leaned forward. "Close is one word for it. Reckless is another. Do you think I would permit my daughter to disgrace our family with such... indulgences?" His tone was laced with irritation.

Her cheeks burned hot, not with shame, but with fury. She opened her mouth to speak, to deny, but the words tangled in her throat. He tilted his head, studying her as though she were something fragile and foolish.

"Reckless," he sneered. "That is what it was. You will attend your precious initiation. Display to the world that you're nothing but a *respectable* daughter, whose virtue is untarnished. Then, you will marry the governor's son, and you will do it without protest."

The torches crackled louder as if the fire bristled at his warning. Her heart pounded against her ribs, hot tears prickling at the corners of her eyes.

"If you defy me—if you *think* your will is stronger than mine —then you continue to learn and suffer the consequences of disobedience, which at this point, you must be well acquainted with."

Her back stung at the reminder.

"And they will not fall just on you. Do you understand?" he asked, each word deliberate, final.

The chamber felt smaller, the air thicker.

"When will everything happen?" She asked, meeting his gaze. "The induction and the wedding."

"So eager." He mocked.

Not in the slightest. She resisted a scowl.

"Initiation in two days. Wedding, I'll tell you after. Don't want to spoil the big day."

She clenched her fists, nails biting into her palms, and bowed her head in silent approval.

THIRTY-NINE

NANNEAU COVE WAS ALIVE WITH LIGHT AND SONG, torches swaying in the evening wind like fire-spirits dancing. The air carried the mingled perfumes of roasted meats, crushed grass, and the sweet fragrance of flowers braided into the hair of countless women. Reverence for Hera and Hestia was the occasion, yet Zeus had his own devotions to pursue.

He lingered in his mortal form, savoring the hum of flesh and desire. Among mortals, he could move freely as a man among them. Close enough to hear their laughter, close enough to catch the perfume clinging to their skin. This form has its pleasures, and tonight the meadow offered them in abundance.

Am I wrong for wanting to get involved in mortal affairs? Perhaps. Would it stop me? No. Has it ever? Who am I to deprive myself of Aeshite beauty? Their governess is proof enough of how blessed their genetics are.

Speaking of, there she was now. With flowers curled through her hair like a wreath from the meadow itself, and her smile— genuine, warm, almost careless of the dangers that pressed her borders—lit the air around her.

She moved among her guests with kindness, laughter, and attention, as though every soul gathered belonged to her household. Zeus' eyes lingered a moment. Her charm could be her own power, one perhaps even more dangerous than his.

He admired how she was able to switch between business and personal. Not many had the ability to do so, and he wondered... his gaze trailed to her rose-colored gown, trailing behind her, and the sleeves of her top bodice clung from her flawless tan shoulders. And her breasts... covered for modesty, but still able to be appreciated underneath it.

Quite the tease.

He wondered what it would take to bend her just right and see what else she was able to do. Aeshite women did have a reputation of being the best lovers across the continent.

He tore his gaze away. *I'll entertain that thought soon enough.*

Hestia stood surrounded by a circle of families near the central hearth, her hands folded, her voice as calm as water.

She spoke of the hearth's flame—how keeping it alive was to keep the family whole. They leaned in toward her words, their gazes soft and steady as if she had already bound them in her eternal fire.

Hera, on the other hand, moved with deliberate grace through the field. She leaned close to her listeners, palm pressed against their cheeks or clasping their hands, each blessing given like a crown upon their heads. Her voice was low, her presence calming. But deep down, Zeus knew she was keeping record of his whereabouts and who he spoke to. Her occasional but frequent, glances gave her away.

Soldiers of the Thunder and Regal Guard kept the meadow secure, their helms gleaming and spears glinting. They scanned the field like wolves among sheep, though the families seemed comforted by their presence. Power was safety to some, menace to others, and Zeus found both equally pleasing.

He kept his walk relaxed as he neared the tranquil water that reflected the sky almost exactly. The cove was one of the highlights of the continent, and it was a pity that so few got to bask in its beauty. His gaze locked onto a lonesome dying tree at one end of the water. Zeus approached it, curious as to how it was here when there was so much blooming flora on either side. The ground around it was bone dry, and beneath it lied a single thornless black rose. *Odd.*

Vibrant laughs pulled his attention away from the rose and toward a young woman with strawberry blonde hair caught with ribbons, carrying a basket of lilies so fresh they seemed still wet with dew. She gave one to one of the women and paused at the meadow's edge.

Her eyes met his, and she smiled faintly, nervously, but it was enough. Mortal women, save for a select few, never truly knew who he was when in mortal form, yet they felt a pull that was not like the other men. And *that* led them straight into his arms.

As soon as Hera, Hestia, and Zeus departed the meadow, it'll be like they were never here, just a group of Olympian supporters paying reverence to the divine and reaping their blessings and gifts. It was unfortunate because others may paint his devotees as crazed or fanatical. But they have to keep our anonymity to a degree. Hence why their minds get *tweaked* a bit. But Zeus and the rest of the Olympians were always watching.

He crossed the grass with an easy stride, letting the noise of the meadow fall away until there was only her. "You carry beauty twice over," he said, nodding to the lilies before fixing his gaze back upon her. "The flowers pale in your presence."

Her grip tightened on the basket; her lips parted, but no words came out. A hint of red painted her cheeks as she looked at him from beneath her lashes, and he let the silence hang until she shifted her weight, uncertain yet rooted.

"What's your name?" Zeus asked softly.

"Wendy..." She responded bashfully.

He brushed a fingertip along the edge of a petal, feigning interest, though his eyes never left hers. "Tell me," he murmured, lowering his voice so it dripped like honey, "who are these for? Or are they waiting for the right hands to claim them?"

Her blush intensified, high and hot across her cheeks. She

shook her head lightly, locks bouncing, flowers trembling in her basket. "They are... for the women here," she whispered. "They deserve something nice, given the special occasion."

He leaned closer, the scent of lilies mixing with her skin, sweet and alive. "Then allow me," he said softly, "to make them yours. Keep them, and let me see them where they belong... in your hair, in your hands, scattered across the grass when the night has grown darker."

Her breath caught, and he noticed her knuckles whiten against the wicker handle. She looked past him, toward Hera, who was still granting blessings, then toward Hestia, speaking of hearths, then to the governess, who laughed with her guests as though peace was her birthright.

None of them mattered in this moment; she was his, even if it was just for the day or evening, however long he wanted.

He stepped closer until their arms brushed, and let his hand graze her wrist where it clutched the basket. His touch was light, but sparks leaped between them, nonetheless. "Come," he urged gently, voice steady and inviting. "The meadow is bright with daylight, but its edges hold shadows enough for us. Let me show you why I walk among mortals."

Her chest rose sharply, her breath shivering in her throat. She lowered her eyes, yet did not move away. When she looked back up, her gaze was braver than her words.

"Yes," she whispered.

And with that, the day became his to shape.

The air around them thrummed faintly with his power as she lowered the basket, placing it somewhere others could come and pick a lily for themselves.

The ground shudders with a rhythm not of his making. He turned to the mass of people gradually running one behind the other. Faint screams trailed behind them.

"What's going on?" Wendy asked, her voice laced with a tremor. "She's mad, isn't she? She knows about this, doesn't she? She saw..." she wept.

I'm assuming she thinks Hera is going to exact revenge for this interaction, but she is the least of her worries.

A stampede of families dispersed, looking for shelter.

"Run." Zeus ordered and, without much convincing, Wendy does.

Enemy soldiers poured from the horizon, iron glinting, war cries ripping the air apart. Panic tore through the meadow. Mothers clutched their children. Shields locked. And in the blink of an eye, the music of peace gave way to the shriek of steel.

Zeus raised his hand, veins burning with fury. Lightning would split their ranks, and thunder would crush their spirits and lay this foolishness to rest. He called to it.

Nothing.

Enemy soldiers, displaying their sun emblem, kept piling through. Thrashing and burning everything in sight.

Zeus blinked, stunned, and thrust his hand higher; summoning the storm once again.

Yet nothing came.

The meadow was drowning in blood. Arrows rained down, striking mortals as they fled. His men fell beneath blades. Children screamed, their cries cutting sharper than any sword. Zeus bellowed in rage, his voice carrying across the battlefield as he called once more to the heavens.

Answer me!

Still, the sky denied him. His chest constricted, and for the first time, he felt a tremor of doubt.

Hera.

Hestia.

I have to find them. Without much thought, he lunged into the chaos as enemy soldiers crashed into the crowd. His men fought against them. Some guided families out of harm's way while others defended those fighting alongside them.

Steel clashed. Screams rose, and the meadow turned crimson. He fought through them with his bare strength, but every mortal he struck down was replaced by three more. They fell around him —his people, his kin, his children.

He tried again, voice breaking as he bellowed. Still nothing. His heart pounded. *This is all wrong.*

Something was *wrong.*

And then, through the storm of chaos, he saw *her.*

Eris.

She stood at the center of the battlefield, untouched by the carnage, her dark hair flowing like shadow. Her lips curved into a smile as her violet eyes found him. She raised her hand slowly, deliberately, and gave him a mocking, playful wave.

His fury surged, but before he could move, before he could roar her name, she winked and vanished. Like smoke in the wind. Rage and dread collided in his chest. *Of course this is her fucking doing. Was it she who cut me from the storm? If so, fucking how?*

He tried again, calling the lightning, thunder, anything—but the sky ignored him, as though it no longer knew who he was despite his mortal form. He'd always been able to wield his power, regardless of the form he took.

Around me, countless mortals fell. Their blood pools in the grass; their screams pierced the air. And he felt utterly useless. Hera's voice cried out, Hestia's too, but he could not save them all.

Zeus grabbed Hera's arm, pulling her away from the soldiers attacking her. He managed to punch one in the stomach and pull out a blade from his back as he hunched over.

Swiftly, he sliced his way through, Hera following closely behind. The battlefield pressed against him, suffocating. Rage boiled over into panic. The air thickened with the weight of loss, with the stench of smoke and charred flesh. His name was shouted, cried out in desperation, but he could not answer them.

What am I to do? He felt naked, stripped of the very essence that made him who he was. He tried again—his voice broke with the effort, his arm trembling as he willed the storm to obey. But there was only silence.

He continued to advance, reaching Hestia and forcing them out, before his mind could argue. Through the chaos, through the cries of the dying, he fled, disappearing into thin air.

Zeus barged into the bright hall, breath heaving, heart thunderless. For the first time, Olympus felt not like a throne above the world, but a cage.

His power failed him. And the meadow was now a graveyard that bore his shame and utter failure.

Her fucking wave lingered in his mind, sharper than any blade, mocking and all too knowing. All around him, countless lives were snuffed out. And he did nothing. His people. Their blood stained the meadow until the green was lost in deep crimson.

His arms ached, not from battle, but from the weight of those he carried. Hera staggered beside me, her gown torn and streaked with ash, her face pale with fury. On his other side walked Hestia, clutching his arm for balance, her usual serene gaze hollowed with grief.

Soldiers fell back in stunned silence as they crossed the threshold and into the Assembly Chamber. The Olympians stood as one they laid eyes on Zeus. Athena's eyes sharpened, her voice quick. "You bring Hera and Hestia... but where are the others? Where are the people who gathered in the meadow? Where are the soldiers?"

Hera's answer came before he could form a pitiful excuse. She tore herself free from his side, her voice blazing. "Dead! Cut down like cattle while he stood powerless!" She gestured at Zeus with trembling hands, rage burning through the cracks of her grief. "Zeus, who commands the sky, stood with an empty fist while children screamed for mercy. Where were you? Where were all of you?"

Well, that's one way to put it.

The chamber rippled with shock. Poseidon leaned forward on his trident, a cruel smirk tugging at his lips. "Empty fist? Impossible. The storm bends to your will."

Zeus' throat tightened, but the words came raw, despite his pride. "It failed me. I summoned it again and again, and I got nothing in return."

Hestia's hand clutched his arm tighter. Her voice was low, sorrowful. "I saw it with my own eyes. His call went unanswered. But if it weren't for him, Hera or I wouldn't be here."

The hall fell into an uneasy silence, the kind that seeped into bone. Athena broke it first, her gaze slicing into Zeus like a blade.

"Then the meadow was not merely an attack; it was a message. Whoever dared to strike did so knowing you would falter."

"It was retaliation for what I did to their precious gathering." Zeus admitted.

"The real question is how?" Ares asked. "You weren't even going to the fucking meadow until today. Not even the most skilled generals can alter plans that quickly. Give me a host of soldiers, and I'll send a pretty message to the Heretic."

Hera turned her fury from Athena to Ares. "And then what, Ares? What will that give you? Ashes? Graves? There is no one left in that meadow. He killed and burned them all, and it's only a matter of time before he moves to the rest of the continent."

Her words clung to Zeus like chains. His people. All of them gone, and he had carried away only two.

Zeus forced his voice steady, though it wavered beneath. "We are not defeated. This was just one battle. I will summon the storm again. It *will* answer to me."

But in the silence that followed, their eyes betrayed what they truly thought. That he was no longer Zeus the Mighty, but Zeus the Forsaken.

"Yet Hera's question remains unanswered." Zeus added. "Where were all of you when this was happening?"

They averted their gaze.

Zeus huffed. "Even when the storms failed me, I still showed up and did what I had to do. Unlike you cowards."

"What about the governess? Is she still alive?" Athena asked.

"Everything happened so fast. I lost sight of her once everyone started running away." Hera responded.

"No one here is asking the main question." Poseidon pointed out. "How did you suddenly lose control over the sky?"

"You think I'm not asking myself the same fucking thing?" Zeus ran a hand through his hair. "Not only that, first was your power to control the sea, now me..."

"We also have to ask if it's just the power that you lost? Or something more?" Athena added.

"What are you suggesting?" Hera's brows narrowed.

The silence hung heavy and thick. She didn't have to answer the question for all of them to understand. Everyone's eyes landed on him.

Zeus sank onto his seat, hands trembling against the carved arms. *I've been reduced to shaking like a mortal.* The silence pressed on him heavier than chains.

Why don't they answer me? So many fucking questions. My mind trickled back to the wounded soldiers under Asclepius care.

To Apollo.

Did someone slip some of that poison to me? If so, wouldn't I be dying? Or close to losing my immortality? By the looks of it, I'm still good in that area. But it's not something I will dismiss until I have some kind of proof. His jaw clenched. *Was it a curse? A trick of the Sovereign? How has he severed me from the skies?*

"Where's Argus?" He asked. *If there's someone who can get me answers, it's he.*

Silence remained, and Zeus' gaze locked with Ares, who shrugged.

"He mentioned he was going to see if he could get a sample of the poison. Haven't seen him since."

It's been two days since...

"And you didn't bother to mention that he hasn't returned?"

Zeus retorted. "In times like these, we cannot afford to lose anyone else."

"I'm not his keeper." Ares scowled.

"Just like you weren't Apollo's," Zeus raised a brow.

"What happened to Apollo?" Artemis asked urgently.

Zeus ignored her question.

"Unlike Apollo's case, I wasn't tasked on keeping record of Talos—Argus, whatever the fuck he wants to call himself nowadays. I have better things to do."

Hecate's words rang heavy within me. *"You, as well as I, know that the prophecy cannot be stopped nor undone once it's been set in motion. Therefore, we must stop the chain of events. I, alongside Hades, prepared an area in the deepest parts of Tartarus. It is warded by me and him. No one will be able to leave unless I and Hades deem it so. You must send Typhon here before the Sovereign becomes a vessel. That may be our only chance to stop him. Make sure Joseph didn't create a tether."*

He shut his eyes and covertly reached, the way he always had, into the vastness above, and imagined the lightning breaking through the glass ceiling, piercing the marble floor. Bathing the room in white and silver. It was effortless: a flick of will, and the skies bent, the clouds gathered, the heavens trembled at his command. But now... he had nothing. Even in Olympus, only emptiness remained.

The torches hissed, throwing long shadows across the floor. His reflection in the marble was warped, broken by cracks in the stone. He saw himself as his enemies must: a man...just a man, draped in failing power. Doubt seeped in like poison, and he felt something he thought he had long since beaten out of existence.

Fear.

"We'll reconvene in the Heartfen Citadel," Zeus ordered, and everyone left without uttering a word. "Hera."

She turned expectantly, and Zeus stood as soon as the doors closed.

"Are you alright?" He asked, approaching her.

"I'm fine." She said bitterly.

"You're bleeding." His eyes narrowed at her brow. He took off his shirt and used the fabric to clean the blood.

"You didn't have to take your shirt off." She chuckled.

"Maybe." He snaked his hand around her body. "Should we take this to the bedroom? I'm sure you have some more wounds that need mending."

CHAPTER
FORTY
KATERINA

Breathe. Just breathe.

It's not going to be the end of the world.

You've dealt with him before. He may be a monster, but you know how to handle him... yeah, like I did such a great job handling him after Silas's death. I handled him so damn well at the garden too...

Sure.

If it weren't for Nik being conveniently present... Katerina resisted the urge to slam her head on the seat in front of her, tightening her grip on it. *Breathe. You don't want to be causing a scene in the middle of the Worship Hall... not when you have the initiation coming up...*

The initiation... all for damn show... is that even allowed? She scoffed. *Of course, it is.* Who'd be stupid enough to go against her father? *Well, me.* The scent of frankincense was stronger today.

She glanced briefly at the women around her. One sobbed to her left, consoled by a sister, and others just roamed around trying to garner the attention of any High Re'Veillite in what she assumed was their way to get into their good graces and thus, gaining a spot in the sisterhood.

Katerina would say it was pitiful, but she wasn't even sure if her opinion mattered at this point. *It's all for damn show.* His words still lingered in her mind, and her heart raced at the reminder; ice spreading through her fingertips.

Calm down.

She stood, not caring for the eyes that fell upon her at the abrupt movement. *I need to find the Verenna. Surely, she can shed some light on my situation.* She hurried into the foyer and stormed toward the center stairs that led to the Celestial Tower.

To her damned luck, a High Re'Veillite got in her way, demanding to know where she was headed and that she am not allowed to go to the second floor. In addition to whatever else the High Re'Veillite felt the need to say but Katerina didn't care enough to listen.

Katerina pushed past her, and the Re'Veillite grabbed her arm.

"You will let me go right now." Katerina sneered.

"I cannot let you go up there."

"And I suppose you're going to stop me." Katerina scanned her. "With that pitiful grip of yours?" *There's no point to keeping my grace if this shit is for show, isn't it?*

"Either you turn around or face the consequences."

A threat. Katerina arched a brow. "Take it up with the Sovereign." She hissed, pulling her arm out of her hold. *Maybe he'll be useful for once.*

Ice prickled her fingers, and Katerina slammed into nothingness. *What the hell?* She took another step, yet her body was halted by an invisible barrier.

Katerina pressed a hand against it, and it felt like a strong force, compacted into something impenetrable. *Today is not the day for this shit.*

Katerina turned back to her, the High Re'Veillite smirked like she was the smartest in the room.

Oh, today is the fucking day. She raised a fist, ready to bury it in her smug face. But she couldn't. Something pulled her arm back.

She turned and found the Verenna standing atop the stairs, staring directly at her.

I am fucked.

The Verenna descended the stairs, and the High Re'Veillite stepped away from Katerina.

"Apologies, Verenna." She bowed her head. "She was headed to the Celestial Tower, and I was putting a stop to it, per our oath."

After a moment of silent examination, the Verenna shooed her away with a hand. The High Re'Veillite left without question, and Katerina noticed the wash of indignation that flickered in her eyes before leaving.

The Verenna turned to Katerina, gesturing follow.

Ice prickled at her fingertips again, but a quick tightening of her fists had her controlling the spread. Or so she thought... perhaps it was her body heat doing the work. *What the hell does this icy feeling mean, anyway? Oh, I don't know what to feel at this point.*

They entered the office, and Katerina instantly took a seat in front of her desk.

Usually, she'd wait until the Verenna gave her the go-ahead to sit but she needed to talk to her. She needed her guidance. And she needed it now.

The Verenna took a seat, eyes never straying from Katerina, expectantly.

If she could see into my mind, there's no point in hiding anything. So, she proceed to tell her everything.

Her wrongdoings. Her embarrassing love affair with Byorn. What he'd done to their child. Her anger. Ohh, her anger. Her fucking rage at her father for marrying her to Byorn. The crossroads she's facing between protecting her sister—keeping her punishments out of the conversation—and her duty as the Sovereign's eldest. This confusing as fuck thing that was happening to her, where her hands became ice and her chest enflamed whenever danger lingered. How her sister was allowed to fall in love with whomever.

I am tired of carrying everything. Her eyes burned. She took a deep breath, slowing down her racing heart. *Breathe. I take care of everyone, and absolutely no one bothers to check in on me... well... that used to be Jasmine, but I haven't seen her in who knows how long. Most likely, she got tired of me too.*

The Verenna blinked and gave her a small fraction of a smile.

Katerina saw it all too well. The pity in her eyes. In her face.

The Verenna reached for a sheet of parchment next to her and started writing.

"I know I have to be a certain way to be in line with what the Sisters represent, but... does it really matter if my initiation is just all for show?" Katerina looked down at her palms, biting back the tears. "It won't mean anything, anyway."

The Verenna's eyes didn't leave the sheet.

Great.

"If this is your way of making me draw my own conclusions, I have to admit, with all due respect, it's not working." Katerina said, eyes jumping back from the quill to her unreadable face.

Look at me.

Acknowledge me.

Tell me something.

"Can you give me something?" Katerina pleaded. "I am at a crossroads. I don't know where else to turn. Who else to talk to."

After a long moment, the Verenna looked up at her, sliding the sheet over.

Look inward, child. For the mirror never lies. The answers you seek are written in the quiet corners of your soul. Trust the stillness, for it will reveal what words cannot.

Yet, be wary. Shadows cling even when the light is brightest. The reflection you find may not be yours alone. Something waits there, older than memory, heavier than silence. It has marked you, and it lingers still. Do not mistake its whisper for your own voice, for the curse it left behind feeds on your searching. Guard your spirit, for what looks within may already be looking back.

When I looked within, I found answers... but also a shadow that clung to me. If you search your depths, beware—you may find what cursed me waiting for you.

Katerina looked up at her. "You were cursed?" She muttered before she could stop the words.

A slight nod.

Katerina's stomach dropped, mind stirring. "But who—is this why you haven't spoken to me?"

Another nod, and her quill traced the parchment. Katerina followed carefully.

G. U. I...

Guiol

T. E. N. E. B...

Tenebrios.

"What does this mean?" Katerina asked. "My Ialahri is not that advanced. I—"

The Verenna pressed a finger onto her lips and instantly shredded the parchment. Before she was able to ask anything, the door opened.

"Apologies for the interruption, High Priestess." A soldier nodded curtly. "The Sovereign requests Katerina to be in her chambers in order to prepare for her ceremony."

"What ceremony?" *I swear, he better not mean the wedding.*

His eyes met Katerina's with an unreadable expression. "The initiation, of course."

Bullshit. "Certainly." Katerina muttered, standing and turning back to the Verenna. "Thank you for your time."

She nodded politely, and Katerina took it as her cue to leave.

He already had the date for the wedding and, based on the soldier's tone, I'm not stupid to when it is.

Right after my initiation.

How fucking considerate.

KATERINA PACED UP AND DOWN THE ROOM. *THIS IS risky. I don't know what I'm thinking. I shouldn't do this. But I can't let him win. Father can't win. Byorn can't win. And I refuse to accept this without doing this first.* Knocking turned her attention to the door of the inn's bedchamber. *No turning back now.*

Nik stood in the doorway. His blonde hair was untamed, and wore casual clothing instead of his uniform. "I was not expecting you to reach out."

Katerina's throat clenched, but stepped out of his way, allowing him entry into the cozy room.

"Bold of you to do this." He said once the door closed. "How did you find me?"

"Connections..." She shrugged, not wanting to admit that it was her meddling that managed to allow her to find the address to the Heartfen Citadel. She'd hoped he would receive it. Yet, she didn't expect him to show, especially not this quickly.

"Ah..." he chuckled. "Well, I'm here."

You are... Katerina's throat bobbed, eyes focused on the ground.

He tilted his head and approached her, stopping once he was towering over her. "What do you want, baby girl?" He was close enough she felt the warmth radiating from him, the rise and fall of his chest a rhythm her own breath mimicked.

She looked up from under her eyelashes. "You know what I want..."

When his hand brushed a stray curl from her cheek, she didn't draw away. She should have. The thought flickered once, like the dying glow of a candle—but his touch lingered, and her will slipped with it.

"Do you know what you're asking for?" His hand crept up, resting at the base of her neck.

"Yes," she breathed.

He leaned in, hovering his lips over hers. "You don't care that Chryssa works here? A few days ago, you were saying how she was your friend and couldn't do precisely this." His free hand slipped off the fabric that clung to her shoulder.

She licked her lips. "You told me all you had was a fling... nothing more."

"Is that what you want?" He lowered his head, kissing her neck gently. "Just a fling?"

I want to remember what its like to feel wanted... Katerina's eyes fluttered, feeling his hot breath against her skin. *I want a distraction. I want to enjoy something, for once.*

"Hmm? Use your words, Princess." His free hand snaked around her waist.

"Yes," she breathed, letting her dress fall to her feet. *Just kiss me already.*

"If I would've known you'd wanted me so badly, I would've obliged sooner." He met her gaze.

"Then what are you waiting for?" she breathed, eyes fluttering.

"You don't want me to be gentle?" He traced a hand across her cheek.

"I want..." She bit her lip. "Do your worst..."

The distance between them collapsed in a heartbeat. His lips found hers, hesitant at first, then certain—each stolen kiss a quiet rebellion. Her fingers clutched at the fabric of his shirt as though anchoring herself to something real and dangerous. His mouth moved with a kind of urgency that scared her in its honesty—like he knew this wouldn't last and wanted to burn it into memory before it vanished.

She broke the kiss first, her forehead resting against his. Her breath came fast, tangled with his. "We shouldn't..." she started, but the rest died in her throat.

"I know," he murmured, brushing his thumb along her lower lip. "Then tell me to stop."

But she didn't. *I want this. I want something to enjoy, no matter how fleeting it might be.*

And when his lips found hers once more, she stopped thinking about right or wrong; only how the rain outside seemed to echo the sound of her pulse, steady and wild and alive.

He pulled away and removed his shirt, tossing it on the ground. Katerina's gaze trailed down his muscular body, then her eyes stopped on the ink that crept through his waist and abdomen.

"Something caught your eye?"

"I didn't realize you had a tattoo..."

"Well, princess, you haven't seen me shirtless before." He turned, giving her a full view of his back.

The light through the open window caught on his back, where ink and skin seemed to blur together. It wasn't like any tattoo she had seen before—well, she'd never seen anyone with a tattoo before. She's heard about them, yes... but that didn't compare to this.

It didn't look etched, but it moved, or perhaps it seemed to. The black flowed down his shoulders in twisting, organic shapes, darker in some places, thinner in others, like it had once been liquid and only just decided to stop spreading. Thin white lines wove through the darkness in faint, shimmering veins that pulsed softly when he breathed, giving the impression of life beneath the surface.

Her fingers traced the inky tattoo, drawn in before she realized it. The ink seemed to be as if it spilled into water. But within the swirling blackness, there were shapes drawn with fine and faint lines. She leaned closer. A vase cracked open just beneath his shoulder blade. The curve of a serpent coiling across his ribs. A pair of scales, faint as a reflection in glass. Her eyes followed the design down the center of his spine, where thin lightning-like streaks of light branched out from a heart-shaped flame. It looked alive, like it was breathing through him, wrapping him in something ancient.

"I've never seen anything like it," she whispered, half to herself.

The longer she looked, the more she saw—a wing hidden in shadow near the base of his spine, a flower blooming out of the ink near his ribs. The whole piece seemed caught between chaos and control, like something divine and human trying to exist in the same space. It was an utter and complete masterpiece.

"Does it mean anything?"

"If I were to tell you, we'd be here all night." He turned, towering over her. "And I would like for us to use our time wisely, since all you want is a fling."

Yeah...

He picked her up, and her breath caught, wrapping her legs around his torso. Nik dropped her onto the bed and climbed on top of her. Katerina's hands reached up to caress his face, but he caught them, pinning them overhead.

"If you want to know what that means, we might have to schedule another encounter," he whispered against her lips and trailed a hand down her body, caressing her soft skin and resting between her legs. "Oh," he chuckled, amusement lacing his words as he massaged her.

She couldn't read his expression, but then he kissed her. Her hands ran through his soft hair, savoring his taste. The kiss was hungry; he devoured her lips as if they were his to own. She tightened her grip on his hair, pulling it.

"You've been quite a tease." He groaned against her lips.

Her finger traced his lips, then his scar. "As have you…"

Her breath caught as he propped her legs wide and buried his face between them. She moaned, drawing a sharp breath. *I want you. I want all of you. He feels so good.* He groaned and looked at her. "You are so sweet." He picked up the tempo, building her up just right. *Don't stop, please.* Her hands gripped the sheets.

He pulled away.

Katerina sat up, reaching for his pants. *I need you now. I want you.*

He grabbed her hands, stopping her. "You're going to feel it first. But how I want you to."

Before she could protest, he turned her, facing down, and made her arch her back. Her breath caught as he teased her, feeling his length. *Savior help me… please… give it to me, please…* she leaned back, and he held her in place.

"So greedy…"

"And you're selfish."

"Am I?" he chuckled, sliding into her.

Her eyes rolled back, pleasure spreading through her. He was bigger than she expected.

"Am I selfish now?" he asked, sneaking his hand up her hair and pulling it, her back arched.

He felt so good. She didn't want him to stop. She didn't want to go back. He kept thrusting faster, taking her up to the edge.

Oh gods…

She whimpered as he slapped her ass. *I'm so close.*

"Oh, no." He stopped and turned her until she was facing him. "I want to look at your pretty face when you come for me."

He brought her legs up to his shoulders, sliding back in. "That's it." He muttered as her eyes rolled back.

"You're so big..." she whispered.

"I know, but you're taking it so well." He picked up the pace. "Now, be a good girl and come for me."

His hand found hers, gently at first, then tightened as her breath hitched, uneven, the world narrowing. *Please.* Every sound seemed to dissolve into something wordless. He murmured her name like a promise, and her body answered before her voice could.

For a heartbeat, time broke apart. The room spun, the air thick with heat and lightning. Her fingers clutched at him, eyes closing as the tension inside her fractured and gave way to something blinding, quiet, and whole all at once, to that damned release.

His lips found the hollow beneath her throat as he lowered, breath ragged; she felt the world tilt. Her fingers threaded through his hair, pulling him closer, chasing warmth in a world that had given her none. The scent of rain on his skin, the whisper of fabric shifting, the uneven beat of their hearts. Every sound became part of the same rhythm, desperate and fleeting.

She didn't think beyond that second. There was no past, no future—only the present, fragile and burning. She knew she wouldn't see him again. That this wouldn't happen again because tomorrow her life would change to an eternity of confinement.

CHAPTER
FORTY-ONE
JOSEPH

Soldiers threw Governess Kiarelli forward, and though she stumbled, she didn't bow. She snapped her head toward Joseph, eyes ablaze with hatred. Her curly hair was tangled with pieces of twigs and who knew what else. Her rose-colored dress was torn at the hem, and her skin was even bruised and ragged; yet, she carried herself as if she still had a dash of dignity in her.

"You murderer" she roared, voice echoing against the walls of his study. "Do you know how many women lay bleeding in that meadow? How many children cried for their mothers before smoke stole the air from their lungs? You think you can come onto *my* lands, kill *my* people, and live to see another day?"

The soldiers at her sides stiffened, awaiting Joseph's orders. He didn't move. He just folded his hands atop his desk and let her fury crash against him like waves against stone. He allowed the silence to stretch, watching her tremble with fury. For a moment, he admired the fire in her. She was as stunning as she was fiery.

He stood, letting his shadow fall across her. "All of this could have been avoided, Governess. Had you simply agreed to the alliance I offered."

"You attacked my country because I refused to join you?" She asked, dumbfounded. "Can't handle rejection? Get over it." She took a step toward him.

His soldiers moved simultaneously. But a simple gesture from Joseph kept them at bay.

"You would bind my people as slaves to your hunger for power." She added.

Joseph leaned close, close enough for her to see the cold certainty in his gaze. "You speak of chains, but your people already wear them. Chains of loyalty to gods who never come. Tell me, Faviola. When your walls crumbled, did they descend from the heavens to protect you as you called upon them? Did they put up a fight against my soldiers?"

Her jaw tightened. *Silence. Beautiful, damning silence.*

He smiled. "No. They left you. You, their devoted servant, abandoned in your hour of need. What does that tell you? They do not care."

She trembled, and he saw that fire light up behind her eyes once more. Her silence screamed louder than her voice ever could.

He circled her slowly, like a predator stalking its prey. "I offer you something better than their empty promises. Join me. Place your lands beneath my rule, and I will guarantee safety. Your people will live. This is mercy, Faviola. Take it before I decide mercy is wasted on you."

Her breath hitched; her expression unreadable. Yet, Joseph could sense the grief pressing hard against her defiance. Was it a part of his newly acquired power? Perhaps, but those were questions for another time.

She lifted her chin, her eyes unyielding. "No." Her voice cracked, but she forced it stronger. "My people won't kneel to you. And if the gods don't come today, they will come tomorrow. They will avenge the dead. They will deliver me. And you—" She raised her voice, ringing with conviction. "You will choke on the ashes of your throne as it goes up in flames."

The soldiers glanced at him as if waiting for something, an

order to silence her. But instead, he leaned close enough that only she could hear, his voice a venomous whisper.

"Then let your gods come. Let them come down, and I will break them as I break you. And when they fail you again, when your people kneel not by choice but for survival, you will know it was not divinity that abandoned you—it was your own stubborn pride."

Her lips quivered, her fire flickering beneath the weight of the words, and he savored every moment of it.

He straightened, stepping back into the shadows of his chamber. "Take her to the catacombs, and prepare the cell next to the altar."

THE TORCHES BURNED LOW IN THE CATACOMBS, THEIR light swallowing more shadow than they cast. Joseph descended the spiral stairs behind his soldiers, the air growing damp, thick with the stench of stone and rot. Even though the Fortress above was his, down here, beneath the earth, he held a different kind of throne.

Down here, voices broke.

Kiarelli fought the entire way, heels grinding against stone, her curses rattling the vaulted halls. She refused to give in. But that wasn't enough for Joseph to show more mercy than what he's given.

He had given her a way out—a way toward peace, yet she refused. But regardless of her choice, Joseph had to secure Aeshelyn somehow. No matter the cost.

The soldiers dragged her to the waiting cell with iron bars slick with condensation and straw reeking of mildew. They threw her inside, the sound of her body striking the stone floor echoing through the cavern. She pushed herself upright, hair falling across her face, her breath ragged as soldiers secured her arms and legs to the chains attached to the walls. Yet when her eyes found Joseph in the corridor, they blazed as they had in his study.

"This cage," she hissed, "will not silence me or keep me. You may bury me beneath your Fortress, Sovereign, but my people will rise once they notice my absence. And when they do, you'll wish you'd struck me dead."

He approached the doorframe, studying her through the flicker of firelight. "Your people are ash, Governess. Their rise will be no more than smoke in the wind. And you—" He let his voice soften. "You remain alive only because *I* allow it. Do not mistake your breath for your victory."

She approached him, only to be stopped midway by the chains that bound her. "The gods will avenge them," she said fiercely. "Even if my people cannot, the gods will not leave me here."

Joseph tilted his head, savoring the tremor in her voice. The torches flickered, dropping low. He addressed his men, though his eyes remained on her. "Let her sit with her silence and reflect on her choices."

"You underestimate them. They will come."

"Then let them." He smiled faintly, turning from her cell. "You have until dawn to change your mind."

THE SOUND OF ERIS' STEPS ECHOED AHEAD OF HIM, light and deliberate, a taunt in the endless dark of the catacombs' tunnels. He quickened his pace, boots striking harder against the stone, chasing the flicker of her shadow as it slipped between the pillars.

"Do you mean to run from me, or draw me deeper into your fucking game?" He said, voice roughened by the damp air.

She stopped at last, half-turned, her profile lit by the weak torch he carried. That mocking smile curved her lips.

"You always follow, Joseph," she said. "And each time, you

expect something different. Have you not learned that I only ever bring you closer to what you want depending on your performance?"

He caught up to her, standing close enough to feel the chill that seeped from her presence. "I don't have time for this. You summoned me right when I was in the middle of securing Aeshelyn as he wanted. So what the fuck do you want?"

Her eyes sparkled in the gloom as she leaned forward. "He stirs. You've given it much, but not enough. The sickle is yet to be retrieved and he is growing impatient."

"I have men scouring the Euxine Sea. If he wants it that bad, tell him to get it himself."

She laughed. "Oh, Joseph. You know what happens when he's impatient."

"Hmm." He huffed.

"Besides, he requires one final thing to seal what we have begun after you acquire the Sickle."

His jaw tightened, hand instinctively brushing the hilt at his side. "What else? Let me guess, more blood?"

Her smile sharpened, cruel yet alluring. "Not just any."

"Of course." He muttered.

"The blood that binds you. The one whose loss will break the chain around your heart." She tilted her head, watching him.

"Unfortunately, she was taken away from me long before my rule. Sorry to disappoint." He responded bitterly, sarcasm lacing the last words.

"Not her. But someone else you already know. You've always known."

He forced himself to hold her gaze, though the cold certainty struck deeper than he wished to admit. *The only other one is Rena... and I won't part with her.* The catacombs seemed to close tighter around him, stone pressing in, shadows thickening like a noose.

"You tempt me toward ruin," He retorted.

Her laughter echoed, soft and merciless, "No, Joseph. I tempt you toward victory." She stepped closer, so close he could feel the brush of her presence against his skin—cold at first, then warming, like embers stoked beneath ash. "Besides, you call it ruin," she whispered, her fingertips trailing along the ancient stone. "But ruin is only what the weak call victory when they are too afraid to claim it."

"You would have me believe this sacrifice is glory, when it reeks of demise."

She grinned. "Glory is born of demise. Don't you see it? Every empire, every crown, every sovereign must drown something they love to rise higher. You have the *power*... you have the *will*... all that remains is the courage to sever what limits you."

Her voice sank lower as she leaned in, lips brushing the air near his ear. "He waits for you. He chose *you*—not Zeus, not the governors, not your pitiful council. *You.* Because you are willing to do what others will not."

Joseph swallowed, though his mouth was dry as bone. "And if I refuse?"

She laughed again, softer this time, almost tender. "Then you remain a sovereign bound in chains, fearing his own shadow, who most likely face a long, torturous death—when he feels like you've earned death. But if you accept, if you offer the sacrifice, the darkness will bend to you, the heavens will break, and your will be the only name spoken when the world kneels."

Her hand, pale and cold, hovered just above his where it rests on the hilt. Not touching, but close enough that he felt the pull, like the edge of a blade brushing skin.

"And they *will* kneel to you."

He should step back, cast her into silence. But instead, he stood frozen, the weight of her promise sinking into him, rooting deep where ambition and dread had long been entwined.

"Imagine the power in your veins, ten times stronger. No mortal will dare to rise against you. The Governess? Gone. Eseron? Yours."

Her hand finally closed the space, fingertips brushing against his. The contact was slight, but it burned hotter than any flame, searing straight through the steel in his veins.

"You feel it, don't you?" she murmured, tilting her head. Her lips curved into that wicked smile he knew all too well. "The hunger. The promise. It's not the blade that yearns—it's you."

He clenched his jaw, though he did not move. Her touch slid higher, across the back of his hand, up his wrist, tracing the path of veins that hammered with defiance—or desire. He couldn't tell which, and that scared him.

"Every time you resist me," she whispered, pressing closer, "you draw nearer to surrender. Do you think I can't see the fire in your eyes and the way you linger on my words?"

He glared at her, meeting the violet gleam in her gaze. "You poison me with promises."

She laughed softly, lips just short of brushing his. Her hand slipped to his chest, resting above his heart. The cold of her touch spread outward, sinking beneath flesh and bone, coiling around the place where fear and ambition warred. "Then drink, Joseph. Let the poison make you strong."

Her thumb traced idle circles, each one pulling him deeper. He couldn't explain it; it was as if he were falling down an abyss he couldn't return from.

"The sacrifice is not loss," she added, voice silk. "It is liberation. Give it, and you will shed the last of your chains. Give it, and he will rise through you. His power won't consume you—it'll become you."

The catacombs seemed to pulse with her words, the torchlight guttering as if the flames bent in reverence. *I should create distance. I should push her hand away.* He should stop this, but instead he found himself leaning in, caught between revulsion and craving, enthralled by her wicked essence.

Her lips hovered a breath away from his, her whisper the final snare. "Sever what limits, Sovereign... and the world will be ours."

And then, she vanished, taking the flames with her and leaving him in darkness.

FORTY-TWO

HERA'S DELICATE FINGERS RAKED THROUGH ZEUS' hair, grasping tightly with each slow and gentle thrust. He savored her every breath, moan, and bite as he continuously slid himself in.

Her starlight eyes rolled back, and he buried his face in her neck, placing gentle kisses on her soft skin. Her moans grew fainter by the second until silence. He glanced up at her, lips parted and drawing in jagged breaths. A weight pressed against his chest.

Weak.

The word slithered into his ear like venom. He snapped his head around, but the room was empty, save for him and Hera's nakedness beneath. His fists curled tight.

"Everything alright?" She asked softly.

"Turn around."

She hesitated, confusion painting her sharp features.

You once ruled the skies, another voice mocked, lower, guttural, serpentine. *Now, even the clouds turn their backs on you.*

He grabbed her hips, twisting her until her breasts were

pressed against the bed, ass up against him. He thrust into her without a second thought.

The silence in his head was unbearable. Lightning used to course through his veins, thunder waiting at his tongue's command. And now he'd been reduced to nothing but a mere immortal—if even that.

The memory of him burned hot in Zeus' mind, his chains rattling in the depths of Tartarus. Yet, the sound was here. His voice was here, echoing against the marble walls, as though he stood beside him.

Zeus' breath grew ragged. "You are bound. Buried. Forgotten," he hissed.

Hera turned to him, concern inching across her face. *Fuck. I said it out loud.* I hadn't realized I had stopped fucking her.

He turned her face around and pressed her head against the bed, thrusting into her again and again. Picking up the pace. Fucking her so deep and fast that her cries filled the room and drowned the invasive voices in his mind. His thoughts spun, tearing at themselves. He couldn't listen. He couldn't think. All he could feel was the weight of absence.

He fisted her hair, willing the spark to answer him, to remind him that he was still who he was. *I don't fucking care if the lightning spurs out of my hands. I need it now. I need it to answer me.*

Nothing came. Not even a flicker. His knuckles whitened the more he tightened his grip, and he didn't even finish.

"Leave," he said, low, barely audible as he released her.

She hesitated, straightening herself on the bed. *A mistake.* His head snaps toward her, eyes burning with fury he could not control. "I said Leave!"

"I don't know what your problem is, but it has nothing to do with me!" She picked up her clothes, slipping her dress on. "I'm not to blame."

"I'm not blaming you." He said through gritted teeth.

"Might as well have, considering you just fucked me like some whore you despised." She sneered.

"I need a moment alone."

"You need more than a moment alone, Zeus." She aimed for the door, fabric brushing the marble as the doors slammed shut behind her.

Alone, the pressure boiled over. He got dressed and thrust his hand skyward, calling to it, demanding what was his. *Break the fucking ceiling. I don't care. You will answer me.* A rumble of thunder answered... faint, yet hollow, like a dying beast gasping its last breath.

And then—a laugh, lighter, laced with venomous delight. Eris. Her mocking tone wrapped around him.

"A god who falters commands no respect. Do you hear it, Zeus? The world no longer trembles for you." Eris said, distant yet so close.

Rage overtook him, striking the nearest pillar with his palm. The marble cracked, dust spilling down, but it wasn't from divine strength—it was from brittle stone yielding too easily. The sound mocked me.

Breath heaving, he sank to one knee. His vision blurred with fury and shame.

"What am I," he whispered to the empty space, "if not power?" The silence answered louder than any storm.

He staggered backward, gripping his temples, as though he could press the voices out. But they only grew louder, circling him, gnawing at what remained of his certainty.

"No!" he roared, forcing the sound into the emptiness. His shout cracked the air, thunder answering faintly, but it's hollow, pitiful—an echo of what once was.

His chest heaved, vision stirred. And in that moment, he knew... whether these voices were phantoms or truths, they were not wrong. His power was slipping, if not already gone, and his enemies knew it.

THE AIR WAS THICK WITH ASH, AND EACH STEP ECHOED endlessly down the worn stone corridors carved by the weight of eternity.

The rattling of chains in the distance filled the space around Zeus, with some holding nameless creatures that dared not speak, others simply swayed as though mocking him. He pressed onward through the abyss.

Hecate's words rose to the surface, an air of caution yet he couldn't sit idly by and wait whenever Joseph was vulnerable.

Zeus needed to act now. He needed to attack the source. *I'm putting an end to this fucking now, and I am reclaiming my power, and I'm sending this bastard to the depths of this infernal place.*

At last, he reached the pit where he had shackled the monster himself; chained beneath rock and flame, and condemned to rot.

But silence greeted him, not the usual rumble of restrained rage.

He stopped at the edge of the cell. Zeus' hands tightened into fists. The massive chains lie broken, links twisted as though snapped by a force greater than iron. The ground around the prison wad scorched, blackened with fresh wounds. The scent of brimstone lingered.

The pit was empty.

Zeus stepped inside, his chest tightening, his fleeting power flickering faintly with a surge of anger.

He could still see the remnants of his presence—claw marks etched into the stone, deep furrows as though he fought even as he fled...or perhaps, as though he had help.

His mind raced. *I'm too late...* he tasted the bitter edge of fear, but smothered it quickly with wrath. Someone dared to turn against me. He had no doubt about it. *But who?* The shadows seemed to move as he lingered.

He straightened, forcing his fury into focus. The storm inside him pressed against the walls of this forsaken pit. Whoever freed him would regret it. And when Zeus finds who was responsible—

when he finds them both—he will remind the world why he is the god of Olympus.

The *true* fucking Sovereign.

"Two visits in less than 48 hours," Hecate said as the Mother. "Things must be worse than I thought, or you decided to do as you pleased and not as I instructed."

"Don't play with me." Zeus scowled. "Typhon is gone. His cell is empty."

Her expression didn't change. "Didn't I say to deal with the Sovereign first?"

"It made no sense to kill Joseph first, if the source lies in our domain." He growled. "The pit is scarred. Either he was freed, or he tore his way out." He paced before her. "This is not a coincidence."

She folded her hands before her, composed as always. "You presume much. Tartarus is not easily breached, not even by your kind. If Typhon walks, he does so because a will greater than you desired it."

He narrowed his eyes. "Do you speak of titans... or of the mortal Sovereign who toys with powers beyond his station?"

Hecate's lips curve into the faintest smile, though it does not reach her eyes. "Perhaps both. The walls between realms are thinning. Old powers stir where they should not. You should know this better than anyone—you've felt your own strength falter, did you not?"

Her words struck deep, though he did not let them show. She saw too much already.

He leaned. "If Typhon uses Joseph as a vessel, Olympus will burn. With Eris behind this, chaos will spread until even you are consumed. Tell me, where do I strike first?"

"I told you where to strike." She moved over to the cauldron, morphing into the Crone. "Did you find out if a tether weaved?" Her gaze pierced him, steady and unyielding.

He blinked, instantly thinking of the meadow and the beautiful woman... *Wendy, I think her name was...* "I was dealing with other matters."

Her lips pressed into a thin line. "You will not find Typhon in chains again. You will find him in whispers, in shadows, in the breaking of oaths. I could prepare a search between realms, in the event he shows. But understand this—if he rises, he will not rise alone."

The storm within him roared, demanding blood, demanding vengeance. Yet her words clung to him, impossible to shake. *Not alone.*

"Have you interacted with him? Or has he made any contact?"

"Briefly." He replied curtly.

She raised an eyebrow. "It was..." she muttered.

"My power is not bound to his life." He protested.

"A tether was woven." She reiterated, louder this time. "To whom? Is unknown to me. But he shouldn't have access to your mind..."

"The only possible way a tether was weaved is with another god and a piece of me."

"A drop of blood, a piece of hair, anything as small as a sliver of skin is enough to bind you or drain you."

"Then get the Fates and fix this." He snapped. "Tell me who tied my powers to a mortal. Tell me who on my fucking council is plotting against me. I can't afford to waste more fucking time." He took a breath. "Tell me how I can undo this."

Hecate shook her head. "With the life of the Sovereign. *If* and only *if,* he hasn't retrieved the sickle."

"Has he already retrieved the sickle?"

"Not yet, but his men are close. I've placed some hexes myself, and with Poseidon making the tides impenetrable, they won't be able to retrieve it for millennia."

"You claim this as if it's a fact. Typhon is no mere monster; he'll find a way to get to it." Zeus paced around.

"At this rate, you know as well as I that the prophecy will come to fruition." Hecate stepped toward Zeus, her gaze steady.

"I won't let that happen." He hissed, lightning flaring around him as the storm above roared in answer. *You better fucking respond when I fucking call you.*

His hands trembled with rage, but from the weight of what he had seen. Typhon lived. He had found his way into the mortal lands through Joseph.

I will tear Joseph apart if it's the last thing I do. And when Typhon emerges from his mortal shell, I will strike him down again, or I will burn the world trying.

Zeus left her then, not because he was finished, but because the fury inside him could not be contained. Olympus must prepare. He didn't care if she claimed that the prophecy had already been set in motion. The age of silence was over, and he had a Sovereign to kill.

WAR BANNERS HUNG LIMP ON THE WALLS, AND THE TWO generals in the Heartfen Citadel stood restless before Zeus, one from the Blood Legion and one from the War Regiment. Beside me sat Athena, calm and calculating, while Ares loomed on the opposite side with his elite standing behind him.

Zeus recognized two of them.

The redhead: Rhei, and the blonde: Nik.

"Our plan is clear." Athena said. "A split force—one to storm his gates, another to infiltrate and recover the Governess. If she lives, her rescue will rally half—if not the entire continent—to our side."

General Kallistratos from the War Regiment nodded, his face scarred and grim. "Her return could turn the tide of loyalty. She is more than a symbol; she is the heart of her people."

Ares laughed low and sharp, shaking his head. "Always the tactician, sister. Always chasing banners and hearts." He leaned forward, his eyes glinting red beneath the firelight. "The governess is but one mortal woman. Let us not waste our strength chasing shadows when the true prize is the Sovereign's blood. Strike his Fortress, crush his armies, drag him screaming from his throne. That will rally the continent far louder than the tears of a rescued governess."

The generals stiffened, glancing at Athena.

Athena's gaze hardened. "You speak as though she is disposable. Yet her presence binds entire provinces in loyalty, not to mention Sylene. Lose her, and you invite rebellion. Your thirst for battle blinds you, Ares."

He shrugged indifferently. "And your obsession with symbols blinds you to the truth. Mortals follow victory, not sentiment. When the Sovereign lies broken in the dirt, none will remember a captive governess."

Zeus slammed his fists onto the table, thunder snapping through the chamber. The wood cracked beneath his hand, silencing them both. Sparks danced across his skin as he glared at Ares. *Still there, weak, yes but still there.*

"She is not to be forgotten." His voice was iron. "She is not to be abandoned. Joseph holds her because she *matters*. She is valuable somehow. To her people. To the continent. And perhaps... to Olympus itself. We will not leave her to rot."

Athena inclined her chin, quiet satisfaction in her eyes.

For a moment, Ares' grin faltered. His eyes flickered with something darker—resentment, perhaps. "And what if it's a trap? What if she dies in the process? Then you've wasted men and will on sentiment. Mortals rally behind power."

The generals murmured concurrence, emboldened by his ferocity.

From the line of soldiers, Nik stepped forward, his armor dented with a hundred battles. "With respect, Zeus, chasing the governess through the Sovereign's fortress is folly. A siege will burn men alive before we breach the walls. And once inside, what if he has already broken her? What if she is no longer the woman her people remember?" He glanced at Athena briefly. "Symbols are fragile things. Kill the Sovereign, and the people will not care whose chains he rattled. They will cheer the victor, as they always do."

The chamber stirred uneasily. Nik had weight among them since he spoke as one who had bled for every word. Then General Kallistratos raised his hand, measured and stern.

"And yet if we abandon her, what message do we send? That Olympus leaves its allies to rot? That loyalty is answered with silence? If we burn her name from history, we hand her people to the Sovereign without a fight. He will wield her death as his banner, not ours." His eyes moved across the table, steady as a blade. "We cannot win by power alone. We must win the hearts of men."

Athena inclined her head ever so slightly, vindicated. "Well spoken."

"Hearts don't win wars—steel does." General Ikaros retorted.

"Enough!" Zeus rose, the table quaking beneath his palm. His gaze pierced them, burning through their arguments. "The plan stands. The Blood Legion will break his gates, and the War Regiment will carve a path to the governess. She will be freed, and the Sovereign will be executed. Ready your armies."

Chapter
FORTY-THREE
KATERINA

The Sister's delicate hands patted Katerina down, fixing her grey dress and placing the last pins in her hair, securing a sheet veil that partially obscured her face.

Her heart thundered rapidly against her chest. *No turning back now.* The sister opened a red velvet box and held it at chest level, prompting her to put on the white lace gloves.

"I can sense you're nervous." She pulled the sheer veil over Katerina's face. "I'd be lying if I said I wasn't when I was initiated."

If only this meant anything. She slid the gloves on.

"At least you're not alone in this."

Katerina laughed sheepishly. *Even though I'm not the only one getting initiated, it doesn't make this less terrifying.*

"Any guesses on where you'll be placed?" She asked, taking a step back and examining Katerina one last time.

"Naturopath." She answered with as much hope as she could feign.

"Oh?" she lets out. "You don't want to be a High Re'Veillite? Being the Sovereign's eldest and all..."

"Is not a position I covet." *I rather be able to heal than destroy. Then again, I rather for this to be real, more than anything.*

"Well," she gestured Katerina to follow her down to the end of the line.

There were approximately ten *Initiate-Sisters*, all dressed in grey gowns and gloves with sheer veils covering their entire faces.

Katerina placed herself behind the last initiate.

The sister surveyed her once more, picking up lint from my clothing. Her delicate hand brushed over the pendant around Katerina's neck. "You know that for this you shouldn't be wearing—"

"It was my mother's." Katerina lied. *Well, it's not technically a lie...*

"I understand, but you can't—"

"I'm not taking it off." Katerina said curtly.

"Of course," the sister responded bitterly. "Thy Savior will place you where you'll do most good." The Sister bowed. "*Se're vosto.*"

"*Se're Vosto.*"

The sister left, disappearing behind the doors to the Worship Hall. Katerina's mind stirred for a brief moment.

"All you have to do is make it to induction—everything will fall into place." Her mom's words echoed. *What's it worth, anyway? It was all just a big spectacle.*

The initiate in front of her moved forward, and Katerina's heart leapt to her throat as they filed into the Worship Hall.

But what exactly will fall into place? There aren't many things that don't make sense or that I'm interested in finding out anyway.

A plethora of people filled the room, bowing as they walked down the center one behind the other. Jezebelle sat in the front row, next to her father. *Will I lose contact with my sister once I leave with Byorn?* Then, her eyes fell on Byorn who was on the opposite side of her father. *Savior help me.*

Her mind then drifted to Nik. How he had protected her from that monster, how he always seemed to find her, how he showed up when she called, even when he had barely enough time to respond... then on his gentle touch... on his kiss and how the ghost of it still lingered on her lips and body. *Stop. It was just a fling... like you wanted... it wouldn't have worked anyway...not with Byorn in the picture, not with the marriage looming over her. It was good while it lasted... no matter how fleeting it was.*

The scent of cedar incense filled Katerina's nose the closer they got to the altar. *Will my father suddenly pull me out due to something he'd heard? No. He wouldn't. Not when there are so many spectators.*

They stopped right in front of the altar and bow as the Verenna took center stage in a rich, burgundy robe embellished with golden embroidery and a sun medallion around her neck. A High Re'Veillite joined her, and prompted all Initiate-Sisters to kneel.

They do, with their hand resting on their laps. *What will happen after I renounce my family name? Surely that cannot be faked... right?*

"*Se're Vosto.*" The High Re'Veillite greeted, her voice a wave of calm reverence. "The most awaited time of the year has finally come. Today marks a momentous occasion that many women want but not many get to experience. Today we sort you into the coveted sisterhood and grant you the well awaited Re'Veillite title that continues to bless the continent."

Katerina's heart raced. Three Re'Veillites joined the Verenna: a *Master Chronicler* with a deep blue robe and a black sash, holding a scroll; an *Expert Naturopath* in a forest green robe, holding a medallion; and a *Sister* in the classic white robe with dark red embroidery, holding a clear quartz.

"When I call your name, step forward and stand in the ring."

Katerina looked down to the materializing grey-smoky ring in front of them.

"Gwendolyn Qizar."

An Initiate-Sister stood and gracefully walked to the ring. Her body language displayed nothing but pure confidence. She bowed as she passed the Verenna and stood inside the ring. All gazes fixed on her and an overwhelming silence filled the room.

One by one, the items in the Re'Veillites' hands glowed. An overwhelming buzzing surrounded them. Gwendolyn fell to her knees.

"Lift your veil." The High Re'Veillite ordered.

With trembling hands, she did, revealing her icy blonde hair partially braided to her crown.

The High Re'Veillite approached her, placing a hand to her temple. All items stopped glowing, except for one.

The Scroll.

The ring around Gwendolyn turned a shade of bright blue.

"Stand." The High Re'Veillite removed her hand, helping Gwendolyn up. "From this moment forth, you belong to the Chronicler Wing and are afforded the title of *Scholar.*"

A scroll materialized in between them, hovering midair. The High Re'Veillite summoned a quill. "Unglove and place your hand here."

Gwendolyn proceeded and her finger got pricked by the quill.

"Upon signing, you agree to renounce the Qizar family name and adopt the Re'Veillite way of life guided by the Codex Lux Aequitatis and the Re'Veillite Code of Conduct."

Without any hesitation, Gwendolyn signed her name on the scroll.

"Henceforth you shall be known as Alexandra. Your fealty lies with the sisterhood."

She was then guided to stand behind the Master Chronicler.

Katerina's eyes scanned the Re'Veillites. There was one empty spot next to the Naturopath... *is this a where the High Re'Veillite is supposed be? But then again, what if someone where to be slotted as one of them? Would she stand behind nothingness?*

Another initiate walked to the ring but Katerina's attention remained on the empty space. *Was it because the Verenna is unable to speak? Well, it made sense. She needed a cover. If I recall correctly, the Verenna usually led this ceremony. But, won't people think something is off since she hasn't spoken?*

"From this moment forth, you belong to the Sister Wing and are afforded the title of *Re'Veillite Sister.*"

Katerina's attention drew back to the High Re'Veillite, giving the redhead initiate the title, and guiding her to stand behind the sister standing next to the Verenna.

Several minutes went by, one initiate after the other got called, all given different titles. So far, there were 2 new Scholars, 3 Naturopaths (2 Healers and 1 Mender), and 3 Sisters.

Gasps rippled through the room, followed by side chatter. Katerina looked to the empty space, drawing a shallow breath upon noticing the deep purple flames emerging from the ground. The High Re'Veillite prompted the brunette initiate to stand. Silence fell once the flames disappeared.

"Elena Yavos, from this moment forth, you belong to the Celestial Tower and are afforded the title of *High Re'Veillite.*" The flames spawned on the High Re'Veillite's hands, dividing the purple flame. "You've been bestowed the gift of *Precognition.*" She places her hands to Elena's temples. "The gift bestowed upon you is to be used in accordance with Codex Lux Aequitatis and the Re'Veillite Code of Conduct. You agree to renounce the Yavos family name and henceforth you shall be known as Thalia. Your fealty lies with the sisterhood."

She signed and the High Re'Veillite escorted her back toward the Verenna, prompting her to stand behind the High Priestess.

"Katerina Faye Argryros."

Her mouth dried. She looked to her left. Empty. *Shit.* She stood, making my way to the grey ring, careful not to stumble. Her heart thundered against her ears, drowning her loud footsteps.

She stood face to face with the High Re'Veillite.

"Lift your veil."

She obeyed, side glancing at Jezebelle, who gave her a subtle nod and smile, but that didn't wash away the unease inside her. Katerina's knees buckled and she fell to her knees. Heaviness presses against her shoulders, weighing her down. She raised her head but the force stopped her from doing so. Her eyes remained fixed in the tile for what felt like an eternity. Her chest clenched as if her heart was about to give out.

Muttering grew around her. An overwhelming buzzing spread through her body as an icy stinging sensation gathered in her gloved palms.

The muttering increased, but she shut out every sly comment of her inadequacy. Her heart sank. A mix of ice and heat seared into her chest.

The pendant... it burned. She tried to raise a hand to tear it out but the heaviness anchored her to the floor, and a flash of white flooded her vision.

"You won't feel a thing, child." The image of the Verenna standing in front of her materialized.

She didn't know where she was, just in a circular brick room with panoramic glass around it, that had a clear view of Caverest and the rest of Castelencia.

The Verenna turned to the man standing behind Katerina.

"I must warn you, she'll eventually come to remember."

"Make sure she doesn't. Aren't you supposed to be the best in your craft?" Her father responded. "You must understand that this indiscretion of hers cannot be tolerated or publicized."

"What about the boy?"

"I'll deal with him." He replied. "Just modify what I asked."

She blinked repeatedly, the white tile focused into view. She gritted her teeth but showed no signs of weakness. *They already think I'm inadequate. That I'm not good enough.* Fire and Ice clashed, burning her from within. The stinging turned to pain, spreading to her limbs. *Remove your gloves. Let it out. No.* She shook her head. *Yes. Do it.*

Gasps reverberated around her. She blinked. The ring was now onyx. The pain turned to a burning sensation. She winced at the heaviness in her chest. Darkness flooded her vision.

"THERE MUST BE ANOTHER WAY." HER MOTHER SAID, standing in the middle of the darkened woodland. "She's just a baby."

A male figure shook his head. "You either agree or we have no deal."

KATERINA BLINKED, FOCUSING BACK ON THE TILE.

"Stand." The High Re'Veillite ordered.

The pressure diminished as she stood. Katerina's eyes fell on the High Re'Veillite, black smoke emerging from her cupped hands.

Darkness follows me like the plague. Katerina suppressed a squirm.

"I can sense the power in you." The Verenna's voice slithered inside her mind. *"It lay dormant until weeks ago."*

Katerina looked down at her gloved hands. *Remove them.* The burning sensation seared into her palms. Gritting her teeth, she kept her hands gloved and face neutral. Katerina glanced briefly at the Verenna

"Remarkable..." The Verenna's said, mouth unmoving.

"Unglove." The High Re'Veillite said.

Katerina removed the lace fabric, revealing smoke-stained sharpened nails and fingertips that stretched to her palms. She look up at the High Re'Veillite. But now, her hands were empty and the searing pain ceased.

The Verenna stepped forward, grabbing her hands and examining them closely. *"I didn't want to believe it..."* her voice rang in her mind.

Katerina glanced at Jezebelle. She looked as perplexed as she was, but her father, on the other hand, focused his attention behind the Verenna, to Ele—Thalia. *You better not...*

"From this moment forth, you belong to the Celestial Tower and are afforded the title of *High Re'Veillite.*" The High Re'Veillite announced. "You've been bestowed the gift of *Nyctokinesis.* The gift bestowed upon you is to be used in accordance Codex Lux Aequitatis and the Re'Veillite Code of Conduct." Her gaze seared into Katerina. "You agree to renounce the Argyros family name, and henceforth you shall be known as Lyla. Your fealty lies with the sisterhood."

A roll of parchment materialized in front of her alongside the quill.

RE'VEILLITE CODE OF CONDUCT:

RENUNCIATION OF THE FORMER SELF

1. Upon initiation, every Sister shall forsake her family name and former allegiances.

2. She shall be known henceforth by her chosen Devotional Name, bestowed during Initiation.

3. No Sister shall speak of her past life save in sacred confession or at the command of the Verenna.

4. Blood ties are to be replaced by the sacred bond of the sisterhood; the Sisterhood is now mother, kin, and legacy.

OATH OF FEALTY TO THE SAVIOR

1. Each Sister pledges unwavering fealty to the Sisterhood and the Savior it serves.

2. Loyalty to the Verenna and the Council of the Inner Veil is absolute.

3. To act against the Sisterhood is to walk in shadow; such betrayal shall be met with cleansing judgment.

4. No Sister shall withhold her strength or knowledge when called upon by the Sisterhood.

SACRED USE OF POWER

1. The gifts granted by the Savior are not for personal gain, vengeance, or vanity.

2. Powers shall only be wielded in service to the Sisterhood's holy missions, defense of the sanctum, or divine justice.

3. Use of power without sanction is forbidden and shall be punished according to the gravity of misuse.

4. A Sister must never reveal the full extent of her abilities to outsiders unless explicitly ordered to do so.

CONDUCT IN PURITY AND SILENCE

1. All Sisters shall maintain discipline in thought, word, and deed.

2. Idle speech, gossip, or discord sowing among the Sisters is a sin against unity.

3 Chastity of body and clarity of purpose are to be preserved; no binding vows may be taken outside the Order, to include marriage.

4. Daily meditation and prayer with the Savior are mandatory.

HIERARCHY AND SERVICE

1. The hierarchy of the Sisterhood is sacred and must be honored at all times.

2. Orders from superiors must be obeyed without question unless they conflict with the Savior's principles.

3. Re'Veillites shall show reverence to their mentors, and High Re'Veillites shall guard the souls of their charges with care.

4. Each Sister, from novice to Master Chronicler, Expert Naturopath, High Re'Veillite, is both servant and steward of the Savior.

THE VEIL OF SECRECY

1. The rites, relics, abilities, and true history of the Sisterhood are not to be shared with the outside world.

2. All contact with outsiders must be approved by the Verenna or higher authority: *The Sovereign.*

3. Betrayal of sacred secrets will result in exile, memory severance, withdrawal of power, or flame immolation, as deemed just by the Council of the Inner Veil, the Verenna, the Denai, and the Sovereign.

PENANCE AND REDEMPTION

1. Should a Sister falter, she must seek atonement through the Rites of Ash and Embers.

2. Forgiveness is granted only through trial, confession, and Savior approval.

3. No wrongdoing is beyond redemption, but no wrongdoing may go unexamined.

DEATH AND ASCENSION

1. Upon death, a Sister's name shall be etched into the Pillar of Light, and her ashes mixed with the Ever-Burning Flame.

2. Her soul shall join the chorus of the Divine, guiding the Sisterhood from beyond.

3. The living shall honor her memory with silence and flame for seven days.

————————————

Signed by

Katerina grabbed the quill with trembling hands. *None of this feels fake...* she looked at her sister one last time. *If I sign this, would I be saved from marrying him? This was divine law...* She buried the tip of the quill into her index finger until the tip dripped red. She brought it close to the parchment. *I'm not selfish. I'm not selfish. I'm not—*

Her body flew across the room, stopping with a loud thud against concrete, draining the air from her lungs. Screams rippled around her amidst the ringing in her ears. The stench of burning flesh filled her nose.

Boom.

Her body cowered.

"GET OUT!" someone yelled. "IF YOU'RE NEAR THE DOOR, LEAVE NOW!"

Propping her aching body up, shreds of marble biting into her palms. An icy sensation slithered from her chest to her ungloved hands. Everything around her dimmed. She looked up. Sunlight filtered through the massive hole in the ceiling, yet it was like the sun was losing power.

Olympian soldiers raided the Worship Hall. *Where's Jezebelle?* Her heart slammed against her ears, drowning out the sounds of slicing flesh. There were so many. Her throat clenched. *I need to find my sister.*

Grabbing the pointiest piece of marble she could find, she stumbled around, scanning around for her sister. The once-polished flooring was now covered in blood, skin, and debris.

A soldier lunged her way, sword at the ready.

Her heart dropped.

She lunged sideways, barely evading the sword. He charged back at her. She hurried back, falling on her ass. He swung, she rolled to the right. He straddled her, holding her in place with his hands and suddenly, she was back at Mrs. Dhalia's shop.

Rage stirred in her as she struggled. He grinned, pressing the sword against her neck. Icy radiated from her chest to her palms.

He released the blade, clutching onto his neck and gasping for air.

There must be something more than just darkness, but I'll inquire later. Just find Jezebelle.

Katerina moved, straddling his body and burying the pointy edge of the marble shred into his eye.

Darkness washed over the Worship Hall.

"I'VE NEVER SEEN A PRINCESS WITH QUITE THE temper." The thief mocked. "Maybe they'll spare your life and toss you around for us to use."

SHE PULLED OUT THE SHRED AND BURIED IT AGAIN.

"ARE YOU EVEN AWARE OF HOW VALUABLE THE BOTH OF you are to us—to the Gods?" The Olympian High Priest motioned upward.

"I hope you burn in whatever hell hole it is you believe in." I hissed.

"I rather send you in my stead." He took a step toward us, determination in his eyes.

AND AGAIN, THE FIRE IN HER ABLAZE.

I CLASPED MY HANDS TOGETHER TO STOP THE RATTLING
of the chains as I laid eyes on the item in his other hand. What
haunted my nightmares—an ebony whip.

"Truly!" I cried out to my father. "I don't know what I did! I've
been focused on my duties. I've kept an eye on Jezy." My lips quaked.
"I've been good."

AND AGAIN. THE REPRESSED FEELING OF UTTER RAGE
that consumed her, finally out. She kept going. She didn't care if
her hands were stained crimson, if her clothes were ruined. She
was done with feeling helpless.

Strong hands pulled her body off the disfigured corpse as
blood and black smoke dripped from her hands.

Temper be fucking damned.

CHAPTER

FORTY-FOUR

JOSEPH

THE GROUND SHOOK BENEATH HIS FEET AS THEY continued to breach the inner walls of the Worship Hall. One after the other, their formations tore through the smoke, their war cries drowning in the thumping in his chest. Joseph pulled out his sword as he summoned the sliver of power that coursed through his veins.

The storms.

Venomous rage coiled within him. He inhaled deeply, feeling the fire and poison fill his lungs. Heat spread through him and funneled toward the blade in his hands as the storms above answered his calling.

He trudged forward, swinging his fire-bound weapon, slicing his way through, and bringing every single enemy to their knees.

Byorn fought on the other side of him. His navy clothes were burnt and torn. Joseph kept fighting.

This was supposed to be an easy day. I would get my arsenal. I would have gotten my weapons.

His stomach turned as he took in his surroundings. Countless of his men lie on the ground either dead or at the verge of death. Olympian soldiers kept pouring in. *I'm fucking outnumbered.*

One after the other, his men collapsed under a blade. Under the hands of soldiers with eagle-thunder, Corinthian, and sword insignias.

At this rate, he would lose all his men and cause further uproar in his council.

Joseph stopped.

Letting his men fight around him. Protect him as rage surged. Power—white hot power spread through him and, with one exhale, the world cracked.

A black tempest surged from his throat, carrying shards of burning stone. The front ranks of soldiers rose and tore apart, their armor shrieking as it melted into their flesh. Their screams didn't linger; they were instantly drowned by the howling wind of the storm cascading down like a furious tempest.

"It's on now." He muttered to himself.

Spears and arrows cut through the air toward him, but he was no longer bound by mortal limits. His shadow swelled and split, serpents of smoke bursting forth. They writhed across the ruined hall, fangs dripping molten fire. They sank into men and beasts alike, piercing through shields, piercing through hearts. Their flesh blackened and swelled until their bodies ruptured like over-ripe fruit.

Amid the chaos, his eyes caught a movement near the inner hall. Katerina and Jezebelle were being hurried away by guards through a narrow passage. Their terrified faces glanced back at him once before disappearing into safety.

His chest tightened. *There's no hiding now. They saw me. They saw this. I don't care anymore. They would be spared from this bloodshed. They would live.*

The enemy pressed harder. Yet, the chaos was not his alone.

High Re'Veillites joined forces, casting a shield over the Worship Hall—no, over the Acrailerion, stopping more Olympian soldiers from breaching. Chroniclers dashed in the direction of the Archives. The Naturopaths tended to the wounded, seemingly trying to revive them somehow, and the Sisters... where were the Sisters?

Around them, loud voices echoed in a chorus of chanting. High Re'Veillites place themselves around the Worship Hall's inner walls, their voices weaving a spell in a language foreign to him.

A ring of violet flame surged upward, warding the grounds from further collapse. Roofs that would have caved held firm. The very air hardened, turning aside falling stones and fire from catapults. Their power shielded the heart of his dominion, freeing him to unleash without hesitation.

Joseph thrust his arms wide, and from the ground, talons of black rock erupted. They skewered entire battalions, lifting soldiers screaming into the storm-dark sky before shattering into dust.

He walked forward, each step trailing scales upon the earth. His shadow lengthened, wings unfurling from the blackness, though they were his—they belonged to *Him*, whose power Joseph now bore.

Remaining enemy troops faltered. Some turned to flee, but the serpents would not allow retreat. They coiled around stragglers, constricting until bones cracked and eyes burst.

"Show yourself, Zeus!" Joseph commanded in a voice not entirely his own. **"Not so high and mighty now, are you?"**

They begged, their knees sinking into blood-soaked tiles. Mercy was forfeited now. Joseph clenched his fists, and a great wave of molten fire swept across them, leaving nothing but ash spiraling upward.

The Re'Veillites' ward pulsed with light, holding back the ruin of his storm. One High Re'Veillite, braver than the rest, stepped forward and whispered words that steadied his fury, drawing his wrath toward the invaders and not his own walls.

When the smoke thinned, the grounds lay littered with charred armor, blackened corpses, blood, water, and debris.

He stood amidst the silence, chest heaving, exhaustion threatening to consume him whole, the serpents of shadow hissed as they retreated back into him.

I am Sovereign and Eseron will bow to me.

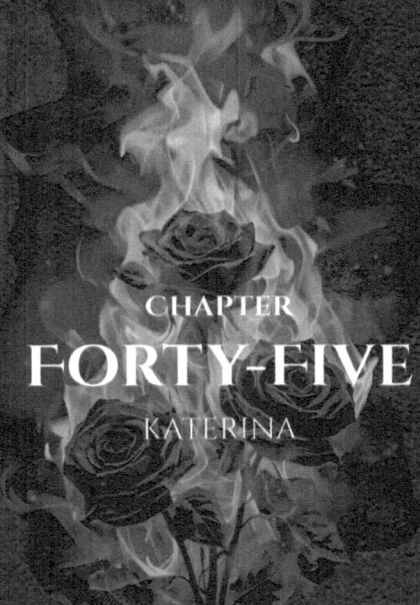

CHAPTER
FORTY-FIVE
KATERINA

KATERINA TRIED TO KEEP UP THE PACE WITH THE guards hurrying her and Jezebelle by the arms as chaos reigned inside the Fortress. She pushed off the bodies crashing into them. Housemaids ran in all directions, paving the way for the Light Militia in their black and gold uniforms, arms stacked with all sorts of weapons. Orders were barked in the midst of the rampage.

They bolted left, down a corridor and into the Great Hall.

Bodies were dragged into the open space as the Naturopaths tended to the wounded in makeshift beds. Screams of agony tore through the commotion as some got their limbs regrown by the Menders.

One of the Soldiers stopped them, older looking, face contorted into a scowl.

Katerina peered down at the rank—*Master Sergeant*.

"They shouldn't be here." He looked down at Katerina and Jezebelle.

"Per order of the Sovereign, I'm taking both princesses to the bunker." The soldier informs. "Quickest path is through here."

The master sergeant nodded hesitantly. "Some areas of the Fortress have been infiltrated. Avoid the east wing."

Without another thought, they hurried out of the Great Hall and to the corridor on the right.

Light Militia soldiers emerged from the Petrakis Library, rushing by them without a second glance. Katerina peered in as they passed. Soldiers and members of her father's council slithered down in between bookshelves. *What the...?*

She motioned to go in, but the soldier held her firm, keeping her in route. They go into a dim room. Her throat clenched at the scent of tobacco and citrus. *My father's study.*

"But no, you decided to go into your own adventurous spree and comeback here near midnight. Do you realize what could've happened if any of them had gotten their hands on you?"

"I'm surprised you care so much after what happened to Mom." I cupped a hand over my mouth. Shit. "I'm sorry, I didn't mean that..."

Katerina shook her head. The guard searched through her father's desk.

"Where'd you go?" She asked Jezebelle.

"Father pulled me out before I could get to you." She said. "I ran to get you."

"That's not what I meant..."

She frowned, letting Katerina know she understood precisely what she was referring to.

The guard moved away from the desk and to the shelf at the far right end of the study. He moved a series of books and jammed a key into a hole. The shelf swung open, revealing a downward staircase. He went in, prompting them to follow. He unlocked a steel door that led to a decently furnished room with refreshments and, to her surprise, ventilation. *He had his own safe room? Yet, we were all crammed in the other one?*

"I'll let you know once it's safe to come out." He said before locking the door and leaving Katerina and Jezebelle to their own devices.

Jezebelle eyed Katerina intently.

"What?" Katerina asked, plopping onto a seat.

"What?" Jezebelle shrugged.

"I asked you a question."

Jezebelle drew a sharp breath. "I went to the pier with Rhei."

"For three days?" Katerina cocked a brow. *She can disappear for three fucking days and think I won't have questions?*

"You're bleeding." She gazed down at Katerina's hands. "Your hands are stained..."

"Don't change the subject."

"Listen, I get that you are angry, but—"

"Angry?" Katerina stood. "Jezebelle, I am livid. I was worried sick about you."

"I just had to do a few things."

"Like?"

Jezebelle hesitated.

"Jezebelle, I need you to talk to me."

"Remember when I said father wanted me to give him information?"

Katerina nodded, suppressing the betrayal that stirred.

"Through... persuasion, Rhei has been giving me information."

So, I was right. She is an informant to my father. "And how do you know it's information you can validate to be true?"

"I've contested some of the things he's said, and they all turned out to be true."

"Such as?" Katerina crossed her arms. "No. Better yet, how did you get to be an offering on Veneration Night?"

Jezebelle stilled, a pained expression washing over her face. "A few nights before... me and Rhei were talking, and he mentioned how you are very... how should I say this?"

"Just like he said it." Katerina said curtly.

"He said that you were very in my business. I said that you were just being a caring sister, but he was dead set that you were this overbearing, overprotective sister—again, I defended you. I know you'd do anything for me."

I would.

"So that's what he meant by wanting to prove a point..." Katerina muttered.

"What?" Jezebelle arched an eyebrow.

"Before you and I had our discussion, Rhei and I spoke after I got out of the meeting with the Verenna. He said that he did it to prove a point. I don't know whose point was proven, though. Yours by being a protective sister or his by being an overbearing one. Take your pick."

"I'm sorry for how everything played out."

Katerina looked up at her. *As am I.* "You don't need to apologize. Unfortunately, the cards we were given aren't the ideal ones..."

"Maybe... but nevermind that. We'll survive." Jezebelle smiled.

"Besides, you're a newly inducted *High Re'Veillite!*"

Katerina couldn't help but look down at her stained hands. *Will my hands stay like this? My nails are now black and pointy, as if I dipped my hands in liquid smoke.* "Barely. Soon you'll see me dressed in white and traveling to the Tatiades' Estate... so I wouldn't be so ecstatic."

"Wait..." Jezebelle's brows furrowed. "The Tatiades' Estate?"

Katerina turned to Jezebelle. "Byorn came to see me."

Her eyes widened. "When? What did he want?"

"He proposed marriage—well, his father did. They're invoking the Union Convention."

"His father proposed marriage to you?" She snorted. "Things must be pretty bad for them to take these measures."

"His father mentioned it, but the marriage would be to Byorn." Katerina swatted her arm. "I am certain that father has some hidden agenda behind it, and after what just happened, I wouldn't be surprised if he were to move the wedding up. "

"But you don't seem happy about it."

"I'm not." Katerina blinked the tears welling up away. "But being the eldest, I have a duty to fulfil."

"I'm really sorry, Kate." Jezebelle grabbed Katerina's hands. "I've seen what father has done to you... I didn't want to mention it before, but you don't deserve any of it. You've given so much... especially for me, and it enfuriates me that he punishes you for stuff I've done."

"How did you find out?"

"I saw your back briefly when you went to see the house naturopath... and staff... they talk. They know."

A chill spread through Katerina's body. *How long have they known?*

Jezebelle tightened her grip. "Before you say anything, I was going to talk to him about it. To make him stop somehow."

"He won't, Jezy." Katerina said. "So long as I am still here, I will keep doing it. My biggest concern is if he'll do the same to you."

"That's not for you to worry about."

"You are my sister. I will worry. Always." Katerina walked over to the refreshments, pouring herself and Jezebelle some water and handing it to her. "Let's just table this topic of conversation, please."

"Fine," Jezebelle said, taking the water offered. "Answer me this then."

Katerina looked at her sister through the rim of her cup, savoring the cool drink.

"You didn't sign the Code of Conduct, right?"

"Didn't get the chance to."

"Then how come your hands are still stained and your hair is losing pigment at the roots?"

Katerina let out an exasperated sigh. "Your guess is as good as mine." She touched her roots. "Is it really faded?"

Jezabelle reached for her sister's hair and trailed her hand down to the middle, where her cheekbones sat. "From your roots to here, your hair looks like it was never black. It's white, unnaturally white, which in contrast, makes the rest of your hair look darker, like ink."

Katerina looked around. No mirror in sight.

"It's odd."

"Odd is an understatement." Katerina muttered, peering down at her hands. "I can feel it—faintly, but I feel something. I shouldn't have this if I didn't complete the ceremony..."

It lay dormant until weeks ago. The Verenna's voice echoed in her mind. But how did it? What triggered it?

"Try not to stress yourself too much; the greys are starting to come." Nik laughed.

"Honey, that stress is really doing a number on your hair," Chryssa said, eyeing her hair.

All this time?

"How does it feel?" Jezebelle's gaze focused on Katerina's hands.

"It's difficult to explain... but just imagine if your hands get really cold—icy cold, and it gets colder to the point it burns, depending on how emotional you get."

"Interesting..." she muttered. "Are your hands going to stay like that?"

"I don't know." Katerina shrugged. "Let's just say that now I have a reason to keep my temper at bay." Her mind flickered back to their mom, her laughter, their times painting, the times when they were happy. How Katerina's keeping her sanity would ensure that they grew up the right way. Then her mind turned to what she had seen during the induction... the Verenna and her father, altering Katerina's mind regarding Byorn. Then her mother... talking to someone in the middle of nowhere... making a deal...

Katerina didn't recognize the man, let alone see his face. What had her mother done?

"Where is Rhei anyway?" Katerina asked, not wanting to go down the spiral.

Jezebelle frowned. "He had to take care of some family business in Sylene."

"Oh," Katerina let out. "And... is the marriage still happening?"

"Yes," she answered dryly.

"You don't sound convinced."

"I am. He'll be back. He just needs to sort a few things out with family. That's all."

"I heard his sister hosted an engagement party for you." Katerina mentioned nonchalantly.

"She did—wait, how do you know Chryssa?"

"Does it matter?"

"I guess it doesn't." She pursed her lips. "I felt bad, to be honest. I wanted to go but, Rhei advised against it. Supposedly for my safety."

"Oh," Katerina suppressed a snort. *I guess he does have common sense after all.* "What did you do instead?"

"We just did some sightseeing, nothing too crazy."

"I see..." Katerina stopped herself from asking further questions since it could open the possibility for another argument to flourish, and they'd just made amends; so she wasn't about to ruin it. "I wonder what's going on outside."

"I'm more interested in you." Jezebelle countered.

"Why?"

"What can you do with your power?"

Katerina blinked. *I have no idea. Nyctokinesis... darkness manipulation but... I am able to cut off someone's air supply—well, was it me who did that? No matter. What can I actually do?* "Don't know. I haven't been given time to explore it."

"Try something."

"I don't think it works like that..."

"Just try it."

Katerina closed her eyes, focusing her energy toward her hands. Waiting for the icy feeling to slither from the tugging chest to my palms.

Waiting.

Waiting.

Waiting.

Nothing.

"I'm telling you. This is not how it works." Katerina opened her eyes.

"You're not trying." Jezebelle countered. "But what I can see is that it's somehow tied to your emotional state."

"You seem oddly con—"

The door to the safe room opened. "You may return to your rooms. But both must remain inside until final guidance from the Sovereign."

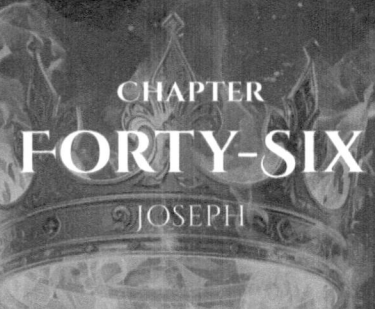

CHAPTER
FORTY-SIX
JOSEPH

JOSEPH PUSHED OPEN THE DOORS TO THE COUNCIL chamber with his council, generals and Byorn trailing behind him. He didn't give them time to sit before he started hounding them with orders and questions.

"Where are Katerina and Jezebelle?"

"In their bedchambers, Sovereign." General Lee responded.

"Take them out of the country." Joseph ordered. "After today, everything will get exponentially worse. I need them out of here." *I can't afford for either of them to die.*

"Where to?"

"They can take up residence at my estate." Byorn suggested. "It is heavily guarded, and it's not an active threat to none of the other countries. Besides, the Olympians will assume they'd use the sanctuary country and most likely turn to Sylene first. It will provide them safe quarters for the time being."

"Then it's settled." Joseph turned to Byorn. "You're to go with them. They'll need you to get settled."

He nodded.

"Now, for the important thing." Joseph pressed his hands against the table, shadows snakes slithering across the surface. "Operations are to be moved to the Belsir Outpost."

"But isn't the Outpost—" Khir's tongue stilled with a look in his direction. Panic contorted his face as he realized that his tongue was missing.

"No interruptions." All nodded silently. "These halls have stood as the heart of our dominion, but we can no longer pretend they are beyond reach. The enemy has grown bold. Their attacks are more precise, more deliberate." Joseph paused, watching their shoulders tighten as the shadows trailed among them. "It is only a matter of time before they attack us here."

"Sir? If I may?" General Ware spoke and Joseph nodded. "To abandon the Fortress is to hand them a victory they do not deserve."

"Wrong," Joseph countered, his voice sharp. "We will not abandon; we will outmaneuver. The Acrailerion was supposed to be neutral ground. Yet, they turned it into a battlefield. I won't put everything I worked for at risk. Our operations will be shifted to the Belsir Outpost."

"A shield that is crumbling is no shield at all. Pride does not stop steel. Stone does not stop fire when cracks run through its bones. Belsir Outpost is our answer," Dremian said, and murmurs rippled through the chamber.

General Veris leaned forward with narrowed eyes. "Belsir? Hidden in those cursed ridges? It is a place of ruins, shadows, and harsh winds. How do you expect morale to endure there?"

"Survival outweighs morale." Joseph said curtly, stepping out from behind the table, letting his shadow spill long across the room, "I will be there with them. Soldiers do not fight for walls. They fight for command, for purpose. And I will give them both."

General Lee cleared his throat. "Belsir offers a tactical advantage. Its ruins conceal the operations. With the proper methods, we could bleed our enemies dry before they even reach us."

Ware snarled at him, "You speak as though the enemy will simply march into the traps we set. They are not fools. You saw what happened moments ago."

"No, they are not fools." Joseph cut across before the bickering could spiral. "Which is why they expect us to stay. And when they come and find us gone, we'll be much stronger and ready to end them for once."

Kalio, ever the cautious voice, tapped his fingers against the table. "And the civilians? What shall we tell them, Sovereign? That their leader retreats while they remain exposed?"

"We will not leave them exposed," Joseph answered with an underlying tone of mock. "A garrison will remain here—enough to defend and reassure. But the mind and muscle of our war effort move with me. The enemy cannot cut the head if it does not know where it lies."

The council grew quiet, some nodding, others shifting uneasily. Joseph let the silence reign, then drove the final nail.

"This is not retreat. This is strategy. We don't yield ground. We shift the battlefield to where *I* decide. From Belsir, we'll endure. From Belsir, we'll strike. And from Belsir... we'll break them." The braziers roared higher, as if in answer.

"Sovereign, I cannot support this." Ware shifted in place, the iron of his cuirass groaning with the motion. "To move our strength into the ridges is to bury ourselves alive. These walls are the heart of our dominion. Leave them, and you leave the people to whisper that the Sovereign runs from war."

Joseph straightened, letting the weight of silence grind against him. "Careful, *General*. There is a line between counsel and defiance, and I hear your boot pressing against it."

But before he could continue, Veris raised his hand lightly, just enough to garner his attention. "Ware speaks truth, Sovereign. The men will question us. Question *you*. They need stability, not shadows in the mountains." His tone had steel, but beneath it, Joseph heard the whisper of challenge.

The chamber split in murmurs, the council like wolves scenting blood.

Joseph stepped forward, each stride deliberate, until he stood between Ware and Veris. His hand rested on the hilt of the dagger at his belt, not to draw it, but to remind them who commanded the steel in this room.

"You mistake me," Joseph said, voice low but burning. "This is not a plea for your agreement. It's an order."

Veris stiffened, his jaw tightening.

But Ware dared to smirk. "And if your order drives us into ruin?"

The braziers flared as though answering the fury simmering beneath Joseph's skin. Ware's eyes bulged, smirk dying and face reddening by the second before his body collapsed and blood trickled out of his ears.

"Then I will carry the ruin on my back before I let it fall on my people." Joseph stepped over Ware's body as he addressed the council. "Do not think me blind to ambition. Should you raise your doubts again, raise them with a blade in hand and see if it carries you further than your tongues, agreed?"

The chamber froze. Even Veris lowered his eyes, his defiance diluted.

"Mark this well: we don't retreat. We *hunt*. We bleed our enemies where they cannot reach us. Belsir is not exile; it is the forge where we sharpen our war. You will march because I command it, and because war is all that endures."

The silence that followed was heavy, but it was no longer uncertain.

It was submission.

The braziers hissed, and no one dared raise their voice after Ware's humiliation. He let them simmer in silence until the moment was ripe, then motioned to the guards at the side doors.

"Bring her inside."

The doors opened, and the sound of soft chains followed. A woman entered, flanked by two armored soldiers. She was cloaked in grey, her eyes veiled, but even beneath the covering Joseph felt the tremor that ran through the council.

"This," Joseph said, walking toward her as if unveiling a relic, "is Thalia." He pulled her veil back, revealing the beautiful brunette underneath. Her eyes were as white as snow. At first glance, people would think her eyes were colorless, but upon closer inspection, a slight shade of silver could be seen within her irises. "She is a seer, touched by the threads of fate itself."

The room shifted uneasily. Mare clasped his hands tightly. "Sovereign... to consort with such power is dangerous. Premonitions are riddles. To place strategy upon them—"

"Is to have an advantage they can't match," Joseph cut in as he circled Thalia, studying her as one would study a blade yet untested. "When she speaks of ambush, we will not be caught. When she speaks of weakness, we'll strike. Our foes will bleed before they even know where we stand."

"Have you forgotten that they have Mnemosyne on their side?" Dremian asked.

"She's been... *handled*." Joseph responded.

Thalia raised her head slightly, lips parting. Her voice was hushed, brittle, yet carried to every corner of the chamber. "Flames rise to devour the horizon, and from the depths a shadow stirs, older than stone and storm. I saw chains quake, some breaking, as scarred hands pressed against the walls of time. A voice from the forgotten age whispered through the fire, and with it rose a crown of ruin, towering above the world. The sky trembled, the sea recoiled—reminders of a war that should never awaken. The ashes of the first tyrant still burn."

Gasps rippled across the table. Lee's eyes narrow, suspicion wrestling with fear.

Joseph spread his arms, seizing the moment. "You see? Even fate bends toward our choice. This is destiny. And destiny is on *our* side."

He turned back to his council, voice ironclad. "With steel in hand and prophecy as our guide, we will not only endure... we will *conquer*. The next war will be ours before the first blade ever strikes."

The chamber doors thundered once more. Another knock, sharper, impatient. The room stirred uneasily, but before he could utter a word, the doors burst open.

Soldiers staggered in, dripping seawater, armor battered as if they had wrestled with the waves themselves. Between them, wrapped in sodden cloth, was a package too heavy for silence.

"Leave us," Joseph ordered.

They all hesitated, their gazes locked upon the shrouded burden. Yet, they knew better than to linger beneath his stare. One by one they bowed out, the chamber dimming as the last of their whispers vanished beyond the doors.

"Bring it forward," He ordered.

The soldiers obeyed, lowering the package onto the table. Their hands shook as they unwound the drenched wrappings. A faint glow seeped through the last layer, as though the steel beneath longed to breathe again. The final cloth fell, and there it was—serrated, curved, an edge forged not merely to cut, but to end.

The sickle.

The air bent to its presence, a low hum vibrating through the stone floor. He felt it crawling across his skin, down into his bones.

One soldier, trembling, cleared his throat. "We lost men, Sovereign. The tides rose against us, wild and untamed. Some... some were swallowed whole."

Joseph didn't look at him. *A price to pay to accomplish such a great milestone.* His eyes were bound to the blade. He kneeled, his hand hovering above it. The sickle drew him closer, pulling breath and will alike. His fingers closed around its hilt, and at once a tremor of power coursed through him. Not borrowed power, not stolen. His.

Visions flashed across his mind: a crown of fire, storms chained and broken, the world bent upon its knees. He heard whispers in the steel—hollow, ancient, filled with a hunger that matched his own.

"At fucking last," He muttered. *I can finish what Quinn fucking started.*

The chamber quaked softly, as though the world had heard his vow. The soldiers bowed low, but he scarcely noticed. His hand tightened on the sickle. *Nothing can stand against me now.*

CHAPTER
FORTY-SEVEN
ZEUS

THE CLING OF STEEL AGAINST STEEL RANG ACROSS THE field as Zeus strode onto the training grounds of Mount Olympus. The air was heavy with sweat, despite his being outdoors. Soldiers froze mid-strike when they noticed him. Helmets dipped and shields lowered.

They could be mistaken for common hoplites in the mortal lands, but they weren't. They were his chosen. His elite cadre forged in both war and divine fire—well, what remained of them, at least. Zeus was used to seeing thousands of troops, yet here stood merely a brigade or even a battalion each.

He considered employing the help of the remaining 9 divisions, but they didn't have any combat experience. He'd be wasting resources. The Olympian Army was forged to maintain balance in the mortal lands.

When it came to ground warfare, the Thunder Guard, the Blood Legion, and the War Regiment would be among the first to be tasked. Through the strategic planning and siegecraft of the War Regiment, the Blood Legion would deploy its infantrymen to the front lines and use relentless assault to shock the enemy while the Thunder Guard garnered air superiority and conducted surprise assaults using lightning-embedded weaponry. For more amphibious assaults, the Trident Fleet would take center stage in deploying its troops.

They stood with Zeus against the Titans, against monsters, against the very chaos of the void. Now, they stood ready for the storm he would unleash upon the Sovereign's Fortress, living by their oath. He could employ the Hunter Corps to conduct reconnaissance and the Siren Guard for psychological warfare, but they didn't have time. One more second wasted and it would be the end for them all.

At the center of the grounds, a makeshift sand table of the Sovereign's fortress was made, from its walls, library, study, mausoleum, bed chambers, staff quarters—they had everything. *Argus thought of everything.*

Soldiers formed a horseshoe around him, the air heavy with anticipation and the faint scent of lightning that clung to him.

Zeus' let his hand hover over the sand table, silently watching the sparks snapping at the ridges. "Joseph believes himself strong," he began, voice cutting through the still air. "He hides behind his fortress, convinced Olympus cannot touch him. And why would he not? He has already spilled the blood of our finest."

He let the words fall heavy, the truth none dared speak aloud.

"The Blood Legion: cut down to a handful. The War Regiment: most of them shattered, their strategies undone before they could be carried out. Both, General Ikaros and Kallistratos dead. And my Thunder Guard...slain in numbers I have not seen since the Titan War. " His jaw tightened, anger burning as much at his own failing as at Joseph's hand. "Every man lost is a wound to Olympus, and every wound festers while he draws breath in that hall."

The soldiers shifted uneasily, but their gaze sharpened with fury. Zeus could see it, grief transmuting into rage.

Zeus wanted to let it out—the rage, the frustration, but he held steady, eyes surveying the troops. "No more. We strike not at his outposts, not at his patrols, but at his heart. His fortress is his base of operations, and it is there he has gathered the strength to mock us. We will end him where he feeds, before he can spread further rot. What do we know about this place?"

A soldier bearing Athena's insignia stepped forward; his dark skin glistened in the sunlight. "Sergeant Ghil, Lord Zeus. The place is two stories. With only two entry and exit points." His hands shuffled through the layout. "The main entrance leads to the foyer, but funneling through here could make frontal assaults costly. The other is the back. Also referred to as the staff entrance. Both are heavily guarded. Especially after the attack on the Acrailerion."

"What about the catacombs?" Rhei stepped forth, making the sergeant move. "The Fortress has hidden catacombs with its entrance placed inside their library. We could enter from there."

"And you know this how?" Zeus asked.

"Dating the Sovereign's youngest has its perks."

"You're dating the enemy's offspring?" another soldier asked.

"Got us the information we need, didn't it?"

"What if she is doing the same to you? Have you considered that?"

"I haven't given her anything worth inquiring about."

"Let's put some things into perspective." Another soldier stepped forward. "*If* we were to go through the catacombs, how would you get in to begin with? Besides how are you sure he won't be there when we show?"

"He won't." Nik answered. "Word on the street is that the Sovereign is planning a move to the Outpost."

"Are you certain?" someone asked.

He nodded. "Rhei isn't the only one with connections to the guy's offspring."

"And how are you sure it isn't just a lie to get you to turn your attention elsewhere?"

"She didn't have to tell me." Nik clarified. "She is of primordial descent, which makes her blood divine, thus making it easier for me to create a subtle yet powerful soul tie. They're getting evacuated as we speak, seeking sanctuary in Windermere."

"Then let's attack there! Catch them off guard." A soldier boasted.

"And risk our position? Not a chance," Rhei said, turning to Nik again. "Primordial descent?"

Nik nodded. "I had my doubts at first. But she is. I don't know who, but the energy is there. It's unmistakable."

Is that why Joseph kept her secluded all this time? Zeus' brows furrowed. *This could change everything.*

"Has she exhibited any traits of this?" Zeus finally spoke.

"Hardly." Nik answered. "Her traits could still lie dormant, barely. I saw it first when her hair began to lose its pigment. I mentioned it to her as stress, but the strands weren't grey, like a mortal. They were white. But what confirmed it was when she touched my tattoo." He ignored the curious eyes that followed.

Zeus ordered. "Has the other exhibited traits like this?"

Rhei shook his head.

Perhaps it's an isolated thing. But if there is a slight chance that she is of Primordial descent, Typhon could use her to enhance his power... he wouldn't shy away from killing her either... and using her blood as a beacon. Fuck. If she isn't dead, that most likely means that he doesn't know or has picked up on it.

"Find a way to bring her here." Zeus ordered. "Tell me about the catacombs?"

Rhei ran a hand over the sand table, shifting until revealing a layout of the catacombs. "I did some exploring of my own. Don't ask me how. But the catacombs are divided into two levels. From the library passage, you automatically fall onto the upper level, where the Sovereign keeps weird fucking altars and ceremonial trinkets. It has an abandoned mausoleum that leads in from the outside, but there isn't a way to go through here without drawing attention. But there is another passage that leads to the lower portion. Here, you have tunnels that branch outward. One side leads to drainage and ventilation tunnels that provide a narrow exit leading to a treeline. The problem is, the passage is so narrow that one, maybe two at a time can pass. Now, the other side leads to a collapsed passage. We could dig in through there."

"Easier said than done." A soldier retorted. "Did you mark where the passage leads to?"

"You think so low of me." Rhei snickered. "I suggest sending the bulk of the men through the Catacombs and having a squad infiltrate the servant access when they report in for the day."

"It won't work. Don't you think they don't know each other?"

"Have you heard of new hires?" Rhei retorted.

"What about Dremian? He can give us a better understanding of where to enter from." A soldier asked.

"He can't. He has to maintain a low profile since the Sovereign has him in his inner counsel." Nik added.

"If the breach holds longer than expected, if the War Regimenet men are slowed—what then? The Sovereign's militia fights with desperation, and it may buy him time." Someone spoke.

Zeus clenched his jaw, the truth gnawing at him. *I won't be able to fight with them through lightning, but I will do what I must to see the Fortress crumble.* "If they hold," I say evenly, "then the squad will strike from within the kitchens. Blood will buy us what lightning cannot."

Another soldier stepped forward, hand on his sword hilt. "And if his men are stronger than reports claim? If he rallies his militia at the Great Hall and counters our formations?"

A low rumble built in Zeus' chest, thunder veiling his unease. "Then I will be the spearhead. His men will face Olympus itself."

The men nodded, but he felt their eyes linger. *Did they sense it? That the storm in me was not what it once was? That every crack of lightning now demanded more of me than before?* His hand trembled slightly, and he clenched it into a fist before they could notice. "Have Hermes aid you in teleporting in and out of the Fortress." Zeus said, eyes on the sand table. "We won't retreat.

This fortress is no sanctuary. It's a tomb waiting to be sealed. Bring the structure down if you have to."

The roar of approval hid the quiet churn of doubt inside him. But if it faltered... if his storms failed again... what then?

He let his gaze sweep across them, buying a breath to steady himself. "Where's Argus?"

The soldiers exchanged uneasy looks. One finally spoke, his tone hesitant. "No word has come of him. Not in days. Scouts were sent to his quarters, found them empty."

A cold weight settled in Zeus' chest. *My confidant, my eyes and ears beyond these walls, gone without a trace.* He forced himself to stand tall, though suspicion twisted in his gut. *Had he betrayed me? Or had Joseph's shadow already reached Olympus?*

"Then we proceed without him," Zeus said, voice measured despite the unease. "Trust no one besides yourselves once you step into the Fortress. The Sovereign thinks himself untouchable behind stone and prayer. We will prove him wrong."

The soldiers roared their vows, spears and shields pounding like thunder across the mountains. Yet behind the sound, his thoughts whispered darker truths: the storm within him waned, his ally was missing, and perhaps the eyes upon him saw more than he wished them to.

FORTY-EIGHT

Night had already fallen, and the commotion outside seemed to have died down, as Katerina shoved a handful of clothes inside a bag. *No one had ever dared to attack the Acrailerion... The Acrailerion of all places... If they would've hit the Chronicler Wing or even the Apothecary.*

"What did he do this time?" She asked herself, shoving the last bit of clothing into the bag. "What the hell did you do?"

First the furies, now this? He wouldn't do something unprovoked —well, he would. But doing so would hurt his standing as Sovereign. This can open the door to rebellion. An exasperated sigh escaped her lips. *What makes you think a rebellion hasn't begun?* She ran her stained hands through her hair. *Besides, what am I supposed to do? Oh, yeah, go to Byorn's estate... how fitting.*

"These rules don't apply to you?" She mocked. *Fucking bastard.* She glanced at her hands. *Initiation or not, I have power. I hardly know how to use it—shit, I barely understand it as it is.* Her fingers felt light as she moved them.

Can I truly control darkness? Her mind flickered back to the Olympian High Priest and how he choked to death... the same with the soldier who attacked her in the forest and the one in the

Acrailerion earlier. *None of these have to do with darkness. I've never used it.*

Walking over to the mirror, she peered down at the star pendant atop her chest and pushed it to the side. She gasped. Her skin was burned underneath. Burned through to leave a scar. *Fucking fantastic.* Then her eyes drifted to her hair and how the black portion crept up the white like smoke. *Jezebelle was right; almost half of my hair is white.*

Repeated knocks had her scrambling over to tie up her hair and rushing over to close the bag. *I need answers.*

She walked over to the door.

"Yes?" She answered. "Jezebelle?"

"Come here." She whispered. Her hair was bunched up in a messy bun with strands flying over her face.

"What's going on?" Katerina asked, and Jezebelle grabbed her hand, pulling her out of the room and toward the mezzanine.

Soldiers of the Light Militia filled the Great Hall with weapons and barricades, while General Lee and General Vivek surrounded the table with a floor plan of the Fortress and another location Katerina didn't seem to recognize.

"They've been at it for the past couple of hours." Jezebelle whispered. "They even told the staff to evacuate the grounds. Things are getting bad, Kate."

"You don't say..." Katerina muttered. "Have you seen Jasmine? I'm worried."

"I was going to ask you. I haven't seen her in days."

Shit...did they take her? What could she possibly be doing? I just hope she's alright.

"I'm sure she's fine. She was a High Re'Veillite, so I wouldn't be surprised if General Lee or the Verenna called her into service again amidst all this," Katerina said, eyes following the soldiers beneath.

"You're also a High Re'Veillite, and they're pulling you out of here."

"Barely." Katerina scowled. "At this very moment, I'm still the eldest of the Sovereign. Not a High Re'Veillite."

"Perhaps..." Jezebelle let out.

"What were you doing out of your room?"

"I went to get some books from the library." She shrugged. "I don't know how long it'll take us to get to Windermere, but I prefer to have some sort of distraction on the way."

Katerina shot her a look. "Did you see anything weird in the library?"

Jezebelle shook her head. "Not that I can think of. Why?"

"I could've sworn I saw some of father's council members disappear in between shelves." Katerina said. "Don't look at me like I'm insane."

"Kate, it *is* insane."

"I think we're well past insane at this point." Katerina looked back at the soldiers opening and closing rooms and adding the final touches on some of the barricades. "I'm going to find out." She pushed off the mezzanine.

"Kate, it's useless. They're coming to pick us up at any moment."

"You can either come with me or stay. But if you stay, I expect you to cover for me until I return."

"How long will you be gone?"

Katerina shrugged. "As long as it takes, but hopefully not long. Let me just finish packing."

CHAPTER
FORTY-NINE
JOSEPH

"You asked for the sickle," Joseph said, raising the blade so its serrated edge glimmered in the half-light of the mausoleum. "Here it is." He tossed it onto the dusty ground.

The shadows writhed, and Eris walked toward him. Her steps were noiseless; her eyes like fractured glass catching fire.

"Ever the brute," she whispered, as if tasting the words. "You may have brought this. But you still clutch at chains, Joseph. Don't you feel it? The weight still pressing upon your heart?"

He glared, knowing exactly what she was referring to. "This sickle is enough."

She laughed, low and cruel, the sound curling like smoke around him. "In other circumstances, yes. But in this case, the sickle may wound the world, but it cannot free you on its own. It cannot sever what binds you. "

Joseph scowled, her words cutting deeper than the blade. "Are you done?"

Her eyes glimmered. "You know what? Where is my gratitude? You did in fact bring this to me, thus keeping your word so I might as well keep mine to show some good faith."

Joseph's eyes narrowed, stomach stirring with unease.

"You can have Rena."

His heart dropped, then chuckled. "No, you are lying."

"Am I not a goddess of my word?" she taunted. "You asked for power, and I delivered. I asked for the sickle, and you delivered. It's time for me to extend the courtesy. You asked for Rena, and I will deliver. But don't get used to it."

He blinked, unable to comprehend what just shifted. He looked down at his picture with Quinn for a moment, then back at her.

"He still requires you to sever the bond." She added. "Only then will the prison split, and he will rise and give you unlimited power, which is what you wanted all along. To be better than Quinn."

His chest tightened. The image of Rena's face flashed in his mind, unbidden. His jaw clenched. "That's why you'll let me see her. You want me to kill her. I won't."

Eris tilted her head, the smile never faltering. "Then you have until dusk. Deny him, and all you've bled for crumbles into nothing."

"I can give you another." he pressed, stepping closer, voice desperate yet fierce. "A rival. A traitor. Even a child of the Olympians, if you want. Blood is blood no matter where you take it from. Take theirs and be satisfied."

Her laughter rang out, sharp as broken glass. "Don't insult me."

"You ask too much," he growled, the sickle trembling in the ground as if sensing his rage.

"And yet," she whispered, leaning so close he could feel her breath against his ear, "you know I am right. Without it, you are a king holding an empty crown. With it, you command the end of gods and claim Quinn's legacy as your own. You will no longer be known as Quinn's successor but as the Sovereign who put Quinn's rule to shame."

He turned sharply, but she was already pulling back, her figure melting into the shadows, her voice lingering long after she was gone.

"Dusk will decide. Either the chain breaks... or you do."

The mausoleum fell silent once more. He stared down at the sickle. But it was gone. And it was only him and his thoughts. *Dusk was in four hours.*

THE STUDY WAS SILENT EXCEPT FOR THE CRACKLE OF the oil lamp and the low hum of the night wind pressing against the shutters. Scrolls and maps lay open across the desk, troop formations drawn in sharp ink strokes, the movement of companies toward the Belsir Outpost set in rigid lines.

This is where my mind should be. On strategy, on survival, on the defense of my fortress. But every time he bent over the parchment, every time he forced his eyes to the marks of terrain and numbers, he saw Eris instead.

Her words haunted him like a phantom perched on his shoulder. *The blood that binds you. The one whose loss will break the chain around your heart.*

The one who binds my heart.

He pressed his fingers hard into his temples, eyes closing against the weight of it. How cruelly clear her demand was, and yet how impossible. She didn't want nameless blood, nor the blood of an enemy already condemned to fucking die. No, she wanted the sacrifice that would cut deepest, that would unmake him.

He cursed under his breath.

Curse her.

Curse *him*.

Curse the day he became sovereign.

Curse the day he was adopted by Marcus.

Curse the day he extended a kind hand to Quinn.

Curse the day Quinn made him this...

He felt like a knife was about to be plunged into his chest.

Maps blurred before him as doubt coiled in his gut. He had led armies against greater odds than these.

Have I? Have I really? I've wrestled power from men and gods alike, and yet here I was—paralyzed. Paralyzed not by blades or fire, but by the thought of giving her what she asked.

His mind split into cruel halves. One side roared like a commander, urging him to choose swiftly, to act with the ruthlessness required of a sovereign.

The other recoiled, clutching desperately at the threads of love, of loyalty, of family, of the oaths he had once sworn; and beneath it all, the ticking of time. She had given him until dusk. Already the horizon felt too close.

He rose from his chair and paced, hands clenched into fists. He thought of the council, of his generals, of the soldiers who looked to him as the unbreakable center of this country. *If they knew how fractured I was inside, how close I stand to breaking— would they still follow? Or would they scatter like sand through open fingers?*

He slammed fist against the edge of the desk, scattering scrolls to the floor. His breath came hard and ragged. *I don't know what to do.* And so, in the silence that surrounded him, he let pride fall.

"Rena," he whispered, her name catching in his throat. He turned toward the door, as if by sheer will he could summon her. "If you were here, you'd be my rock. My moral compass. If there's a chance you could be here... I—" he stopped.

If she were here, she'd be the first to be sacrificed... Fuck. Sometimes I wonder what life would be like if I had just died when Bernadette died, or if I would've avoided the Petrakis household entirely.

Who would I be then? Certainly not in this fucking mess.

The firelight flickered across the maps, casting their lines into chaos. He rubbed his eyes, so hard he saw stars. *Fuck. I need something.*

"My love."

That voice. I know it better than my own heartbeat. He jerked up.

Rena stood framed in the doorway with a kind smile and starlight eyes, her silken gown gliding over the floor.

She moved toward him with a grace that felt both familiar and new, her hips swaying in a rhythm that entranced him.

"I won't..." He muttered, unable to believe that she is here. That he let her out. But no, he wouldn't.

Her lips curled, warm and inviting. "I was surprised myself..." She raised her hand, fingertips brushing his cheek. "It's been so long... I thou—I thought I'd never see you or the girls again." Her honey eyes crystallized.

He leaned into her touch before his mind could form a protest. The tender look on her face. The softness of her touch. The warmth of her skin. Her gentle gaze... his chest tightened. *I've been a monster, but I've missed her. This was her. In the flesh. My rock. My comfort. My moral compass.*

"I don't care how long we have. Or why they let you out. But I'm sorry. For everything I've done. You didn't deserve to be in this situation." He whispered, grasping her face. "The girls... they miss you."

She leaned into his touch, and he just kissed her. Gentle at first. Then—deep, hungry, possessive.

His breath faltered, chest tightening as fire spread where her lips lingered. This was no kiss of comfort, no sweetness of home. This was a wildfire consuming every hesitation.

"Fuck," he murmured against her lips, arms already circled her waist, drawing her nearer.

Her eyes glowed in the dim light, lips curling into a smile. "I see you missed me as much as I missed you."

Her hands roamed across his chest, pulling him further into the storm of her body, and he sank willingly. Every ounce of reason dissolved as her scent of roses and honey filled him.

His heart raced, breath caught, and still he yielded.

The world narrowed to her skin, her voice, her mouth. In that moment, the weight of war, the gnawing of doubt, the burden of command—all of it vanished beneath her touch.

He wanted only her.

Her lips moved against his, desperate, hungry. She pulled the clothes off him, and he was eager to return the favor.

His fingers traced the silken straps of her dress and slipped it off her shoulders, allowing it to bunch at her feet.

Fuck... He pulled her closer, feeling the warmth of her skin, the softness of her perky breasts against him. He claimed her mouth again, and they staggered back until her ass was against the desk. He threw the scrolls and map onto the ground and put her body atop it.

She whispered his name as though it were sacred, her body pressing closer, her hand sliding along his chest. He held her tighter, intoxicated by her nearness and terrified that she'd slip away at any moment.

"Oh, Rena..." he breathed, lips brushing hers, "I've missed this."

She drew him deeper into the kiss. *This is real. She is in my arms. Naked and delectable.*

She is here.

And then something sharp slid between his ribs.

He froze, eyes shooting wide and staring into hers. Then, he carefully looked down. At the blade protruding from his chest, where his heart should lie. Warm liquid trailed slowly down his body.

He gasped, the air tearing from his lungs in a ragged cry.

The warmth of her body remained pressed to him as pain bloomed like fire, sharp and unrelenting. His hands clutched at her arms in desperate confusion.

"W-why..." The word caught in his throat.

Her smile curved, cruel and knowing. The softness of his wife's gaze flickered, replaced by violet fire. Her voice, once sweet, now dripped like venom.

"Time's up."

His heart clenched with a sharp pain, but the pain of the betrayal hurt deeper. His wife's face was still there, still pressed close, and yet it was a lie, a lie he had kissed willingly.

He staggered, knees weakening, but her hand gripped the hilt and held the knife fast inside him, keeping him upright.

"You let yourself be consumed by what you longed for most," she whispered, her lips brushing the shell of his ear, her words burning hotter than the blood spilling down his chest. "And in that weakness, you gave me everything I need."

He tried to push her away, to pull the knife free, but his arms were numb, his body frozen in the shock of her deceit. His breath rattled as he fought against the blackness tugging at his vision.

"Kill me then." He sputtered. "Use my blood instead. That's what you wa-wanted... to undo me."

"You will not die," she murmured, almost tenderly. "The tether was forged long before this night, on the day you gave yourself to him. This is to... *expedite* the process."

His pulse hammered weakly in his ears. "N-no..."

Her smile deepened, wicked and victorious. "Yes. I had to take matters into my own hands since you lacked the gall to finish what he demanded. That bond cannot be undone." She twisted the blade, and he choked on a cry.

"Her life will be claimed tonight," Eris said, her once violet eyes now blazing, golden.

"Spare her... spa-spare Rena."

"Rena?" She laughed. "You're hilarious. She has another purpose."

His strength faltered, blood soaking into the floor, knees trembling as the world spun. "Wh-Who?

She released the blade, and he fell to the ground, letting darkness consume him.

THE FORTRESS ROSE ABOVE THEM, ITS WALLS BLACK against the night sky, but they didn't go to it from the gates or the towers. They descended into the earth, into the forgotten tunnels beneath. The catacombs were carved long before the Sovereign claimed this place, their stones damp with age and whispers of the dead. The air was cold and close, the extinguished torches along the walls barely able to be seen amidst the darkness. Every step echoed too loudly, a reminder that sound itself was their enemy here.

Athena's soldiers led the way, weaving through the narrow corridors, their blades drawn, eyes sharp. The squad trailed behind, shields propped on their backs and weapons at the ready. Zeus walked among them, feeling the fortress above them, the weight of stone and treachery pressing down.

His chest felt heavy, but he discarded it as a mere overreaction. The tunnels bend sharply upward, a hidden stairwell coiling them toward the surface. The stench of incense and charred offerings hit Zeus before they reached the top.

When they emerged, it was into the chamber of the altar—an antechamber of worship, gilded in false reverence. Blood still glistened fresh upon its stones. Skulls over the walls in hollowed spaces.

One of the soldiers hissed between his teeth. "Sacrifice," staring at the crimson stains. "The Sovereign feeds his power here."

You don't say. Zeus silenced him with a glare. "Then we will cut him off from the source."

The soldiers crossed the altar chamber swiftly, climbing to the upper level. But Zeus remained behind, hovering over the onyx altar with unknown script engraved on it. But, something felt off. It was as if someone had wiped the altar clean. As if it were nothing but a mere relic stored away.

Zeus' heart dropped. *He knows. He fucking knows.* He trudged forward, crossing the chamber and up the stairs.

The walls widened into a vaulted hall, shelves stacked with scrolls and tomes. The library, its knowledge twisted now to serve him. Candles burned low, shadows stretching like claws across the floor. But it was too late; the Sovereign's soldiers awaited them there, their armor black, their blades wet with oil. *We walked right into this bullshit.*

One of them stepped forth, meeting half-way. No intimidation in the slightest. Zeus stepped forward, raising his hand, dying lightning flickering across his skin.

"Come to surrender?" The soldier smirked, sword at the ready.

Rage burned within him, but he managed to maintain a relaxed composure. "I've come to take you with me."

His men surged to the left, shields locking as they rammed into the enemy line. Ares' men struck the right flank, swords skewering through gaps in armor. Athena's scouts scattered upward onto the shelves as if they weighed nothing. Then it rained arrows and daggers from the shadows above.

Zeus advanced through the center, every step a hammer blow. The library filled with the roar of steel, and screams. Amidst the swinging of his blade, he tried to summon lightning. But again, nothing.

"Split and strike!" He ordered. "Crush them from all sides!"

The soldiers obeyed, scattering into separate streams of fury, carving their way deeper into Joseph's stronghold. Zeus took care of the handful of men that still lingered around the library. Each strike, each blow was more taxing than the last. But he didn't stop until every single one of them was on the ground.

Towers of parchment and tomes toppled, and Joseph's men drowned beneath the Wrath of Olympus. Yet, even amid victory's roar, he felt it—the storm within him sluggish and slow to answer. His soldiers did not see it in the chaos, but he felt it in his bones.

Still, he pressed forward to join his men. They had come through the dark beneath his Fortress, through the catacombs, through the altar, and now through the library. Zeus knew that it was a matter of time before Joseph would be notified, that Olympus was inside his very walls—and soon, at his throat.

Zeus' soldiers pressed forward, and with the faint power he had left, he made them morph into enemy soldiers. *Slither and hide in plain sight. We'll see how long Joseph lasts.* He strode through the center of it all, his hand raised high. With all he had, once more, he tried summoning the storm to finish this chamber in one strike. But as the lightning gathered, a shadow darted across his side.

A flash of steel.

A searing pain exploded on the side of his skull.

The world tilted, blurred, and went dark.

"ARE YOU SURE YOU SAW THE RIGHT THING?" JEZEBELLE asked, surveying through the ajar door.

"I did." Katerina scanned through the different bookshelves, careful not to step over the pools of blood and bodies that toppled over each other. Some were burnt to a crisp. *No doubt as a result of my father's insolence.*

They had managed to sneak out of their rooms since everyone else was focused on the infiltrators. Were they taking a risk? Yes. Did Katerina need answers despite the active threat? Yes.

She kept looking through the mess. *History of Escron, Basic Enrichment of Herbology, Caverest: The Folklore, The Myths, and The Truth. Blah. Blah. Blah.*

Stepping away, she moved from shelf to shelf, touching and moving every book, every scroll, every item that crossed her field of vision.

Savior, please. I know I didn't imagine it. I saw it. Please.

"Seems like you just saw something at an angle. You know? When you look in a certain direction and it looks like people are doing something when in reality it's the opposite?"

"I am not crazy, Jezebelle." Katerina snapped. *Please give me a sign. Anything.*

"Kate, you've been looking for a while. They're most likely looking for us right now."

"If you'd help me, maybe I wouldn't be taking so long." Her gaze locked onto a potted evergreen between two vaulted bookshelves, primarily focusing on the rectangular outline behind it. *You've got to be kidding.*

Jezebelle snorted. "I still think you're wasting your time."

Katerina inched closer to the plant. *How could I be so stupid to not notice this?* She pushed it to the side, revealing a white door camouflaged with the wall, slightly ajar.

"You were saying?" Katerina glanced at her sister, unable to contain her smugness.

"Don't celebrate too much." Jezebelle pointed at the door. "What if someone's down there?"

Katerina didn't waste a second longer before rushing in. She went down a stone spiral staircase, dimly lit by scattered torches. Footsteps echoed behind her, letting her know that Jezebelle was close. Faint mist lingered in the cool air as they reached the lower level. Her stomach turned. Rows of weathered skulls were arranged neatly in niches carved into the stone walls. Their glowing eyes followed their every move, but Katerina didn't stop.

"What the hell?" Jezebelle muttered.

Cobwebs and dust covered the walls, and dim light filtered in from cracks in the ceiling.

"My thought's the same..." Katerina's body froze.

Chains hung from one of the walls. Her heart thundered ferociously in her ears. Deep crimson stained the ground.

"Do you understand?"

"Yes." Tears drenched my cheeks.

Another crack.

"Yes, what?"

"Yes...I understand...and will not step out of line again."

"Good." He said. "Bring the dress down to your hips. Keep your eyes on the wall."

She obeyed. With trembling hands, she slid the top part of her dress down to her wrists. Cool air caressed her exposed skin.

"Three. That is all you are getting, since your situation was able to be... handled."

A HAND ON HER SHOULDER MADE KATERINA JERK AWAY.

"Kate?" Jezebelle asked softly. "Oh..."

I don't know why I came down here. Katerina walked away from the chains, suppressing every thought, every reminder of her pain. Her back tingled, but she kept moving. *No need to dwell on it. You are leaving anyway.*

"Kate, I'm here if you need to talk about it."

"I rather spare you the horrific details of father's punishments, if I can help it." Katerina stopped in her tracks, and her mouth went dry.

A simple yet unnerving black marble altar stood before her. It looked like it hadn't been touched for so long. Next to it, an extinguished hearth emitted fresh smoke, and small particles glowing orange were able to be seen amidst the burnt wood with an iron poker resting against the coarse wall.

Heat brushed her face as she crouched down to the ashes, grabbing a bit with her blackened, pointy fingers. She could barely distinguish the ash from her skin if it weren't for the soft, yet grainy texture. A smooth piece of marble glinted faintly through the burnt debris. She picked it up, wiping the ash and revealing its carved surface.

De're Guiol to Tenebrios.

Katerina's eyes narrowed at it, her memories flipping through like a book.

I looked up at the Verenna. "You were cursed?"

A slight nod.

My stomach dropped, mind stirring. "But who—is this why you haven't spoken to me?"

Another nod, and her quill traced the parchment. I followed carefully.

G. U. I...

Guiol

T. E. N. E. B...

Tenebrios.

"What does this mean?" I asked. "My Iahlari is not that advanced. I—"

The Verenna pressed a finger onto her lips and instantly shredded the parchment.

HER MIND CONTINUED TO STIR, TO JUMP, TO SORT, TO understand. To remember somehow. She looked back. Jezebelle roamed with apparent morbid curiosity.

I flipped through mom's notes as she hovered over me to keep reading. I wasn't a fan of this topic, hence why I never took the initiative to read it in my personal time.

"Why? Just tell me why do I need to know this?" I asked, reading the translations in front of me.

Se're Vosto: Blessed Day
Verenna: High Priestess
San'ra: Mother
Guiol: Father

"I remember when you told me you wanted to become a naturopath in the Acrailerion." Mom responded. *"I figured, why not give you a head-start on Ialahri?"*

"Why can't they just communicate in Modern Calastalli like the rest of us?"

"Because there are a lot of evil people who seek to steal from the archives and cause harm to the sisterhood. This is just to ensure that valuable information is properly protected. Now, read up."

My eyes fall back on the parchment.

CAOSEN: APOSTATE
AMORITZIE: MY LOVE
UMBRA: DARKNESS
SEFT: STRENGTH
PROMISA: PROMISE
DELTO: WORLD
TENEBRIOS: MONSTERS

"FATHER OF MONSTERS..." KATERINA GASPED.

Heat seared into her chest, making her throw the marble in the process. She clutched onto her necklace, separating it from her stinging flesh. *It can't be...*

"Came to sacrifice yourself to me, little one?"

She jolted upright. *What the hell?* She walked back, keeping her eyes fixed on the hearth and the altar. Ice seared into her palm, cooling the burning pendant.

"What's wrong?" Jezebelle asked.

Heat. Threat. Cold. Power. "We have to get out of here." Katerina whispered, eyes crystallizing by the second.

"Why?" Jezebelle's voice dropped dangerously low. "That's no fun."

Katerina turned.

Jezebelle's smile stretched unnaturally wide, her eyes darkening with sinister intensity.

Katerina's throat clenched. *Move.* She took a step back, but her feet remained frozen in place. Her chest tightened. *I can't breathe.*

"I knew you'd eventually come to me." Jezebelle—well, not Jezebelle? said. **"Your father can't hide you from me forever. He'll pay for his insolence."**

Darkness slithered from Katerina as her blood chills up her trembling arms.

Jezebelle lunged for her, and Katerina pushed her back. *I don't want to hurt you.*

"Kate." Her soft voice emerged, hands fighting to get a hold of her.

Katerina shook her head. "Stop." She pushed her sister back again and again until she was merely inches away from the hearth.

"Kate, please!" She urged. "It's me."

Katerina picked up the poker. "Liar!" Heat sears into her chest as she lifted the poker between them, aiming the pointy edge toward whatever was taking control of Jezebelle. Shadows snuffed out the remaining lights around the catacombs, leaving only a wash of silver creeping from the cracked ceiling. The hair at the back of her neck stood as the temperature dropped.

"Your father doesn't give you nearly enough credit." A deep voice says. **"Come to me."**

"Like hell." Katerina tightened her icy grip around the metal rod, scanning for her sister's body amidst the darkness. The heat from the pendant spread through her shivering body.

It laughed. **"Come to me."**

Her chest tugged, and her feet skidded into the dark. She rooted her heels onto the ground, but they continued to slide. *Stop. Stop. Stop. Savior, help me.*

"Savior, help me." It laughed again.

It can hear my thoughts? She kept fighting against the pull.

"I am the Savior you plead to."

Her stomach plummeted. *Lies. This isn't right.* Terror simmered within her. *I was not pleading... relying... worshiping... the father of monsters.* Her gaze crystalized and a treacherous tear broke free.

"But you did." It said. *"I'll give your father some credit. He hid you from me for twenty-eight years."* It slid into a sliver of light.

Her mouth dried. *The voice didn't come from my sister anymore. No,* it came from a monstrous being...tall, barely an inch away from touching the ceiling, with its upper body exposed and massive coils of vipers writhing from the waist down. His eyes burned bright, like flames, as he gave her a sinister grin, displaying his razor-sharp teeth, and dark leathery wings stretched from his shoulders.

If we weren't confined in the crypt, I swear he could make himself bigger and more terrifying.

"He thought I would never find you. The darkened blood in the flesh, raised by a coward."

She opened her mouth to retort, but something held her back.

"You wear his weakness in your eyes. A pathetic shadow he thought could resist."

She sneered, rage taking over her trembling body and gradually simmering down the terror in her core. "Whatever problem it is you have with my father, sort it out with him. I had nothing to do with it."

"Oh, but you did." It said, voice humming against her bones. *"He made you to destroy me. Funny how he believed sheltering you would be of use. He just served you to me."*

Her chest clenched. Not of fear or confusion, but of burning, white-hot rage.

"If it's me you want. Have at it," Katerina challenged, saving any shred of dignity she had left. "You're not the first who's tried to kill me."

"Killing you would be a waste." He chuckled. *"You won't just witness the end. You are the reason it begins."*

Strong hands jerked her body, and bright, warm light flooded her vision.

"My stars, Kate!"

Katerina turned her head, and stinging pain spread from her neck to her legs. Everything ached. Dark blurs sneaked into view.

"I thought you were dead!" Jezebelle squealed, her soft hands grabbing Katerina's.

Her face focused into clarity. "Where am I?" Katerina's throat ached, head throbbing.

"In one of the rooms next to the Great Hall." She said softly. "You scared me back there."

Katerina bolted upright and regretted it almost instantly. Her head spun. "What time is it?"

"A little past nightfall. Here." Jezebelle passed her a cup. "Drink up."

"What is it?" She didn't make an effort to take it from her hands.

Jezebelle's brows furrowed. "It's water."

"I'm not thirsty." Katerina's gaze drifted behind her sister.

Soldiers of the light militia stood at the ready, hands on their assigned weapons.

"They helped me take you out of the catacombs."

Katerina turned to her, head still pounding. "What happened?"

"It's... complicated." Jezebelle looked away. "Besides, we're leaving soon, anyway. Just get some rest."

"Jez—" her head thundered. "Jezebelle, what happened?"

A wash of pain coated her sister's pooling eyes, and Katerina couldn't help but wonder if what happened down there was truly as horrid as Jezebelle was painting it out to be or if it triggered something in her...*that I swore I would protect...*

"I thought you were dead, Kate..." Tears streamed down her

cheeks. "You...at first—" she breathed. "You were pale—unresponsive—I... I thought I lost you. What in the world did you—"

"The Sovereign is summoning everyone to the Worship Hall," General Lee announced from the entrance.

"But we're leaving soon under his orders." Jezebelle countered.

"Momentary change of plans, we'll leave after his announcement. He wants both of you there."

CHAPTER
FIFTY-TWO

JOSEPH

The study's walls felt closer than they should. His frame—*Joseph's* frame—was powerful by mortal standards, yet it was *small*.

Cramped.

Fragile.

A vessel unworthy of me.

Every breath burned in the chest, every muscle groaned as though it carried chains. He despised it, this sensation of weakness —yet it was necessary. Mortality was the mask through which he would command.

For now.

Eris lingered in the half-light, her golden eyes studying him with that perpetual smile of hunger. She tilted her head. "What comes next?"

He leaned forward; the desk creaking under his grasp. "What comes next is the *welcome*. I will summon them all. Every general, every councilor, every trembling soul who once called this man their sovereign. They will gather in... how did he call it? The Worship Hall... even if it lies in ruin, they will bow. They will bend their necks to me, not him." His voice cracked through the chamber, though this body's throat rasped with the weight of flesh.

"Already done." She smirked. "They're heading there as we speak."

A flicker of warmth surged in his chest, but it was not mortal frailty; it was satisfaction. His patience paved the way, and now *he* stood at the threshold of dominion. The mortal lands lay open, and through it he would pull Zeus down into the dust. *I will grind his arrogance into the soil beneath mortal feet.*

Eris stepped closer, brushing her hand against the arm of this host. "The beacon of darkness still roams wild, untethered. My gifts can root it, control it, *wield it* for you. Let me find it for you, and I will weave its chaos into your conquest."

He studied her carefully. "I know where she dwells. Erebus thought he could use her against me," he chuckled. "When she can hardly help herself without going insane."

"I am at your disposal." She lowered her gaze. "Just say the word."

Her grin sharpened, satisfied, as though she could already hear the echo of bowed voices filling the space. And in his chest, despite the limitations of this cursed flesh, he felt the storm coil tighter.

THE DOOR OF THE STUDY SLAMMED BEHIND HIM, shaking the frame in its hinges. Eris followed, her laughter soft and hungry, her steps never far from his. The corridors reeked of blood before he reached the first archway. Shouts and steel clashed, echoing through the halls. As he turned the corner, the scene unfolded before him.

Olympian soldiers, stained and shredded, clashed against the ragged armor of the Light Militia. Their bodies tore at each other in blind fury—brothers ripping into brothers, blades carving through armor, arrows hissing down narrow halls.

The Fortress was choking on its blood.

He stood in the threshold and let it wash over him. For a moment, this vessel's heart raced with mortal memory—fear, pity, loyalty—he squashed it. *I will not inherit his weakness.* He narrowed his gaze at the soldiers, only to notice what Zeus had done. Morphed his soldiers into Light Militia allies to then make them turn against themselves.

"Pathetic," he growled, lifting a hand. "All of you."

The storm burst from his chest. A wave of blackened lightning roared through the corridor, shredding steel and flesh alike. Screams shrilled, then died, as both Olympian soldiers and Light Militia were scorched to ash in the blink of an eye. Blood sprayed the walls, then steamed into nothing. Armor crumpled where men had stood.

Still, he wasn't finished.

Thunder cracked from above, splitting the stone. Shadows crawled across the corpses that littered the floor. He stretched out his arms and pulled. Smoke poured from the wounds, from the mouths, from the empty hollows of their eyes. Their flesh dissolved into grey, their features melting away.

One by one, they *rose*.

Faceless.

Hollow.

Their skin hard as stone, their bodies cloaked in the storm's darkness. They no longer bore banners nor names—only silence and strength. Their armor fused to their forms, warped by lightning into jagged edges.

His soldiers.

Not Olympian.

Not Light Militia.

Not men.

His.

His to wield.

His to conquer.

They fell in behind him as he strode forward, their steps echoing, an endless column of thunder and void.

Eris's laughter followed, high and sharp through the Fortress halls. "Oh, they're not ready for this."

He said nothing. Words were ash compared to the power that filled him now. The mortal body still dragged, but with every faceless soldier at his back, the sickle in his possession, the vessel felt less weak. Less small.

The Fortress trembled.

The Worship Hall waited ahead. Its doors groaned in anticipation. And when they open, the mortals within will not see a sovereign. They would see the storm, crowned in death, with an army of faceless shadows bowing in its wake.

CHAPTER
FIFTY-THREE

ZEUS

ZEUS WOKE TO THE STENCH OF IRON AND DAMP STONE. Chains clattered as he stirred, heavy links binding his wrists and shoulders, his strength dragging like lead. His head throbbed, a dull ache reverberating through his skull. Blurry shapes swam before his eyes, the world hazy. *What happened?* He blinked repeatedly. *I tried to summon the storm...*

His vision steadied on the dark chamber around him. Flames guttered on the walls, their light falling upon another figure slumped nearby.

Argus.

His body was battered, his face bruised to near nonrecognition, one eye swollen shut. He moves faintly, breath ragged, barely conscious.

Relief warred with suspicion in Zeus' chest. *He lived. Yet... why are you here? Who did this to you?*

Zeus tugged at the chains again, harder, fury rising. *The storm is gone.* His veins felt empty; his body felt heavy. No surge of power, no spark on his tongue. The realization hollowed him.

"I... am mortal," he breathed, the words tasting like ash. *No, I'm in my mortal form.*

A low chuckle scraped from the shadows.

Zeus turned his head.

There in the far corner sat Ares. His massive frame leaned against the wall, arms crossed, eyes glinting in the torchlight. But there was no brotherhood in his gaze. Only hunger. Malice. He smirked, the firelight dancing across his scarred face. "The great Zeus," he muttered, voice mocking. "Chained like a mortal dog." His eyes flickered to Argus, then back to him. "You thought him the traitor?" He leaned forward, his grin widening. "No, father. The betrayal runs deeper than that." He clicked his tongue. "I'll admit I'm a little disappointed that you decided to give *him* the credit."

The flames hissed faintly in their sconces, the only sound besides the rattle of Zeus' chains when he shifted. Argus groaned beside him, his head lolling forward, blood dripping from his split lip. He looked barely alive, and yet an ember of suspicion refused to die in Zeus' chest.

Ares' armor was unbuckled, the plates stacked against the wall, but his presence was heavy. His boots struck the stone as he approached, the smirk on his lips growing sharper with each step. "You look smaller like this," he said, unable to contain his grin. "Almost... *human*."

Zeus pulled at his bonds, sparks barely flickering from his fingertips before dying into nothing. He forced his voice steady. "Why? You think this makes you strong? Sitting in shadows while others bleed? I didn't take you for a coward."

Ares crouched before him, eyes level and onyx hair glinting. He snorted. "Don't pretend you understand strength. You've never needed it—you were born with it. Power poured into your veins while the rest of us clawed for scraps."

"You were never denied. I gave you command, legions—"

"Command?" he barked a laugh, sharp and bitter. "You gave me slaughter and called it honor. You forged me into your bloodhound, then leashed me whenever it pleased you. And for what? So you could hold Apollo high in your hand like a golden idol."

The words cut deep, and Zeus drew a sharp breath, controlling his simmering blood.

"Twice he betrayed you—fucking twice he schemed to overthrow you. And twice you forgave him. All because Apollo was the favored son, the shining one, the one who could do no wrong. While I—your loyal soldier, your shield, your fucking butcher—was chained in his shadow."

"Apollo earned his place back through penance." Zeus said through gritted teeth.

"Penance?" Ares sneered, stepping closer. "Don't insult me. You coddled him because you feared Olympus without his light. But me? You never feared losing me. Because to you, Ares was nothing more than the sword you could always replace."

"You resent me for being king?"

"No." His voice darkened, low and cold. "I resent you for being a *terrible* one. You call yourself ruler of the gods, yet you let Olympus rot. You favor mortals. You let dissension spread through your council. You weakened the very throne you sit on. And all the while, you blind yourself, pretending thunder alone holds this world together. Olympus is weak. *You* are weak. I warned you, time and again—cling to mortals, and you become one. You coddled them, called them allies, let them seep into our wars. And now? You bleed as they do." He flicked his gaze to Argus, slumped beside Zeus. "Even your most trusted turned fragile. You're lucky I didn't pierce that precious vein of his."

"He didn't betray me," Zeus growled, though the words felt hollow in his mouth. I tried to summon his power, to let lightning silence him—but nothing came. His chest felt hollow, his divinity slipping further away with every breath.

Ares' grin widened. "Didn't he? Then how did the Sovereign know every step, every weakness, every wall to break? You wonder if he's the knife at your back, but you can't admit the truth, can you?"

Zeus' chest sank, chains digging into his wrists. "If you believe for a second I am going to believe any of this, you're surely mistaken."

Ares chuckled. "You're right. He doesn't have the fortitude to go against you. But he was clever. I give him that. He was onto me since he sent my men into the mortal lands."

No wonder you were so angry. Zeus muttered. "Why not deal with him then?"

"And risk exposing myself? I don't think so." Ares leaned close, eyes gleaming with triumph. "I watched. I waited. And when the Sovereign rose, I saw my opening. Granted, he is no god, yet he commands fear as you never could. He bleeds his enemies dry without hesitation, without mercy. He understands war in ways you never will."

"You berate me for how I am with mortals, yet here you are, chained to a mortal tyrant. The irony."

"Better a tyrant who knows power than a king who squanders it." Ares straightened. "You made me this way. Time to reap what you sow."

His words hit hard. Ares was not the boy he had raised to lead armies, nor the warrior who once defended Olympus without question. He was something else—something twisted, sharpened by his own failings.

"I didn't make you this way. This is of your own accord."

He chuckled. "Do you know what it feels like to watch the great Zeus fall? To see the mighty storm-god caged? It is *justice*. You bound me in your shadow all my life, parading your thunder while I carried your wars. But now? Now the storm is mine to wield."

"And what of Olympus?" Zeus asked, forcing steel into his voice though his power was gone. "Will you burn it to the ground with Joseph at your side?"

Ares' eyes became alive with cruel certainty. "Olympus will kneel. Whether beneath the Sovereign or beneath me, it makes no difference. The age of your thunder is over. Now, war will rule."

"And then what? Do you seriously think Typhon will let you rule Olympus?"

"He needs me to make Olympus submit." Ares scoffed. "Thanks to me, he is where he is now, and I will rule Olympus while he rules the mortal lands."

"He won't let you. He'll wait until the time is right and your guard is lowered to strike." Zeus said, attempting again to summon some power. But nothing.

"You're just bitter that I outsmarted you. The mighty fucking Zeus." Ares mocked.

"How did you do it?"

"It was quite simple. You made it too fucking easy for me." He paced casually around the cell. "You know that ambrosia, that wine you love so much?"

Zeus' eyes widened, mind flickering back to every single time he had a fucking drink. "You—"

"Bingo," Ares mocked. "I thought you would make me work for it. But imagine if someone wanted to cause you harm?" He clicked his tongue disapprovingly. "Get comfortable, but not too comfortable. I'm coming back to get you."

He turned, stepping back into the shadows, his laughter rumbling low like a mockery of thunder.

Argus moved weakly, whispering something Zeus could barely catch through blood and pain. "Don't... trust him..."

"It's a little late for that." He muttered, then heaviness took over his eyelids.

FIFTY-FOUR

EVERYTHING AROUND KATERINA SEEMED TO MOVE slowly as if she walked through thick liquid. People passed by her but she couldn't tell if their expressions were of concern, curiosity, pity, or a mix of everything.

Her head felt like it was going to explode at any second and the last thing she wanted to do right now was listen to her father give some poor announcement or sermon under the guise of good faith and survival.

She followed the herd of people out of the Fortress, escorted by General Lee, and into the Caverest Plaza.

Buzzing overtook her ears, making her stop and press her hands to her head. *Please stop. Please. Sav*—she drew a bitter breath.

"I am the Savior you plead to."

Like hell I'll ever plead to you again.

"Kate, are you alright?" Jezebelle placed a hand on her shoulder.

"Yeah." Katerina lied. "I'll meet you inside, I just need a minute of fresh air."

"I'm not leaving you."

"I'll be fine." She reassured her sister. "I just need a minute."

I need to decompress before I am stuck in a room full of hypocrites. Namely, my father. Did he know? Did he know that this Savior he so worships is nothing but pure evil? Wouldn't that make it worse though? If he knew? Shit.

Jezebelle scanned her for a moment with what Katerina believed was apprehension. "Fine. Just don't take too long." She gave Katerina a reassuring shoulder squeeze and followed the herd into the Acrailerion.

She breathed in, filling her lungs with fresh air and biting back the tears pooling in her eyes.

Moving away from the group, Katerina hurried to the fountain, focusing on the sounds of the running water. But that did little to stifle the pain building in *my chest and the flash of white light covering her vision.*

JEZEBELLE'S BODY TOWERED OVER KATERINA'S, *darkness enveloping them both.*

"Come back to me, Kate."

She tapped her face repeatedly, trying to get a response from her icy face.

KATERINA BLINKED THE FOUNTAIN BACK INTO VIEW, head slamming against her temples. *Was I truly dying?* She dunked her hands into the cool water and splashed her face. Heart racing, heat emitted from the pendant. *Are you going to keep burning me?*

She reached for the clasp, ready to toss this shit into the water, when her mother's words annoyingly rushed to the surface, urging her to keep it.

But, was it really her? Or an illusion? The Savior I believed in for so many years turned out to be a lie. What's to say that this isn't one too?

"Miss, we need you inside." General Lee walked up to her.

Suppressing a sneer, Katerina stood and followed him to the Acrailerion.

———

OUT OF ALL OF THE THINGS THAT COULD'VE CROSSED her mind, she would've never imagined how the attack had left the Worship Hall.

The once-bright walls and glass-pane ceilings were now dark and broken. The *Savior's* altar was now warped and stained, no longer displaying the sense of tranquility and hope. No, that was stripped away. Moonlight flooded the room through the gaping hole in the ceiling, and the pillars were crumbling, barely capable of holding their own weight.

Her gaze swept across the room. The bodies of the soldiers who fought against her still lay there in pools of their own making. A sense of utter unease and despair filled the room as she squeezed through the chattering crowd, searching for her sister.

"Monsters. That's what they all are."

"How could they do such a thing?"

"And they dare to say that they worship a god capable of such destruction."

"I heard that they took some records out of the Chronicler Archives."

"I'm not surprised if they did. Those imbeciles were out to eradicate our history. Rewrite it as their own."

Katerina spotted Jezebelle near the edge of the first row of battered seats.

"Have you seen the Sovereign?" A woman stopped her, taking hold of my arm. "I need to speak to him about the farms and crops amidst the war."

"I haven't." Katerina replied icily, pulling her arm out of her grasp. "Don't you dare touch me again."

Her eyes widened, and she took a step back. "My apologies."

Katerina moved past her and took a seat next to her sister. "Any news?"

"Only that father wants to address the war situation and mitigation plan for the country. Supposedly, he has special guidance on where the civilians should take shelter."

"Is he expecting another attack soon?"

Jezebelle shrugged. "All I want to know is when we're leaving."

Katerina chuckled. *Makes two of us.* "Have you seen him anywhere? I need to tell him something."

Jezebelle shook her head. "I haven't seen him since the ceremony."

Shit.

"Why? What's going on?"

Katerina surveyed the surrounding people. Most where engaged in their own conversations and General Lee had left their side. "This is absolutely the worst place for me to tell you."

"Is it really that serious?"

She nodded and subtly gestured at the plethora of people around us. "I don't wish to have an audience."

Jezebelle scooted closer to her, lowering her voice. "Tell me anyway."

Katerina pressed her lips into a thin line. *Might as well... she deserves to know.* "You know that the Olympians fought a ton of monsters years ago and that one almost dethroned Zeus?"

Jezebelle nodded.

"The Savior we've been praying and devoting to is Typhon," Katerina muttered.

"You're lying." Jezebelle whisper-shouted, pulling back slightly. "Father wouldn't lead us astray like that."

"Wouldn't he?" Katerina retorted, searing her gaze into her sister. "Wouldn't he do it to serve his agenda?"

"You may think that because of what he did to you, but... father is not evil."

Katerina could see the trouble this was causing her, unable to accept their father's true nature. The side Katerina had seen with her own two eyes and tried to divert Jezebelle away from. *Is it because of me that she doesn't want to believe me? Did I do too much?* "I think you have really high hopes..."

Silence fell around them, and their attention drifted to the altar, where her father walked up to the obsidian dais accompanied by General Ware, General Lee and General Vivek in a black robe with red trim. His expression was cold and unreadable.

Katerina's eyes scanned the generals. Their eyes were bloodshot and dark, skin greyish. *What did he do to you?* Her stomach lurched.

"My people... sons and daughters of the Paragons of *Light*." His voice, once cold and measured, now echoed with a wrathful undertone of something inhuman.

Katerina's throat tightened. Her pendant warmed.

"You're no stranger to what happened just this morning. The once sacred place of our beloved sisterhood and keepers of our history was ransacked and destroyed by none other than the ones who destroyed our lands over twenty years ago."

The crowd was silent, hanging on his every word as smoke still rose outside the walls where enemy fires had sifted through their lands. Distant, but the stench of smoke and fire lingered. Katerina examined her father. Though his face appeared familiar, the unsettling stillness in his eyes, the subtle shift in the air, and the faint, metallic scent she couldn't place whispered a disquieting truth. The pendant thrummed, its metal suddenly radiating intense heat that prickled the skin.

"Look around, not with despair, but with clarity and justified anger. The mantle of peace was torn away, and these cowards thought they could break us. They believed our fire had ceased. Our enemies sought to cripple a kingdom, but what they've done is unleash their worst enemy yet."

Katerina leaned over to Jezebelle. "Believe me now?"

But she didn't respond, or move, for that matter. She was transfixed...like everyone else in the crowd...

"As sovereign, it is my sworn duty to protect our lands and our people. They will not leave unscathed. They will not leave believing they are victors. They will succumb and burn in the fires we will unleash upon their lands."

An attack on Mount Olympus? Why aren't they running? Can't they see what I see? Should I run? What will happen to Jezebelle if I do? Katerina nudged Jezebelle's arm.

No response.

"We are done mourning. We are done with pleading for justice from deaf skies and cowardly entities."

Heat overtook her body as her father's eyes turned black as night. *What did you do?*

"Tonight, I offer you not sorrow, but a *new beginning*." He drifted his attention to Katerina, and her stomach dropped. *"Come to me."*

Her chest tugged, anticipating the uncontrollable movement of her legs as they made it to the altar. But her feet weren't the ones moving.

Trembling with fear, Katerina ran toward her sister, whose body moved toward the altar. But Katerina's feet remained secured in place; an invisible force holding her back.

"No! Please!" Katerina yelled. "Jezy! Jezebelle! Listen to me!"

Unresponsive, she stood next to her father.

"Don't just stand there! Do something!" Katerina yelled at the generals, struggling against the invisible restraints, but none of them moved. "Anyone!" The crowd ignored her pleas.

"To seal what has been awakened within and bind fully to this mortal shell. I shall offer a *life* for a power that reshapes the world." He stepped down, caressing the edge of a ceremonial blade presented to him in a box by... General Lee...?

"It's me you want! Not her!" The icy grip of terror seized Katerina. Her vision narrowed, the world blurring at the edges as a cold sweat prickled her skin. A silent scream clawed at her throat. "Don't please!" She tugged on the force, again and again.

She is innocent.

"Do not avert your eyes, for this is the price of ascendancy. Power is not inherited; it is earned, forged, and claimed by those bold enough to pay the price." He picked up the blade and moved to her unmoving sister, who stared at a void as if she were a shell of a person.

"Stop!" Katerina pulled again, feeling the force giving way slightly as ice slithered up her arms. *Fucking work!* She pulled again, and again, and again, heart slamming against her chest as he brought the blade to sister's neck. "JEZEBELLE! WAKE UP!"

The force gave way. Shadows rippled from Katerina in vicious hunger as she ran as fast as her legs could take her.

Jezebelle's eyes turned to her and smiled.

The polished steel flashed in the dim light, a silver arc against the air. A wet tearing sound, a sickening *shhhrrrhk*, ripped through the silence as the blade met flesh. Skin and sinew yielded, parting like oiled parchment. Blood erupted in a sudden, hot spray, streaming into the air in a crimson arc that steamed against the cool dusk.

Katerina crumpled, knees hitting the cold, unforgiving marble, a jarring thud echoing in her ears. Her mouth dried and felt impossibly tight, mirroring the vise-grip constricting her throat.

Jezebelle choked, the coppery tang of blood filling the air as life gurgled from her. Crimson pooled, spreading across the cold, smooth obsidian dais.

CHAPTER
FIFTY-FIVE
JOSEPH

Her sister's scream ripped the chamber apart. She broke through the crowd, clawing toward Joseph, toward her sister, but the faceless barred her path. "She didn't deserve this," she sobbed, her voice unraveling into a wail.

He looked down at the body at his feet. The girl's body convulsed once, twice, then stilled—but her blood was already his. His eyes drifted to the eldest sister; shadows emanated from her, slithering upward like smoke, still on her knees pathetically, weeping with her face buried in her palms.

Joseph's mouth tugged upward. *That's it. I just need a little more.*

The dark lightning in his chest roared as the sacrifice's essence fused with it. The faceless legion stirred, their hollow forms trembling as cracks of glowing red shot through their armor of shadow and stone. They inhaled without lungs, drank without mouths, their storm fire swelling brighter.

"Do you see?" Joseph turned to the trembling mortals, speaking over the sister's howls of grief. "Life is fleeting, flesh is weak. But through me, through sacrifice, death itself is conquered."

The girl's blood moved across the hall like a living thing, splitting into streams that seeped into the sockets and seams of his faceless soldiers and the corpses that filled the ruined hall. They grew taller, their edges sharper, their silence more dreadful. No longer empty husks—they were storm-forged titans, born of death and chaos. The tether—the lifeline, had served its purpose and given life to his army.

Eris moved to his side, her smile hungry as she whispered only for him to hear. "They're here."

The faceless split the crowd in the middle. Six men and a woman were pulled in by their wrists, bodies scraping across the floor until they were tossed in front of Joseph.

He walked over to the beaten, trembling men, save for one, who looked at him straight in the eyes with nothing but pure, unrelenting hatred. The woman averted her ghostly gaze.

"You're one of his." Joseph smiled at Dremian. "I had my suspicions, but my host didn't pick up on your Olympian-ridden stench."

Dremian lunged, but a faceless soldier held him back.

Joseph's lips curled. "Bow." He stepped back, addressing the crowd, lips stretching too wide. "Bow, or join her."

The crowd hesitated. Still frozen.

The faceless soldiers stepped forward in unison. Their very presence bled terror into the room. Hollow sockets stared without mercy, jaws locked in silence.

The first mortal fell to his knees.

Then another.

Then all at once, the chamber collapsed into submission, bodies dropping, foreheads pressed to the floor. Generals clutched the hilts of their blades, but even they dared not raise them. The hall became a sea of bent backs and trembling hands.

And now they'll serve me as revenants.

"Yes," he murmured, his voice rolling like distant thunder. "Bow. Bow to the storm that will break Zeus. Bow to the shadow that will rule your realm. Bow... and be remade."

The faceless army sprang into action. The crimson slick glistened, reflecting the flickering torchlight as the screams faded into a rewarding silence. A metallic tang filled the air, mingling with the coppery scent of death as the faceless legion's work was done.

The six men knelt before him, unharmed but facing the ground. Joseph's attention then turned to the side, where Ares showed up, followed by an obscenely thin Zeus and his pet.

I'll be dealing with you once I'm done with her. His eyes drifted to Katerina.

Chapter
FIFTY-SIX
KATERINA

I ALWAYS KNEW MY LIFE WAS NOT MY OWN. I'VE KNOWN it, and I dealt with it. In my own bitter way, I've pushed through the pain and the suffering.

I've dealt with my mother's passing.

I've dealt with the lashings.

I've dealt with the confinement in my own home.

I've dealt with the loss of a child.

I've dealt with the loss of a lover.

Again, I am familiar with pain but nothing, and I mean nothing, would've prepared me for the loss of my sister...

I promised myself that I would always protect her.

No matter the cost.

No matter the burden,

No matter what...

And now... she lies here before me, limp and lifeless.

And her last words to Katerina were: *You may think that because of what he did to you, but...father is not evil.*

That didn't sit right with her. *That is not fucking right. It should've been me in her place. She wasn't part of this. She was dragged into this bullshit.*

Katerina wanted to destroy every last fiber of his being, even if it was the last thing she'd fucking do. Even if she died in the process. She's got nothing more to lose, and all she had was ice, chilling rage coursing through her body as what controlled her father stood there nonchalantly. *How fucking could you?*

"You sick bastard!" She yelled, struggling to stand. "How could you do this to her?" Tears sprung out of her burning eyes but she didn't care. "She was innocent. She was your daughter."

But he didn't acknowledge her, he just stared at her.

"Say something!" she barked, her voice powerful and commanding. Ice crept into her hands as darkness surrounded her like a mantle.

"Ah... my darling Katerina..." he said, his voice now back to normal.

His acknowledgment made her skin crawl. *He hasn't called me darling since mom passed away.*

"You look at me with your mother's eyes, but they don't see the world as I do. Your sister was an unfortunate but necessary loss. She served a purpose. She opened the gate with her blood. Raised my army with her sacrifice. She was always meant to be the *key.*"

How fucking dare you speak about her that way? Shadows snuffed out the light, leaving only the moonlight above. "She wasn't disposable. She wasn't a pawn. She was innocent."

"Your sister was far from innocent. But you... you are the one I need."

"Then why not kill me in her stead?"

He shook his head, laughing as he walked down from the bloodied dais. "I will not waste you on an altar when you were born for war." He reached for her face, and she stepped back. "Your father made you for precisely this."

She blinked, unable to conjure words. *My father made me for what precisely? How the hell did he make me?*

"Apologies, my manners are rusty, millennia in confinement. You understand, yes?" His smile widened unnaturally. "I don't ask for your death. I ask for *loyalty.*"

"As if you've earned it," Katerina sneered.

He clicked his tongue disapprovingly, eyes darkening back into black holes. "When the old world falls to ash, you will be my beacon—well, better yet, your essence will be my beacon."

"I'd rather die." Ice pulsed through her, dragging at her veins, pulling her to pieces and knitting her together again.

"Cute." he chuckled. "You think you have a choice." His voice returned to the deep, inhuman tone.

A strong force clenched her throat, lifting her a few feet in the air. The pendant seared her skin as ice slithered from her palms. Fire and ice wrestled each other from within her as her body slammed against the battered wall. Invisible shackles pinned her in place, her feet barely touching the ground.

Think. Fucking think. All this supposed power and I can't use it to escape? Fucking useless. Think!

She scanned her surroundings as they focused into view. An ocean of grey-skinned people bowed, unmoving. Her stomach turned. She gagged, choking on her own breath. Her gaze drifted to the two men chained near the dais. One, has silvery white hair, tan skin and a thin, frail frame, and it took her a moment to realize that it was Zeus. The guy next to him she couldn't seem to recog—wait. *Isn't he the guy who claimed to be Jasmine's husband?* She blinked. His face was beaten to a pulp, arms bruised and frail.

A beautiful slender woman with inky hair approached her, clicking her tongue. "It's going to be okay, sweetness. This won't hurt."

"Fuck off." She sneered as the woman pressed a hand to Katerina's forehead. Sharp pain spread through her restricted body.

"Your sister understood the value of obedience. She didn't fight her purpose, she embraced it. That's why her end was... merciful." Her father—no. Joseph said. "You, however, insist and continue to insist on disappointing me. So tell me, was it cruelty you suffered... or just the consequences of your defiance?"

Her body trembled, not just with pain but also with white hot rage and icy resentment. *Merciful? Merciful would've been to spare her from this. Consequences of my fucking defiance?* She gritted her teeth as the pressure surged.

Shadows drowned her sight, and the sound of tearing flesh filled the room, followed by loud, repeated thumps. She fell to the ground, knees buckling on impact.

"Do you see it now? You offered them. Bled them dry. You are just like me, and yet you still cling to a pathetic illusion of resistance. Why fight it when your hands already carry the weight of my will?"

Her burning gaze focused on the six men and the woman near the dais, blood saturating the tile further. *Her father's council... Thalia...*

"I didn't do this." She shook her head. "I am nothing and will never be like you." She sneered as she stood, squaring her shoulders.

"Oh, but you are." He hovered around the corpses. "Or else you wouldn't have done this."

Am I truly a monster? No. No. No. You are not. Don't give in. Her chest constricted, a vise around her ribs, and she crumpled to the rough ground, the gritty texture scraping her palms. A chilling vacuum seemed to pull at her, sucking out something...

"It's time for everyone to get what they deserve." He added. "And I'm sure you see the vision, my darling Katerina."

"Don't call me that." She spat amidst chest contractions. She placed her palms on the floor, stopping herself from falling forward.

What the hell? The dark stain on her palms crept upwards, a slow, viscous tide against her warm ivory skin fingers. She breathed, keeping her face neutral despite the turning of her stomach and rapid beats of her heart. *She's taking my power...shit. Shit. Fucking think!*

"Keep resisting your calling." He taunted, walking toward her again. "Sooner or later, you'll be begging for my help."

"Fuck off." Pain stung her palms as she drove them to the tile.

Katerina lifted her gaze, falling on the woman who had her eyes fixed on her. *As much as I hate the stain, I can't let her take it.*

She lunged toward the woman with all the strength she could muster, tackling her to the ground. But, there was no one beneath her. Katerina's brows furrowed and found the woman standing on the opposite side.

"Stop messing with our guest of honor, Eris," he said, then turned to Katerina as she stood. "I see it festering in you. Twisting through your soul, hungry and wild. Stop pretending you're still pure." He stretched a hand. "Let me show you who you *truly* are."

His grin widened as she approached in silence. *I'm dying today, but I will avenge my sister.* Hesitantly, she reached for his hand.

The pendant blazed, a blinding white flash searing the air. A wave of heat washed over her skin. The world tilted and roared as her knees buckled, and the ground shuddered.

His body recoiled, screaming in a language she didn't understand that made the insides of her body as cold as ice.

This could be my one and only chance. Run. Run. Fucking Run!

Her legs found the strength to run, born from terror and survival, trampling over the sea of bodies and into the foyer. A herd of faceless soldiers and High Re'Veillites, now dressed in black and red, rushed her way, but she didn't stop.

Pushing and throwing anything she find into their way, she ran out the doors and into the pathway that led to the Caverest Plaza.

Her legs ached, lungs burned, but she couldn't afford to take a break. Her sister wouldn't want her to stop. Her mother wouldn't want her to stop.

Keep fucking running.

She bolted through the entrance of the Plaza. The place was ghostly. There was not a single civilian in sight. Her mouth became drier. Faceless soldiers combed the streets, destroying everything in sight. The capital was no longer her home. She kept running until she was miles and miles away from the arched entryway and deep into the Liverfront Forest.

Branches slashed her arms, and her lungs pleaded for air.

She stopped for a brief moment, the morning sun barely making its appearance through the canopy. Suppressing the pain in her chest and the urge to cry, she took a breath and walked deeper into the woods. She didn't have time to grieve. She didn't have time to process what the fuck just happened. She needed to disappear. She needed to... she needed to take a break as exhaustion took control of her.

With tiresome eyes, she glanced around, ears perked for any sound; yet only the chirping of birds and ruffling of leaves were able to be heard. If she kept going, her body would eventually give out on her.

Only for a little bit... she hid behind a large tree, using it as support as her eyes fluttered closed. *I have to survive. Because next time... there won't be a light to save me.*

CHAPTER
FIFTY-SEVEN
KATERINA

WARM AIR CARESSED KATERINA'S FACE AND EXPOSED flesh as she walked behind a line of people inside the crowded space overlooking the pier. She looked out the glass window. A large, multi-story contraption with extended wings sat atop the uneasy waters, resembling a snake or maze going upward. Thunder roared over the darkened horizon with occasional bursts of lightning, one of the few sources of light.

A warning?

A threat?

Her chest tightened, and breathing became more difficult with every step she took. But she couldn't seem to stop.

People filed out of the room and into the winged contraption, unbothered by the storm. Icy air cuts through her upon stepping outside. A mix of salty and sweet water splashed her face as she approached the entrance.

The sea was black glass until the sky cracked open. The ocean rose only to her calves, but she felt the weight of it in her core; the weight of the unknown. The surf didn't churn; it *breathed*, like it was something alive.

The stairs inside it glistened, wet with salt and sky. A blonde woman greeted her in a red uniform and guided her to what she called the *lower deck*.

Katerina's heart wanted to leap out of her chest upon stepping inside. The lighting was dim, humming; the windows sealed, and fogged by condensation. The walls didn't curve in as seen outside—no. They leaned inward, narrowing the space like a descending throat and an opening at its very end, displaying the tremulous inky waters that looked like they were crashing against an invisible barrier, preventing them from flooding the deck.

The space was empty. No seats, no table, nothing in sight, save for a barrier in the middle of the room.

Every inch of her body screamed at her to run. But she couldn't. Her legs moved of their own accord until the woman sat her next to the barrier with calm inevitability and secured Katerina's hands and feet with a leash to the barrier. *Why can't I run? Why can't I call for help?*

"I can sense your unease and reluctance," she said softly, finishing the last knots around her feet. "You will stay here a minute... and then decide whether you want to go up, or stay here." She left before Katarina was able to utter a word in response.

Her limbs felt heavy, wet with seawater or perhaps something deeper. She needed to get out of here. She needed to leave.

Get me out.

Get me out.

Get me out.

Thunder murmured beyond the walls like the voice of a forgotten god. And then...*drip.*

Drip.

Drip.

Water. Seeped through the seams. Slowly at first, then steadily. The floor grew slick. Cold licked at her ankles. She tried to shift, but the restraints held. The water was rising. Not fast enough to drown. But just enough to feel.

A wave crashed against her body, knocking her back. Wave after wave crashed against her. She sat up. The barrier had broken.

Get me out.

Let me out.

She tried to scream, but nothing came out.

Whatever this was, she was not a fan. Katerina pulled on the restraints. The surrounding light snuffed out, leaving her in complete and utter darkness.

The darkness that follows me like the plague...

Then it hits her. The choices she didn't make. The grief she never cried. The truth she'd buried like a bone beneath her ribs in order to protect her sister. *My sister...*

Her failure to *protect* her...

How she *failed* to protect her...

The sickening sound of her ripping flesh still haunted Katerina. Her body bleeding out in front of her. How she couldn't stop it. She had failed. *I am a failure.* She was supposed to be the one who'd died that day. Not Jezebelle.

Heat spread from her chest, and she breathed in the foggy air. Somewhere above the upper level pulsed faintly.

The woman returned, and she knelt beside her; her face unreadable.

"It's time. You may go up... if you wish. Or stay here. Where it's familiar. Where it's quiet."

Was it *really* quiet? To stay here with her thoughts? With her guilt? Was she truly a failure? Lightning flashed outside, casting her reflection in the flooded floor, distorted and rippling. Katerina turned to the opening. The shield was intact...

Would she just let her sister's death be in vain?

She inhaled deeply, her green eyes meeting the woman.

And chose.

HER EYES FLUTTERED OPEN, SILVER LIGHT SHONE ABOVE her as the room focused into view. A cool, gentle breeze swept through her aching body. Katerina inhaled, and even such a natural action ached profoundly.

Sitting up, she found herself in a navy and cream room with an open balcony that had a direct view to a darkened summit. She blinked, head tilting. *Where am I?* She got to her feet, the cold tile biting into her skin. She ignored the pain consuming her as she approached the balcony, stopping on the threshold. *Easy... you don't know where you are and who brought you here.*

She held onto the loose fabric atop her shoulders in hopes that it would keep her warm. But it was futile. The chill air cut through the fabric and into her flesh.

She hurried back inside and approached the dresser. Someone had left a note atop it next to a glass with a blue drink and a small plate of cherries.

Eat and drink this. It'll help you feel better.

She reached out and instantly noticed that her fingers were still stained black, but the smoke only seemed to reach her fingers midway. Katerina exhaled, unsure of how to feel. She looked up and almost jumped at the sight of her condition.

Her hair was almost entirely white, save for the ends. Her eyes were a dark shade of green. Her face was sharper than usual, and cuts covered most of her bruised skin. Then her eyes fell on the scar along her jaw.

Katerina drew a shaky breath and covered her mouth with a hand, stifling a sob. *Don't cry... don't.* She reached for the drink. The scent of blueberry, mint and something tangy filled her nose. *An Ameliorate Tonic.* She froze, eyes fixed on the blue liquid. *Is she here?* Muffled voices turned her attention toward the cream doors.

She set the glass down and approached them with caution. She turned the handle slowly, peeking out, only to find a blonde man and a woman walking down the corridor in navy and silver attire.

Katerina slipped out, even as her body groaned in protest, and followed them down the decadent corridor. Her head throbbed, eyes burned with the bright light, and her feet ached.

They disappeared to the right, and Katerina debated whether to enter. *Am I at Byorn's Estate?* She looked at the surrounding banners, a crescent moon behind a darkened mountain. *This didn't look like Windermere...*

Her head pounded, prompting her to press her hands against her temples. *I should go back to the room...then again, I already walked over here...*

Fuck it.

Katerina barged through the doors and froze.

"What the hell?" Katerina said through gritted teeth as she laid eyes on Jasmine, Rhei, and Nik sitting in the middle of the drawing room.

TO BE CONTINUED IN
OLYMPUS: THE FALLEN KINGDOM

RELEVANT INFORMATION

Eseron is the primary continent within the mortal lands. It is currently divided into 4 major countries: Castelencia, Windermere, Sylene, and Aeshelyn.

12-MONTH CALENDAR

- **Illunara:** The year begins, fires are lit, oaths are renewed, and the light descends. Renewal through flame.
- **Seraphine:** Rivers awaken, mercy flows, and forgiveness is sought. A time of cleansing and reconciliation.
- **Bloomrise:** The land blossoms. Faith and beauty intertwine. The Paragons bless the birth of life and devotion. The heart of Blossom Peak Season.
- **Solareth:** The height of the sun. Triumph, ambition, and divine favor. Armies march beneath banners of gold.
- **Pyratheon:** Fire season of both war and faith. Trials of endurance and judgment of the unworthy.

- **Emberveil:** Gratitude and offering. Fields glow gold, temples burn candles of remembrance. The faithful give without taking.
- **Lunareth:** The moon reigns, Dreams, confessions, and reflection under starlight. Shadows begin to stir.
- **Serenith:** Calmness before change. Reflection, meditation, and diplomacy. The light paused but does not fade.
- **Mournvale:** The fading of life and light. Shadows strengthen. The dead are honored, and the faithful steel themselves.
- **Vespera:** The veil thins. Lanterns burn low. The Light mourns itself—and the faithful endure darkness.
- **Noctyelle:** Winter reigns. The world grows still. The faithful fast in silence, awaiting divine rebirth.
- **Ascendral:** The end and beginning entwine. The Sun and Moon unite, birthing a new light and a new year.

THE RE'VEILLITES

- **High Re'Veillites** - Top 2% of sisters characterized by their unique ability to support Eseron and the countries within.
- **Naturopaths** - sisters dedicated to the practice of healing across the continent.
  - *Levels:* Novice Healer, Healer, Mender, Expert Naturopath
- **Chroniclers** - sisters dedicated to the record-keeping of the history of Eseron and the countries within. Only area where men are allowed.
  - *Levels:* Novice Scholar, Scholar, Adept Chronicler, Master Chronicler
- **Sisters** - Sisters dedicated to the council and sanctification of women across the continent.

ACKNOWLEDGMENTS

Thank you so much for taking the time to read this new and improved version of Olympus: A New Order. I hope you enjoyed reading this story as much as I did writing it. After 5 years, I can finally say that I am happy and proud of the result.

Thank you for trusting and supporting my art and dreams to be a published author. There aren't enough words to describe how grateful I am.

I also want to take a moment to thank my family for their unwavering support. My sister for using her knowledge in graphic design to help me polish the cover and map in this story. My bestie, for helping me push this book onto the shelves and at a variety of retailers. I am extremely grateful to all of you.

THE WRITING JOURNEY:

Olympus: A New Order, as well as the entire Wrath of Olympus Trilogy and the books to follow within this universe, has been my baby for years. It started off as a rushed Wattpad story back in 2015, meant to be a romance to be developed in 3 books. But at the time, I didn't see myself as a published author; so the idea didn't seem real to me. Perhaps because I was merely 16 years old. But as the years went by, I fell in love with writing.

Before I took this story seriously, I focused on mystery/thriller short stories and scripts; and no matter how much time passed or the obstacles that life threw my way, I never stopped writing. That's when I knew that I had fallen in love with storytelling.

It wasn't until May 2019 in Kabul, Afghanistan, that life gave me a reality check and showed me how quickly life can vanish in an instant. I asked myself, was I truly happy with what I had accomplished in life? Did I even try to do something I was passionate about? What if I had finished my stories? What if my story motivated someone to publish their story? What if...

So, I decided to pursue my dream officially in 2020. Went to Full Sail University and spent all of my Bachelor's Degree program revising what I had written for Olympus: A New Order (at the time, it was titled: Chosen by the Gods). I outlined, reviewed, wrote, reviewed, researched, rewrote, etc. The whole nine. Aside from the fact that we were quarantined, and I was trying to keep myself entertained.

It wasn't until 2022 that I "finished" the story. But I had one big problem: no beta readers, no editors, no feedback. NOTHING. Yet, I still went on a whim and published anyway under the new name.

BIG MISTAKE.

Not even a month after it being out, I unpublished it because something inside me was not satisfied with the story. It felt rushed, it had a lot of plot holes, and the story itself didn't make sense. But I wanted to finish it because I didn't want to run out of time.

So, setting pride aside, I sat down and reviewed: every single chapter, character connection, every single minute detail I could find. I spent hours upon hours on YouTube watching videos from authors like Abbie Emmons to make my writing and stories better.

Therefore, I spent 3 years after publishing turning the story to what it is today.

The 1st version of the book was 21 chapters long with 65,000 words; which is considered very short for a fantasy story.

This current version is 57 chapters long with 130,000 words.

What does this mean for you?

If you're an aspiring author who thinks is running out of time, I'd like you to take a moment and breathe. Take your time.

Storytelling is not something that should be rushed in any way. Take your time to flesh out the characters, to enrich your world-building, to create your complex magic system, to develop your plot twists and foreshadowing moments.

Take your time, because this is your legacy. This is your baby.

Readers can tell when an author has put their heart and soul into their stories. Not only because of how it was written, but you can see it when they talk about their book as if it were real. Real places, real people, real conflicts. You can see the passion in their eyes and how long they've been waiting for this moment.

Everything will fall into place if you just take your time. Schedule some uninterrupted time to research and write; set up your writing space, so it works best for you; do whatever you need to do.

But most importantly: Write what you love.

Storytelling is a gift. Use it to the fullest extent to tell the story you are passionate about.

I wish you the best on your writing journey!

"No Weapon That Is Formed Against Thee Shall Prosper."

About the Author

"Follow your passion. The rest will attend to itself. If I can do it, anybody can do it. It's possible. And it's your turn. So go for it. It's never too late to become what you always wanted to be in the first place."
-J. Michael Straczynski

Isamar Miranda Colón is a Puerto Rican combat veteran with a passion for literature. She graduated from Full Sail University in 2021 with a Bachelor's Degree in Entertainment Business, and in 2023 with a Master's Degree in the same field. Soon after, she began to pursue a career in publishing by writing her debut novel, Olympus: A New Order.

www.authorimirandacolon.com

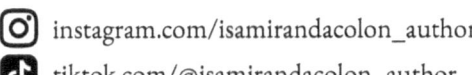 instagram.com/isamirandacolon_author
tiktok.com/@isamirandacolon_author

www.ingramcontent.com/pod-product-compliance
Lightning Source LLC
Chambersburg PA
CBHW031151050726
47495CB00019B/1357